GRAHAM GREENE

GRAHAM GREENE

BRIGHTON ROCK

THE END OF THE AFFAIR

Brighton Rock first published in Great Britain in 1938
by William Heinemann Limited
The End of the Affair first published in Great Britain in 1951
by William Heinemann Limited

This edition first published in Great Britain in 1987
jointly by

William Heinemann Limited
10 Upper Grosvenor Street
London W1

and

Octopus Books Limited
59 Grosvenor Street
London W1

ISBN 0 7064 3059 X

Printed at The Bath Press, Avon

CONTENTS

BRIGHTON ROCK

Brighton Rock

'This were a fine reign:
To do ill and not hear of it again.'

The Witch of Edmonton

Chapter One

Hale knew, before he had been in Brighton three hours, that they meant to murder him. With his inky fingers and his bitten nails, his manner cynical and nervous, anybody could tell he didn't belong – belong to the early summer sun, the cool Whitsun wind off the sea, the holiday crowd. They came in by train from Victoria every five minutes, rocked down Queen's Road standing on the tops of the little local trams, stepped off in bewildered multitudes into fresh and glittering air: the new silver paint sparkled on the piers, the cream houses ran away into the west like a pale Victorian water-colour; a race in miniature motors, a band playing, flower gardens in bloom below the front, an aeroplane advertising something for the health in pale vanishing clouds across the sky.

It had seemed quite easy to Hale to be lost in Brighton. Fifty thousand people besides himself were down for the day, and for quite a while he gave himself up to the good day, drinking gins and tonics wherever his programme allowed. For he had to stick closely to a programme: from ten till eleven Queen's Road and Castle Square, from eleven till twelve the Aquarium and Palace Pier, twelve till one the front between the Old Ship and West Pier, back for lunch between one and two in any restaurant he chose round the Castle Square, and after that he had to make his way all down the parade to the West Pier and then to the station by the Hove streets. These were the limits of his absurd and widely advertised sentry-go.

Advertised on every *Messenger* poster: 'Kolley Kibber in Brighton to-day.' In his pocket he had a packet of cards to distribute in hidden places along his route; those who found them would receive ten shillings from the *Messenger*, but the big prize was reserved for whoever challenged Hale in the proper form of words and with a copy of the *Messenger* in his hand: 'You are Mr Kolley Kibber. I claim the *Daily Messenger* prize.'

This was Hale's job to do sentry-go, until a challenger released him, in every seaside town in turn: yesterday Southend, to-day Brighton, to-morrow—

He drank his gin and tonic hastily as a clock struck eleven and moved out of Castle Square. Kolley Kibber always played fair, always wore the same kind of hat as in the photograph the *Messenger* printed, was always on time. Yesterday in Southend he had been unchallenged: the paper liked to save its guineas occasionally, but not too often. It was his duty to-day to be spotted – and it was his inclination too. There were reasons why he didn't feel too safe in Brighton, even in a Whitsun crowd.

He leant against the rail near the Palace Pier and showed his face to the crowd as it uncoiled endlessly past him, like a twisted piece of wire, two by two, each with an air of sober and determined gaiety. They had stood all the way from Victoria in crowded carriages, they would have to wait in queues for lunch, at midnight half asleep they would rock back in trains to the cramped streets and the closed pubs and the weary walk home. With immense labour and immense patience they extricated from the long day the grain of pleasure: this sun, this music, the rattle of the miniature cars, the ghost train diving between the grinning skeletons under the Aquarium promenade, the sticks of Brighton rock, the paper sailors' caps.

Nobody paid any attention to Hale; no one seemed to be carrying a *Messenger*. He deposited one of his cards carefully on the top of a little basket and moved on, with his bitten nails and his inky fingers, alone. He only felt his loneliness after his third gin; until then he despised the crowd, but afterwards he felt his kinship. He had come out of the same streets, but he was condemned by his higher pay to pretend to want other things, and all the time the piers, the peepshows pulled at his heart. He wanted to get back – but all he could do was to carry his sneer along the front, the badge of loneliness. Somewhere out of sight a woman was singing, 'When I came up from Brighton by the train': a rich Guinness voice, a voice from a public bar. Hale turned into the private saloon and watched her big blown charms across two bars and through a glass partition.

She wasn't old, somewhere in the late thirties or the early forties, and she was only a little drunk in a friendly accommodating way. You thought of sucking babies when you looked at her, but if she'd borne them she hadn't let them pull her down: she took care of herself. Her lipstick told you that, the confidence of her big body. She was well-covered, but she wasn't careless; she kept her lines for those who cared for lines.

Hale did. He was a small man and he watched her with covetous envy over the empty glasses tipped up in the lead trough, over the beer handles, between the shoulders of the two serving in the public bar. 'Give us another, Lily,' one of them said and she began, 'One night – in an alley – Lord Rothschild said to me.' She never got beyond a few lines. She wanted to laugh too much to give her voice a chance, but she had an inexhaustible memory for ballads. Hale had never heard one of them before. With his glass to his lips he watched her with nostalgia: she was off again on a song which must have dated back to the Australian gold rush.

'Fred,' a voice said behind him, 'Fred.'

The gin slopped out of Hale's glass on to the bar. A boy of about seventeen watched him from the door – a shabby smart suit, the cloth too thin for much wear, a face of starved intensity, a kind of hideous and unnatural pride.

'Who are you Freding?' Hale said. 'I'm not Fred.'

'It don't make any difference,' the boy said. He turned back towards the door, keeping an eye on Hale over his narrow shoulder.

'Where are you going?'

'Got to tell your friends,' the boy said.

They were alone in the saloon bar except for an old commissionaire, who slept over a pint glass of old and mild. 'Listen,' Hale said, 'have a drink. Come and sit down over here and have a drink.'

'Got to be going,' the boy said. 'You know I don't drink, Fred. You forget a lot, don't you?'

'It won't make any difference having one drink. A soft drink.'

'It'll have to be a quick one,' the boy said. He watched Hale all the time closely and with wonder: you might expect a hunter searching through the jungle for some half-fabulous beast to look like that – at the spotted lion or the pygmy elephant – before the kill. 'A grape-fruit squash,' he said.

'Go on, Lily,' the voices implored in the public bar. 'Give us another, Lily,' and the boy took his eyes for the first time from Hale and looked across the partition at the big breasts and the blown charm.

'A double whisky and a grape-fruit squash,' Hale said. He carried them to a table, but the boy didn't follow. He was watching the woman with an expression of furious distaste. Hale felt as if hatred had been momentarily loosened like handcuffs to be fastened round another's wrists. He tried to joke, 'A cheery soul.'

'Soul,' the boy said. 'You've no cause to talk about souls.' He turned his hatred back on Hale, drinking down the grape-fruit squash in a single draught.

Hale said, 'I'm only here for my job. Just for the day. I'm Kolley Kibber.'

'You're Fred,' the boy said.

'All right,' Hale said, 'I'm Fred. But I've got a card in my pocket which'll be worth ten bob to you.'

'I know all about the cards,' the boy said. He had a fair smooth skin, the faintest down, and his grey eyes had an effect of heartlessness like an old man's in which human feeling has died. 'We were all reading about you,' he said, 'in the paper this morning,' and suddenly he sniggered as if he'd just seen the point of a dirty story.

'You can have one,' Hale said. 'Look, take this *Messenger*. Read what it says there. You can have the whole prize. Ten guineas,' he said. 'You'll only have to send this form to the *Messenger*.'

'Then they don't trust you with the cash,' the boy said, and in the other bar Lily began to sing, 'We met – 'twas in a crowd – and I thought he would shun me.' 'Christ,' the boy said, 'won't anybody stop that buer's mouth?'

'I'll give you a fiver,' Hale said. 'It's all I've got on me. That and my ticket.'

'You won't want your ticket,' the boy said.

'I wore my bridal robe, and I rivall'd its whiteness.'

The boy rose furiously, and giving way to a little vicious spurt of hatred – at the song? at the man? – he dropped his empty glass on to the floor. 'The gentleman'll pay,' he said to the barman and swung through the door of the private lounge. It was then Hale realized that they meant to murder him.

> 'A wreath of orange blossoms,
> When next we met, she wore;
> The expression of her features
> Was more thoughtful than before.'

The commissionaire slept on and Hale watched her from the deserted elegant lounge. Her big breasts pointed through the thin vulgar summer dress, and he thought: I must get away from here, I must get away: sadly and desperately watching her, as if he were gazing at life itself in the public bar. But he couldn't get away, he had his job to do: they were particular on the *Messenger*. It was a good paper to be on, and a little flare of pride went up in Hale's heart when he thought of the long pilgrimage behind him: selling newspapers at street corners, the reporter's job at thirty bob a week on the little local paper with a circulation of ten thousand, the five years in Sheffield. He was damned, he told himself with the temporary courage of another whisky, if he'd let that mob frighten him into spoiling his job. What could they do while he had people round him? They hadn't the nerve to kill him in broad day before witnesses; he was safe with the fifty thousand visitors.

'Come on over here, lonely heart.' He didn't realize at first she was speaking to him, until he saw all the faces in the public bar grinning across at him, and suddenly he thought how easily the mob could get at him with only the sleeping commissionaire to keep him company. There was no need to go outside to reach the other bar, he had only to make a semicircle through three doors, by way of the saloon bar, the 'ladies only'. 'What'll you have?' he said, approaching the big woman with starved gratitude. She could save my life, he thought, if she'd let me stick to her.

'I'll have a port,' she said.

'One port,' Hale said.

'Aren't you having one?'

'No,' Hale said, 'I've drunk enough. I mustn't get sleepy.'

'Why ever not – on a holiday? Have a Bass on me.'

'I don't like Bass.' He looked at his watch. It was one o'clock. His programme fretted at his mind. He had to leave cards in every section: the paper in that way kept a check on him; they could always tell if he scamped his job. 'Come and have a bite,' he implored her.

'Hark at him,' she called to her friends. Her warm port-winey laugh filled all the bars. 'Getting fresh, eh? I wouldn't trust myself.'

'Don't you go, Lily,' they told her. 'He's not safe.'

'I wouldn't trust myself,' she repeated, closing one soft friendly cowlike eye.

There was a way, Hale knew, to make her come. He had known the way once. On thirty bob a week he would have been at home with her; he would have known the right phrase, the right joke, to cut her out from among her friends, to be friendly at a snack-bar. But he'd lost touch. He had nothing to say; he could only repeat, 'Come and have a bite.'

'Where shall we go, Sir Horace? To the Old Ship?'

'Yes,' Hale said. 'If you like. The Old Ship.'

'Hear that,' she told them in all the bars, the two old dames in black bonnets in the ladies, the commissionaire who slept on alone in the private, her own half dozen cronies. 'This gentleman's invited me to the Old Ship,' she said in a mock-refined voice. 'Tomorrow I shall be delighted, but to-day I have a prior engagement at the Dirty Dog.'

Hale turned hopelessly to the door. The boy, he thought, would not have had time to warn the others yet. He would be safe at lunch; it was the hour he had to pass after lunch he dreaded most.

The woman said, 'Are you sick or something?'

His eyes turned to the big breasts; she was like darkness to him, shelter, knowledge, common-sense; his heart ached at the sight; but, in his little inky cynical framework of bone, pride bobbed up again, taunting him, 'Back to the womb . . . be a mother to you . . . no more standing on your own feet.'

'No,' he said, 'I'm not sick. I'm all right.'

'You look queer,' she said in a friendly concerned way.

'I'm all right,' he said. 'Hungry. That's all.'

'Why not have a bite here?' the woman said. 'You could do him a ham sandwich, couldn't you, Bell,' and the barman said, Yes, he could do a ham sandwich.

'No,' Hale said, 'I've got to be getting on.'

– Getting on. Down the front, mixing as quickly as possible with the current of the crowd, glancing to right and left of him and over each shoulder in turn. He could see no familiar face anywhere, but he felt no relief. He thought he could lose himself safely in a crowd, but now the people he was among seemed like a thick forest in which a native could arrange his poisoned ambush. He couldn't see beyond the man in flannels just in front, and when he turned his vision was blocked by a brilliant scarlet blouse. Three old ladies went driving by in an open horse-drawn carriage: the gentle clatter faded like peace. That was how some people still lived.

Hale crossed the road away from the front. There were fewer people there: he could walk faster and go further. They were drinking cocktails on the terrace of the Grand, a delicate pastiche of a Victorian sunshade twisted its ribbons and flowers in the sun, and a man like a retired statesman, all silver hair and powdered skin and double old-fashioned eyeglass, let life slip naturally, with dignity, away from him, sitting over a sherry. Down the broad steps of the Cosmopolitan came a couple of women with bright brass hair and ermine coats and heads close together like parrots, exchanging metallic confidences. ' "My dear," I said quite coldly, "if you haven't learnt the Del Rey perm, all I can say – " ' and they flashed their pointed painted nails at each other and cackled. For the first time for five years Kolley Kibber was late in his programme. At the foot of the Cosmopolitan steps, in the shadow the huge bizarre building cast, he remembered that the mob had bought his paper. They hadn't needed to watch the public house for him: they knew where to expect him.

A mounted policeman came up the road, the lovely cared-for chestnut beast stepping delicately on the hot macadam, like an expensive toy a millionaire buys for his children; you admired the finish, the leather as deeply glowing as an old mahogany table top, the bright silver badge; it never occurred to you that the toy was for use. It never occurred to Hale watching the policeman pass; he couldn't appeal to him. A man stood by the kerb selling objects on a tray; he had lost the whole of one side of the body: leg and arm and shoulder, and the beautiful horse as it paced by turned its head aside delicately like a dowager. 'Shoelaces,' the man said hopelessly to Hale, 'matches.' Hale didn't hear him. 'Razor blades.' Hale went by, the words lodged securely in his brain: the thought of the thin wound and the sharp pain. That was how Kite was killed.

Twenty yards down the road he saw Cubitt. Cubitt was a big man, with red hair cut *en brosse* and freckles. He saw Hale, but he made no sign of recognition, leaning carelessly against a pillar-box watching him. A postman came to collect and Cubitt shifted. Hale could see him exchanging a joke with the postman and the postman laughed and filled his bag and all the time Cubitt looked away from him down the street waiting for Hale. Hale knew exactly what he'd do; he knew the whole bunch; Cubitt was slow and had a friendly way with him. He'd simply link his arm with Hale's and draw him on where he wanted him to go.

But the old desperate pride persisted, a pride of intellect. He was scared sick, but he told himself, 'I'm not going to die.' He jested hollowly, 'I'm not front page stuff.' This was real: the two women getting into a taxi, the band playing on the Palace Pier, 'tablets' fading in white smoke on the pale pure sky: not red-haired Cubitt waiting by the pillar-box. Hale turned again and crossed the road, made back towards the West Pier walking fast; he wasn't running away, he had a plan.

He had only, he told himself, to find a girl: there must be hundreds waiting to be picked up on a Whitsun holiday, to be given a drink and taken to dance at Sherry's and presently home, drunk and affectionate, in the corridor carriage. That was the best way: to carry a witness round with him. It would be no good, even if his pride allowed him, to go to the station now. They would be watching it for certain, and it was always easy to kill a lonely man at a railway station: they had only to gather close round a carriage door or fix you in the crush at the barrier; it was at a station that Colleoni's mob had killed Kite. All down the front the girls sat in the twopenny deck-chairs, waiting to be picked, all who had not brought their boys with them; clerks, shop-girls, hairdressers – you could pick out the hairdressers by their new and daring perms, by their beautifully manicured nails: they had all waited late at their shops the night before, preparing each other till midnight. Now they were sleepy and sleek in the sun.

In front of the chairs the men strolled in twos and threes, wearing their summer suits for the first time, knife-edged silver-grey trousers and elegant shirts; they didn't look as if they cared a damn whether they got a girl or not, and among them Hale went in his seedy suit and his string tie and his striped shirt and his inkstains, ten years older, and desperate for a girl. He offered them cigarettes and they stared at him like duchesses with large cold eyes and said, 'I don't smoke, thenk you,' and twenty yards behind him he knew, without turning his head, that Cubitt strolled.

It made Hale's manner strange. He couldn't help showing his desperation. He could hear the girls laughing at him after he'd gone, at his clothes and the way he talked. There was a deep humility in Hale; his pride was only in his profession: he disliked himself before the glass – the bony legs and the pigeon breast, and he dressed shabbily and carelessly as a sign – a sign that he didn't expect any woman to be interested. Now he gave up the pretty ones, the smart ones, and looked despairingly down the chairs for someone plain enough to be glad of even his attentions.

Surely he thought, *this* girl, and he smiled with hungry hope at a fat spotty creature in pink whose feet hardly touched the ground. He sat down in an empty chair beside her and gazed at the remote and neglected sea coiling round the piles of the West Pier.

'Cigarette?' he asked presently.

'I don't mind if I do,' the girl said. The words were sweet like a reprieve.

'It's nice here,' the fat girl said.

'Down from town?'

'Yes.'

'Well,' Hale said, 'you aren't going to sit here alone all day, are you?'

'Oh, I don't know,' the girl said.

'I thought of going to have something to eat, and then we might—'

'*We*,' the girl said, 'you're a fresh one.'

'Well, you aren't going to sit here alone all day, are you?'

'Who said I was?' the fat girl said. 'Doesn't mean I'm going with *you*.'

'Come and have a drink anyway and talk about it.'

'I wouldn't mind,' she said, opening a compact and covering her spots deeper.

'Come along then,' Hale said.

'Got a friend?'

'I'm all alone.'

'Oh then, I couldn't,' the girl said. 'Not possibly. I couldn't leave my friend all alone,' and for the first time Hale observed in the chair beyond her a pale bloodless creature waiting avidly for his reply.

'But you'd like to come,' Hale implored.

'Oh, yes, but I couldn't possibly.'

'Your friend won't mind. She'll find someone.'

'Oh, no. I couldn't leave her alone.' She stared pastily and impassively at the sea.

'You wouldn't mind, would you?' Hale leaned forward and begged the bloodless image, and it screeched with embarrassed laughter back at him.

'She doesn't know anyone,' the fat girl said.

'She'll find somebody.'

'Would you, Delia?' The pasty girl leant her head close to her friend's and they consulted together: every now and then Delia squealed.

'That's all right then,' Hale said, 'you'll come?'

'Couldn't you find a friend?'

'I don't know anyone here,' Hale said. 'Come along. I'll take you anywhere for lunch. All I want—' he grinned miserably – 'is for you to stick close.'

'No,' the fat girl said. 'I couldn't possibly – not without my friend.'

'Well, both of you come along then,' Hale said.

'It wouldn't be much fun for Delia,' the fat girl said.

A boy's voice interrupted them. 'So there you are, Fred,' and Hale looked up at the grey inhuman seventeen-year-old eyes.

'Why,' the fat girl squealed, 'he said he hadn't got a friend.'

'You can't believe what Fred says,' the voice said.

'Now we can make a proper party,' the fat girl said. 'This is my friend Delia. I'm Molly.'

'Pleased to meet you,' the boy said. 'Where are we going, Fred?'

'I'm hungry,' the fat girl said. 'I bet you're hungry too, Delia?' and Delia wriggled and squealed.

'I know a good place,' the boy said.

'Do they have sundaes?'

'The best sundaes,' he reassured her in his serious dead voice.

'That's what I want, a sundae. Delia likes splits best.'

'We'll be going, Fred,' the boy said.

Hale rose. His hands were shaking. This was real now: the boy, the razor cut, life going out with the blood in pain: not the deck chairs and the permanent waves, the miniature cars tearing round the curve on the Palace Pier. The ground moved under his feet, and only the thought of where they might take him while he was unconscious saved him from fainting. But even then common pride, the instinct not to make a scene, remained overpoweringly strong; embarrassment had more force than terror, it prevented him crying his fear aloud, it even urged him to go quietly. If the boy had not spoken again he might have gone.

'We'd better get moving, Fred,' the boy said.

'No,' Hale said. 'I'm not coming. I don't know him. My name's not Fred. I've never seen him before. He's just getting fresh,' and he walked rapidly away, with his head down, hopeless now – there wasn't time – only anxious to keep moving, to keep out in the clear sun; until from far down the front he heard a woman's winey voice singing, singing of brides and bouquets, of lilies and mourning shrouds, a Victorian ballad, and he moved towards it like someone who has been lost a long while in a desert makes for the glow of a fire.

'Why,' she said, 'if it isn't lonely heart,' and to his astonishment she was all by herself in a wilderness of chairs. 'They've gone to the gents,' she said.

'Can I sit down?' Hale asked. His voice broke with relief.

'If you've got twopence,' she said. 'I haven't.' She began to laugh, the great breasts pushing at her dress. 'Someone pinched my bag,' she said. 'Every penny I've got.' He watched her with astonishment. 'Oh,' she said, 'that's not the funny part. It's the letters. He'll have had all Tom's letters to read. Were they passionate? Tom'll be crazy when he hears.'

'You'll be wanting some money,' Hale said.

'Oh,' she said, 'I'm not worrying. Some nice feller will lend me ten bob when they come out of the gents.'

'They your friends?' Hale asked.

'I met 'em in the pub,' she said.

'You think,' Hale said, 'they'll come back from the gents?'

'My,' she said, 'you don't think—' She gazed up the parade, then looked at Hale and began to laugh again. 'You win,' she said. 'They've pulled my leg properly. But there was only ten bob – and Tom's letters.'

'Will you have lunch with me now?' Hale said.

'I had a snack in the pub,' she said. 'They treated me to that, so I got something out of my ten bob.'

'Have a little more.'

'No, I don't fancy any more,' she said, and leaning far back in the deck-chair with her skirt pulled up to her knees exposing her fine legs, with an air of ribald luxury, she added, 'What a day,' sparkling back at the bright sea. 'All the same,' she said, 'they'll wish they'd never been born. I'm a sticker where right's concerned.'

'Your name's Lily?' Hale asked. He couldn't see the boy any more: he'd gone: Cubitt had gone. There was nobody he could recognize as far as he could see.

'That's what *they* called me,' she said. 'My real name's Ida.' The old and vulgarized Grecian name recovered a little dignity. She said, 'You look poorly. You ought to go off and eat somewhere.'

'Not if you won't come,' Hale said. 'I only want to stay here with you.'

'Why, that's a nice speech,' she said. 'I wish Tom could hear you – he writes passionate, but when it comes to talking—'

'Does he want to marry you?' Hale asked. She smelt of soap and wine: comfort and peace and a slow sleepy physical enjoyment, a touch of the nursery and the mother, stole from the big tipsy mouth, the magnificent breasts and legs, and reached Hale's withered and frightened and bitter little brain.

'He *was* married to me once,' Ida said. 'But he didn't know when he was lucky. Now he wants to come back. You should see his letters. I'd show them you if they hadn't been stolen. He ought to be ashamed,' she said, laughing with pleasure, 'writing such things. You'd never think. And he was such a quiet fellow too. Well, I always say it's fun to be alive.'

'Will you take him back?' Hale asked, peering out from the valley of the shadow with sourness and envy.

'I should think not,' Ida said. 'I know all about him. There'd be no thrill. If I wanted a man I could do better than that now.' She wasn't boastful: only a little drunk and happy. 'I could marry money if I chose.'

'And how do you live now?' Hale said.

'From hand to mouth,' she said and winked at him and made the motion of tipping a glass. 'What's your name?'

'Fred,' He said it automatically: it was the name he always gave to chance acquaintances. From some obscure motive of secrecy he shielded his own name, Charles. From childhood he had loved secrecy, a hiding place, the dark, but it was in the dark he had met Kite, the boy, Cubitt, the whole mob.

'And how do you live?' she asked cheerfully. Men always liked to tell, and she liked to hear. She had an immense store of masculine experiences.

'Betting,' he said promptly, putting up his barrier of evasion.

'I like a flutter myself. Could you give me a tip, I wonder, for Brighton on Saturday?'

'Black Boy,' Hale said, 'in the four o'clock.'

'He's twenty to one.'

Hale looked at her with respect. 'Take it or leave it.'

'Oh, I'll take it,' Ida said.'I always take a tip.'

'Whoever gives it you?'

'That's my system. Will you be there?'

'No,' Hale said. 'I can't make it.' He put his hand on her wrist. He wasn't going to run any more risks. He'd tell the news-editor he was taken ill: he'd resign: he'd do anything. Life was here beside him, he wasn't going to play around with death. 'Come to the station with me,' he said. 'Come back to town with me.'

'On a day like this,' Ida said. 'Not me. You've had too much town. You look stuffed up. A blow along the front'll do you good. Besides, there's lots of things I want to see. I want to see the Aquarium and Black Rock and I haven't been on the Palace Pier yet to-day. There's always something new on the Palace Pier. I'm out for a bit of fun.'

'We'll do those and then—'

'When I make a day of it,' Ida said, 'I like to make a real day of it. I told you – I'm a sticker.'

'I don't mind,' Hale said, 'if you'll stay with me.'

'Well, *you* can't steal my bag,' Ida said. 'But I warn you – I like to spend. I'm not satisfied with a ring here and a shot there: I want all the shows.'

'It's a long walk,' Hale said, 'to the Palace Pier in this sun. We'd better take a taxi.' But he made no immediate pass at Ida in the taxi, sitting there bonily crouched with his eyes on the parade: no sign of the boy or Cubitt in the bright broad day sweeping by. He turned reluctantly back, and, with the sense of her great open friendly breasts, fastened his mouth on hers and received the taste of port wine on his tongue and saw in the driver's mirror the old 1925 Morris following behind, with its split and flapping hood, its bent fender and cracked and discoloured windscreen. He watched it with his mouth on hers, shaking against her as the taxi ground slowly along beside the parade.

'Give me breath,' she said at last, pushing him off and straightening her hat. 'You believe in hard work,' she said. 'It's you little fellows—' she could feel his nerves jumping under her hand, and she shouted quickly through the tube at the driver, 'Don't stop. Go on back and round again.' He was like a man with fever.

'You're sick,' she said. 'You oughtn't to be alone. What's the matter with you?'

He couldn't keep it in. 'I'm going to die. I'm scared.'

'Have you seen a doctor?'

'They are no good. They can't do anything.'

'You oughtn't to be out alone,' Ida said. 'Did they tell you that – the doctors, I mean?'

'Yes,' he said and put his mouth on hers again because when he kissed her he could watch in the mirror the old Morris vibrating after them down the parade.

She pushed him off but kept her arms round him. 'They're crazy. You aren't that sick. You can't tell me I wouldn't know if you were that sick,' she said. 'I don't like to see a fellow throw up the sponge that way. It's a good world if you don't weaken.'

'It's all right,' he said, 'long as you are here.'

'That's better,' she said, 'be yourself,' and letting down the window with a rush for the air to come in, she pushed her arm through his and said in a frightened gentle way, 'You were just kidding, weren't you, when you said that about the doctors? It wasn't true, was it?'

'No,' Hale said wearily, 'it wasn't true.'

'That's a boy,' Ida said. 'You nearly had me scared for a moment. Nice thing it would have been for me if you'd passed out in this taxi. Something for Tom to read about in the paper, I'd say. But men are funny with me that way. Always trying to make out there's something wrong, money or the wife or the heart. You aren't the first who said he was dying. Never anything infectious though. Want to make the most of their last hours and all the rest of it. It comes of me being so big, I suppose. They think I'll mother them. I'm not saying I didn't fall for it the first time. "The doctors only give me a month," he said to me – that was five years ago. I see him regular now in Henekey's. "Hullo, you old ghost," I always say to him, and he stands me oysters and a Guinness.'

'No, I'm not sick,' Hale said. 'You needn't be scared.' He wasn't going to let his pride down as much as that again, even in return for the peaceful and natural embrace. The Grand went by, the old statesman dozing out the day, the Metropole. 'Here we are,' Hale said. 'You'll stay with me, won't you, even if I'm not sick.'

'Of course I will,' Ida said, hiccuping gently as she stepped out. 'I like you, Fred. I liked you the moment I saw you. You're a good sport, Fred. What's that crowd, there?' she asked with joyful curiosity, pointing to the gathering of neat and natty trousers, of bright blouses and bare arms and bleached and perfumed hair.

'With every watch I sell,' a man was shouting in the middle of it all, 'I give a free gift worth twenty times the value of the watch. Only a shilling, ladies and gents, only a shilling. With every watch I sell . . .'

'Get me a watch, Fred,' Ida said, pushing him gently, 'and give me threepence before you go. I want to get a wash.' They stood on the pavement at the entrance to the Palace Pier; the crowd was thick around them, passing in and out of the turnstiles, watching the pedlar: there was no sign anywhere of the Morris car.

'You don't want a wash, Ida,' Hale implored her. 'You're fine.'

'I've got to get a wash,' she said, 'I'm sweating all over. You just wait here. I'll only be two minutes.'

'You won't get a good wash here,' Hale said. 'Come to a hotel and have a drink—'

'I can't wait, Fred. Really I can't. Be a sport.'

Hale said, 'That ten shillings. You'd better have that too while I remember it.'

'It's real good of you, Fred. Can you spare it?'

'Be quick, Ida,' Hale said. 'I'll be here. Just here. By this turnstile. You won't be long, will you? I'll be here,' he repeated, putting his hand on a rail of the turnstile.

'Why,' Ida said, 'anyone'd think you were in love,' and she carried the image of him quite tenderly in her mind down the steps of the ladies' lavatory: the small rather battered man with the nails bitten close (she missed nothing) and the inkstains and the hand clutching the rail. He's a good geezer, she said to herself, I liked the way he looked even in that bar if I did laugh at him, and she began to sing again, softly this time, in her warm winey voice, 'One night – in an alley – Lord Rothschild said to me. . . .' It was a long time since she'd hurried herself so for a man, and it wasn't more than four minutes before, cool and powdered and serene, she mounted into the bright Whitsun afternoon to find him gone. He wasn't by the turnstile, he wasn't in the crowd by the pedlar; she forced herself into that to make sure and found herself facing the flushed, permanently irritated salesman. 'What? Not give a shilling for a watch, and a free gift worth exactly twenty times the watch. I'm not saying the watch is worth much more than a shilling, though it's worth that for the looks alone, but with it a free gift twenty times—' She held out the ten-shilling note and got her small package and the change, thinking: he's probably gone to the gents, he'll be back; and taking up her place by the turnstile, she opened the little envelope which wrapped the watch round. 'Black Boy,' she read, 'in the four o'clock at Brighton,' and thought tenderly and proudly, 'That was his tip. He's a fellow who knows things,' and prepared patiently and happily to wait for him to return. She was a sticker. A clock away in the town struck half-past one.

Chapter Two

The Boy paid his threepence and went through the turnstile. He moved rigidly past the rows of deck-chairs four deep where people were waiting for the orchestra to play. From behind he looked younger than he was in his dark thin ready-made suit a little too big for him at the hips, but when you met him face to face he looked older, the slatey eyes were touched with the annihilating eternity from which he had come and to which he went. The orchestra began to play: he felt the music as a movement in his belly: the violins wailed in his guts. He looked neither right nor left but went on.

In the Palace of Pleasure he made his way past the peepshows, the slot-machines and the quoits to a shooting-booth. The shelves of dolls stared down with glassy innocence, like Virgins in a church repository. The Boy looked up: chestnut ringlets, blue orbs and painted cheeks: he thought – Hail Mary . . . in the hour of our death. 'I'll have six shots,' he said.

'Oh, it's you, is it?' the stall-holder said, eyeing him with uneasy distaste.

'Yes, it's me,' the Boy said. 'Have you got the time on you, Bill?'

'What do you mean – the time? There's a clock up there in the hall, isn't there?'

'It says nearly a quarter-to-two. I didn't think it was that late.'

'That clock's always right,' the man said. He came down to the end of the booth pistol in hand. 'It's always right, see,' he said. 'It doesn't stand for any phoney alibis. A quarter-to-two, that's the time.'

'That's all right, Bill,' the Boy said. 'A quarter-to-two. I just wanted to know. Give me that pistol.' He raised it: the young bony hand was steady as a rock: he put six shots inside the bull. 'That's worth a prize,' he said.

'You can take your bloody prize,' Bill said, 'and hop it. What do you want? Chocolates?'

'I don't eat chocolates,' the Boy said.

'Packet of Players?'

'I don't smoke.'

'You'll have to have a doll then or a glass vase.'

'The doll'll do,' the Boy said. 'I'll have that one – the one up there with the brown hair.'

'You getting a family?' the man said, but the Boy didn't answer, walking rigidly away past the other booths, with the smell of gunpowder on his fingers, holding the Mother of God by the hair. The water washed round the piles at the end of the pier, dark poison-bottle green, mottled with seaweed, and the salt wind smarted on his lips. He climbed the ladder on to the tea-terrace and looked around; nearly every table was full. He went inside the glass shelter and round into the long narrow tea-room which faced west, perched fifty feet above the slow withdrawing tide. A table was free and he sat down where he could see all the room and across the water to the pale parade.

'I'll wait,' he said to the girl who came for his order. 'I've got friends coming.' The window was open and he could hear the low waves beating at the pier and the music of the orchestra – faint and sad, borne away on the wind towards the shore. He said, 'They are late. What time is it?' His fingers pulled absentmindedly at the doll's hair, detaching the brown wool.

'It's nearly ten-to-two,' the girl said.

'All the clocks on this pier are fast,' he said.

'Oh, no,' the girl said. 'It's reel London time.'

'Take the doll,' the Boy said. 'It's no good to me. I just won it in one of those shooting booths. It's no good to me.'

'Can I reely?' the girl said.

'Go on. Take it. Stick it up in your room and pray.' He tossed it at her, watching the door impatiently. His body was stiffly controlled. The only sign of nervousness he showed was a slight tick in his cheek through the soft chicken down, where you might have expected a dimple. It beat more impatiently when Cubitt appeared, and with him Dallow, a stout muscular man with a broken nose and an expression of brutal simplicity.

'Well?' the Boy said.

'It's all right,' Cubitt said.

'Where's Spicer?'

'He's coming,' Dallow said. 'He's just gone into the gents to have a wash.'

'He ought to have come straight,' the Boy said. 'You're late. I said a quarter-to-two sharp.'

'Don't take on so,' Cubitt said. 'All you'd got to do was to come straight across.'

'I had to tidy up,' the Boy said. He beckoned to the waitress. 'Four fish and chips and a pot of tea. There's another coming.'

'Spicer won't want fish and chips,' Dallow said. 'He's got no appetite.'

'He'd better have an appetite,' the Boy said, and leaning his face on his hands, he watched Spicer's pale-faced progress up the tea-room and felt anger grinding at his guts like the tide at the piles below. 'It's five-to-two,' he said. 'That's right, isn't it? It's five-to-two?' he called to the waitress.

'It took longer than we thought,' Spicer said, dropping into the chair, dark and pallid and spotty. He looked with nausea at the brown crackling slab of fish the girl set before him. 'I'm not hungry,' he said. 'I can't eat this. What do you think I am?' and they all three left their fish untasted as they stared at the Boy – like children before his ageless eyes.

The Boy poured anchovy sauce out over his chips. 'Eat,' he said. 'Go on. Eat.' Dallow suddenly grinned. 'He's got no appetite,' he said and stuffed his mouth with fish. They all talked low, their words lost to those around in the hubbub of plates and voices and the steady surge of the sea. Cubitt followed suit, picking at his fish: only Spicer wouldn't eat. He sat stubbornly there, grey-haired and sea-sick.

'Give me a drink, Pinkie,' he said. 'I can't swallow this stuff.'

'You aren't going to have a drink, not to-day,' the Boy said. 'Go on. Eat.'

Spicer put some fish to his mouth. 'I'll be sick,' he said, 'if I eat.'

'Spew then,' the Boy said. 'Spew if you like. You haven't any guts to
spew.' He said to Dallow, 'Did it go all right?'

'It was beautiful,' Dallow said. 'Me and Cubitt planted him. We gave the
cards to Spicer.'

'You put 'em out all right?' the Boy said.

'Of course I put 'em out,' Spicer said.

'All along the parade?'

'Of course I put 'em out. I don't see why you get so fussed about the
cards.'

'You don't see much,' the boy said. 'They're an alibi, aren't they?' He
dropped his voice and whispered it over the fish. 'They prove he kept to
programme. They show he died after two.' He raised his voice again. 'Listen.
Do you hear that?'

Very faintly in the town a clock chimed and struck twice.

'Suppose they found him already?' Spicer said.

'Then that's just too bad for us,' the Boy said.

'What about that polony he was with?'

'She doesn't matter,' the Boy said. 'She's just a buer – he gave her a half.
I saw him hand it out.'

'You take account of most things,' Dallow said with admiration. He
poured himself a cup of black tea and helped himself to five lumps of sugar.

'I take account of what I do myself,' the Boy said. 'Where did you put the
cards?' he said to Spicer.

'I put one of 'em in Snow's,' Spicer said.

'What do you mean? Snow's?'

'He had to eat, hadn't he?' Spicer said. 'The paper said so. You said I
was to follow the paper. It'd look odd, wouldn't it, if he didn't eat, and he
always put one where he eats.'

'It'd look odder,' the boy said, 'if the waitress spotted your face wasn't
right and she found it soon as you left. Where did you put it in Snow's?'

'Under the table-cloth,' Spicer said. 'That's what he always does. There'll
have been plenty at that table since me. She won't know it wasn't him. I
don't suppose she'll find it before night, when she takes off the cloth. Maybe
it'll even be another girl.'

'You go back,' the Boy said, 'and bring that card here. I'm not taking
chances.'

'I'll not go back.' Spicer's voice rose above a whisper, and once again they
all three stared at the Boy in silence.

'You go, Cubitt,' the Boy said. 'Maybe it had better not be him again.'

'Not me,' Cubitt said. 'Suppose they'd found the card and saw me looking.
Better take a chance and leave it alone,' he urged in a whisper.

'Talk natural,' the boy said, 'talk natural,' as the waitress came back to
the table.

'Do you boys want any more?' she asked.

'Yes,' the Boy said, 'we'll have ice-cream.'

'Stow it, Pinkie,' Dallow protested when the girl had left them, 'we don't
want ice-cream. We ain't a lot of tarts, Pinkie.'

'If you don't want ice-cream, Dallow,' the Boy said, 'you go to Snow's
and get that card. You've got guts, haven't you?'

'I thought we was done with it all,' Dallow said. 'I've done enough. I've got guts, you know that, but I was scared stiff . . . Why, if they've found him before time, it'd be crazy to go into Snow's.'

'Don't talk so loud,' the Boy said. 'If nobody else'll go,' he said, 'I'll go. I'm not scared. Only I get tired sometimes of working with a mob like you. Sometimes I think I'd be better alone.' Afternoon moved across the water. He said, 'Kite was all right, but Kite's dead. Which was your table?' he asked Spicer.

'Just inside. On the right of the door. A table for one. It's got flowers on it.'

'What flowers?'

'I don't know what flowers,' Spicer said. 'Yellow flowers.'

'Don't go, Pinkie,' Dallow said, 'better leave it alone. You can't tell what'll happen,' but the Boy was already on his feet, moving stiffly down the long narrow room above the sea. You couldn't tell if he was scared; his young ancient poker-face told nothing.

In Snow's the rush was over and the table free. The wireless droned a programme of weary music, broadcast by a cinema organist – a great *vox humana* trembled across the crumby stained desert of used cloths: the world's wet mouth lamenting over life. The waitress whipped the cloths off as soon as the tables were free and laid tea things. Nobody paid any attention to the Boy; they turned their back when he looked at them. He slipped his hand under the cloth and found nothing there. Suddenly the little spurt of vicious anger rose again in the Boy's brain and he smashed a salt sprinkler down on the table so hard that the base cracked. A waitress detached herself from the gossiping group and came towards him, cold-eyed, acquisitive, ash-blonde. 'Well?' she said, taking in the shabby suit, the too young face.

'I want service,' the Boy said.

'You're late for the Lunch.'

'I don't want lunch,' the Boy said. 'I want a cup of tea and a plate of biscuits.'

'Will you go to one of the tables laid for tea, please?'

'No,' the Boy said. 'This table suits me.'

She sailed away again, superior and disapproving, and he called after her, 'Will you take that order?'

'The waitress serving your table will be here in a minute,' she said and moved away to the gossips by the service door. The Boy shifted his chair, the nerve in his cheek twitched, again he put his hand under the cloth: it was a tiny action, but it might hang him if he was observed. But he could feel nothing, and he thought with fury of Spicer: he'll muddle once too often, we'd be better without him.

'Was it tea you wanted, sir?' He looked sharply up with his hand under the cloth: one of those girls who creep about, he thought, as if they were afraid of their own footsteps: a pale thin girl younger than himself.

He said, 'I gave the order once.'

She apologized abjectly. 'There's been such a rush. And it's my first day. This was the only breathing spell. Have you lost something?'

He withdrew his hand, watching her with dangerous and unfeeling eyes. His cheek twitched again; it was the little things which tripped you up, he could think of no reason at all for having his hand under the table. She went on helpfully, 'I'll have to change the cloth again for tea, so if you've lost—'

In no time she had cleared the table of pepper and salt and mustard, the cutlery and the O.K. sauce, the yellow flowers, had nipped together the corners of the cloth and lifted it in one movement from the table, crumbs and all.

'There's nothing there, sir,' she said. He looked at the bare table-top and said, 'I hadn't lost anything.' She began to lay a fresh cloth for tea. She seemed to find something agreeable about him which made her talk, something in common perhaps – youth and shabbiness and a kind of ignorance in the dapper café. Already she had apparently forgotten his exploring hand. But would she remember, he wondered, if later people asked her questions? He despised her quiet, her pallor, her desire to please: did she also observe, remember . . .? 'You wouldn't guess,' she said, 'what I found here only ten minutes ago. When I changed the cloth.'

'Do you always change the cloth?' the Boy asked.

'Oh, no,' she said, putting out the tea things, 'but a customer upset his drink and when I changed it, there was one of Kolley Kibber's cards, worth ten shillings. It was quite a shock,' she said, lingering gratefully with the tray, 'and the others don't like it. You see it's only my second day here. They say I was a fool not to challenge him and get the prize.'

'Why didn't you challenge him?'

'Because I never thought. He wasn't a bit like the photograph.'

'Maybe the card had been there all the morning.'

'Oh, no,' she said, 'it couldn't have been. He was the first man at this table.'

'Well,' the Boy said, 'it don't make any odds. You've *got* the card.'

'Oh yes, I've got it. Only it don't seem quite fair – you see what I mean – him being so different. I *might* have got the prize. I can tell you I ran to the door when I saw the card: I didn't wait.'

'And did you see him?'

She shook her head.

'I suppose,' the Boy said, 'you hadn't looked at him close. Else you'd have known.'

'I always look at you close,' the girl said, 'the customer, I mean. You see, I'm new. I get a bit scared. I don't want to do anything to offend. Oh,' she said aghast, 'like standing here talking when you want a cup of tea.'

'That's all right,' the Boy said. He smiled at her stiffly; he couldn't use those muscles with any naturalness. 'You're the kind of girl I like—' The words were the wrong ones; he saw it at once and altered them. 'I mean,' he said, 'I like a girl who's friendly. Some of these here – they freeze you.'

'They freeze me.'

'You're sensitive, that's what it is,' the Boy said, 'like me.' He said abruptly, 'I suppose you wouldn't recognize that newspaper man again? I mean, he may be still about.'

'Oh, yes,' she said, 'I'd know him. I've got a memory for faces.'

The Boy's cheek twitched. He said, 'I see you and I've got a bit in common. We ought to get together one evening. What's your name?'

'Rose.'

He put a coin on the table and got up. 'But your tea,' she said.

'Here we been talking, and I had an appointment at two sharp.'

'Oh, I'm so sorry,' Rose said. 'You should've stopped me.'

'That's all right,' the Boy said. 'I liked it. It's only ten-past anyway – by your clock. When do you get off of an evening?'

'We don't close till half-past ten except on Sundays.'

'I'll be seeing you,' the Boy said. 'You an' me have things in common.'

Chapter Three

Ida Arnold broke her way across the Strand; she couldn't be bothered to wait for the signals, and she didn't trust the Belisha beacons. She made her way under the radiators of the buses; the drivers ground their brakes and glared at her, and she grinned back at them. She was always a little flushed as the clock struck eleven and she reached Henekey's, as if she had emerged from some adventure which had given her a better opinion of herself. But she wasn't the first in Henekey's. 'Hullo, you old ghost,' she said, and the sombre thin man in black with a bowler hat sitting beside a wine barrel said, 'Oh, forget it, Ida. Forget it.'

'You in mourning for yourself?' Ida asked, cocking her hat at a better angle in a mirror which advertised White Horse: she didn't look a day over forty.

'My wife's dead. Have a Guinness, Ida?'

'Yes. I'll have a Guinness. I didn't even know you had a wife.'

'We don't know much about each other, that's what it is, Ida,' he said. 'Why, I don't even know how you live or how many husbands you've had.'

'Oh, there's only been one Tom,' Ida said.

'There's been more than Tom in *your* life.'

'You ought to know,' Ida said.

'Give me a glass of Ruby,' the sombre man said. 'I was just thinking when you came in, Ida, why shouldn't we two come together again?'

'You and Tom always want to start again,' Ida said. 'Why don't you keep tight hold when you've got a girl?'

'What with my little bit of money and yours—'

'I like to start something fresh,' Ida said. 'Not off with the new and on with the old.'

'But you've a kind heart, Ida.'

'That's what you call it,' Ida said, and in the dark depth of her Guinness kindness winked up at her, a bit sly, a bit earthy, having a good time. 'Do you ever have a bit on the horses?' she asked.

'I don't believe in betting. It's a mug's game.'

'That's it,' Ida said. 'A mug's game. You never know whether you'll be up or down. I like it,' she said with passion, looking across the wine barrel at the thin pale man, her face more flushed than ever, more young, more kind. 'Black Boy,' she said softly.

'Eh, what's that?' the ghost said sharply, snatching a glance at his face in the White Horse mirror.

'It's the name of a horse,' she said, 'that's all. A fellow gave it me at Brighton. I was wondering if maybe I'd see him at the races. He got lost somehow. I liked him. You didn't know whatever he'd be saying next. I owe him money, too.'

'You saw about this Kolley Kibber at Brighton the other day?'

'Found him dead, didn't they? I saw a poster.'

'They've had the inquest.'

'Did he kill himself?'

'Oh no. Just his heart. The heat knocked him over. But the paper's paid the prize to the man who found him. Ten guineas,' the ghost said, 'for finding a corpse.' He laid the paper bitterly down on the wine barrel. 'Give me another Ruby.'

'Why,' Ida said. 'Is that picture the man who found him? The little rat. That's where he went to. No wonder he didn't need his money back.'

'No, no, that's not *him*,' the ghost said. 'That's Kolley Kibber.' He took a little wooden pick out of a paper packet and began to scrape his teeth.

'Oh,' Ida said. It was like a blow. 'Then he wasn't trying it on,' she said. 'He *was* sick.' She remembered how his hand had shaken in the taxi and how he had implored her not to leave him, just as if he had known he was going to die before she came back. But he hadn't made a scene. 'He was a gentleman,' she said gently. He must have fallen there by the turnstile as soon as she had turned her back, and she had gone on down without knowing into the ladies. A sense of tears came to her now in Henekey's; she measured those polished white steps down to the wash-basins as if they were the slow stages of a tragedy.

'Ah well,' the ghost said gloomily, 'we've all got to die.'

'Yes,' Ida said, 'but he wouldn't've wanted to die any more than I want to die.' She began to read and exclaimed almost at once: 'What made him walk all that way in that heat?' For he hadn't dropped at the turnstile: he'd gone back all the way they'd come, sat in a shelter. . . .

'He'd got his job to do.'

'He didn't say anything to me about a job. He said, "I'll be here. I'll stay right here by this turnstile." He said, "Be quick, Ida. I'll be just here," ' and as she repeated what she could remember of his words she had a feeling that later in an hour or two, when things got straightened out, she would want to cry a bit for the death of that scared passionate bag of bones who called himself—

'Why,' she said, 'whatever do they mean? Read here.'

'What about it?' the man said.

'The bitches,' Ida said, 'what would they go and tell a lie like that for?'

'What lie? Have another Guinness. You don't want to fuss about that.'

'I don't mind if I do,' Ida said, but when she had taken a long draught she returned to the paper. She had instincts, and now her instincts told her there was something odd, something which didn't smell right. 'These girls,' she said, 'he tried to pick up, they say a man came along who called him "Fred", and he said he wasn't Fred and he didn't know the man.'

'What about it? Listen, Ida, let's go to the pictures.'

'But he *was* Fred. He told me he was Fred.'

'He was Charles. You can read it there. Charles Hale.'

'That don't signify,' Ida said. 'A man always has a different name for strangers. You aren't telling me your real name's Clarence. And a man don't have a different name for every girl. He'd get confused. You know you always stick to Clarence. You can't tell me much about men I don't know.'

'It don't mean anything. You can read how it was. They just happened to mention it. Nobody took any notice of that.'

She said sadly, 'Nobody's taken any notice of anything. You can read it here. He hadn't got any folks to make a fuss. "The Coroner asked if any relation of the deceased was present, and the police witness stated that they could trace no relations other than a second cousin in Middlesbrough." It sounds sort of lonely,' she said. 'Nobody there to ask questions.'

'I know what loneliness is, Ida,' the sombre man said. 'I've been alone a month now.'

She took no notice of him: she was back at Brighton on Whit Monday, thinking how while she waited there, he must have been dying, walking along the front to Hove, dying, and the cheap drama and pathos of the thought weakened her heart towards him. She was of the people, she cried in cinemas at *David Copperfield*, when she was drunk all the old ballads her mother had known came easily to her lips, her homely heart was touched by the word 'tragedy'. 'The second cousin in Middlesbrough – he was represented by counsel,' she said. 'What does that mean?'

'I suppose if this Kolley Kibber hasn't left a will, he gets any money there is. He wouldn't want any talk of suicide because of the life assurance.'

'He didn't ask any questions.'

'There wasn't any need. No one made out he'd killed himself.'

'Perhaps he did all the same,' Ida said. 'There was something queer about him. I'd like to 'ave asked some questions.'

'What about? It's plain enough.'

A man in plus-fours and a striped tie came to the bar. 'Hullo, Ida,' he called.

'Hullo, Harry,' she said sadly, staring at the paper.

'Have a drink?'

'I've got a drink, thank you.'

'Swallow it down and have another.'

'No, I don't want any more, thank you,' she said. 'If I'd been there—'

'What'd have been the good?' the sombre man said.

'I could've asked questions.'

'Questions, questions,' he said irritably. 'You keep on saying questions. What about beats me.'

'Why he said he wasn't Fred.'

'He wasn't Fred. He was Charles.'

'It's not natural.' The more she thought about it the more she wished she had been there: it was like a pain in the heart, the thought that no one at the inquest was interested, the second cousin stayed in Middlesbrough, his counsel asked no questions, and Fred's own paper only gave him half a column. On the front page was another photograph – the new Kolley Kibber: he was going to be at Bournemouth to-morrow. They might have waited, she thought, a week. It would have shown respect.

'I'd liked to have asked them why he left me like that, to go scampering down the front in that sun.'

'He had his job to do. He had to leave those cards.'

'Why did he tell me he'd wait?'

'Ah,' the sombre man said, 'you'd have to ask *him* that,' and at the words it was almost as if he *was* trying to answer her, answer her in his own kind of hieroglyphics, in the obscure pain, speaking in her nerves as a ghost would have to speak. Ida believed in ghosts.

'There's a lot he'd say if he could,' she said. She took up the paper again and read slowly. 'He did his job to the end,' she said tenderly. She liked men who did their jobs: there was a kind of vitality about it. He'd dropped his cards all the way down the front: they'd come back to the office: from under a boat, from a litter basket, a child's pail. He had only a few left when 'Mr Alfred Jefferson, described as a chief clerk, of Clapham' found him. 'If he did kill himself,' she said (she was the only counsel to represent the dead), 'he did his job first.'

'But he didn't kill himself,' Clarence said. 'You've only got to read. They cut him up and they say he died natural.'

'That's queer,' Ida said. 'He went and left one in a restaurant. I knew he was hungry. He kept on wanting to eat, but whatever made him slip away like that all by himself and leave me waiting. It sounds crazy.'

'I suppose he changed his mind about you, Ida.'

'I don't like it,' Ida said. 'It sounds strange to me. I wish I'd been there. I'd have asked 'em a few questions.'

'What about you and me going across to the flickers, Ida?'

'I'm not in the mood,' Ida said. 'It's not every day you lose a friend. And you oughtn't to be in the mood either with your wife just dead.'

'She's been gone a month now,' Clarence said. 'You can't expect anyone to go on mourning for ever.'

'A month's not so long,' Ida said sadly, brooding over the paper. A day, she thought, that's all he's been gone, and I dare say there's not another soul but me thinking about him: just someone he picked up for a drink and a cuddle, and again the easy pathos touched her friendly and popular heart. She wouldn't have given it all another thought if there had been other relations, besides the second cousin in Middlesbrough, if he hadn't been so alone as well as dead. But there *was* something fishy to her nose, though there was nothing she could put her finger on except that 'Fred' – and everyone would say the same: 'He wasn't Fred. You've only to read. Charles Hale.'

'You oughtn't to fuss about that, Ida. It's none of your business.'

'I know,' she said. 'It's none of mine.' But it's none of anybody's, her heart repeated to her: that was the trouble: no one but her to ask questions. She knew a woman once who'd seen her husband after he was dead standing by the wireless set trying to twiddle the knob: she twiddled the way he wanted and he disappeared and immediately she heard an announcer say on Midland Regional: 'Gale Warning in the Channel.' She had been thinking of taking one of the Sunday trips to Calais, that was the point. It just showed: you couldn't laugh at the idea of ghosts. And if Fred, she thought, wanted to tell someone something, it wouldn't be to his second cousin in Middlesbrough that he'd go; why shouldn't he come to me? He had left her waiting there, she had waited nearly half an hour: perhaps he wanted to tell her why. 'He was a gentleman,' she said aloud, and with bolder resolution she cocked her hat and smoothed her hair and rose from the wine barrel. 'I've got to be going,' she said. 'So long, Clarence.'

'Where to? I've never known you in such a hurry. Ida,' he complained bitterly over the Guinness.

Ida put her finger on the paper. 'Someone ought to be *there*,' she said, 'even if the second cousins aren't.'

'He won't care who's putting him in the ground.'

'You never know,' Ida said, remembering the ghost by the radio set. 'It shows respect. Besides – I *like* a funeral.'

But he wasn't exactly being put in the ground in the bright new flowery suburb where he had lodged. There were no unhygienic buryings in that place. Two brick towers like those of a Scandinavian town hall, cloisters with little plaques along the walls like school war memorials, a bare cold secular chapel which could be adapted quietly and conveniently to any creed: no cemetery, wax flowers, impoverished jam-pots of wilting flowers. Ida was late. Hesitating a moment outside the door for fear the place might be full of Fred's friends, she thought someone had turned on the National Programme. She knew that cultured inexpressive voice, but when she opened the door, a man, not a machine, stood up in a black cassock saying 'Heaven'. There was nobody there but someone who looked like a landlady, a servant who had parked a pram outside, two men impatiently whispering.

'Our belief in heaven,' the clergyman went on, 'is not qualified by our disbelief in the old medieval hell. We believe,' he said, glancing swiftly along the smooth polished slipway towards the New Art doors through which the coffin would be launched into the flames, 'we believe that this our brother is already at one with the One.' He stamped his words like little pats of butter with his personal mark. 'He has attained unity. We do not know what that One is with whom (or with which) he is now at one. We do not retain the old medieval beliefs in glassy seas and golden crowns. Truth is beauty and there is more beauty for us, a truth-loving generation, in the certainty that our brother is at this moment reabsorbed in the universal spirit.' He touched a little buzzer, the New Art doors opened, the flames flapped and the coffin slid smoothly down into the fiery sea. The doors closed, the nurse rose and made for the door, the clergyman smiled gently from behind the slipway, like a conjurer who has produced his nine hundred and fortieth rabbit without a hitch.

It was all over. Ida squeezed out with difficulty a last tear into a handkerchief scented with Californian Poppy. She liked a funeral – but it was with horror – as other people like a ghost story. Death shocked her, life was so important. She wasn't religious. She didn't believe in heaven or hell, only in ghosts, ouija boards, tables which rapped and little inept voices speaking plaintively of flowers. Let Papists treat death with flippancy: life wasn't so important perhaps to them as what came after: but to her death was the end of everything. At one with the One – it didn't mean a thing beside a glass of Guinness on a sunny day. She believed in ghosts, but you couldn't call that thin transparent existence life eternal: the squeak of a board, a piece of ectoplasm in a glass cupboard at the psychical research headquarters, a voice she'd heard once at a séance saying, 'Everything is very beautiful on the upper plane. There are flowers everywhere.'

Flowers, Ida thought scornfully; that wasn't life. Life was sunlight on brass bedposts, Ruby port, the leap of the heart when the outsider you have backed passes the post and the colours go bobbing up. Life was poor Fred's mouth pressed down on hers in the taxi, vibrating with the engine along the parade. What was the sense of dying if it made you babble of flowers? Fred didn't want flowers, he wanted— and the enjoyable distress she had felt in Henekey's returned. She took life with a deadly seriousness: she was prepared to cause any amount of unhappiness to anyone in order to defend the only thing she believed in. To lose your lover – 'broken hearts,' she would say, 'always mend,' to be maimed or blinded – 'lucky,' she'd tell you, 'to be alive at all.' There was something dangerous and remorseless in her optimism, whether she was laughing in Henekey's or weeping at a funeral or a marriage.

She came out of the crematorium, and there from the twin towers above her head fumed the very last of Fred, a thin stream of grey smoke from the ovens. People passing up the flowery suburban road looked up and noted the smoke; it had been a busy day at the furnaces. Fred dropped in indistinguishable grey ash on the pink blossoms: he became part of the smoke nuisance over London, and Ida wept.

But while she wept a determination grew; it grew all the way to the tram lines which would lead her back to her familiar territory, to the bars and the electric signs and the variety theatres. Man is made by the places in which he lives, and Ida's mind worked with the simplicity and the regularity of a sky sign: the ever-tipping glass, the ever-revolving wheel, the plain question flashing on and off: 'Do You Use Forhams for the Gums?' I'd do as much for Tom, she thought, for Clarence, that old deceitful ghost in Henekey's, for Harry. It's the least you can do for anyone – ask questions, questions at inquests, questions at séances. Somebody had made Fred unhappy, and somebody was going to be made unhappy in turn. An eye for an eye. If you believed in God, you might leave vengeance to him, but you couldn't trust the One, the universal spirit. Vengeance was Ida's, just as much as reward was Ida's, the soft gluey mouth affixed in taxis, the warm handclasp in cinemas, the only reward there was. And vengeance and reward – they both were fun.

The tram tingled and sparked down the Embankment. If it was a woman who had made Fred unhappy, she'd tell her what she thought. If Fred had killed himself, she'd find it out, the papers would print the news, someone would suffer. Ida was going to begin at the beginning and work right on. She was a sticker.

The first stage (she had held the paper in her hand all through the service) was Molly Pink, 'described as a private secretary', employed by Messrs Carter & Galloway.

Ida came up from Charing Cross Station, into the hot and windy light in the Strand flickering on the carburettors; in an upper room of Stanley Gibbons a man with a long grey Edwardian moustache sat in a window examining a postage stamp through a magnifying glass; a great dray laden with barrels stamped by, and the fountains played in Trafalgar Square, a cool translucent flower blooming and dropping into the drab sooty basins.

It'll cost money, Ida repeated to herself, it always costs money if you want to know the truth, and she walked slowly up St Martin's Lane calculating, while all the time beneath the melancholy and the resolution, her heart beat faster to the refrain: it's exciting, it's fun, it's living. In Seven Dials the negroes were hanging round the public house doors in tight natty suitings and old school ties, and Ida recognized one of them and passed the time of day. 'How's business, Joe?' The great white teeth went on like a row of lights in the darkness above the bright striped shirt. 'Fine, Ida, fine.'

'And the hay fever?'

'Tur'ble, Ida, tur'ble.'

'So long, Joe.'

'So long, Ida.'

It was a quarter of an hour's walk to Messrs Carter & Galloway who lived at the very top of a tall building on the outskirts of Grays Inn. She had to economize now: she wouldn't even take a bus, and when she got to the dusty antiquated building, there wasn't a lift. The long flights of stone stairs wearied Ida. She'd had a long day and nothing to eat but a bun at the station. She sat down on a window-sill and took off her shoes. Her feet were hot, she wiggled her toes. An old gentleman came down. He had a long moustache and a sidelong raffish look. He wore a check coat, a yellow waistcoat and a grey bowler. He took off his bowler. 'In distress, madam?' he asked peering down at Ida with little bleary eyes. 'Be of assistance?'

'I don't allow anyone else to scratch my toes,' Ida said.

'Ha, ha,' the old gentleman said, 'a card. After my own heart. Up or down?'

'Up. All the way to the top.'

'Carter & Galloway. Good firm. Tell 'em I sent you.'

'What's your name?'

'Moyne. Charlie Moyne. Seen you here before.'

'Never.'

'Some place else. Never forget fine figure of a woman. Tell 'em Moyne sent you. Give you special terms.'

'Why don't they have a lift in this place?'

'Old-fashioned people. Old-fashioned myself. Seen you at Epsom.'

'You might have.'

'Always tell a sporting woman. Ask you round the corner to split a bottle of fizz if those beggars hadn't taken the last fiver I came out with. Wanted to go and lay a couple. Have to go home first. Odds'll go down while I'm doing it. You'll see. You couldn't oblige me, I suppose? Two quid, Charlie Moyne.' The bloodshot eyes watched her without hope, a little aloof and careless; the buttons on the yellow waistcoat stirred as the old heart hammered.

'Here,' Ida said, 'you can have a quid; now run along.'

'Awfully kind of you. Give me your card. Post you a cheque to-night.'

'I haven't got a card,' Ida said.

'Came out without mine, too. Never mind. Charlie Moyne. Care of Carter & Galloway. All know me here.'

'That's all right,' Ida said. 'I'll see you again. I've got to be going on up.'

'Take my arm.' He helped her up. 'Tell 'em Moyne sent you. Special terms.' She looked back at the turn of the stairs. He was tucking the pound note away in his waistcoat, smoothing the moustache which was still golden at the tips, like a cigarette smoker's fingers, setting his bowler at an angle. Poor old geezer, Ida thought, he never expected to get that, watching him go down the stairs in his jaunty and ancient despair.

There were only two doors on the top landing. She opened one marked 'Enquiries', and there without a doubt was Molly Pink. In a little room hardly larger than a broom cupboard she sat beside a gas-ring sucking a sweet. A kettle hissed at Ida as she entered. A swollen spotty face glared back at her without a word.

'Excuse me,' Ida said.

'The partners is out.'

'I came to see *you*.'

The mouth fell a little open, a lump of toffee stirred on the tongue, the kettle whistled.

'Me?'

'Yes,' Ida said. 'You'd better look out. The kettle'll boil over. You *are* Molly Pink?'

'You want a cup?' The room was lined from floor to ceiling with files. A little window disclosed through the undisturbed dust of many years another block of buildings with the same arrangement of windows staring dustily back like a reflection. A dead fly hung in a broken web.

'I don't like tea,' Ida said.

'That's lucky. There's only one cup,' Molly said, filling a thick brown teapot with a chipped spout.

'A friend of mine called Moyne . . .' Ida began.

'Oh, him!' Molly said. 'We just turned him out of house and home.' A copy of *Woman and Beauty* was propped open on her typewriter, and her eyes slid continually back to it.

'Out of house and home?'

'House and home. He came to see the partners. He tried to blarney.'

'Did he see them?'

'The partners is out. Have a toffee?'

'It's bad for the figure,' Ida said.

'I make up for it. I don't eat breakfast.'

Over Molly's head Ida could see the labels on the files:'Rents of 1–6 Mud Lane.' 'Rents of Wainage Estate, Balham.' 'Rents of . . .' They were surrounded by the pride of ownership, property . . .

'I came here,' Ida said, 'because you met a friend of mine.'

'Sit down,' Molly said. 'That's the client's chair. I has to entertain 'em. Mr Moyne's not a friend.'

'Not Moyne. Someone called Hale.'

'I don't want any more to do with that business You ought to 'ave seen the partners. They was furious. I had to have a day off for the inquest. They kept me hours late next day.'

'I just want to hear what happened.'

'What happened! The partners is awful when roused.'

'I mean about Fred – Hale.'

'I didn't exactly know him.'

'That man you said at the inquest came up—'

'He wasn't a man. He was just a kid. He knew Mr Hale.'

'But in the paper it said—'

'Oh, Mr Hale *said* he didn't know him. I didn't tell them different. They didn't ask me. Except was there anything odd in his manner? Well, there wasn't anything you'd call odd. He was just scared, that's all. We get lots like that in here.'

'But you didn't tell them that?'

'That's nothing uncommon. I knew what it was at once. He owed the kid money. We get lots like that. Like Charlie Moyne.'

'He was scared was he? Poor old Fred.'

' "I'm not Fred," he said, sharp as you please. But I could tell all right. So could my friend.'

'What was the kid like?'

'Oh, just a kid.'

'Tall?'

'Not particularly.'

'Fair?'

'I couldn't say that.'

'How old was he?'

''Bout my age, I dessay.'

'What's that?'

'Eighteen,' Molly said, staring defiantly across the typewriter and the steaming kettle, sucking a toffee.

'Did he ask for money?'

'He didn't have time to ask for money.'

'You didn't notice anything else?'

'He was awful anxious for me to go along with him. But I couldn't, not with my friend there.'

'Thanks,' Ida said, 'it's something learnt.'

'You a woman detective?' Molly asked.

'Oh, no, I'm just a friend of his.'

There *was* something fishy: she was convinced of it now. She remembered again how scared he'd been in the taxi, and going down Holborn towards her digs behind Russell Square, in the late afternoon sun, she thought again of the way in which he had handed her the ten shillings before she went down into the ladies. He was a real gentleman: perhaps it was the last few shillings he had: and those people – that boy – dunning him for money. Perhaps he was another one ruined like Charlie Moyne, and now that her memory of his face was getting a bit dim, she couldn't help lending him a few of Charlie Moyne's features, the bloodshot eyes if nothing else. Sporting gentlemen, freehanded gentlemen, real gentlemen. The dewlaps of the commercials drooped in the hall of the Imperial, the sun lay flat across the plane trees, and a bell rang and rang for tea in a boarding-house in Coram Street.

I'll try the Board, Ida thought, and then I'll know.

When she got in, there was a card on the hall table, a card of Brighton Pier: if I was superstitious, she thought, if I was superstitious. She turned it over. It was only from Phil Corkery, asking her to come down. She had the same every year from Eastbourne, Hastings and once from Aberystwyth. But she never went. He wasn't someone she liked to encourage. Too quiet. Not what she called a man.

She went to the basement stairs and called Old Crowe. She needed two
sets of fingers for the Board and she knew it would give the old man pleasure.
'Old Crowe,' she called, peering down the stone stairs. 'Old Crowe.'

'What is it, Ida?'

'I'm going to have a turn at the Board.'

She didn't wait for him, but went on up to her bed-sitting-room to make
ready. The room faced east and the sun had gone. It was cold and dusk. Ida
turned on the gas-fire and drew the old scarlet velvet curtains to shut out the
grey sky and the chimney-pots. Then she patted the divan bed into shape
and drew two chairs to the table. In a glass-fronted cupboard her life stared
back at her – a good life: pieces of china bought at the seaside, a photograph
of Tom, an Edgar Wallace, a Netta Syrett from a second-hand stall, some
sheets of music, *The Good Companions*, her mother's picture, more china,
a few jointed animals made of wood and elastic, trinkets given her by this,
that and the other, *Sorrell and Son*, the Board.

She took the Board gently down and locked the cupboard. A flat oval
piece of polished wood on tiny wheels, it looked like something which had
crept out of a cupboard in a basement kitchen. But in fact it was Old Crowe
who had done that, knocking gently on the door, sidling in, white hair, grey
face, short-sighted pit-pony eyes, blinking at the bare globe in Ida's reading-
lamp. Ida tossed a pink netty scarf over the light and dimmed it for him.

'You got something to ask it, Ida?' Old Crowe said. He shivered a little,
frightened and fascinated. Ida sharpened a pencil and inserted it in the prow
of the little board.

'Sit down, Old Crowe. What you been doing all day?'

'They had a funeral at twenty-seven. One of those Indian students.'

'I been to a funeral, too. Was yours a good one?'

'There aren't any good funerals these days. Not with plumes.'

Ida gave the little board a push. It slid sideways across the polished table
more than ever like a beetle. 'The pencil's too long,' Old Crowe said. He sat,
hugging his hands between his knees, bent forward watching the board. Ida
screwed the pencil a little higher. 'Past or future?' Old Crowe asked, panting
a little.

'I want to get into touch to-day,' Ida said.

'Dead or alive?' Old Crowe said.

'Dead. I seen him burnt this afternoon. Cremated. Come on, Old Crowe,
put your fingers on.'

'Better take off your rings,' Old Crowe said. 'Gold confuses it.'

Ida unclothed her fingers, laid the tips on the board which squeaked away
from her across the sheet of foolscap. 'Come on, Old Crowe,' she said.

Old Crowe giggled. He said, 'It's naughty,' and placed his bony digits on
the very rim, where they throbbed a tiny nervous tattoo. 'What you going
to ask it, Ida?'

'Are you there, Fred?'

The board squeaked away under their fingers drawing long lines across
the paper this way and that. 'It's got a will of its own,' Ida said.

'Hush,' said Old Crowe.

The board bucked a little with its hind wheel and came to a stop. 'We
might look now,' Ida said. She pushed the board to one side, and they stared
together at the network of pencilling.

'You might make out a Y there,' Ida said.

'Or it might be an N.'

'Anyway something's there. We'll try again.' She put her fingers firmly on the board. 'What happened to you, Fred?' and immediately the board was off and away. All her indomitable will worked through her fingers: she wasn't going to have any nonsense this time, and across the board the grey face of Old Crowe frowned with concentration.

'It's writing – real letters,' Ida said with triumph, and as her own fingers momentarily loosened their grip she could feel the board slide firmly away as if on another's errand.

'Hush,' said Old Crowe, but it bucked and stopped. They pushed the board away, and there, unmistakably, in large thin letters was a word, but not a word they knew: 'SUKILL'.

'It looks like a name,' Old Crowe said.

'It must mean something,' Ida said. 'The Board always means something. We'll try again,' and again the wooden beetle scampered off, drawing its tortuous trail. The globe burnt red under the scarf, and Old Crowe whistled between his teeth. 'Now,' Ida said and lifted the Board. A long ragged word ran diagonally across the paper: 'FRESUICILLEYE.'

'Well,' Old Crowe said, 'that's a mouthful. You can't make anything of that, Ida.'

'Can't I though,' Ida said. 'Why, it's clear as clear. Fre is short for Fred and Suici for Suicide and Eye; that's what I always say – an eye for an eye and a tooth for a tooth.'

'What about those two L's?'

'I don't know yet, but I'll bear them in mind.' She leant back in her chair with a sense of power and triumph. 'I'm not superstitious,' she said, 'but you can't get over that. The Board knows.'

'She knows,' Old Crowe said, sucking his teeth.

'One more try?' The board slid and squeaked and abruptly stopped. Clear as clear the name stared up at her: 'PHIL'.

'Well,' Ida said, 'well.' She blushed a little. 'Like a sugar biscuit?'

'Thank you, Ida, thank you.'

Ida took a tin out of the cupboard drawer and pushed it over to Old Crowe. 'They drove him to death,' Ida said happily. 'I knew there was something fishy. See that EYE. That as good as tells me what to do.' Her eye lingered on Phil. 'I'm going to make those people sorry they was ever born.' She drew in her breath luxuriously and stretched her monumental legs. 'Right and wrong,' she said. 'I believe in right and wrong,' and delving a little deeper, with a sigh of happy satiety, she said, 'It's going to be exciting, it's going to be fun, it's going to be a bit of life, Old Crowe,' giving the highest praise she could give to anything, while the old man sucked his tooth and the pink light wavered on the Warwick Deeping.

Chapter One

The Boy stood with his back to Spicer staring out across the dark wash of sea. They had the end of the pier to themselves; everyone else at that hour and in that weather was in the concert hall. The lightning went on and off above the horizon and the rain dripped. 'Where've you been?' the Boy asked.

'Walking around,' Spicer said.

'You been There?'

'I wanted to see it was all safe, that there wasn't anything you'd forgotten.'

The Boy said slowly, leaning out across the rail into the doubtful rain, 'When people do one murder, I've read they sometimes have to do another – to tidy up.' The word murder conveyed no more to him than the word 'box', 'collar', 'giraffe'. He said, 'Spicer, you keep away from there.'

The imagination hadn't awoken. That was his strength. He couldn't see through other people's eyes, or feel with their nerves. Only the music made him uneasy, the catgut vibrating in the heart; it was like nerves losing their freshness, it was like age coming on, other people's experience battering on the brain. 'Where are the rest of the mob?'

'In Sam's, drinking.'

'Why aren't you drinking too?'

'I'm not thirsty, Pinkie. I wanted some fresh air. This thunder makes you feel queer.'

'Why don't they stop that bloody noise in there?' the Boy said.

'You not going to Sam's?'

'I've got a job of work to do,' the Boy said.

'It's all right, Pinkie, ain't it? After that verdict it's all right? Nobody asked questions.'

'I just want to be sure,' the Boy said.

'The mob won't stand for any more killing.'

'Who said there was going to be any killing?' The lightning flared up and showed his tight shabby jacket, the bunch of soft hair at the nape. 'I've got a date, that's all. You be careful what you say, Spicer. You aren't milky, are you?'

'I'm not milky. You got me wrong, Pinkie. I just don't want another killing. That verdict sort of shook us all. What did they mean by it? We *did* kill him, Pinkie?'

'We got to go on being careful, that's all.'

'What did they mean by it, though? I don't trust the doctors. A break like that's *too* good.'

'We got to be careful.'

'What's that in your pocket, Pinkie?'

'I don't carry a gun,' the Boy said. 'You're fancying things.' In the town a clock struck eleven: three strokes were lost in the thunder coming down across the Channel. 'You better be off,' the Boy said, 'She's late already.'

'You've got a razor there, Pinkie.'

'I don't need a razor with a polony. If you want to know what it is, it's a bottle.'

'You don't drink, Pinkie.'

'Nobody would want to drink this.'

'What is it, Pinkie?'

'Vitriol,' the Boy said. 'It scares a polony more than a knife.' He turned impatiently away from the sea and complained again, 'That music.' It moaned in his head in the hot electric night, it was the nearest he knew to sorrow, just as a faint secret sensual pleasure he felt, touching the bottle of vitriol with his fingers, as Rose came hurrying by the concert hall, was his nearest approach to passion. 'Get out,' he said to Spicer. 'She's here.'

'Oh,' Rose said, 'I'm late. I've run all the way,' she said. 'I thought you might have thought—'

'I'd have waited,' the Boy said.

'It was an awful night in the cafe,' the girl said. 'Everything went wrong. I broke two plates. And the cream was sour.' It all came out in a breath. 'Who was your friend?' she asked, peering into the darkness.

'He don't matter,' the Boy said.

'I thought somehow— I couldn't see properly—'

'He don't matter,' the Boy repeated.

'What are we going to do?'

'Why, I thought we'd talk a little here first,' the Boy said, 'and then go on somewhere – Sherry's? I don't care.'

'I'd love Sherry's,' Rose said.

'You got your money yet for that card?'

'Yes. I got it this morning.'

'Nobody came and asked you questions?'

'Oh no. But wasn't it dreadful, his being dead like that?'

'You saw his photograph?'

Rose came close to the rail and peered palely up at the Boy. 'But it wasn't him. That's what I don't understand.'

'People look different in photographs.'

'I've got a memory for faces. It wasn't him. They must have cheated. You can't trust the newspapers.'

'Come here,' the Boy said. He drew her round the corner until they were a little farther from the music, more alone with the lightning on the horizon and the thunder coming closer. 'I like you,' the Boy said, an unconvincing smile forking his mouth, 'and I want to warn you. This fellow Hale, I've heard a lot about him. He got himself mixed up with things.'

'What sort of things?' Rose whispered.

'Never mind what things,' the Boy said. 'Only I'd warn you for your own good – you've got the money – if I was you I'd forget it, forget all about that fellow who left the card. He's dead, see. You've got the money. That's all that matters.'

'Anything you say,' Rose said.

'You can call me Pinkie if you like. That's what my friends call me.'

'Pinkie,' Rose repeated, trying it shyly out as the thunder cracked overhead.

'You read about Peggy Baron, didn't you?'

'No, Pinkie.'

'It was in all the papers.'

'I didn't see any papers till I got this job. We couldn't afford papers at home.'

'She got mixed up with a mob,' the Boy said, 'and people came asking her questions. It's not safe.'

'I wouldn't get mixed up with a mob like that,' Rose said.

'You can't always help it. It sort of comes that way.'

'What happened to her?' Rose said.

'They spoilt her looks. She lost one eye. They splashed vitriol on her face.'

Rose whispered, 'Vitriol? What's vitriol?' and the lightning showed a strut of tarred wood, a wave breaking and her pale, bony, terrified face.

'You never seen vitriol?' the Boy said, grinning through the dark. He showed her the little bottle. 'That's vitriol.' He took the cork out and spilled a little on the wooden plank of the pier: it hissed like steam. 'It burns,' the Boy said. 'Smell it,' and he thrust the bottle under her nose.

She gasped at him. 'Pinkie, *you* wouldn't—' and 'I was pulling your leg,' he smoothly lied to her. 'That's not vitriol, that's just spirit. I wanted to warn you, that's all. You and me's going to be friends. I don't want a friend with her skin burned off. You tell me if anyone asks questions. Anyone – mind. Get me on the blower at Frank's straight off. Three sixes. You can remember that.' He took her arm and propelled her away from the lonely pier-end, back by the lit concert-hall, the music drifting landwards, grief in the guts. 'Pinkie,' she said, 'I wouldn't want to interfere. I don't interfere in anyone's business. I've never been nosy. Cross my heart.'

'You're a good kid,' he said.

'You know an awful lot about things, Pinkie,' she said with horror and admiration, and suddenly at the stale romantic tune the orchestra was playing – 'lovely to look at, beautiful to hold, and heaven itself –' a little venom of anger and hatred came out on the Boy's lips: 'You've got to know a lot,' he said, 'if you get around. Come on, we'll go to Sherry's.'

Once off the pier they had to run for it; taxis splashed them with water; the strings of coloured bulbs down the Hove parade gleamed like pools of petrol through the rain. They shook the water off on to the floor of Sherry's and Rose saw the queue waiting all the way upstairs for the gallery. 'It's full,' she said, with disappointment.

'We'll go on the floor,' the Boy said, paying his three shillings as carelessly as if he always went there, and walked out among the little tables, the dancing partners with bright metallic hair and little black bags, while the coloured lights flashed green and pink and blue. Rose said, 'It's lovely here. It reminds me,' and all the way to their table she counted over aloud all the things of which it reminded her, the lights, the tune the band was playing, the crowd on the floor trying to rumba. She had an immense store of trivial memories and when she wasn't living in the future she was living in the past. As for the present – she got through that as quickly as she could, running away from things, running towards things, so that her voice was always a little breathless, her heart pounding at an escape or an expectation. 'I whipped the plate under the apron and she said. "Rose, what are you hiding there?" ' and a moment later she was turning wide unfledged eyes back to the Boy with a look of the deepest admiration, the most respectful hope.

'What'll you drink?' the Boy said.

She didn't even know the name of a drink. In Nelson Place from which she had emerged like a mole into the daylight of Snow's restaurant and the Palace Pier, she had never known a boy with enough money to offer her a drink. She would have said 'beer', but she had had no opportunity of discovering whether she liked beer. A twopenny ice from an Everest tricycle was the whole extent of her knowledge of luxury. She goggled hopelessly at the Boy. He asked her sharply, 'What d'you like? *I* don't know what you like.'

'An ice,' she said with disappointment, but she couldn't keep him waiting.

'What kind of an ice?'

'Just an ordinary ice,' she said. Everest hadn't in all the slum years offered her a choice.

'Vanilla?' the waiter said. She nodded; she supposed that that was what she had always had, and so it proved – only a size larger; otherwise she might just as well have been sucking it between wafers by a tricycle.

'You're a soft sort of kid,' the Boy said. 'How old are you?'

'I'm seventeen,' she said defiantly; there was a law which said a man couldn't go with you before you were seventeen.

'I'm seventeen too,' the Boy said, and the eyes which had never been young stared with grey contempt into the eyes which had only just begun to learn a thing or two. He said, 'Do you dance?' and she replied humbly, 'I haven't danced much.'

'It don't matter,' the Boy said, 'I'm not one for dancing.' He eyed the slow movement of the two-backed beasts: pleasure, he thought, they call it pleasure: he was shaken by a sense of loneliness, an awful lack of under-standing. The floor was cleared for the last cabaret of the evening. A spotlight picked out a patch of floor, a crooner in a dinner jacket, a microphone on a long black movable stand. He held it tenderly as if it were a woman, swinging it gently this way and that, wooing it with his lips while from the loudspeaker under the gallery his whisper reverberated hoarsely over the hall, like a dictator announcing victory, like the official news following a long censorship. 'It gets you,' the Boy said, 'it gets you,' surrendering himself to the huge brazen suggestion.

'Music talks, talks of our love.
The starling on our walks, talks, talks of our love.
The taxis tooting,
The last owl hooting,
The tube train rumbling,
Busy bee bumbling,
   Talk of our love.

Music talks, talks of our love,
The west wind on our walks, talks, talks of our love.
The nightingale singing,
The postmen ringing,

Electric drill groaning,
Office telephoning,
    Talk of our love.'

The Boy stared at the spotlight: music, love, nightingale, postmen: the words stirred in his brain like poetry: one hand caressed the vitriol bottle in his pocket, the other touched Rose's wrist. The inhuman voice whistled round the gallery and the Boy sat silent. It was he this time who was being warned; life held the vitriol bottle and warned him: I'll spoil your looks. It spoke to him in the music, and when he protested that he for one would never get mixed up, the music had its own retort at hand: 'You can't always help it. It sort of comes that way.'

    'The watchdog on our walks, talks, talks of our love.'

The crowd stood at attention six deep behind the tables (there wasn't enough room on the floor for so many). They were dead quiet. It was like the anthem on Armistice Day when the King has deposited his wreath, the hats off, and the troops turned to stone. It was love of a kind, music of a kind, truth of a kind they listened to.

    'Gracie Fields funning,
    The gangsters gunning,
        Talk of our love.'

The music pealed on under the Chinese lanterns and the pink spotlight featured the singer holding the microphone closer to his starched shirt. 'You been in love?' the Boy asked sharply and uneasily.

'Oh yes,' Rose said.

The Boy retorted with sudden venom, 'You would have been. You're green. You don't know what people do.' The music came to an end and in the silence he laughed aloud. 'You're innocent.' People turned in their chairs and looked at them: a girl giggled. His fingers pinched her wrist. 'You're green,' he said again. He was working himself into a little sensual rage, as he had done with the soft kids at the council school. 'You don't know anything,' he said, with contempt in his nails.

'Oh no,' she protested. 'I know a lot.'

The Boy grinned at her, 'Not a thing,' pinching the skin of her wrist until his nails nearly met. 'You'd like me for your boy, eh? We'll keep company?'

'Oh,' she said, 'I'd love it.' Tears of pride and pain pricked behind her lids. 'If you like doing that,' she said, 'go on.'

The Boy let go. 'Don't be soft,' he said. 'Why should I like it? You think you know too much,' he complained. He sat there, anger like a live coal in his belly, as the music came on again: all the good times he'd had in the old days with nails and splinters: the tricks he'd learnt later with a razor blade: what would be the fun if people didn't squeal? He said furiously, 'We'll be going. I can't stand this place,' and obediently Rose began to pack her handbag, putting back her Woolworth compact and her handkerchief. 'What's that?' the Boy said when something clinked in her bag; she showed him the end of a string of beads.

'You a Roman?' the Boy asked.

'Yes,' Rose said.

'I'm one too,' the Boy said. He gripped her arm and pushed her out into the dark dripping street. He turned up the collar of his jacket and ran as the lightning flapped and the thunder filled the air. They ran from doorway to doorway until they were back on the parade in one of the empty glass shelters. They had it to themselves in the noisy stifling night. 'Why, I was in a choir once,' the Boy confided and suddenly he began to sing softly in his spoilt boy's voice: 'Agnus dei qui tollis peccata mundi, dona nobis pacem.' In his voice a whole lost world moved – the lighted corner below the organ, the smell of incense and laundered surplices, and the music. Music – it didn't matter what music – 'Agnus dei', 'lovely to look at, beautiful to hold', 'the starling on our walks', 'credo in unum Dominum' – any music moved him, speaking of things he didn't understand.

'Do you go to Mass?' he asked.

'Sometimes,' Rose said. 'It depends on work. Most weeks I wouldn't get much sleep if I went to Mass.'

'I don't care what you do,' the Boy said sharply. 'I don't go to Mass.'

'But you believe, don't you,' Rose implored him, 'you think it's true?'

'Of course it's true,' the Boy said. 'What else could there be?' he went scornfully on. 'Why,' he said, 'it's the only thing that fits. These atheists, they don't know nothing. Of course there's Hell. Flames and damnation,' he said with his eyes on the dark shifting water and the lightning and the lamps going out above the black struts of the Palace Pier, 'torments.'

'And Heaven too,' Rose said with anxiety, while the rain fell interminably on.

'Oh, maybe,' the Boy said, 'maybe.'

Wet to the skin, the trousers sticking to his thin legs the Boy went up the long unmatted flight to his bedroom at Frank's. The banister shook under his hand, and when he opened the door and found the mob there, sitting on his brass bedstead smoking, he said furiously, 'When's that banister going to be mended. It's not safe. Someone'll take a fall one day.' The curtain wasn't drawn, the window was open, and the last lightning flapped across the grey roofs stretching to the sea. The Boy went to his bed and swept off the crumbs of Cubitt's sausage roll. 'What's this,' he said, 'a meeting?'

'There's trouble about the subscriptions, Pinkie,' Cubitt said. 'There's two not come in. Brewer and Tate. They say now Kite's dead—'

'Do we carve 'em up, Pinkie?' Dallow asked. Spicer stood at the window watching the storm. He said nothing, staring out at the flames and chasms of the sky.

'Ask Spicer,' the Boy said. 'He's been doing a lot of thinking lately.' They all turned and watched Spicer. Spicer said, 'Maybe we ought to lay off a while. You know a lot of the boys cleared out when Kite got killed.'

'Go on,' the Boy said. 'Listen to him. He's what they call a philosopher.'

'Well,' Spicer said angrily, 'there's free speech in this mob, ain't there? Those that cleared out, they didn't see how a kid could run this show.'

The Boy sat on the bed watching him with his hands in his damp pockets. He shivered once.

'I was always against murder,' Spicer said. 'I don't care who knows it.'

'Sour and milky,' the Boy said.

Spicer came into the middle of the room. 'Listen, Pinkie,' he said. 'Be reasonable.' He appealed to them all, 'Be reasonable.'

'There's things in what he says,' Cubitt suddenly put in. 'We had a lucky break. We don't want to draw attention to ourselves. We'd better let Brewer and Tate be for a while.'

The Boy got up. A few crumbs stuck to his wet suit. 'You ready, Dallow?' he said.

'What you say, Pinkie,' Dallow said, grinning like a large friendly dog.

'Where you going, Pinkie?' Spicer asked.

'I'm going to see Brewer.'

Cubitt said, 'You act as if it was last year we killed Hale, not last week. We got to act cautious.'

'That's over and done,' the Boy said. 'You heard the verdict. Natural causes,' he said, looking out at the dying storm.

'You forget that girl in Snow's. She could hang us.'

'I'm looking after the girl. She won't talk.'

'You're marrying her, aren't you?' Cubitt said. Dallow laughed.

The Boy's hands came out of his pockets, the knuckles clenched white. He said, 'Who told you I was marrying her?'

'Spicer,' Cubitt said.

Spicer backed away from the Boy. He said, 'Listen, Pinkie. I only said as it would make her safe. A wife can't give evidence . . .'

'I don't need to marry a squirt to make her safe. How do we make you safe, Spicer?' His tongue came out between his teeth, licking the edges of his dry cracked lips. 'If carving'd do it . . .'

'It was just a joke,' Cubitt said. 'You don't need to take it so solemn. You want a sense of humour, Pinkie.'

'You think that was funny, eh?' the Boy said. 'Me – marrying – that cheap polony.' He croaked 'Ha, ha,' at them, 'I'll learn. Come on, Dallow.'

'Wait till morning,' Cubitt said. 'Wait till some of the other boys come in.'

'You milky too?'

'You don't believe that, Pinkie. But we got to go slow.'

'You with me, Dallow?' the Boy asked.

'I'm with you, Pinkie.'

'Then we'll be going,' the Boy said. He went across to the washstand and opened the little door where the jerry stood. He felt at the back behind the jerry and pulled out a tiny blade, like the blades women shave with, but blunt along one edge and mounted with sticking-plaster. He stuck it under his long thumb-nail, the only nail not bitten close, and drew on his glove. He said, 'We'll be back with the sub. in half an hour,' and led the way bang straight down Frank's stairs. The cold of his drenching had got under his skin: he came out on to the front a pace ahead of Dallow, his face contorted with ague, a shiver twisting the narrow shoulders. He said over his shoulder to Dallow, 'We'll go to Brewer's. One lesson'll be enough.'

'What you say, Pinkie,' Dallow said, plodding after. The rain had stopped: it was low tide and the shallow edge of the sea scraped far out at the rim of the shingle. A clock struck midnight. Dallow suddenly began to laugh.

'What's got you, Dallow?'

'I was just thinking,' Dallow said. 'You're a grand little geezer, Pinkie. Kite was right to take you on. You go straight for things, Pinkie.'

'You're all right,' the Boy said, staring ahead, the ague wringing his face. They passed the Cosmopolitan, the lights on here and there all the way up the tall front to the turrets against the clouded moving sky. In Snow's when they passed a single light went out. They turned up the Old Steyne. Brewer had a house near the tram lines on the Lewes road almost under the railway viaduct.

'He's gone to bed,' Dallow said. Pinkie rang the bell, holding his finger on the switch. Low shuttered shops ran off on either hand, a tram went by with nobody in it, labelled 'Depot Only', ringing and swinging down the empty road, the conductor drowsing on a seat inside, the roof gleaming from the storm. Pinkie kept his finger on the bell.

'What made Spicer say that – about me marrying?' the Boy asked.

'He just thought it'd close her clapper,' Dallow said.

'She's not what keeps me awake,' the Boy said, pressing on the bell. A light went on upstairs, a window creaked up, and a voice called, 'Who's that?'

'It's me,' the Boy said. 'Pinkie.'

'What do you want? Why don't you come around in the morning?'

'I want to talk to you, Brewer.'

'I've got nothing to talk about, Pinkie, that can't wait.'

'You'd better open up, Brewer. You don't want the mob along here.'

'The old woman's awful sick, Pinkie. I don't want any trouble. She's asleep. She hasn't slept for three nights.'

'This'll wake her,' the Boy said with his finger on the bell. A slow goods train went by across the viaduct, shaking smoke down into the Lewes road.

'Leave off, Pinkie, and I'll open up.'

Pinkie shivered as he waited, his gloved hand deep in his damp pocket. Brewer opened the door, a stout elderly man in soiled white pyjamas. The bottom button was missing and the coat swung from the bulging belly and the deep navel. 'Come in, Pinkie,' he said, 'and walk quiet. The old woman's bad. I've been worrying my head off.'

'That why you haven't paid your subscription, Brewer?' the Boy said. He looked with contempt down the narrow hall – the shell case converted into an umbrella-stand, the moth-eaten stag's head bearing on one horn a bowler hat, a steel helmet used for ferns. Kite ought to have got them into better money than this. Brewer had only just graduated from the street corner, saloon-bar betting. A welsher. It was no good trying to draw more than ten per cent of his bets.

Brewer said, 'Come in here and be snug. It's warm in here. What a cold night.' He had a hollow cheery manner even in pyjamas. He was like a legend on a racing card – The Old Firm. You can Trust Bill Brewer. He lit the gas-fire, turned on a stand lamp in a red silk shade with a bobble fringe. The light glowed on a silver-plated biscuit-box, a framed wedding group. 'Have a spot of Scotch?' Brewer invited them.

'You know I don't drink,' the Boy said.

'Ted will,' Brewer said.

'I don't mind a spot,' Dallow said. He grinned and said, 'Here's how.'

'We've called for that subscription, Brewer,' the Boy said.

The man in white pyjamas hissed soda into his glass. His back turned he watched Pinkie in the glass above the sideboard until he caught the other's eye. He said, 'I been worried, Pinkie. Ever since Kite was croaked.'

'Well?' the Boy said.

'It's like this. I said to myself if Kite's mob can't even protect—' he stopped suddenly and listened. 'Was that the old woman?' Very faintly from the room above came the sound of coughing. Brewer said, 'She's woke up. I got to go and see her.'

'You stay here,' the Boy said, 'and talk.'

'She'll want turning.'

'When we've finished you can go'.

Cough, cough, cough: it was like a machine trying to start and failing. Brewer said desperately, 'Be human. She won't know where I've got to. I'll only be a minute.'

'You don't need to be longer than a minute here,' the Boy said. 'All we want's what's due to us. Twenty pounds.'

'I haven't got it in the house. Honest I haven't.'

'That's too bad for you.' The Boy drew off his right glove.

'It's like this, Pinkie. I paid it all out yesterday. To Colleoni.'

'What in Jesus' name,' the Boy said, 'has Colleoni to do with it?'

Brewer went rapidly and desperately on, listening to the cough, cough, cough upstairs. 'Be reasonable, Pinkie. I can't pay both of you. I'd have been carved if I hadn't paid Colleoni.'

'Is he in Brighton?'

'He's stopping at the Cosmopolitan.'

'And Tate – Tate's paid Colleoni too?'

'That's right, Pinkie. He's running the business in a big way.' A big way it was like an accusation, a reminder of the brass bedstead at Frank's, the crumbs on the mattress.

'You think I'm finished?' the Boy said.

'Take my advice, Pinkie, and go in with Colleoni.'

The Boy suddenly drew his hand back and slashed with his razored nail at Brewer's cheek. He struck blood out along the cheek bone. 'Don't,' Brewer said, 'don't,' backing against the sideboard, upsetting the biscuit-box. He said, 'I've got protection. You be careful. I've got protection.'

The Boy laughed. Dallow refilled his glass with Brewer's whisky. The Boy said, 'Look at him. He's got protection.' Dallow took a splash of soda.

'You want any more?' the Boy said. 'That was just to show you who's protecting you.'

'I can't pay you both, Pinkie. God's sake, keep back.'

'Twenty pounds is what we've come for, Brewer.'

'Colleoni'll have my blood, Pinkie.'

'You needn't worry. We'll protect you.'

Cough, cough, cough went the woman upstairs, and then a faint cry like a sleeping child's. 'She's calling me,' Brewer said.

'Twenty pounds.'

'I don't keep my money in here. Let me fetch it.'

'You go with him, Dallow,' the Boy said. 'I'll wait here,' and he sat down on a straight carved dining-room chair and stared out – at the mean street, the dustbins along the pavement, the vast shadow of the viaduct. He sat perfectly still with his grey ancient eyes giving nothing away.

A big way – Colleoni come into it in a big way – he knew there wasn't a soul in the mob he could trust – except perhaps Dallow. That didn't matter. You couldn't make mistakes when you trusted nobody. A cat coasted cautiously round a bin on the pavement, stopped suddenly, crouched back, and in the semi-dark its agate eyes stared up at the Boy. Boy and cat, they didn't stir, watching each other, until Dallow returned.

'I've got the money, Pinkie,' Dallow said. The Boy turned his head and grinned at Dallow. Suddenly his face was convulsed: he sneezed twice, violently. Overhead the coughing died away. 'He won't forget this visit,' Dallow said. He added anxiously, 'You ought to have a spot of whisky, Pinkie. You've caught cold.'

'I'm all right,' the Boy said. He got up. 'We won't stop and say good-bye.'

The Boy led the way down the middle of the empty road, between the tram lines. He said suddenly, 'Do you think I'm finished, Dallow?'

'You?' Dallow said. 'Why, you haven't even begun.' They walked for a while in silence, the water from the gutters dripped on the pavement. Then Dallow spoke.

'You worrying about Colleoni?'

'I'm not worrying.'

Dallow said suddenly, 'You're worth a dozen Colleonis. The Cosmopolitan,' he exclaimed and spat.

'Kite thought he'd go in for the automatic machines. He learned different. Now Colleoni thinks the coast's clear. *He's* branching out.'

'He ought to have learned from Hale.'

'Hale died natural.'

Dallow laughed. 'Tell that to Spicer.' They turned the corner by the Royal Albion and the sea was with them again – the tide had turned – a movement, a splashing, a darkness. The Boy looked suddenly sideways and up at Dallow – he could trust Dallow – receiving from the ugly and broken face a sense of triumph and companionship and superiority. He felt as a physically weak but cunning schoolboy feels who has attached to himself in an indiscriminating fidelity the strongest boy in the school. 'You mug,' he said and pinched Dallow's arm. It was almost like affection.

A light still burned in Frank's, and Spicer was waiting in the hall. 'Anything happened?' he asked anxiously. His pale face had come out in spots round the mouth and nose.

'What do you think?' the Boy said, going upstairs. 'We brought the subscription.'

Spicer followed him into his bedroom. 'There was a call for you just after you'd gone.'

'Who from?'

'A girl called Rose.'

The Boy sat on the bed undoing his shoe. 'What did she want?' he asked.

'She said while she was out with you, somebody had been in asking for her.'

The Boy sat still with the shoe in his hand. 'Pinkie,' Spicer said, 'was it *the* girl? The girl from Snow's?'

'Of course it was.'

'I answered the phone, Pinkie.'

'Did she know your voice?'

'How do I know, Pinkie?'

'Who was asking for her?'

'She didn't know. She said tell you because you wanted to hear. Pinkie, suppose the bogies have got that far?'

'The bogies aren't as smart as that,' Pinkie said. 'Maybe it's one of Colleoni's men, poking around after their pal Fred.' He took off his other shoe. 'You don't need to turn milky, Spicer.'

'It was a woman, Pinkie.'

'I'm not troubling. Fred died natural. That's the verdict. You can forget it. There's other things to think of now.' He put his shoes side by side under the bed, took off his coat, hung it on a bed ball, took off his trousers, lay back in his pants and shirt on top of the bed. 'I'm thinking, Spicer, you oughter take a holiday. You look all in. I wouldn't want anyone seeing you like that.' He closed his eyes. 'You be off Spicer, and take things easy.'

'If that girl ever knew *who* put the card . . .'

'She'll never know. Turn out the light and get.'

The light went out and the moon went on like a lamp outside, slanting across the roofs, laying the shadow of clouds across the downs, illuminating the white empty stands of the racecourse above Whitehawk Bottom like the monoliths of Stonehenge, shining across the tide which drove up from Boulogne and washed against the piles of the Palace Pier. It lit the washstand, the open door where the jerry stood, the brass balls at the bed end.

Chapter Two

The Boy lay on the bed. A cup of coffee went cold on the washstand, and the bed was sprinkled with flakes of pastry. The Boy licked an indelible pencil, his mouth was stained purple at the corners, he wrote: 'Refer you to my previous letter,' and concluded it at last, 'P. Brown, Secretary, the Bookmakers' Protection . . .' The envelope addressed 'Mr J. Tate' lay on the washstand, the corner soiled with coffee. When he had finished writing he put his head back on the pillow and closed his eyes. He fell asleep at once: it was like the falling of a shutter, the pressure of the bulb which ends a time exposure. He had no dreams. His sleep was functional. When Dallow opened the door he woke at once. 'Well?' he said, lying there without moving, fully dressed among the pastry crumbs.

'There's a letter for you, Pinkie. Judy brought it up.'

The Boy took the letter. Dallow said, 'It's an elegant letter, Pinkie. Smell it.'

The Boy held the mauve envelope to his nose. It smelt like a cachou for bad breath. He said, 'Can't you keep off that bitch? If Frank knew . . .'

'Who'd be writing an elegant letter like that, Pinkie?'

'Colleoni. He wants me to call in for a talk at the Cosmopolitan.'

'The Cosmopolitan,' Dallow repeated with disgust. 'You won't go, will you?'

'Of course I'll go.'

'It's not the sort of place where you'd feel at home.'

'Elegant,' the Boy said, 'like his notepaper. Costs a lot of money. He thinks he can scare me.'

'Perhaps we'd better lay off Tate.'

'Take that jacket down to Frank. Tell him to sponge it quick and put an iron over it. Give these shoes a brush.' He kicked them out from under the bed and sat up. 'He thinks he'll have the laugh on us.' In the tipped mirror on the washstand he could see himself, but his eyes shifted quickly from the image of smooth, never shaven cheek, soft hair, old eyes: he wasn't interested. He had too much pride to worry about appearances.

So that later he was quite at ease waiting in the great lounge under the domed lights for Colleoni: young men kept on arriving in huge motoring coats accompanied by small tinted creatures, who rang like expensive glass when they were touched but who conveyed an impression of being as sharp and tough as tin. They looked at nobody, sweeping through the lounge as they had swept in racing models down the Brighton Road, ending on high stools in the American Bar. A stout woman in a white fox fur came out of a lift and stared at the Boy, then she got back into the lift again and moved weightily upwards. A little bitch sniffed at him and then talked him over with another little bitch on a settee. Mr Colleoni came across an acre of deep carpet from the Louis Seize writing room, walking on tiptoe in glacé shoes.

He was small with a neat round belly; he wore a grey double-breasted waistcoat, and his eyes gleamed like raisins. His hair was thin and grey. The little bitches on the settee stopped talking as he passed and concentrated. He clinked very gently as he moved; it was the only sound.

'You were asking for me?' he said.

'You asked for me,' the Boy said. 'I got your letter.'

'Surely,' Mr Colleoni said, making a little bewildered motion with his hands, 'you are not Mr P. Brown?' He explained, 'I expected someone a good deal older.'

'You asked for me,' the Boy said.

The little raisin eyes took him in: the sponged suit and the narrow shoulders, the cheap black shoes. 'I thought Mr Kite . . .'

'Kite's dead,' the Boy said. 'You know that.'

'I missed it,' Mr Colleoni said. 'Of course that makes a difference.'

'You can talk to me,' the Boy said, 'instead of Kite.'

Mr Colleoni smiled. 'I don't think it's necessary,' he said.

'You'd better,' the Boy said. Little chimes of laughter came from the American Bar and the chink, chink, chink of ice. A page came out of the Louis Seize writing room, called, 'Sir Joseph Montagu, Sir Joseph Montagu,' and passed into the Pompadour Boudoir. The spot of damp, where Frank's iron had failed to pass, above the Boy's breast-pocket, was slowly fading out in the hot Cosmopolitan air.

Mr Colleoni put out a hand and gave him a quick pat, pat, pat on the arm. 'Come with me,' he said. He led the way, walking on glacé tiptoe past the settee, where the bitches whispered, past a little table where a man was saying 'I told him ten thousand's my limit' to an old man who sat with closed eyes above his chilling tea. Mr Colleoni looked over his shoulder and said gently, 'The service here is not what it used to be.'

He looked into the Louis Seize writing room. A woman in mauve with an untimely tiara was writing a letter in a vast jumble of chinoiserie. Mr Colleoni withdrew. 'We'll go where we can talk in peace,' he said and tiptoed back across the lounge. The old man had opened his eyes and was testing his tea with his finger. Mr Colleoni led the way to the gilt grill of the lift. 'Number Fifteen,' he said. They rose angelically towards peace. 'Cigar?' Mr Colleoni asked.

'I don't smoke,' the Boy said. A last squeal of gaiety came from below, from the American Bar, the last syllable of the page boy returning from the Pompadour Boudoir, 'Gue,' before the gates slid back and they were in the padded sound-proof passage. Mr Colleoni paused and lit his cigar.

'Let's have a look at that lighter,' the Boy said.

Mr Colleoni's small shrewd eyes shone blankly under the concealed pervasive electric glow. He held it out. The Boy turned it over and looked at the hallmark. 'Real gold,' he said.

'I like things good,' Mr Colleoni said, unlocking a door. 'Take a chair.' The arm-chairs, stately red velvet couches stamped with crowns in gold and silver thread, faced the wide seaward windows and the wrought-iron balconies. 'Have a drink?'

'I don't drink,' the Boy said.

'Now,' Mr Colleoni said, 'who sent you?'

'No one sent me.'

'I mean, who's running your mob if Kite's dead?'

'I'm running it,' the Boy said.

Mr Colleoni politely checked a smile, tapping his thumb-nail with the gold lighter.

'What happened to Kite?'

'You know that story,' the Boy said. He gazed across at the Napoleonic crowns, the silver thread. '*You* won't want to hear the details. It wouldn't have happened if we hadn't been crossed. A journalist thought he could put one over on us.'

'What journalist's that?'

'You oughter read the inquests,' the Boy said, staring out through the window at the pale arch of sky against which a few light clouds blew up.

Mr Colleoni looked at the ash on his cigar; it was half an inch long; he sat deep down in his arm-chair and crossed his little plump thighs contentedly.

'I'm not saying anything about Kite,' the Boy said. 'He trespassed.'

'You mean,' Mr Colleoni said, 'you aren't interested in automatic machines?'

'I mean,' the Boy said, 'that trespassing's not healthy.'

A little wave of musk came over the room from the handkerchief in Mr Colleoni's breast-pocket.

'It'd be you who'd need protection,' the Boy said.

'I've got all the protection I need,' Mr Colleoni said. He shut his eyes; he was snug; the huge moneyed hotel lapped him round; he was at home. The

Boy sat on the edge of his chair because he didn't believe in relaxing during business hours; it was he who looked like an alien in this room, not Mr Colleoni.

'You are wasting your time, my child,' Mr Colleoni said. 'You can't do me any harm.' He laughed gently. 'If you want a job though, come to me. I like push. I dare say I could find room for you. The World needs young people with energy.' The hand with the cigar moved expansively, mapping out the World as Mr Colleoni visualized it: lots of little electric clocks controlled by Greenwich, buttons on a desk, a good suite on the first floor, accounts audited, reports from agents, silver, cutlery, glass.

'I'll be seeing you on the course,' the Boy said.

'You'll hardly do that,' Mr Colleoni said. 'I haven't been to a racecourse, let me see, it must be twenty years.' There wasn't a point, he seemed to be indicating, fingering his gold lighter, at which their worlds touched: the week-end at the Cosmopolitan, the portable dictaphone beside the desk, had not the smallest connection with Kite slashed quickly with razors on a railway platform, the grubby hand against the skyline signalling to the bookie from the stand, the heat, the dust fuming up over the half-crown enclosure, the smell of bottled beer.

'I'm just a business man,' Mr Colleoni softly explained. 'I don't need to see a race. And nothing you might try to do to my men could affect me. I've got two in hospital now. It doesn't matter. They have the best attention. Flowers, grapes . . . I can afford it. I don't have to worry. I'm a business man,' Mr Colleoni went expansively and good-humouredly on. 'I like you. You're a promising youngster. That's why I'm talking to you like a father. You can't damage a business like mine.'

'I could damage you,' the Boy said.

'It wouldn't pay. There wouldn't be any faked alibis for you. It would be *your* witnesses who'd be scared. I'm a business man.' The raisin eyes blinked as the sun slanted in across a bowl of flowers and fell on the deep carpet. 'Napoleon the Third used to have this room,' Mr Colleoni said, 'and Eugenie.'

'Who was she?'

'Oh,' Mr Colleoni said vaguely, 'one of those foreign polonies.' He plucked a flower and stuck it in his buttonhole, and something a little doggish peeped out of the black buttony eyes, a hint of the seraglio.

'I'll be going,' the Boy said. He rose and moved to the door.

'You do understand me don't you?' Mr Colleoni said without moving; holding his hand very still he kept the cigar ash, quite a long ash now, suspended. 'Brewer's been complaining. You don't do that again. And Tate . . . you mustn't try tricks with Tate.' His old Italian face showed few emotions but a mild amusement, a mild friendliness; but suddenly sitting there in the rich Victorian room, with the gold lighter in his pocket and the cigar-case on his lap, he looked as a man might look who owned the whole world, the whole visible world that is, the cash registers and policemen and prostitutes, Parliament and the laws which say 'this is Right and this is Wrong'.

'I understand all right,' the Boy said. 'You think our mob's too small for you.'

'I employ a great many people,' Mr Colleoni said.

The Boy closed the door; a loose shoe-lace tapped all the way down the passage: the huge lounge was almost empty: a man in plus-fours waited for a girl. The visible world was all Mr Colleoni's. The spot where the iron hadn't passed was still a little damp over the Boy's breast.

A hand touched the Boy's arm. He looked round and recognized the man in a bowler hat. He nodded guardedly. 'Morning.'

'They told me at Frank's,' the man said, 'you'd come here.'

The Boy's heart missed a beat: for almost the first time it occurred to him that the law could hang him, take him out in a yard, drop him in a pit, bury him in lime, put an end to the great future . . .

'You want me?'

'That's right.'

He thought: Rose, the girl, someone asking questions. His memory flashed back: he remembered how she caught him with his hand under the table, feeling for something. He grinned dully and said, 'Well, they haven't sent the Big Four, anyway.'

'Mind coming round to the station?'

'Got a warrant?'

'It's only Brewer been complaining you hit him. You left your scar all right.'

The Boy began to laugh. 'Brewer? Me? I wouldn't touch him.'

'Come round and see the inspector?'

'Of course I will.'

They came out on to the parade. A pavement photographer saw them coming and lifted the cap from his camera. The Boy put his hands in front of his face and went by. 'You oughter put a stop to those things,' he said. 'Fine thing it'd be to have a picture postcard stuck up on the pier, you and me walking to the station.'

'They caught a murderer once in town with one of those snaps.'

'I read about it,' the Boy said and fell silent. This is Colleoni's doing, he thought, he's showing off: he put Brewer up to this.

'Brewer's wife's pretty bad they say,' the detective remarked softly.

'Is she?' the Boy said. 'I wouldn't know.'

'Got your alibi ready, I suppose?'

'How do I know? I don't know when he said I hit him. A geezer can't have an alibi for every minute of the day.'

'You're a wide kid,' the detective said, 'but you needn't get fussed about this. The inspector wants to have a friendly chat, that's all.'

He led the way through the charge-room. A man with a tired ageing face sat behind a desk. 'Sit down, Brown,' he said. He opened a cigarette box and pushed it across.

'I don't smoke,' the Boy said. He sat down and watched the inspector alertly. 'Aren't you going to charge me?'

'There's no charge,' the inspector said. 'Brewer thought better of it.' He paused. He looked more tired than ever. He said: 'I want to talk straight for once. We know more about each other than we admit. I don't interfere with you and Brewer: I've got more important things to do than prevent you and Brewer – arguing. But you know just as well as I do that Brewer wouldn't come here to complain if he hadn't been put up to it.'

'You've certainly got ideas,' the Boy said.

'Put up to it by someone who's not afraid of your mob.'

'There's not much escapes the bogies,' the Boy said, grimacing derisively.

'The races start next week, and I don't want to have any big scale mob fighting in Brighton. I don't mind you carving each other up in a quiet way, I don't give a penny for your worthless skins, but when two mobs start scrapping people who matter may get hurt.

'Meaning who?' the Boy said.

'Meaning decent innocent people. Poor people out to put a shilling on the tote. Clerks, charwomen, dustmen. People who wouldn't be seen dead talking to you – or to Colleoni.'

'What are you getting at?' the Boy said.

'I'm getting at this. You aren't big enough for your job, Brown. You can't stand against Colleoni. If there's any fighting I shall come down like a ton of bricks on both of you – but it will be Colleoni who'll have the alibis. No one's going to fake you an alibi against Colleoni. You take my advice. Clear out of Brighton.'

'Fine,' the Boy said. 'A bogy doing Colleoni's job for him.'

'This is private and unofficial,' the inspector said. 'I'm being human for once. I don't care if you get carved or Colleoni gets carved, but I'm not going to have innocent people hurt if I can help it.'

'You think I'm finished?' the Boy said. He grinned uneasily, looking away, looking at the walls plastered with notices. Dog Licences. Gun Licences. Found Drowned. A dead face met his eye staring from the wall, unnaturally pasty. Unbrushed hair. A scar by the mouth. 'You think Colleoni'll keep the peace better?' He could read the writing: 'one nickel watch, waistcoat of grey cloth, blue-striped shirt, aertex vest, aertex pants'.

'Well?'

'It's valuable advice,' the Boy said, grinning down at the polished desk, the box of Players, a crystal paper-weight. 'I'll have to think it over. I'm young to retire.'

'You're too young to run a racket if you ask me.'

'So Brewer's not bringing a charge?'

'He's not afraid to. I talked him out of it. I wanted to have a chance to speak to you straight.'

'Well,' the Boy said, standing up, 'maybe I'll be seeing you: maybe not.' He grinned again, passing through the charge-room, but a bright spot of colour stood out on each cheek-bone. There was poison in his veins, though he grinned and bore it. He had been insulted. He was going to show the world. They thought because he was only seventeen . . . he jerked his narrow shoulders back at the memory that he'd killed his man, and these bogies who thought they were clever weren't clever enough to discover that. He trailed the clouds of his own glory after him: hell lay about him in his infancy. He was ready for more deaths.

Chapter One

Ida Arnold sat up in the boarding-house bed. For a moment she didn't know where she was. Her head ached with the thick night at Sherry's. It came slowly back to her as she stared at the thick ewer on the floor, the basin of grey water in which she had perfunctorily washed, the bright pink roses on the wallpaper, a wedding group – Phil Corkery dithering outside the front door, pecking at her lips, swaying off down the parade as if that was all he could expect, while the tide receded. She looked round the room; it didn't look so good in the morning light as when she had booked it, but 'it's homely,' she thought with satisfaction, 'it's what I like.'

The sun was shining; Brighton was at its best. The passage outside her room was gritty with sand, she felt it under her shoes all the way down stairs, and in the hall there was a pail, two spades, and a long piece of seaweed hanging by the door as a barometer. There were a lot of sandshoes lying about, and from the dining-room came a child's querulous voice repeating over and over, 'I don't want to dig. I want to go to the pictures. I don't want to dig.'

At one she was meeting Phil Corkery at Snow's. Before that there were things to do; she had to go easy on the money, not put away too much in the way of Guinness. It wasn't cheap living down at Brighton, and she wasn't going to take cash from Corkery – she had a conscience, she had a code, and if she took cash she gave something in return. Black Boy was the answer: she had to see about it first before the odds shortened: sinews of war, and she made her way towards Kemp Town to the only bookie she knew, old Jim Tate, 'Honest Jim' of the half-crown enclosure.

He bellowed at her as soon as she got inside his office, 'Here's Ida. Sit down, Mrs Turner,' getting her name wrong. He pushed a box of Gold Flake across to her. 'Inhale a cheroot.' He was a little more than life-size. His voice, after the race meetings of twenty years, could hit no tone which wasn't loud and hoarse. He was a man you needed to look at through the wrong end of a telescope if you were to believe him the fine healthy fellow he made himself out to be. When you were close to him, you saw the thick blue veins on the left forehead, the red money-spider's web across the eyeballs. 'Well, Mrs Turner – Ida – what is it you fancy?'

'Black Boy,' Ida said.

'Black Boy,' Jim Tate repeated. 'That's ten to one.'

'Twelve to one.'

'The odds have shortened. There's been quite a packet laid on Black Boy this week. You wouldn't get ten to one from anyone but your old friend.'

'All right,' Ida said. 'Put me on twenty pounds. And my name's not Turner. It's Arnold.'

'Twenty nicker. That's a fat bet for you, Mrs What-ever-you-are.' He licked his thumb and began to comb the notes. Half-way through he paused, sat still like a large toad over his desk, listening. A lot of noise came in through the open window, feet on stone, voices, distant music, bells ringing, the continuous whisper of the Channel. He sat quite still with half the notes in his hand. He looked uneasy. The telephone rang. He let it ring for two seconds, his veined eyes on Ida; then he lifted the receiver. 'Hullo. Hullo. This is Jim Tate.' It was an old-fashioned telephone. He screwed the receiver close into his ear and sat still while a low voice burred like a bee.

One hand holding the receiver to his ear, Jim Tate shuffled the notes together, wrote out a slip. He said hoarsely, 'That's all right, Mr Colleoni. I'll do that, Mr Colleoni,' and planked the receiver down.

'You've written Black Dog,' Ida said.

He looked across at her. It took him a moment to understand. 'Black Dog,' he said, and then laughed, hoarse and hollow. 'What was I thinking of? Black Dog, indeed.'

'That means Care,' Ida said.

'Well,' he barked with unconvincing geniality, 'we've always something to worry about.' The telephone rang again. Jim Tate looked as if it might sting him.

'You're busy', Ida said. 'I'll be going.'

When she went out into the street she looked this way and that to see if she could see any cause for Jim Tate's uneasiness, but there was nothing visible: just Brighton about its own business on a beautiful day.

Ida went into a pub and had a glass of Douro port. It went down sweet and warm and heavy. She had another. 'Who's Mr Colleoni?' she asked the barman.

'You don't know who Colleoni is?'

'I never heard of him till just now.'

The barman said, 'He's taking over from Kite.'

'Who's Kite?'

'Who *was* Kite? You saw how he got croaked at St Pancras?'

'No.'

'I don't suppose they meant to do it,' the barman said. 'They just meant to carve him up, but a razor slipped.'

'Have a drink?'

'Thanks. I'll have a gin.'

'Cheeryo.'

'Cheeryo.'

'I hadn't heard all this,' Ida said. She looked over his shoulder at the clock: nothing to do till one: she might as well have another and gossip awhile. 'Give me another port. When did all this happen?'

'Oh, before Whitsun.' The word Whitsun always caught her ear now: it meant a lot of things, a grubby ten shilling note, the white steps down to the ladies', Tragedy in capital letters. 'And what about Kite's friends?' she asked.

'They don't stand a chance now Kite's dead. The mob's got no leader. Why, they tag round after a kid of seventeen. What's a kid like that going to do against Colleoni?' He bent across the bar and whispered, 'He cut up Brewer last night.'

'Who? Colleoni?'

'No, the kid.'

'I dunno who Brewer is,' Ida said, 'but things seem lively.'

'You wait till the races start,' the man said. 'They'll be lively all right then. Colleoni's out for a monopoly. Quick, look through the window there and you'll see him.'

Ida went to the window and looked out, and again she saw only the Brighton she knew; she hadn't seen anything different even the day Fred died: two girls in beach pyjamas arm-in-arm, the buses going by to Rottingdean, a man selling papers, a woman with a shopping basket, a boy in a shabby suit, an excursion steamer edging off from the pier, which lay long, luminous and transparent, like a shrimp in the sunlight. She said, 'I don't see anyone.'

'He's gone now.'

'Who? Colleoni?'

'No, the kid.'

'Oh,' Ida said, 'that boy,' coming back to the bar, drinking up her port. 'I bet he's worried plenty.'

'A kid like that oughtn't to be mixed up with things,' Ida said. 'If he was mine I'd just larrup it out of him.' With those words she was about to dismiss him, to turn her attention away from him, moving her mind on its axis like a great steel dredger, when she remembered: a face in a bar seen over Fred's shoulder, the sound of a glass breaking: 'The gentleman will pay.' She had a royal memory. 'You ever come across this Kolley Kibber?' she asked.

'No such luck,' the barman said.

'It seemed odd his dying like that. Must have made a bit of gossip.'

'None I heard of,' the barman said. 'He wasn't a Brighton man. No one knew him round these parts. He was a stranger.'

A stranger: the word meant nothing to her: there was no place in the world where she felt a stranger. She circulated the dregs of the cheap port in her glass and remarked to no one in particular, 'It's a good life.' There was nothing with which she didn't claim kinship: the advertising mirror behind the barman's back flashed her own image at her: the beach girls went giggling across the parade: the gong beat on the steamer for Boulogne: it was a good life. Only the darkness in which the Boy walked, going from Frank's, going back to Frank's, was alien to her; she had no pity for something she didn't understand. She said, 'I'll be getting on.'

It wasn't one yet, but there were questions she wanted to ask before Mr Corkery arrived. She said to the first waitress she saw, 'Are you the lucky one?'

'Not that I know of,' the waitress said coldly.

'I mean the one who found the card – the Kolley Kibber card.'

'Oh, that was *her*,' the waitress said, nodding a pointed powdered contemptuous chin.

Ida changed her table. She said, 'I've got a friend coming. I'll have to wait for him, but I'll try to pick. Is the shepherd's pie good?'

'It looks lovely.'

'Nice and brown on top?'

'It's a picture.'

'What's your name, dear?'

'Rose.'

'Why, I do believe,' Ida said, 'you were the lucky one who found the card?'

'Did *they* tell you that?' Rose said. 'They haven't forgiven me. They think I didn't ought to be lucky like that my first day.'

'Your first day? That *was* a bit of luck. You won't forget that day in a hurry.'

'No,' Rose said, I'll remember that always.'

'I mustn't keep you here talking.'

'If you only would. If you'd sort of look as if you was ordering things. There's no one else wants to be attended to and I'm ready to drop with these trays.'

'You don't like the job?'

'Oh,' Rose said quickly, 'I didn't say that. It's a good job. I wouldn't have anything different for the world. I wouldn't be in a hotel, or in Chessman's, not if they paid me twice as much. It's elegant here,' Rose said, gazing over the waste of green-painted tables, the daffodils, the paper napkins, the sauce bottles.

'Are you a local?'

'I've always lived here – all my life,' Rose said, 'in Nelson Place. This is a fine situation for me because they have us sleep in. There's only three of us in my room, and we have two looking-glasses.'

'How old are you?'

Rose leant gratefully across the table. 'Sixteen,' she said. 'I don't tell them that. I say seventeen. They'd say I wasn't old enough if they knew. They'd send me—' she hesitated a long while at the grim word, 'home.'

'You must have been glad,' Ida said, 'when you found that card.'

'Oh, I was.'

'Do you think I could have a glass of stout, dear?'

'We have to send out,' Rose said. 'If you give me the money—'

Ida opened her purse. 'I don't suppose you'll ever forget the little fellow.'

'Oh, he wasn't so . . .' Rose began and suddenly stopped, staring out through Snow's window across the parade to the pier.

'He wasn't what?' Ida said. 'What was it you were going to say?'

'I don't remember.'

'I just asked if you'd ever forget the little fellow.'

'It's gone out of my head,' Rose said. 'I'll get your drink. Does it cost all that – a glass of stout?' she asked, picking up the two shilling pieces.

'One of them's for you, dear,' Ida said. 'I'm inquisitive. I can't help it. I'm made that way. Tell me how he looked?'

'I don't know. I can't remember. I haven't got any memory for faces.'

'You can't have, can you, dear, or you'd have challenged him. You must have seen his picture in the papers.'

'I know. I'm silly that way.' She stood there, pale and determined and out of breath and guilty.

'And then it would have been ten pounds not ten shillings.'

'I'll get your drink.'

'Perhaps I'll wait after all. The gentleman who's giving me lunch, he can pay.' Ida picked up the shillings again, and Rose's eyes followed her hand back to her bag. 'Waste not, want not,' Ida said gently, taking in the details of the bony face, the large mouth, the eyes too far apart, the pallor, the immature body, and then suddenly she was loud and cheerful again, calling out, 'Phil Corkery, Phil Corkery,' waving her hand.

Mr Corkery wore a blazer with a badge and a stiff collar underneath. He looked as if he needed feeding up, as if he was wasted with passions he had never had the courage to express.

'Cheer up, Phil. What are you having?'

'Steak and kidney,' Mr Corkery said gloomily. 'Waitress, we want a drink.'

'We have to send out.'

'Well, in that case, make it two large bottles of Guinness,' Mr Corkery said.

When Rose came back Ida introduced her to Mr Corkery. 'This is the lucky girl who found a card.'

Rose backed away, but Ida detained her, grasping firmly her black cotton sleeve. 'Did he eat much?' she asked.

'I don't remember a thing,' Rose said, 'really I don't.' Their faces, flushed a little with the warm summer sun, were like posters announcing danger.

'Did he look,' Ida said, 'as if he was going to die?'

'How can I tell?'

'I suppose you talked to him?'

'I didn't talk to him. I was rushed. I just fetched him a Bass and a sausage roll, and I never saw him again.' She snatched her sleeve from Ida's hand and was gone.

'You can't get much from her,' Mr Corkery said.

'Oh yes I can,' Ida said, 'more than I bargained for.'

'Why, whatever's wrong?'

'It's what that girl said.'

'She didn't say much.'

'She said enough. I always had a feeling it was fishy. You see he told me in the taxi he was dying and I believed him for a moment: it gave me quite a turn till he told me he was just spinning a tale.'

'Well, he *was* dying.'

'He didn't mean it that way. I have my instincts.'

'Anyway,' Mr Corkery said, 'there's the evidence, he died natural. I don't see as there's anything to worry about. It's a fine day, Ida. Let's go on the *Brighton Belle* and talk it over there. No closing hours at sea. After all, if he did kill himself, it's his business.'

'If he killed himself,' Ida said, 'he was driven to it. I heard what the girl said, and I know this – it wasn't him that left the ticket here.'

'Good God,' Mr Corkery said. 'What do you mean? You oughtn't to talk like that. It's dangerous.' He swallowed nervously and the Adam's apple bobbed up and down under the skin of his scrawny neck.

'It's dangerous all right,' Ida said, watching the thin sixteen-year-old body shrink by in its black cotton dress, hearing the clink, clink, clink of a glass on a tray carried by an unsteady hand, 'but who to's another matter.'

'Let's go out in the sun,' Mr Corkery said. 'It's not so warm here.' He hadn't got a vest on, or a tie; he shivered a little in his cricket shirt and blazer.

'I've got to think,' Ida repeated.

'I shouldn't get mixed up in anything, Ida. He wasn't anything to you.'

'He wasn't anything to anyone, that's the trouble,' Ida said. She dug down into her deepest mind, the plane of memories, instincts, hopes, and brought up from them the only philosophy she lived by. 'I like fair play,' she said. She felt better when she'd said that and added with terrible lightheartedness, 'An eye for an eye, Phil. Will you stick by me?'

The Adam's apple bobbed. A draught from which all the sun had been sifted swung through the revolving door and Mr Corkery felt it on his bony breast. He said, 'I don't know what's given you the idea, Ida, but I'm for law and order. I'll stick by you.' His daring went to his head. He put a hand on her knee. 'I'd do anything for you, Ida.'

'There's only one thing to do after what *she* told me,' Ida said.

'What's that?'

'The police.'

Ida blew into the police-station with a laugh to this man and a wave of the hand to that. She didn't know them from Adam. She was cheerful and determined, and she carried Phil along in her wake.

'I want to see the inspector,' she told the sergeant at the desk.

'He's busy, ma'am. What was it you wanted to see him about?'

'I can wait,' Ida said, sitting down between the police capes. 'Sit down, Phil.' She grinned at them all with brassy assurance. 'Pubs don't open till six,' she said. 'Phil and I haven't anything to do till then.'

'What was it you wanted to see him about, ma'am?'

'Suicide,' Ida said, 'right under your noses and you call it natural death.'

The sergeant stared at her, and Ida stared back. Her large clear eyes (a spot of drink now and then didn't affect them) told nothing, gave away no secrets. Camaraderie, good nature, cheeriness fell like shutters before a plate-glass window. You could only guess at the goods behind: sound old-fashioned hallmarked goods, justice, an eye for an eye, law and order, capital punishment, a bit of fun now and then, nothing nasty, nothing shady, nothing you'd be ashamed to own, nothing mysterious.

'You aren't pulling my leg, are you?' the sergeant said.

'Not this time, sarge.'

He passed through a door and shut it behind him, and Ida settled herself more firmly on the bench, made herself at home. 'Bit stuffy in here, boys,' she said. 'What about opening another window?' and obediently they opened one.

The sergeant called to her from the door. 'You can go in,' he said.

'Come on, Phil,' Ida said and bore him with her into the tiny cramped official room which smelt of French polish and fish glue.

'And so,' the inspector said, 'you wanted to tell me about a suicide, Mrs —?' He looked tired and old and shy. He had tried to hide a tin of fruit drops behind a telephone and a manuscript book.

'Arnold, Ida Arnold. I thought it might be your line, inspector,' she said with heavy sarcasm.

'This your husband?'

'Oh no, a friend. I wanted a witness, that's all.'

'And who is it you're concerned about, Mrs Arnold?'

'Hale's the name, Fred Hale. I beg your pardon. Charles Hale.'

'We know all about Hale, Mrs Arnold. He died quite naturally.'

'Oh no,' Ida said, 'you don't know all. You don't know he was with me, two hours before he was found.'

'You weren't at the inquest?'

'I didn't know it was him till I saw his picture.'

'And why do you think there's anything wrong?'

'Listen,' Ida said. 'He was with me and he was scared about something. We were at the Palace Pier. I had to have a wash and brush up, but he didn't want me to leave him. I was only away five minutes and he'd gone. Where'd he gone to? You say he went and had lunch at Snow's and then went on down the pier to the shelter in Hove. You think he just gave me the slip, but it wasn't Fred – I mean Hale – who had lunch at Snow's and left that card. I've just seen the waitress. Hale didn't like Bass – he wouldn't drink Bass – but the man at Snow's sent out for a bottle.'

'That's nothing,' the inspector said. 'It was a hot day. He was feeling bad, too. He got tired of doing all the thing's he'd got to do. I wouldn't be surprised if he cheated and got someone else to go into Snow's.'

'The girl won't say a thing about him. She knows but she won't say.'

'I can think of an explanation easily enough, Mrs Arnold. The man may have left a card on condition she didn't say anything.'

'It's not that. She's scared. Someone's scared her. Maybe the same person who drove Fred. . . And there are other things.'

'I'm sorry, Mrs Arnold. It's just a waste of time getting fussed like this. You see there was a post-mortem. The medical evidence shows without any doubt that he died naturally. He had a bad heart. The medical name for it is coronary thrombosis. I'd call it just heat and crowds and exertion – and a weak heart.'

'Could I see the report?'

'It wouldn't be usual.'

'I was a friend of his, you see,' Ida said softly. 'I'd like to be satisfied.'

'Well, to put your mind at rest, I'll stretch a point. It's here now on my desk.'

Ida read it carefully. 'This doctor,' she said, 'he knows his stuff?'

'He's a first-class doctor.'

'It seems clear, doesn't it?' Ida said. She began to read it all over again. 'They do go into details, don't they. Why, I wouldn't know more about him if I'd married him. Appendix scar, supernumerary nipples, whatever they are, suffered from wind – I do that myself on a Bank Holiday. It's almost disrespectful, isn't it? He wouldn't have liked this,' she brooded over the report with easy kindliness. 'Varicose veins. Poor old Fred. What's this mean about the liver?'

'Drank too much, that's all.'

'I wouldn't be surprised. Poor Fred. So he had ingrowing toe-nails. It doesn't seem right to know that.'

'You were a great friend of his?'

'Well, we only knew each other that day. But I liked him. He was a real gentleman. If I hadn't been a bit lit this wouldn't have happened.' She blew out her bust. 'He wouldn't have come to any harm with me.'

'Have you quite finished with the report, Mrs Arnold?'

'He does mention everything, this doctor of yours, doesn't he? Bruises, superficial whatever that means, on the arms. What do you think of that, inspector?'

'Nothing at all. Bank Holiday crowds, that's all. Pushed here and there.'

'Oh, come off it,' Ida said, 'come off it.' Her tongue flared up. 'Be human. Were *you* out on Bank Holiday? Where do you find a crowd like that? Brighton's big enough, isn't it? It's not a tube lift. I was here. I know.'

The inspector said stubbornly, 'You've got fancies, Mrs Arnold.'

'So the police won't do a thing? You won't question that girl in Snow's?'

'The case is closed, Mrs Arnold. And even if it had been suicide, why open old wounds?'

'Someone drove him . . . perhaps it wasn't suicide at all . . . perhaps. . . .'

'I've told you, Mrs Arnold, the case is closed.'

'That's what you think,' Ida said. She rose to her feet; she summoned Phil with a jerk of the chin. 'Not half it isn't,' she said. 'I'll be seeing you.' She looked back from the door at the elderly man behind the desk and threatened him with her ruthless vitality. 'Or perhaps not,' she said. 'I can manage this my own way. I don't need your police' (the constables in the outer room stirred uneasily; somebody laughed; somebody dropped a tin of boot polish). 'I've got my friends.'

Her friends – they were everywhere under the bright glittering Brighton air. They followed their wives obediently into fishmongers, they carried the children's buckets to the beach, they lingered round the bars waiting for opening time, they took a penny peep on the pier at 'A Night of Love'. She had only to appeal to any of them, for Ida Arnold was on the right side. She was cheery, she was healthy, she could get a bit lit with the best of them. She liked a good time, her big breasts bore their carnality frankly down the Old Steyne, but you had only to look at her to know that you could rely on her. She wouldn't tell tales to your wife, she wouldn't remind you next morning of what you wanted to forget, she was honest, she was kindly, she belonged to the great middle law-abiding class, her amusements were their amusements, her superstitions their superstitions (the planchette scratching the French polish on the occasional table, and the salt over the shoulder), she had no more love for anyone than they had.

'Expenses mounting up,' Ida said. 'Never mind. Everthing will be all right after the races.'

'You got a tip?' Mr Corkery asked.

'Straight from the horse's mouth. I shouldn't say that. Poor Fred.'

'Tell a pal,' Mr Corkery implored.

'All in good time,' Ida said. 'Be a good boy and you don't know what mayn't happen.'

'You don't still think, do you?' Mr Corkery sounded her. 'Not after what the doctor wrote?'

'I've never paid any attention to doctors.'

'But why?'

'We've got to find out.'

'And how?'

'Give me time. I haven't started yet.'

The sea stretched like a piece of gay common washing in a tenement square across the end of the street. 'The colour of your eyes,' Mr Corkery interjected thoughtfully and with a touch of nostalgia. He said, 'Couldn't we now – just go for a while on the pier, Ida?'

'Yes,' Ida said. 'The pier. We'll go to the Palace Pier, Phil,' but when they got there she wouldn't go through the turnstile, but took up her stand like a huckster facing the Aquarium, the ladies' lavatory. 'This is where I start from,' she said. 'He waited for me here, Phil,' and she stared out over the red and green lights, the heavy traffic of her battlefield, laying her plans, marshalling her cannon fodder, while five yards away Spicer stood too waiting for an enemy to appear. Only a slight doubt troubled her optimism. 'That horse has got to win, Phil,' she said. 'I can't hold out else.'

Chapter Two

Spicer was restless these days. There was nothing for him to do. When the races began again he wouldn't feel so bad, he wouldn't think so much about Hale. It was the medical evidence which upset him: 'death from natural causes', when with his own eyes he'd seen the Boy . . . It was fishy, it wasn't straight. He told himself that he could face a police inquiry, but he couldn't stand this not knowing, the false security of the verdict. There was a catch in it somewhere, and all through the long summer sunlight Spicer wandered uneasily, watching out for trouble: the police-station, the Place where It had been done, even Snow's came into his promenade. He wanted to be satisfied that the cops were doing nothing (he knew every plain-clothes man in the Brighton force), that no one was asking questions or loitering where they had no reason to loiter. He knew it was just nerves. 'I'll be all right when the races start,' he told himself, like a man with a poisoned body who believes that all will be well when a single tooth is drawn.

He came up the parade cautiously, from the Hove end, from the glass shelter where Hale's body had been set, pale with bloodshot eyes and nicotined finger-ends. He had a corn on his left foot and limped a little, dragging after him a bright orange-brown shoe. He had come out in spots, too, round his mouth, and that also was caused by Hale's death. Fear upset his bowels, and the spots came: it was always the way.

He limped cautiously across the road when he was close to Snow's: that was another vulnerable place. The sun caught the great panes of plate-glass and flashed back at him like headlamps. He sweated a little passing by. A voice said, 'Well, if it isn't Spicey?' He had had his eyes on Snow's across the road, he hadn't noticed who was beside him on the parade, leaning on the green railing above the shingle. He turned his damp face sharply. 'What are you doing here, Crab?'

'It's good to be back,' Crab said, a young man in a mauve suit, with shoulders like coat-hangers and a small waist.

'We ran you out once, Crab. I thought you'd stay out. You've altered.'

His hair was carroty, except at the roots, and his nose was straightened and scarred. He had been a Jew once, but a hairdresser and a surgeon had altered that. 'Afraid we'd lamp you if you didn't change your mug?'

'Why, Spicey, me afraid of your lot? You'll be saying "sir" to me one of these days. I'm Colleoni's right-hand man.'

'I always heard as how he was left-handed,' Spicer said. 'Wait till Pinkie knows you're back.'

Crab laughed. 'Pinkie's at the police-station,' he said.

The police-station: Spicer's chin went down, he was off, his orange shoe sliding on the paving, his corn shooting. He heard Crab laugh behind him, the smell of dead fish was in his nostrils, he was a sick man. The police-station: the police-station: it was like an abscess jetting its poison through the nerves. When he got to Frank's there was no one there. He creaked his tortured way up the stairs, past the rotten banister, to Pinkie's room: the door stood open, vacancy stared in the swing mirror: no message, crumbs on the floor: it looked as a room would look if someone had been called suddenly away.

Spicer stood by the chest of drawers (the walnut stain splashed unevenly): no scrap of written reassurance in a drawer: no warning. He looked up and down, the corn shooting through his whole body to the brain, and suddenly there was his own face in the glass – the coarse black hair greying at the roots, the small eruptions on the face, the bloodshot eyeballs, and it occurred to him, as if he were looking at a close-up on a screen, that that was the kind of face a nark might have, a man who grassed to the bogies.

He moved away: flakes of pastry ground under his foot; he told himself he wasn't a man to grass: Pinkie, Cubitt and Dallow, they were his pals. He wouldn't let them down – even though it wasn't he who'd done the killing. He'd been against it from the first: he'd only laid the cards: he only *knew*. He stood at the head of the stairs looking down past the shaky banister. He would rather kill himself than squeal, he told the empty landing in a whisper, but he knew really that he hadn't got that courage. Better run for it: and he thought with nostalgia of Nottingham and a pub he knew, a pub he had once hoped to buy when he had made his pile. It was a good spot, Nottingham, the air was good, none of this salt smart on the dry mouth, and the girls were kind. If he could get away – but the others would never let him go: he knew too much about too many things. He was in the mob for life now, and he looked down the drop of the staircase to the tiny hall, the strip of linoleum, the old-fashioned telephone on a bracket by the door.

As he watched, it began to ring. He looked down at it with fear and suspicion. He couldn't stand any more bad news. Where had everybody gone to? Had they run and left him without a warning? Even Frank wasn't in the basement. There was a smell of scorching as if he'd left his iron burning. The bell rang on and on. Let them ring, he thought. They'll tire of it in time: why should I do all the work of this bloody gaff? On and on and on. Whoever it was didn't tire easily. He came to the head of the stairs and scowled down at the vulcanite spitting noise through the quiet house. 'The trouble is,' he said aloud, as if he were rehearsing a speech to Pinkie and the others, 'I'm getting too old for this game. I got to retire. Look at my hair. I'm grey, ain't I? I got to retire.' But the only answer was the regular ring, ring, ring.

'Why can't someone answer the bloody blower?' he shouted down the well of the stairs. 'I got to do all the work, have I?' and he saw himself dropping a ticket into the child's bucket, slipping a ticket under an upturned boat, tickets which could have hanged him. He suddenly ran down the stairs in a kind of simulated fury and lifted the receiver. 'Well,' he bellowed, 'well, who the hell's there?'

'Is that Frank's?' a voice said. He knew the voice now. It was the girl in Snow's. He lowered the receiver in a panic and waited, and a thin doll's voice came out at him from the orifice: 'Please, I've got to speak to Pinkie.' It was almost as if listening betrayed him. He listened again and the voice repeated with desperate anxiety, 'Is that Frank's?'

Keeping his mouth away from the phone, curling his tongue in an odd way, mouthing hoarsely and crookedly, Spicer in disguise replied, 'Pinkie's out. What do you want?'

'I've got to speak to him.'

'He's out I tell you.'

'Who's that?' the girl asked in a scared voice.

'That's what I want to know. Who are you?'

'I'm a friend of Pinkie's. I got to find him. It's urgent.'

'I can't help you.'

'Please. You've got to find Pinkie. He told me I was to tell him – if ever—' The voice died away.

Spicer shouted down the phone. 'Hullo. Where you gone? If ever what?' There was no reply. He listened, with the receiver pressed against his ear, to silence buzzing up the wires. He began to jerk at the hook: 'Exchange. Hullo. Hullo. Exchange,' and then suddenly the voice came on again as if somebody had dropped a needle into place on a record. 'Are you there? Please, are you there?'

'Of course I'm here. What did Pinkie tell you?'

'You got to find Pinkie. He said he wanted to know. It's a woman. She was in here with a man.'

'What do you mean – a woman?'

'Asking questions,' the voice said. Spicer put down the receiver; whatever else the girl had to say was strangled on the wire. Find Pinkie? What was the good of finding Pinkie? It was the others who had done the finding. And Cubitt and Dallow: they'd slipped away without even warning him. If he did squeal it would be only returning them their own coin. But he wasn't going to squeal. He wasn't a nark. They thought he was yellow. *They'd think* he'd squeal. He wouldn't even get the credit . . . a little moisture of self-pity came pricking out of the dry ageing ducts.

I got to think, he repeated to himself. I got to think. He opened the street door and went out. He didn't even wait to fetch his hat. His hair was thin on top, dry and brittle under the dandruff. He walked rapidly, going nowhere in particular, but every road in Brighton ended on the front. I'm too old for the game, I got to get out, Nottingham; he wanted to be alone, he went down the stone steps to the level of the beach; it was early closing and the small shops facing the sea under the promenade were closed. He walked on the edge of the asphalt, scuffling in the shingle. I wouldn't grass, he remarked dumbly to the tide as it lifted and withdrew, but it wasn't my doing. I never wanted to kill Fred. He passed into shadow under the pier, and a cheap photographer with a box camera snapped him as the shadow fell and pressed a paper into his hand. Spicer didn't notice. The iron pillars stretched down across the wet dimmed shingle holding up above his head the motor-track, the shooting booths and peep machines, mechanical models, 'the Robot Man will tell your fortune'. A seagull flew straight towards him between the pillars like a scared bird caught in a cathedral, then swerved out into the sunlight from the dark iron nave. I wouldn't grass, Spicer said, unless I had to. . . . He stumbled on an old boot and put his hand on the stones to save himself: they had all the cold of the sea and had never been warmed by sun under these pillars.

He thought: that woman – how does she know anything – what's she doing asking questions? I didn't want to have Hale killed; it wouldn't be fair if I took the drop with the others; I told 'em not to do it. He came out into the sunlight and climbed back on to the parade. It'll be this way the bogies will come, he thought, if they know anything; they always reconstruct the crime. He took up his stand between the turnstile of the pier and the ladies' lavatory. There weren't many people about: he could spot the bogies easily enough – if they came. Over there was the Royal Albion; he could see all the way up the Grand Parade to Old Steyne; the pale green domes of the Pavilion floated above the dusty trees; he could see anyone in the hot empty mid-week afternoon who went down below the Aquarium, the white deck ready for dancing, to the little covered arcade where the cheap shops stood between the sea and the stone wall, selling Brighton rock.

Chapter Three

The poison twisted in the Boy's veins. He had been insulted. He had to show someone he was – a man. He went scowling into Snow's, young, shabby and untrustworthy, and the waitresses with one accord turned their backs. He stood there looking for a table (the place was full), and no one attended to him. It was as if they doubted whether he had the money to pay for his meal. He thought of Colleoni padding through the enormous rooms, the embroidered crowns on the chair-backs. He suddenly shouted aloud: 'I want service,' and the pulse beat in his cheek. All the faces round him shivered into motion, and then were still again like water. Everyone looked away. He was ignored. Suddenly a sense of weariness overtook him. He felt as if he had travelled a great many miles to be ignored like this.

A voice said, 'There isn't a table.' They were still such strangers that he didn't recognize the voice, until it added: 'Pinkie'. He looked round and there was Rose, dressed to go out in a shabby black straw which made her face look as it would look in twenty years' time, after the work and the child-bearing.

'They got to serve me,' the Boy said. 'Who do they think they are?'

'There isn't a table.'

Everyone was watching them now – with disapproval.

'Come outside, Pinkie.'

'What are you all dressed up for?'

'It's my afternoon off. Come outside.'

He followed her out and suddenly taking her wrist he brought the poison on to his lips. 'I could break your arm.'

'What have I done, Pinkie?'

'No table. They don't like serving me in there, I'm no class. They'll see – one day—'

'What?'

But his mind staggered before the extent of his ambitions. He said, 'Never mind – they'll learn—'

'Did you get the message, Pinkie?'

'What message?'

'I phoned you at Frank's. I told him to tell you.'

'Told who?'

'I don't know.' She added casually, 'I think it was the man who left the ticket.'

He gripped her wrist again. He said, 'The man who left the ticket's dead. You read it all.' But she showed no sign of fear this time. He'd been too friendly. She ignored his reminder.

'Did he find you?' she asked, and he thought to himself: she's got to be scared again.

'No one found me,' he said. He pushed her roughly forward. 'Come on. We'll walk. I'll take you out.'

'I was going home.'

'You won't go home. You'll come with me. I want exercise,' he said, looking down at his pointed shoes which had never walked further than the length of the parade.

'Where'll we go, Pinkie?'

'Somewhere,' Pinkie said, 'out in the country. That's where you go on a day like this.' He tried to think for a moment of where the country was: the racecourse, that was country; and then a bus came by marked Peacehaven, and he waved his hand to it. 'There you are,' he said, 'that's country. We can talk there. There's things we got to get straight.'

'I thought we were going to walk.'

'This is walking,' he said roughly, pushing her up the steps. 'You're green. You don't know a thing. You don't think people really *walk*. Why – it's miles.'

'When people say, "Come for a walk", they mean a bus?'

'Or a car. I'd have taken you in the car, but the mob are out in it.'

'You got a car?'

'I couldn't get on without a car,' the Boy said, as the bus climbed up behind Rottingdean: red-brick buildings behind a wall, a great stretch of parkland, one girl with a hockey-stick staring at something in the sky, with cropped expensive turf all round her. The poison drained back into its proper glands: he was admired, no one insulted him, but when he looked at the girl who admired him, the poison oozed out again. He said, 'Take off that hat. You look awful.' She obeyed him: her mousy hair lay flat on the small scalp: he watched her with distaste. That was what they'd joked about him marrying: that. He watched her with his soured virginity, as one might watch a draught of medicine offered that one would never, never take; one would die first – or let others die. The chalky dust blew up round the windows.

'You told me to ring up,' Rose said, 'so when . . .'

'Not here,' the Boy said. 'Wait till we're alone.' The driver's head rose slowly against a waste of sky: a few white feathers blown backward into the blue: they were on top of the downs and turned eastwards. The Boy sat with his pointed shoes side by side, his hands in his pockets, feeling the throb of the engine come up through the thin soles.

'It's lovely,' Rose said, 'being out here – in the country with you.' Little tarred bungalows with tin roofs paraded backwards, gardens scratched in the chalk, dry flower-beds like Saxon emblems carved on the downs. Notices read: 'Pull in Here', 'Mazawattee tea', 'Genuine Antiques', and hundreds of feet below the pale green sea washed into the scarred and shabby side of England. Peacehaven itself dwindled out against the downs: half-made streets turned into grass tracks. They walked down between the bungalows to the cliff-edge. There was nobody about: one of the bungalows had broken windows, in another the blinds were down for a death. 'It makes me giddy,' Rose said, 'looking down.' It was early closing and the store was shut; closing time and no drinks obtainable at the hotel; a vista of To Let boards running back along the chalky ruts of unfinished roads. The Boy could see over her shoulder the rough drop to the shingle. 'It makes me feel I'll fall,' Rose said, turning from the sea. He let her turn; no need to act prematurely; the draught might never be offered.

'Tell me,' he said, 'now – who rang up who and why?'

'I rang up *you*, but you weren't in. *He* answered.'

'He?' the Boy repeated.

'The one who left the ticket that day you came in. You remember – you were looking for something.' He remembered all right – the hand under the cloth, the stupid innocent face he had expected would so easily forget. 'You remember a lot,' he said, frowning at the thought.

'I wouldn't forget that day,' she said abruptly and stopped.

'You forget a lot, too. I just told you that wasn't the man you heard speak. That man's dead.'

'It doesn't matter anyway,' she said. 'What matters is – someone was in asking questions.'

'About the ticket?'

'Yes.'

'A man?'

'A woman. A big one with a laugh. You should have heard the laugh. Just as if she'd never had a care. I didn't trust her. She wasn't our kind.'

'Our kind': he frowned again towards the shallow wrinkled tide at the suggestion that they had something in common and spoke sharply. 'What did she want?'

'She wanted to know everything. What the man who left the card looked like.'

'What did you tell her?'

'I didn't tell her a thing, Pinkie.'

The Boy dug with his pointed shoe into the thin dry turf and sent an empty corned-beef tin rattling down the ruts. 'It's only you I'm thinking of,' he said. 'It don't matter to me. I'm not concerned. But I wouldn't want you getting mixed up in things that might be dangerous.' He looked quickly up at her, sideways. 'You don't seem scared. It's serious what I'm telling you.'

'I wouldn't be scared, Pinkie – not with you about.'

He dug his nails into his hands with vexation. She remembered everything she ought to forget, and forgot all that she should remember – the vitriol bottle. He'd scared her all right then: he'd been too friendly since: she really believed that he was fond of her. Why, this, he supposed, was 'walking out', and he thought again of Spicer's joke. He looked at the mousy skull, the bony body and the shabby dress, and shuddered – involuntarily, a goose flying across the final bed. 'Saturday,' he thought, 'to-day's Saturday,' remembering the room at home, the frightening weekly exercise of his parents which he watched from his single bed. That was what they expected of you, every polony you met had her eye on the bed: his virginity straightened in him like sex. That was how they judged you: not by whether you had the guts to kill a man, to run a mob, to conquer Colleoni. He said, 'We don't want to stay round here. We'll be getting back.'

'We've only just come,' the girl said. 'Let's stay a bit, Pinkie. I like the country,' she said.

'You've had a look,' he said. 'You can't *do* anything with the country. The pub's closed.'

'We could just sit. We've got to wait for the bus anyway. You're funny. You aren't scared of anything, are you?'

He laughed queerly, sitting awkwardly down in front of the bungalow with the shattered glass. 'Me scared? That's funny.' He lay back against the bank, his waistcoat undone, his thin frayed tie bright and striped against the chalk.

'This is better than going home,' Rose said.

'Where's home?'

'Nelson Place. Do you know it?'

'Oh, I've passed through,' he said airily, but he could have drawn its plan as accurately as a surveyor on the turf: the barred and battlemented Salvation Army gaff at the corner: his own home beyond in Paradise Piece: the houses which looked as if they had passed through an intensive bombardment, flapping gutters and glassless windows, an iron bedstead rusting in a front garden, the smashed and wasted ground in front where houses had been pulled down for model flats which had never gone up.

They lay on the chalk bank side by side with a common geography, and a little hate mixed with his contempt. He thought he had made his escape, and here his home was: back beside him, making claims.

Rose said suddenly, '*She's* never lived there.'

'Who?'

'That woman asking questions. Never a care.'

'Well,' he said, 'we can't all 'ave been born in Nelson Place.'

'You weren't born there – or somewhere round?'

'Me. Of course not. What do you think?'

'I thought – maybe you were. You're a Roman too. We were all Romans in Nelson Place. You believe in things. Like Hell. But you can see she don't believe a thing.' She said bitterly, 'You can tell the world's all dandy with her.'

He defended himself from any connection with Paradise Piece: 'I don't take any stock in religion. Hell – it's just there. You don't need to think of it – not before you die.'

'You might die sudden.'

He closed his eyes under the bright empty arch, and a memory floated up imperfectly into speech. 'You know what they say – "Between the stirrup and the ground, he something sought and something found".'

'Mercy.'

'That's right: Mercy.'

'It would be awful, though,' she said slowly, 'if they didn't give you time.' She turned her cheek on to the chalk towards him and added, as if he could help her, 'That's what I always pray. That I won't die sudden. What do you pray?'

'I don't,' he said, but he was praying even while he spoke to someone or something: that he wouldn't need to carry on any further with her, get mixed up again with that drab dynamited plot of ground they both called home.

'You angry about anything?' Rose asked.

'A man wants to be quiet sometimes,' he said, lying rigidly against the chalk bank, giving nothing away. In the silence a shutter flapped, and the tide lisped: two people walking out: that's what they were, and the memory of Colleoni's luxury, the crowned chairs at the Cosmopolitan, came back to taunt him. He said, 'Talk, can't you? Say something.'

'You wanted to be quiet,' she retorted with a sudden anger which took him by surprise. He hadn't thought her capable of that. 'If I don't suit you,' she said, 'you can leave me alone. I didn't ask to come out.' She sat with her hands round her knees and her cheeks burned on the tip of the bone: anger was as good as rouge on her thin face. 'If I'm not grand enough – your car and all—'

'Who said—'

'Oh,' she said, 'I'm not that dumb. I've seen you looking at me. My hat—'

It occurred to him suddenly that she might even get up and leave him, go back to Snow's with her secret for the first comer who questioned her kindly: he had to conciliate her, they were walking out, he'd got to do the things expected of him. He put out his hand with repulsion; it lay like a cold paddock on her knee. 'You took me up wrong,' he said, 'you're a sweet girl. I've been worried, that's all. Business worries. You and me' – he swallowed painfully – 'we suit each other down to the ground.' He saw the colour go, the face turn to him with a blind willingness to be deceived, saw the lips waiting. He drew her hand up quickly and put his mouth against her fingers: anything was better than the lips: the fingers were rough on his skin and tasted a little of soap. She said, 'Pinkie, I'm sorry. You're sweet to me.'

He laughed nervously, 'You and me,' and heard the hoot of a bus with the joy of a besieged man listening to the bugles of the relieving force. 'There,' he said, 'the bus. Let's be going. I'm not much of a one for the country. A city bird. You too.' She got up and he saw the skin of her thigh for a moment above the artificial silk, and a prick of sexual desire disturbed him like a sickness. That was what happened to a man in the end: the stuffy room, the wakeful children, the Saturday night movements from the other bed. Was there no escape – anywhere – for anyone? It was worth murdering a world.

'It's beautiful here all the same,' she said, staring up the chalky ruts between the To Let boards, and the Boy laughed again at the fine words people gave to a dirty act: love, beauty . . . All his pride coiled like a watch spring round the thought that *he* wasn't deceived, that *he* wasn't going to give himself up to marriage and the birth of children, he was going to be where Colleoni now was and higher . . . He knew everything, he had watched every detail of the act of sex, you couldn't deceive him with lovely words, there was nothing to be excited about, no gain to recompense you for what you lost; but when Rose turned to him again, with the expectation of a kiss, he was aware all the same of a horrifying ignorance. His mouth missed hers and recoiled. He'd never yet kissed a girl.

She said, 'I'm sorry. I'm stupid. I've never had—' and suddenly broke off to watch a gull rise from one of the little parched gardens and drop over the cliff towards the sea.

He didn't speak to her in the bus, sullen and ill-at-ease, sitting with his hands in his pockets, his feet close together, not knowing why he'd come this far out with her, only to go back again with nothing settled, the secret, the memory still lodged securely in her skull. The country unwound the other way: Mazawattee tea, antique dealers, pull-ins, the thin grass petering out on the first asphalt.

From the pier the Brighton anglers flung their floats. A little music ground mournfully out into the windy sunlight. They walked on the sunny side past 'A Night of Love', 'For Men Only', 'The Fan Dancer'. Rose asked, 'Is business bad?'

'There's always worries,' the Boy said.

'I wish I could help, be of use.' He said nothing, walking on. She put out a hand towards the thin rigid figure, seeing the smooth cheek, the fluff of fair hair at the nape. 'You're so young, Pinkie, to get worries.' She put her hand through his arm. 'We're both young, Pinkie,' and felt his body stonily withdrawn.

A photographer said, 'Snap you together against the sea,' raising the cap from his camera, and the Boy flung up his hands before his face and went on.

'Don't you like being snapped, Pinkie? We might have had our pictures stuck up for people to see. It wouldn't have *cost* anything.'

'I don't mind what things cost,' the Boy said, rattling his pockets, showing how much cash he had.

'We might 'ave been stuck up there,' Rose said, halting at the photographer's kiosk, at the pictures of the bathing belles and the famous comedians and the anonymous couples, 'next—' and exclaimed with surprise, 'why – there *he* is.'

The Boy was staring over the side where the green tide sucked and slid like a wet mouth round the piles. He turned unwillingly to look and there was Spicer fixed in the photographer's window for the world to gaze at, striding out of the sunlight into the shadow under the pier, worried and hunted and in haste, a comic figure at which strangers could laugh and say, 'He's worried right enough. They caught *him* unawares.'

'The one who left the card,' Rose said. 'The one you said was dead. *He's* not dead. Though it almost looks—' she laughed with amusement at the blurred black-and-white haste – 'that he's afraid he will be if he doesn't hurry.'

'An old picture,' the Boy said.

'Oh no, it's not. This is where to-day's pictures go. For you to buy.'

'You know a lot.'

'You can't miss it, can you?' Rose said. 'It's comic. Striding along. All fussed up. Not even seeing the camera.'

'Stay here,' the Boy said. Inside the kiosk it was dark after the sun. A man with a thin moustache and steel-rimmed spectacles sorted piles of prints.

'I want a picture that's up outside,' the Boy said.

'Slip, please,' the man said, and put out yellow fingers which smelt faintly of hypo.

'I haven't got a slip.'

'You can't have the picture without the slip,' the man said and held a negative up to the electric globe.

'What right have you,' the Boy said, 'to stick up pictures without a by-your leave? You let me have that picture,' but the steel rims glittered back at him, without interest – a fractious boy. 'You bring that slip,' the man said, 'and you can have the picture. Now run along. I'm busy.' Behind his head were framed snapshots of King Edward VIII (Prince of Wales) in a yachting cap and a background of peep machines, going yellow from inferior chemicals and age; Vesta Tilley signing autographs; Henry Irving muffled against the Channel winds; a nation's history. Lily Langtry wore ostrich feathers, Mrs Pankhurst hobble skirts, the English Beauty Queen of 1923 a bathing dress. It was little comfort to know that Spicer was among the immortals.

Chapter Four

'Spicer,' the Boy called, 'Spicer.' He climbed up from Frank's small dark hall towards the landing, leaving a smear of country, of the downs, white on the linoleum. 'Spicer.' He felt the broken banister tremble under his hand. He opened the door of Spicer's room and there he was upon the bed, asleep face down. The window was closed, an insect buzzed through the stale air, and there was a smell of whisky from the bed. Pinkie stood looking down on the grying hair. He felt no pity at all; he wasn't old enough for pity. He pulled Spicer round; the skin round his mouth was in eruption. 'Spicer.'

Spicer opened his eyes. He saw nothing for a while in the dim room.

'I want a word with you, Spicer.'

Spicer sat up. 'My God, Pinkie, I'm glad to see you.'

'Always glad to see a pal, eh, Spicer?'

'I saw Crab. He said you were at the police-station.'

'Crab?'

'You weren't at the station, then?'

'I was having a friendly talk – about Brewer.'

'Not about—?'

'About Brewer.' The Boy suddenly put his hand on Spicer's wrist. 'Your nerves are all wrong, Spicer. You want a holiday.' He sniffed with contempt the tainted air. 'You drink too much.' He went to the window and threw it open on the vista of grey wall. A leather-jacket buzzed up the pane and the Boy caught it in his hand. It vibrated like a tiny watchspring in his palm. He began to pull off the legs and wings one by one. 'She loves me,' he said, 'she loves me not. I've been out with my girl, Spicer.'

'The one from Snow's?'

The Boy turned the denuded body over on his palm and puffed it away over Spicer's bed. 'You know who I mean,' he said. 'You had a message for me, Spicer. Why didn't you bring it?'

'I couldn't find you, Pinkie. Honest I couldn't. And anyway it wasn't that important. Some old busybody asking questions.'

'It scared you all the same,' the Boy said. He sat down on the hard deal chair before the mirror, his hands on his knees, watching Spicer. The pulse beat in his cheek.

'Oh, it didn't scare me,' Spicer said.

'You went walking blind straight to There.'

'What do you mean – There?'

'There's only one There to you, Spicer. You think about it and you dream about it. You're too old for this life.'

'This life?' Spicer said, glaring back at him from the bed.

'This racket, of course I mean. You get nervous and then you get rash. First there was that card in Snow's and now you let your picture be stuck up on the pier for anyone to see. For Rose to see.'

'Honest to God, Pinkie, I never knew that.'

'You forget to walk on your toes.'

'She's safe. She's stuck on you, Pinkie.'

'I don't know anything about women. I leave that to you and Cubitt and the rest. I only know what you tell me. You've told me time and again there never was a safe polony yet.'

'That's just talk.'

'You mean I'm a kid and you tell me good-night stories. But I've got so I believe them, Spicer. It don't seem safe to me that you and Rose are in the same town. Apart from this other buer asking questions. You'll have to disappear, Spicer.'

'What do you mean?' Spicer said. 'Disappear?' He fumbled inside his jacket and the Boy watched him, his hands flat on his knees. 'You wouldn't do anything,' he said, fumbling in his pocket.

'Why,' the Boy said, 'what do you think I mean? I mean take a holiday, go away somewhere for a while.'

Spicer's hand came out of his pocket. He held out a silver watch towards the Boy. 'You can trust me, Pinkie. Look there, what the boys gave me. Read the inscription. "Ten Years a Pal. From the boys at the Stadium." I

don't let people down. That was fifteen years ago, Pinkie. Twenty-five years
on the tracks. You weren't born when I started.'

'You need a holiday,' the Boy said. 'That's all I said.'

'I'd be glad to take a holiday,' Spicer said, 'but I wouldn't want you to
think I'm milky. I'll go at once. I'll pack a bag and clear out to-night. Why,
I'd be glad to be gone.'

'No,' the Boy said, staring down at his shoes. 'There's not all that hurry.'
He lifted a foot. The sole was worn through in a piece the size of a shilling.
He thought again of the crowns on Colleoni's chairs at the Cosmopolitan.
'I'll need you at the races.' He smiled across the room at Spicer. 'A pal I can
trust.'

'You can trust me, Pinkie.' Spicer's fingers smoothed the silver watch.
'What are you smiling at? Have I got a smut or something?'

'I was just thinking of the races,' the Boy said. 'They mean a lot to me.'
He got up and stood with his back to the greying light, the tenement wall,
the smut-smeared pane, looking down at Spicer with a kind of curiosity.
'And where will you go, Spicer?' he said. His mind was quite made up, and
for the second time in a few weeks he looked at a dying man. He couldn't
help feeling inquisitive. Why, it was even possible that old Spicer was not
set for the flames, he'd been a loyal old geezer, he hadn't done as much harm
as the next man, he might slip through the gates into – but the Boy couldn't
picture any eternity except in terms of pain. He frowned a little in the effort:
a glassy sea, a golden crown, old Spicer.

'Nottingham,' Spicer said. 'A pal of mine keeps the "Blue Anchor" in
Union Street. A free house. High class. Lunches served. He's often said to
me, "Spicer, why don't you come into partnership? We'd make the old place
into a hotel with a few more nickers in the till." If it wasn't for you and the
boys,' Spicer said, 'I wouldn't want to come back. I wouldn't mind staying
away for keeps.'

'Well,' the Boy said, 'I'll be off. We know where we are now, anyway.'
Spicer lay back on the pillow and put up the foot with the shooting corn.
There was a hole in his woollen stocking, and a big toe showed through,
hard skin calcined with middle age. 'Sleep well,' the Boy said.

He went downstairs, the front door faced east, and the hall was dark. He
switched on a light by the telephone and then switched it out again: he didn't
know why. Then he rang up the Cosmopolitan. When the hotel exchange
answered he could hear the dance music in the distance, all the way from
the Palm House (*thés dansants* three shillings), behind the Louis Seize
lounge. 'I want Mr Colleoni.' 'The nightingale singing, the postmen ringing'
– the tune was abruptly cut off, and a low voice purred up the line.

'That Mr Colleoni?'

He could hear a glass chink and ice move in a shaker. He said, 'This is
Mr P. Brown. I've been thinking things over, Mr Colleoni.' Outside the
little dark linoleumed hall a bus slid by, the lights faint in the grey end of
the day. The Boy put his mouth close to the mouth of the telephone and
said: 'He won't listen to reason, Mr Colleoni.' The voice purred happily
back at him. The Boy explained slowly and carefully, 'I'll wish him good
luck and pat him on the back.' He stopped and asked sharply, 'What's that
you say, Mr Colleoni? No I just thought you laughed. Hullo. Hullo.' He
banged the receiver down and turned with a sense of uneasiness towards the

stairs. The gold cigar-lighter, the grey double-breasted waistcoat, the feeling of a racket luxuriously successful for a moment dominated him: the brass bedstead upstairs, the little pot of violet ink on the washstand, the flakes of sausage-roll. His board school cunning wilted for awhile; then he turned on the light, he was at home. He climbed the stairs, humming softly: 'the nightingale singing, the postman ringing,' but as his thoughts circled closer to the dark, dangerous and deathly centre the tune changed: 'Agnus dei qui tollis peccata mundi . . .' He walked stiffly, the jacket sagging across his immature shoulders, but when he opened the door of his room – 'dona novis pacem' – his pallid face peered dimly back at him full of pride from the mirror over the ewer, the soap-dish, the basin of stale water.

BOOK FOUR

Chapter One

It was a fine day for the races. People poured into Brighton by the first train. It was like Bank Holiday all over again, except that these people didn't spend their money; they harboured it. They stood packed deep on the tops of the trams rocking down to the Aquarium, they surged like some natural and irrational migration of insects up and down the front. By eleven o'clock it was impossible to get a seat on the buses going out to the course. A negro wearing a bright striped tie sat on a bench in the Pavilion garden and smoked a cigar. Some children played touch wood from seat to seat, and he called out to them hilariously, holding his cigar at arm's length with an air of pride and caution, his great teeth gleaming like an advertisement. They stopped playing and stared at him, backing slowly. He called out to them again in their own tongue, the words hollow and unformed and childish like theirs, and they eyed him uneasily and backed farther away. He put his cigar patiently back between the cushiony lips and went on smoking. A band came up the pavement through Old Steyne, a blind band playing drums and trumpets, walking in the gutter, feeling the kerb with the edge of their shoes, in Indian file. You heard the music a long way off, persisting through the rumble of the crowd, the shots of exhaust pipes, and the grinding of the buses starting uphill for the racecourse. It rang out with spirit, marched like a regiment, and you raised your eyes in expectation of the tiger skin and the twirling drumsticks and saw the pale blind eyes, like those of pit ponies, going by along the gutter.

In the public school grounds above the sea the girls trooped solemnly out to hockey: stout goal-keepers padded like armadillos; captains discussing tactics with their lieutenants; junior girls running amok in the bright day. Beyond the aristocratic turf, through the wrought-iron main gates they could see the plebeian procession, those whom the buses wouldn't hold, plodding up the down, kicking up the dust, eating buns out of paper bags. The buses took the long way round through Kemp Town, but up the steep hill came the crammed taxicabs – a seat for anyone at ninepence a time – a Packard for the members' enclosure, old Morrises, strange high cars with family parties, keeping the road after twenty years. It was as if the whole road moved upwards like an Underground staircase in the dusty sunlight, a creaking, shouting, jostling crowd of cars moving with it. The junior girls took to their heels like ponies racing on the turf, feeling the excitement going on outside, as if this were a day on which life for many people reached a kind of climax. The odds on Black Boy had shortened, nothing could ever make life quite the same after that rash bet of a fiver on Merry Monarch. A scarlet racing model, a tiny rakish car which carried about it the atmosphere of innumerable road-houses, of totsies gathered round swimming pools, of furtive encounters in by-lanes off the Great North Road, wormed through the traffic with incredible dexterity. The sun caught it: it winked as far as the dining-hall windows of the girls' school. It was crammed tight: a woman sat on a man's knee, and another man clung on the running board as it swayed and hooted and cut in and out uphill towards the downs. The woman was singing, her voice faint and disjointed through the horns, something traditional about brides and bouquets, something which went with Guinness and oysters and the old Leicester Lounge, something out of place in the little bright racing car. Upon the top of the down the words blew back along the dusty road to meet an ancient Morris rocking and receding in their wake at forty miles an hour, with flapping hood, bent fender and discoloured windscreen.

The words came through the flap, flap, flap of the old hood to the Boy's ears. He sat beside Spicer who drove the car. Brides and bouquets: and he thought of Rose with sullen disgust. He couldn't get the suggestion of Spicer out of his mind; it was like an invisible power working against him: Spicer's stupidity, the photograph on the pier, that woman – who the hell was she? – asking questions. . . . If he married her, of course, it wouldn't be for long: only as a last resort to close her mouth and give him time. He didn't want *that* relationship with anyone: the double bed, the intimacy, it sickened him like the idea of age. He crouched in the corner away from where the ticking pierced the seat, vibrating up and down in bitter virginity. To marry – it was like ordure on the hands.

'Where's Dallow and Cubitt?' Spicer asked.

'I didn't want them here today,' the Boy said. 'We've got something to do today the mob are better out of.' Like a cruel child who hides the dividers behind him, he put his hand with spurious affection on Spicer's arm. 'I don't mind telling you. I'm going to make it up with Colleoni. I wouldn't trust *them*. They are violent. You and I, we'll handle it properly between us.'

'I'm all for peace,' Spicer said, 'I always have been.'

The Boy grinned through the broken windscreen at the long disorder of cars. 'That's what I'm going to arrange,' he said.

'A peace that lasts,' Spicer said.

'No one's going to break this peace,' the Boy said. The faint singing died in the dust and the bright sun: a final bride, a final bouquet, a word which sounded like 'wreath'. 'How do you set about getting married?' the Boy unwillingly asked. 'If you've got to in a hurry?'

'Not so easy for you,' Spicer said. 'There's your age.' He ground the old gears as they climbed a final spur towards the white enclosure on the chalky soil, the gipsy vans. 'I'd have to think about it.'

'Think quick,' the Boy said. 'You don't forget you're clearing out to-night.'

'That's right,' Spicer said. Departure made him a little sentimental. 'The eight-ten. You ought to see that pub. You'd be welcome. Nottingham's a fine town. It'll be good to rest up there a while. The air's fine, and you couldn't ask for a better bitter than you get at the "Blue Anchor".' He grinned. 'I forgot you didn't drink.'

'Have a good time,' the Boy said.

'You'll be always welcome, Pinkie.'

They rolled the old car up into the park and got out. The Boy passed his arm through Spicer's. Life was good walking outside the white sun-drenched wall, past the loud-speaker vans, the man who believed in a second coming, towards the finest of all sensations, the infliction of pain. 'You're a fine fellow, Spicer,' the Boy said, squeezing his arm, and Spicer began to tell him in a low friendly confiding way all about the 'Blue Anchor'. 'It's not a tied house,' he said, 'they've a reputation. I've always thought when I'd made enough money I'd go in with my friend. He still wants me to. I nearly went when they killed Kite.'

'You get scared easy, don't you?' the Boy said. The loud-speakers on the vans advised them whom to put their money with, and gipsy children chased a rabbit with cries across the trampled chalk. They went down into the tunnel under the course and came up into the light and the short grey grass sloping down by the bungalow houses to the sea. Old bookies' tickets rotted into the chalk: 'Barker for the Odds', a smug smiling nonconformist face printed in yellow: 'Don't Worry I Pay', and old tote tickets among the stunted plantains. They went through the wire fence into the half-crown enclosure. 'Have a glass of beer, Spicer,' the Boy said, pressing him on.

'Why, that's good of you, Pinkie. I wouldn't mind a glass,' and while Spicer drank it by the wooden trestles, the Boy looked down the line of bookies. There was Barker and Macpherson and George Beale ('The Old Firm') and Bob Tavell of Clapton, all the familiar faces, full of blarney and fake good humour. The first two races had been run: there were long queues at the tote windows. The sun lit the white Tattersall stand across the course, and a few horses cantered by to the start. 'There goes General Burgoyne,' a man said, 'he's restless,' starting off to Bob Tavell's stand to cover his bet. The bookies rubbed out and altered the odds as the horses went by, their hoofs padding like boxing gloves on the turf.

'You going to take a plunge?' Spicer asked, finishing his Bass, blowing a little gaseous malted breath towards the bookies.

'I don't bet,' the Boy said.

'It's the last chance for me,' Spicer said, 'in good old Brighton. I wouldn't mind risking a couple of nicker. Not more. I'm saving my cash for Nottingham.'

'Go on,' the Boy said, 'have a good time while you can.'

They walked down the row of bookies towards Brewer's stand: there were a lot of men about. 'He's doing good business,' Spicer said. 'Did you see the Merry Monarch? He's going up,' and while he spoke, all down the line the bookies rubbed out the old sixteen to one odds. 'Ten's,' Spicer said.

'Have a good time while you're here,' the Boy said.

'Might as well patronize the old firm,' Spicer said, detaching his arm and walking across to Tate's stand. The Boy smiled. It was as easy as shelling peas. 'Memento Mori,' Spicer said, coming away card in hand. 'That's a funny name to give a horse. Five to one, a place. What does Memento Mori mean?'

'It's foreign,' the Boy said. 'Black Boy's shortening.'

'I wish I'd covered myself on Black Boy,' Spicer said. 'There was a woman down there says she's backed Black Boy for a pony. It sounds crazy to me. But think if he wins,' Spicer said. 'My God, what wouldn't I do with two hundred and fifty pounds? I'd take a share in the "Blue Anchor" straight away. You wouldn't see me back here,' he added, staring round at the brilliant sky, the dust over the course, the torn betting cards and the short grass towards the dark sea beneath the down.

'Black Boy won't win,' the Boy said. 'Who was it put the pony on?'

'Some polony or other. She was over there at the bar. Why don't you have a fiver on Black Boy? Have a bet for once to celebrate?'

'Celebrate what?' the Boy asked quickly.

'I forgot,' Spicer said. 'This holiday's perked me up, so's I think everyone's got something to celebrate.'

'If I did want to celebrate,' the Boy said, 'it wouldn't be with Black Boy. Why, that used to be Fred's favourite. Said he'd be a Derby winner yet. I wouldn't call that a lucky horse,' but he couldn't help watching him canter up by the rails: a little too fresh, a little too restless. A man on top of the half-crown stand tic-tacked to Bob Tavell of Clapton and a tiny Jew, who was studying the ten shilling enclosure through binoculars, suddenly began to saw the air, to attract the attention of the Old Firm. 'There,' the Boy said, 'what did I tell you? Black Boy's going out again.'

'Hundred to eight, Black Boy, hundred to eight,' George Beale's representative called, and 'They're off,' somebody said. People pressed out from the refreshment booth towards the rails carrying glasses of Bass and currant buns. Barker, Macpherson, Bob Tavell, all wiped the odds from their boards, but the Old Firm remained game to the last: 'Hundred to six Black Boy': while the little Jew made masonic passes from the top of the stand. The horses came by in a bunch, with a sharp sound like splintering wood, and were gone. 'General Burgoyne,' somebody said, and somebody said: 'Merry Monarch.' The beer drinkers went back to the trestle boards and had another glass, and the bookies put up the runners in the four o'clock and began to chalk a few odds.

'There,' the Boy said, 'what did I tell you? Fred never knew a good horse from a bad one. That crazy polony's dropped a pony. It's not *her* lucky day. Why' – but the silence, the inaction after a race is run and before the results go up, had a daunting quality. The queues waited outside the totes. Everything on the course was suddenly still, waiting for a signal to begin again; in the silence you could hear a horse whinny all the way across from the weighing-in. A sense of uneasiness gripped the Boy in the quiet and the brightness. The soured false age, the concentrated and limited experience of the Brighton slum drained out of him. He wished he had Cubitt there and Dallow. There was too much to tackle by himself at seventeen. It wasn't only Spicer. He had started something on Whit Monday which had no end. Death wasn't an end; the censer swung and the priest raised the Host, and the loud-speaker intoned the winners: 'Black Boy. Memento Mori. General Burgoyne.'

'By God,' Spicer said, 'I've won. Memento Mori for a place,' and remembering what the Boy had said, 'And she's won too. A pony. What a break. Now what about Black Boy?' Pinkie was silent. He told himself: Fred's horse. If I was one of those crazy geezers who touch wood, throw salt, won't go under ladders, I might be scared to—

Spicer plucked at him. 'I've won, Pinkie. A tenner. What do you know about that?'

– to go on with what he'd planned with care. Somewhere from farther down the enclosure he heard a laugh, a female laugh, mellow and confident, perhaps the polony who'd put a pony on Fred's horse. He turned on Spicer with secret venom, cruelty straightening his body like lust. 'Yes,' he said, putting his arm round Spicer's shoulder, 'you'd better collect now.'

They moved together towards Tate's stand. A young man with oiled hair stood on a wooden step paying out money. Tate himself was away in the ten shilling enclosure, but they both knew Samuel. Spicer called out to him quite jovially as he advanced, 'Well, Sammy, now the pay-off.'

Samuel watched them, Spicer and the Boy, come across the shallow threadbare turf, arm-in-arm like very old friends. Half a dozen men collected and stood round, waiting, the last creditor slipped away, they waited in silence, a little man holding an account book put out a tip of tongue and licked a sore lip.

'You're in luck, Spicer,' the Boy said, squeezing his arm. 'Have a good time with your tenner.'

'You aren't saying good-bye yet, are you?' Spicer asked.

'I'm not waiting for the four-thirty. I won't be seeing you again.'

'What about Colleoni?' Spicer said. 'Aren't you and I . . .?' The horses cantered by for another start; the odds were going up; the crowd moved in towards the tote and left them a clear lane. At the end of the lane the little group waited.

'I've changed my mind,' the Boy said. 'I'll see Colleoni at his hotel. You get your money.' A hatless tout delayed them: 'A tip for the next race. Only a shilling. I've tipped two winners to-day.' His toes showed through his shoes. 'Tip yourself off,' the Boy said. Spicer didn't like good-byes: he was a sentimental soul: he shifted on his corn-sore foot. 'Why,' he said, looking down the lane to the fence, 'Tate's lot haven't written up the odds yet.'

'Tate always was slow. Slow in paying out, too. Better get your money.' He urged him nearer, his hand on Spicer's elbow.

'There's not anything wrong, is there?' Spicer asked. He looked at the waiting men: they stared through him.

'Well, this is good-bye,' the Boy said.

'You remember the address,' Spicer said. 'The "Blue Anchor", you remember, Union Street. Send me any news. I don't suppose there'll be any for *me* to send.'

The Boy put his hand up as if to pat Spicer on the back and let it fall again; the group of men stood in a bunch waiting. 'Maybe –' the Boy said: he looked round: there wasn't any end to what he had begun. A passion of cruelty stirred in his belly. He put up his hand again and patted Spicer on the back. 'Good luck to you,' he said in a high broken adolescent voice and patted him again.

The men with one accord came round them. He heard Spicer scream, 'Pinkie,' and saw him fall: a boot with heavy nails was lifted, and then he felt pain run like blood down on his own neck.

The surprise at first was far worse than the pain (a nettle could sting as badly). 'You fools,' he said, 'it's not me, it's him you want,' and turned and saw the faces ringing him all round. They grinned back at him: every man had his razor out: and he remembered for the first time Colleoni laughing up the telephone wire. The crowd had scattered at the first sign of trouble; he heard Spicer call out, 'Pinkie. For Christ's sake'; an obscure struggle reached its climax out of his sight. He had other things to watch: the long cut-throat razors which the sun caught slanting low down over the downs from Shoreham. He put his hand to his pocket to get his blade, and the man immediately facing him leant across and slashed his knuckles. Pain happened to him, and he was filled with horror and astonishment as if one of the bullied brats at school had stabbed first with the dividers.

They made no attempt to come in and finish him. He sobbed at them, 'I'll get Colleoni for this.' He shouted 'Spicer' twice before he remembered that Spicer couldn't answer. The mob were enjoying themselves, just as he had always enjoyed himself. One of them leant forward to cut his cheek, and when he put up his hand to shield himself they slashed his knuckles again. He began to weep, as the four-thirty went by in a drumbeat of hooves beyond the rail.

Then somebody from the stand shouted 'Bogies' and they all moved together, coming quickly at him in a bunch. Somebody kicked him on the thigh, he clutched a razor in his hand and was cut to the bone. Then they scattered as the police ran up the edge of the course, slow in their heavy boots, and he broke through them. A few followed him, out of the wire gate and straight down the side of the Down towards the houses and the sea. He wept as he ran, lame in one leg from the kick, he even tried to pray. You could be saved between the stirrup and the ground, but you couldn't be saved if you didn't repent and he hadn't time, scrambling down the chalk down, to feel the least remorse. He ran awkwardly, tripping, bleeding down his face and from both hands.

Only two men followed him now, and they followed him for the fun of it, shooing him as they might shoo a cat. He reached the first houses in the bottom, but there was no one about. The races had emptied every house: nothing but crazy paving and little lawns, stained-glass doors and a lawn mower abandoned on a gravel path. He didn't dare to take refuge in a house; while he rang and waited they would reach him. He had his razor blade out now, but he had never yet used it on an armed enemy. He had to hide, but he left a track of blood along the road.

The two men were out of breath; they had wasted it on laughter, and he had young lungs. He gained on them; he wrapped his hand in a handkerchief and held his head back so that the blood ran down his clothes. He turned a corner and was into an empty garage before they had reached it. There he stood in the dusky interior with his razor out, trying to repent. He thought 'Spicer', 'Fred', but his thoughts would carry him no further than the corner where his pursuers might reappear: he discovered that he hadn't the energy to repent.

And when a long while later the danger seemed to be over, and there was a long dusk on his hands, it wasn't eternity he thought about but his own humiliation. He had wept, begged, run: Dallow and Cubitt would hear of it. What would happen to Kite's mob now? He tried to think of Spicer, but the world held him. He couldn't order his thoughts. He stood with weak knees against the concrete wall with the blade advanced and watched the corner. A few people passed, the faintest sound of music bit, like an abscess, into his brain from the Palace Pier, the lights came out in the neat barren bourgeois road.

The garage had never been used for a garage; it had become a kind of potting shed. Little green shoots crept, like caterpillars, out of shallow boxes of earth: a spade, a rusty lawn mower, and all the junk the owner had no room for in the tiny house; an old rocking horse, a pram which had been converted into a wheelbarrow, a pile of ancient records – 'Alexander's Rag Time Band', 'Pack Up Your Troubles', 'If You Were the Only Girl'; they lay with the trowels, what was left of the crazy paving, a doll with one glass eye and a dress soiled with mould. He took it all in with quick glances, his razor blade ready, the blood clotting on his neck, dripping from his hand, where the handkerchief had slipped. Whatever jackdaw owned this house would have that much added to his possessions – the little drying stain on the concrete floor.

Whoever the owner was, he had come a long way to land up here. The pram-wheelbarrow was covered with labels – the marks of innumerable train journeys – Doncaster, Lichfield, Clacton (that must have been a summer holiday), Ipswich, Northampton – roughly torn off for the next journey they left, in the litter which remained, an unmistakable trail. And this, the small villa under the racecourse, was the best finish he could manage. You couldn't have any doubt that this was the end, the mortgaged home in the bottom; like the untidy tidemark on a beach, the junk was piled up here and would never go farther.

And the Boy hated him. He was nameless, faceless, but the Boy hated him, the doll, the pram, the broken rocking horse. The small pricked-out plants irritated him like ignorance. He felt hungry and faint and shaken. He had known pain and fear.

Now, of course, was the time, while darkness drained into the bottom, for him to make his peace. Between the stirrup and the ground there wasn't time: you couldn't break in a moment the habit of thought: habit held you closely while you died, and he remembered Kite, after they'd got him at St Pancras, passing out in the waiting-room, while a porter poured coal-dust on the dead grate, talking all the time about someone's tits.

But 'Spicer', the Boy's thoughts came inevitably back with a sense of relief, 'they've got Spicer.' It was impossible to repent of something which made him safe. The nosy woman hadn't got a witness now, except for Rose, and he could deal with Rose; and then, when he was thoroughly secure, he could begin to think of making peace, of going home, and his heart weakened with a faint nostalgia for the tiny dark confessional box, the priest's voice, and the people waiting under the statue, before the bright lights burning down in the pink glasses, to be made safe from eternal pain. Eternal pain had not meant much to him: now it meant the slash of razor blades infinitely prolonged.

He sidled out of the garage. The new raw street cut in the chalk was empty except for a couple pressed against each other out of the lamplight by a wooden fence. The sight pricked him with nausea and cruelty. He limped by them, his cut hand closed on the razor, with his cruel virginity which demanded some satisfaction different from theirs, habitual, brutish and short.

He knew where he was going. He wasn't going to return to Frank's like this with the cobwebs from the garage on his clothes, defeat cut in his face and hand. They were dancing in the open air on the white stone deck above the Aquarium, and he got down on to the beach where he was more alone, the dry seaweed left by last winter's gales cracking under his shoes. He could hear the music – 'The One I Love'. Wrap it up in cellophane, he thought, put it in silver paper. A moth wounded against one of the lamps crawled across a piece of driftwood and he crushed it out of existence under his chalky shoe. One day – one day – he limped along the sand with his bleeding hand hidden, a young dictator. He was head of Kite's gang, this was a temporary defeat. One confession, when he was safe, to wipe out everything. The yellow moon slanted up over Hove, the exact mathematical Regency Square, and he day-dreamed, limping in the dry unwashed sand, by the closed bathing-huts: I'll give a statue.

He climbed up from the sand just past the Palace Pier and made his painful way across the parade. Snow's Restaurant was all lit up. A radio was playing. He stood on the pavement outside until he saw Rose serve a table close to the window, then went and pressed his face to it. She saw him at once; his attention rang in her brain as quickly as if he had dialled her. He took his hand from his pocket, but his wounded face was anxiety enough for her. She tried to tell him something through the glass: he couldn't understand her; it was as if he were listening to a foreign language. She had to repeat it three times, 'Go to the back,' before he could read her lips. The pain in his leg was worse; he trailed round the building, and as he turned, a car went by, a Lancia, a uniformed chauffeur, and Mr Colleoni – Mr Colleoni in a dinner jacket with a white waistcoat, who leant back and smiled and smiled in the face of an old lady in purple silk. Or perhaps it was not Mr Colleoni at all, they went so smoothly and swiftly past, but any rich middle-aged tycoon returning to the Cosmopolitan after a concert in the Pavilion.

He bent and looked through the letter-box of the back door: Rose came down the passage towards him with her hands clenched and a look of anger on her face. He lost some of his confidence; she's noticed, he thought, how done in ... he'd always known a girl looked at your shoes and coat: if she sends me away, he thought, I'll crack this vitriol bottle ... but when she opened the door she was as dumb and devoted as ever she'd been. 'Who's done it?' she whispered. 'If I could get at them.'

'Never mind,' the Boy said and boasted experimentally, 'you can leave them to me.'

'Your dear face.' He remembered with disgust that they were always said to like a scar, that they took it as a mark of manhood, of potency.

'Is there somewhere,' he asked, 'where I can wash?'

She whispered, 'Come quietly. Through here's the cellar,' and she led the way into a little closet, where the hot pipes ran and a few bottles lay in a small bin.

'Won't they be coming here?' he asked.

'No one here orders wine,' she said. 'We haven't got a licence. It's what was left when we took over. The manageress drinks it for her health.' Every time she mentioned Snow's she said 'we' with faint self-consciousness. 'Sit down,' she said. 'I'll fetch some water. I'll have to put the light out or someone might see.' But the moon lit the room enough for him to look around; he could even read the labels on the bottles: Empire wines, Australian hocks and harvest Burgundies.

She was gone only a little while, but immediately she returned she began humbly to apologize, 'Someone wanted a bill and cook was watching.' She had a white pudding basin of hot water and three handerchiefs. 'They're all I've got,' she said, tearing them up, 'the laundry's not back,' and added firmly, as she dabbed the long shallow cut, like a line drawn with a pin down his neck: 'If I could get at them . . .'

'Don't talk so much,' he said and held out his slashed hand. The blood was beginning to clot: she tied it unskilfully.

'Has anyone been around again talking, asking questions?'

'That man the woman was with.'

'A bogy?'

'I don't think so. He said his name was Phil.'

'*You* seem to have done the asking.'

'They all tell you things.'

'I don't understand it,' the Boy said. 'What do they want if they aren't bogies?' He put out his unwounded hand and pinched her arm. 'You don't tell them a thing?'

'Not a thing,' she said and watched him with devotion through the dark. 'Were you afraid?'

'They can't put anything on me.'

'I mean,' she said, 'when they did this,' touching his hand.

'Afraid,' he lied, 'of course I wasn't afraid.'

'Why did they do it?'

'I told you not to ask questions.' He got up, unsteady on his bruised leg. 'Brush my coat. I can't go out like this. I've got to be respectable.' He leant against the harvest Burgundy while she brushed him down with the flat of her hand. The moonlight shadowed the room, the small bin, the bottles, the narrow shoulders, the smooth scared adolescent face.

He was aware of an unwillingness to go out again into the street, back to Frank's and the unending calculations with Cubitt and Dallow of the next move. Life was a series of complicated tactical exercises, as complicated as the alignments at Waterloo, thought out on a brass bedstead among the crumbs of sausage roll. Your clothes continually needed ironing, Cubitt and Dallow quarrelled or else Dallow went after Frank's wife, the old box telephone under the stairs range and rang, and the extras were always being brought in and thrown on the bed by Judy who smoked too much and wanted a tip – a tip – a tip. How could you think out a larger strategy under those conditions? He had a sudden nostalgia for the small dark cupboard room, the silence, the pale light on the harvest Burgundy. To be alone a while . . .

But he wasn't alone. Rose put her hand on his and asked him with fear, 'They aren't waiting for you, are they, out there?'

He shrank away and boasted. 'They aren't waiting anywhere. They got more than they gave. They didn't reckon on me, only on poor Spicer.'

'Poor Spicer?'

'Poor Spicer's dead,' and just as he spoke a loud laugh came down the passage from the restaurant, a woman's laugh, full of beer and good fellowship and no regrets. '*She*'s back,' the Boy said.

'It's her all right.' One had heard that laugh in a hundred places: dry-eyed, uncaring, looking on the bright side, when boats drew out and other people wept: saluting the bawdy joke in music halls: beside sick beds and in crowded Southern Railway compartments: when the wrong horse won, a good sportswoman's laugh. 'She scares me,' Rose whispered. 'I don't know what she wants.'

The Boy pulled her up to him. Tactics, tactics, there was never any time for strategy, and in the grey night light he could see her face lifted for a kiss. He hesitated, with repulsion, but tactics. He wanted to strike her, to make her scream, but he kissed her inexpertly, missing her lips. He took his crinkling mouth away, and said, 'Listen.'

She said, 'You haven't had many girls, have you?'

'Of course I have,' he said, 'but listen . . .'

'You're my first,' she said. 'I'm glad.' When she said that, he began again to hate her. She wouldn't even be something to boast of: her first: he'd robbed nobody, he had no rival, no one else would look at her, Cubitt and Dallow wouldn't give her a glance: her indeterminate natural hair, her simpleness, the cheap clothes he could feel under his hand. He hated her as he had hated Spicer and it made him circumspect; he pressed her breasts awkwardly under his palms, with a grim opportunist pretence of another man's passion, and thought: it wouldn't be so bad if she was more dolled up, a bit of paint and henna, but this – the cheapest, youngest, least experienced skirt in all Brighton – to have *me* in her power.

'O God,' she said, 'you're sweet to me, Pinkie. I love you.'

'You wouldn't give me away – to *her*?'

Somebody in the passage shouted 'Rose'; a door slammed.

'I'll have to go,' she said. 'What do you mean – give you away?'

'What I said. Talk. Tell her who left that ticket. That it wasn't you know who.'

'I won't tell her.' A bus went by in West Street. The lights came through a little barred window straight on to her white determined face: she was like a child who crosses her fingers and swears her private oath. She said gently, 'I don't care what you've done' as she might have denied interest in a broken window-pane or a smutty word chalked on someone else's door. He was speechless; and some knowledge of the astuteness of her simplicity, the long experience of her sixteen years, the possible depths of her fidelity touched him like cheap music, as the light shifted from cheek-bone to cheek-bone and across the wall, as the gears ground outside.

He said, 'What do you mean? I've done nothing.'

'I don't know,' she said. 'I don't care.'

'Rose,' a voice cried, 'Rose.'

'It's her,' she said, 'I'm sure it's Her. Asking questions. Soft as butter. What does she know about *us*?' She came closer. She said, 'I did something once too. A mortal sin. When I was twelve. But she – she doesn't know what a mortal sin is.'

'Rose. Where are you? Rose.'

The shadow of her sixteen-year-old face shifted in the moonlight on the wall. 'Right and wrong. That's what she talks about. I've heard her at the table. Right and wrong. As if she knew.' She whispered with contempt, 'Oh, she won't burn. She couldn't burn if she tried.' She might have been discussing a damp Catherine wheel. 'Molly Carthew burnt. She was lovely. She killed herself. Despair. That's mortal sin. It's unforgivable. Unless – what is it you said about the stirrup?'

He told her unwillingly. 'The stirrup and the ground. That doesn't work.'

'What you did,' she persisted, 'did you confess it?'

He said evasively, a dark stubborn figure resting his bandaged hand on the Australian hock, 'I haven't been to Mass for years.'

'I don't care,' she repeated. 'I'd rather burn with you than be like Her.' Her immature voice stumbled on the word, 'She's ignorant.'

'Rose.' The door opened on their hiding-place. A manageress in a sage-green uniform, glasses hanging from a button on her breast, brought in with her the light, the voices, the radio, the laugh, dispelled the dark theology between them. 'Child,' she said, 'what are you doing here? And who's the other child?' she added peering at the thin figure in the shadows, but when he moved into the light she corrected herself: 'This boy.' Her eye ran along the bottles counting them. 'You can't have followers here.'

'I'm going,' the Boy said.

The woman watched him with suspicion and distaste: the cobwebs had not all gone. 'If you weren't so young,' she said, 'I'd call the police.'

He said with the only flash of humour he ever showed, 'I'd have an alibi.'

'And as for you,' the manageress turned on Rose, 'we'll talk about you later.' She watched the Boy out of the room and said with disgust, 'You're both too young for this sort of thing.'

Too young – that was the difficulty. Spicer hadn't solved that difficulty before he died. Too young to close her mouth with marriage, too young to stop the police putting her in the witness box, if it ever came to that. To give evidence that – why, to say that Hale had never left the card, that Spicer had left it, that he himself had come and felt for it under the cloth. She remembered even that detail. Spicer's death would add suspicion. He'd got to close her mouth one way or another: he had to have peace.

He slowly climbed the stairs to the bed-sitting-room at Frank's. He had the sense that he was losing grip, the telephone rang and rang, and as he lost grip he began to realize all the things he hadn't years enough to know. Cubitt came out of a downstairs room, his cheek was stuffed with apple, he had a broken penknife in his hand. 'No,' he said, 'Spicer's not here. He's not back yet.'

The Boy called down from the first landing, 'Who wants Spicer?'

'She's rung off.'

'Who was she?'

'I don't know. Some skirt of his. He's soft on a girl he sees at the Queen of Hearts. Where *is* Spicer, Pinkie?'

'He's dead. Colleoni's men killed him.'

'God,' Cubitt said. He shut the knife and spat the apple out. 'I said we ought to lay off Brewer. What are we going to do?'

'Come up here,' the Boy said. 'Where's Dallow?'

'He's out.'

The Boy led the way into the bed-sitting-room and turned on the single globe. He thought of Colleoni's room in the Cosmopolitan. But you had to begin somewhere. He said, 'You've been eating on my bed again.'

'It wasn't me, Pinkie. It was Dallow. Why, Pinkie, they've cut *you* up.'

Again the Boy lied. 'I gave them as good.' But lying was a weakness. He wasn't used to lying. He said, 'We needn't get worked up about Spicer. He was milky. It's a good thing he's dead. The girl at Snow's saw him leave the ticket. Well, when he's buried, no one's going to identify him. We might even have him cremated.'

'You don't think the bogies—'

'I'm not afraid of the bogies. It's others who are nosing round.'

'They can't get over what the doctors said.'

'You know we killed him and the doctors knew he died natural. Work it out for yourself. I can't.' He sat down on the bed and swept off Dallow's crumbs. 'We're safer without Spicer.'

'Maybe you know best, Pinkie. But what made Colleoni—'

'He was scared, I suppose, that we'd let Tate have it on the course. I want Mr Prewitt fetched. I want him to fix me something. He's the only lawyer we can trust round here – if we can trust him.'

'What's the trouble, Pinkie? Anything serious?'

The Boy leant his head back against the brass bedpost. 'Maybe I'll have to get married after all.'

Cubitt suddenly bellowed with laughter, his large mouth wide, his teeth carious. Behind his head the blind was half-drawn down, shutting out the night sky, leaving the chimney-pots black and phallic, smoking palely up into the moonlit air. The Boy was silent, watching Cubitt, listening to his laughter as if it were the world's contempt.

When Cubitt stopped he said, 'Go on. Ring Mr Prewitt up. He's got to come round here,' staring past Cubitt at the acorn gently tapping on the pane at the end of the blind cord, at the chimneys and the early summer night.

'He won't come here.'

'He's got to come. I can't go out like *this*.' He touched the marks on his neck where the razors had cut him. 'I've got to get things fixed.'

'You dog, you,' Cubitt said. 'You're a young one at the game.' The game: and the Boy's mind turned with curiosity and loathing to the small cheap ready-for-anyone face, the bottles catching the moonlight on the bin, and the word 'burn', 'burn' repeated. What did people mean by 'the game'? He knew everything in theory, nothing in practice; he was only old with the knowledge of other people's lusts, those of strangers who wrote their desires on the walls in public lavatories. He knew the moves, he'd never played the game. 'Maybe,' he said, 'it won't come to that. But fetch Mr Prewitt. He knows.'

Mr Prewitt knew. You were certain of that at the first sight of him. He was a stranger to no wangle, twist, contradictory clause, ambiguous word. His yellow shaven middle-aged face was deeply lined with legal decisions. He carried a brown leather portfolio and wore striped trousers which seemed a little too new for the rest of him. He came into the room with hollow joviality, a dockside manner: he had long pointed polished shoes which caught the light. Everything about him, from his breeziness to his morning coat, was brand new, except himself and that had aged in many law courts, with many victories more damaging than defeats. He had acquired the habit of not listening: innumerable rebukes from the bench had taught him that. He was deprecating, discreet, sympathetic and as tough as leather.

The Boy nodded to him without getting up, sitting on the bed. 'Evening, Mr Prewitt,' and Mr Prewitt smiled sympathetically, put his portfolio on the floor, and sat down on the hard chair by the dressing-table. 'It's a lovely night,' he said. 'O dear, O dear, you've been in the wars.' The sympathy didn't belong; it could be peeled off his eyes like an auction ticket from an ancient flint instrument.

'It's not *that* I want to see you about,' the Boy said. 'You needn't be scared. I just want information.'

'No trouble, I hope?' Mr Prewitt asked.

'I want to avoid trouble. If I wanted to get married, what'd I do?'

'Wait a few years,' Mr Prewitt said promptly, as if he were calling a hand in cards.

'Next week,' the Boy said.

'The trouble is,' Mr Prewitt thoughtfully remarked, 'you're under age.'

'That's why I've called *you* in.'

'There are cases,' Mr Prewitt said, 'of people who give their ages wrong. I'm not suggesting it, mind you. What age is the girl?'

'Sixteen.'

'You're sure of that? Because if she was under sixteen you could be married in Canterbury Cathedral by the Archbishop himself, and it wouldn't be legal.'

'That's all right,' the Boy said. 'But if we give our ages wrong, are we married all right – legally?'

'Hard and fast.'

'The police wouldn't be able to call the girl—'

'In evidence against you? Not without her consent. Of course you'd have committed a misdemeanour. You could be sent to prison. And then – there are other difficulties.' Mr Prewitt leant back against the wash-stand, his grey neat legal hair brushing the ewer and eyed the Boy.

'You know I pay,' the Boy said.

'First,' Mr Prewitt said, 'you've got to remember it takes time.'

'It mustn't take long.'

'Do you want to be married in a church?'

'Of course I don't,' the Boy said. 'This won't be a real marriage.'

'Real enough.'

'Not real like when the priest says it.'

'Your religious feelings do you credit,' Mr Prewitt said. 'This I take it then will be a civil marriage. You could get a licence – fifteen days' residence – you qualify for that – and one day's notice. As far as that's concerned you could be married the day after to-morrow – in your own district. Then comes the next difficulty. A marriage of a minor's not easy.'

'Go on. I'll pay.'

'It's no good just saying you're twenty-one. No one would believe you. But if you said you were eighteen you could be married provided you had your parents' or your guardian's consent. Are your parents alive?'

'No.'

'Who's your guardian?'

'I don't know that you mean.'

Mr Prewitt said thoughtfully, 'We might arrange a guardian. It's risky though. It might be better if you'd lost touch. He'd gone to South Africa and left you. We might make quite a good thing out of that,' Mr Prewitt added softly. 'Flung on the world at an early age you've bravely made your own way.' His eyes shifted from bedball to bedball. 'We'd ask for the discretion of the registrar.'

'I never knew it was all that difficult,' the Boy said. 'Maybe I can manage some other way.'

'Given time,' Mr Prewitt said, 'anything can be managed.' He showed his tartar-coated teeth in a fatherly smile. 'Give the word, my boy, and I'll see you married. Trust me.' He stood up, his striped trousers were like a wedding guest's, hired for the day at Moss's; when he crossed the room, yellowly smiling, he might have been about to kiss the bride. 'If you'll let me have a guinea now for the consultation, there are one or two little purchases – for the spouse . . .'

'Are *you* married?' the Boy asked with sudden eagerness. It had never occurred to him that Prewitt . . . He gazed at the smile, the yellow teeth, the lined and wasted and unreliable face as if *there* possibly he might learn . . .

'It's my silver wedding next year,' Mr Prewitt said. Twenty-five years at the game. Cubitt put his head in at the door and said, 'I'm going out for a turn.' He grinned. 'How's the marriage?'

'Progressing,' Mr Prewitt said, 'progressing,' patting the portfolio as if it had been the plump cheek of a promising infant. 'We shall see our young friend spliced yet.'

Just till it all blows over, the Boy thought, leaning back on the grey pillow, resting one shoe on the mauve eiderdown: not a real marriage, just something to keep her mouth shut for a time. 'So long,' Cubitt said, giggling at the bed end. Rose, the small devoted cockney face, the sweet taste of human skin, emotion in the dark room by the bin of harvest Burgundy: lying on the bed he wanted to protest 'not yet' and 'not with her'. If it had to come some time, if he had to follow everyone else into the brutish game, let it be when he was old, with nothing else to gain, and with someone other men could envy him. Not someone immature, simple, as ignorant as himself.

'You've only to give the word,' Mr Prewitt said. 'We'll fix it together.' Cubitt had gone. The Boy said, 'You'll find a nicker on the washstand.'

'I don't see one,' Mr Prewitt said anxiously, shifting a tooth-brush.

'In the soap-dish – under the cover.'

Dallow put his head into the room. 'Evening,' he said to Mr Prewitt. He said to the Boy, 'What's up with Spicer?'

'It was Colleoni. They got him on the course,' the Boy said. 'They nearly got me too,' and he rasied his bandaged hand to his scarred neck.

'But Spicer's in his room now. I heard him.'

'*Heard?*' the Boy said. 'You're imagining things.' He was afraid for the second time that day: a dim globe lit the passage and the stairs: the walls were unevenly splashed with walnut paint. He felt the skin of his face contract as if something repulsive had touched him. He wanted to ask whether you could do more than hear this Spicer, if he was sensible to the sight and the touch. He stood up: it had to be faced whatever it was: passed Dallow without another word. The door of Spicer's room swung in a draught to and fro. He couldn't see inside. It was a tiny room; they had all had tiny rooms but Kite, and he had inherited that. That was why his room was the common room for them all. In Spicer's there would be space for no one but himself – and Spicer. He could hear little creaking leathery movements as the door swung. The words 'Dona nobis pacem' came again to mind; for the second time he felt a faint nostalgia, as if for something he had lost or forgotten or rejected.

He walked down the passage and into Spicer's room. His first feeling when he saw Spicer bent and tightening the straps of his suitcase was relief – that it was undoubtedly the living Spicer, whom you could touch and scare and command. A long stripe of sticking-plaster lined Spicer's cheek. The Boy watched it from the doorway with a rising cruelty: he wanted to tear it away and see the skin break. Spicer looked up, put down the suitcase, shifted uneasily towards the wall. He said, 'I thought – I was afraid – Colleoni had got you.' His fear gave away his knowledge. The Boy said nothing, watching him from the door. As if he were apologizing for being alive at all Spicer explained, 'I got away. . . .' His words wilted out like a line of seaweed, along the edge of the Boy's silence, indifference and purpose.

Down the passage came the voice of Mr Prewitt, 'In the soap-dish. He said it was in the soap-dish', and the clatter of china noisily moved about.

Chapter Two

'I'm going to work on that kid every hour of the day until I get something.' She rose formidably and moved across the restaurant, like a warship going into action, a warship on the right side in a war to end wars, the signal flags proclaiming that every man would do his duty. Her big breasts, which had never suckled a child of her own, felt a merciless compassion. Rose fled at the sight of her, but Ida moved relentlessly towards the service door. Everything now was in train, she had begun to ask the questions she had wanted to ask when she had read about the inquest in Henekey's, and she was getting the answers. And Fred too had done his part, had tipped the right horse, so that now she had funds as well as friends: an infinite capacity for corruption: two hundred pounds.

'Good evening, Rose,' she said, standing in the kitchen doorway, blocking it. Rose put down a tray and turned with all the fear, obstinacy, incomprehension of a wild animal who will not recognize kindness.

'You again,' she said. 'I'm busy. I can't talk to you.'

'But the manageress, dear, has given me leave.'

'We can't talk here.'

'Where can we talk?'

'In my room if you'll let me out.'

Rose went ahead up the stairs behind the restaurant to the little linoleumed landing. 'They do you well here, don't they?' Ida said. 'I once lived in at a public, that was before I met Tom – Tom's my husband,' she patiently, sweetly, implacably explained to Rose's back. 'They didn't do you so well there. Flowers on the landing,' she exclaimed with pleasure at the withered bunch on a deal table, pulling at the petals, when a door slammed. Rose had shut her out, and as she gently knocked she heard an obstinate whisper, 'Go away. I don't want to talk to you.'

'It's serious. Very serious.' The stout which Ida had been drinking returned a little: she put her hand up to her mouth and said mechanically, 'Pardon,' belching towards the closed door.

'I can't help you. I don't know anything.'

'Let me in, dear, and I'll explain. I can't shout things on the landing.'

'Why should you care about *me*?'

'I don't want the Innocent to suffer.'

'As if you knew,' the soft voice accused her, 'who was innocent.'

'Open the door, dear.' She began, but only a little, to lose her patience: her patience was almost as deep as her good will. She felt the handle and pushed; she knew that waitresses were not allowed keys, but a chair had been wedged under the handle. She said with irritation, 'You won't escape me this way.' She put her weight against the door and the chair creaked and shifted, the door opened a crack.

'I'm going to make you listen,' Ida said. When you were life-saving you must never hesitate, so they taught you, to stun the one you rescued. She put her hand in and detached the chair, then went in through the open door. Three iron bed-steads, a chest of drawers, two chairs and a couple of cheap mirrors: she took it all in and Rose against the wall as far as she could get, watching the door with terror through her innocent and experienced eyes, as if there was nothing which mightn't come through.

'Don't be silly now,' Ida said. 'I'm your friend. I only want to save you from that boy. You're crazy about him, aren't you? But don't you understand – he's wicked.' She sat down on the bed and went gently and mercilessly on.

Rose whispered, 'You don't know a thing.'

'I've got my evidence.'

'I don't mean *that*,' the child said.

'He doesn't care for you,' Ida said. 'Listen, I'm human. You can take my word I've loved a boy or two in my time. Why, it's natural. It's like breathing. Only you don't want to get all worked up about it. There's not one who's worth it – leave alone *him*. He's wicked. I'm not a Puritan, mind. I've done a thing or two in my time – that's *natural*. Why,' she said, extending towards the child her plump and patronizing paw, 'it's in my hand: the girdle of Venus. But I've always been on the side of Right. You're young. You'll have plenty of boys before you've finished. You'll have plenty of fun – if you don't let them get a grip on you. It's natural. Like breathing. Don't take away the notion I'm against Love. I should say not. Me. Ida Arnold. They'd laugh.' The stout came back up her throat again and she put a hand before her mouth. 'Pardon, dear. You see we can get along all right when we are together. I've never had a child of my own and somehow I've taken to you. You're a sweet little thing.' She suddenly barked, 'Come away from that wall and act sensible. He doesn't love you.'

'I don't care,' the childish voice stubbornly murmured.

'What do you mean, you don't care.'

'I love *him*.'

'You're acting morbid,' Ida said. 'If I was your mother I'd give you a good hiding. What'd your father and mother say if they knew?'

'*They* wouldn't care.'

'And how do you think it will all end?'

'I don't know.'

'You're young. That's what it is,' Ida said, 'romantic. I was like you once. You'll grow out of it. All you need is a bit of experience.' The Nelson Place eyes stared back at her without understanding. Driven to her hole the small animal peered out at the bright and breezy world; in the hole were murder, copulation, extreme poverty, fidelity and the love and fear of God, but the small animal had not the knowledge to deny that only in the glare and open world outside was something which people called experience.

Chapter Three

The Boy looked down at the body, spread-eagled like Prometheus, at the bottom of Frank's stairs. 'Good God,' Mr Prewitt said, 'how did it happen?'

The Boy said, 'These stairs have needed mending a long while. I've told Frank about it, but you can't make the bastard spend money.' He put his bound hand on the rail and pushed until it gave. The rotten wood lay across Spicer's body, a walnut-stained eagle couched over the kidneys.

'But that happened *after* he fell,' Mr Prewitt protested; his legal voice was tremulous.

'You've got it wrong,' the Boy said. 'You were here in the passage and you saw him lean his suitcase against the rail. He shouldn't have done that. The case was too heavy.'

'My God, you can't mix me up in this,' Mr Prewitt said. 'I saw nothing. I was looking in the soap-dish, I was with Dallow.'

'You both saw it,' the Boy said. 'That's fine. It's a good thing we have a respectable lawyer like you on the spot. Your word will do the trick.'

'I'll deny it,' Mr Prewitt said. 'I'm getting out of here. I'll swear I was never in the house.'

'Stay where you are,' the Boy said. 'We don't want another accident. Dallow, go and telephone for the police – and a doctor, it looks well.'

'You can keep me here,' Mr Prewitt said, 'but you can't make me say—'

'I only want you to say what you want to say. But it wouldn't look good, would it, if I was taken up for killing Spicer, and you were here – looking in the soap-dish. It would be enough to ruin some lawyers.'

Mr Prewitt stared over the broken gap at the turn of the stairs where the body lay. He said slowly, 'You'd better lift that body and put the wood under it. The police would have a lot to ask if they found it that way.' He went back into the bedroom and sat down on the bed and put his head in his hands. 'I've got a headache,' he said, 'I ought to be at home.' Nobody paid him any attention. Spicer's door rattled in the draught. 'I've got a splitting headache,' Mr Prewitt said.

Dallow came lugging the suitcase down the passage: the cord of Spicer's pyjamas squeezed out of it like tooth-paste. 'Where was he going?' Dallow asked.

'The "Blue Anchor", Union Street, Nottingham,' the Boy said. 'We'd better wire them. They might want to send flowers.'

'Be careful about finger-prints,' Mr Prewitt implored them from the washstand without raising his aching head, but the Boy's steps on the stairs made him look up. 'Where are you going?' he asked sharply. The Boy stared up at him from the turn in the stairs. 'Out,' he said.

'You can't go now,' Mr Prewitt said.

'I wasn't here,' the Boy said. 'It was just you and Dallow. You were waiting for me to come in.'

'You'll be seen.'

'That's your risk,' the Boy said. 'I've got things to do.'

'Don't tell me,' Mr Prewitt cried hastily and checked himself. 'Don't tell me,' he repeated in a low voice, 'what things. . . .'

'We'll have to fix that marriage,' the Boy said sombrely. He gazed at Mr Prewitt for a moment – the spouse, twenty-five years at the game – with the air of someone who wanted to ask a question, almost as if he were prepared to accept advice from a man so much older, as if he expected a little human wisdom from the old shady legal mind.

'It had better be soon,' the Boy went softly and sadly on. He still watched Mr Prewitt's face for some reflection of the wisdom the game must have given him in twenty-five years, but saw only a frightened face, boarded up like a store when a riot is on. He went on down the stairs, dropping into the dark well where Spicer's body had fallen. He had made his decision; he had only to move towards his aim; he could feel his blood pumped from the heart and moving indifferently back along the arteries like trains on the inner circle. Every station was one nearer safety, and then one farther away, until the bend was turned and safety again approached, like Notting Hill, and afterwards receded. The middle-aged whore on Hove front never troubled to look round as he came up behind her: like electric trains moving on the same track there was no collision. They both had the same end in view, if you could talk of an end in connection with that circle. Outside the Norfolk bar two smart scarlet racing models lay along the kerb like twin beds. The Boy was not conscious of them, but their image passed automatically into his brain, released his secretion of envy.

Snow's was nearly empty. He sat down at the table where once Spicer had sat, but he was not served by Rose. A strange girl came to take his order. He said awkwardly, 'Isn't Rose here?'

'She's busy.'

'Could I see her?'

'She's talking to someone up in her room. You can't go there. You'll have to wait.'

The Boy put half a crown on the table. 'Where is it?'

The girl hesitated. 'The manageress would bawl Hell.'

'Where's the manageress?'

'She's out.'

The Boy put another half-crown on the table.

'Through the service door,' the girl said, 'and straight up the stairs. There's a woman with her though—'

He heard the woman's voice before he reached the top of the stairs. She was saying, 'I only want to speak to you for your own good,' but he had to strain to catch Rose's reply.

'Let me be, why won't you let me be?'

'It's the business of anyone who thinks right.'

The Boy could see into the room now from the head of the stairs, though the broad back, the large loose dress, the square hips of the woman nearly blocked his view of Rose who stood back against the wall in an attitude of sullen defiance. Small and bony in the black cotton dress and the white apron, her eyes stained but tearless, startled and determined, she carried her courage with a kind of comic inadequacy, like the little man in the bowler put up by the management to challenge the strong man at a fair. She said, 'You'd better let me be.'

It was Nelson Place and Manor Street which stood there in the servant's bedroom, and for a moment he felt no antagonism but a faint nostalgia. He was aware that she belonged to his life, like a room or a chair: she was something which completed him. He thought: She's got more guts than Spicer. What was most evil in him needed her: it couldn't get along without goodness. He said softly, 'What are you worrying my girl about?' and the claim he made was curiously sweet to his ears, like a refinement of cruelty. After all, though he had aimed higher than Rose, he had this comfort: she couldn't have gone lower than himself. He stood there, with a smirk on his face, when the woman turned. 'Between the stirrup and the ground' – he had learnt the fallacy of that comfort: if he had attached to himself some bright brassy skirt, like the ones he'd seen at the Cosmopolitan, his triumph after all wouldn't have been so great. He smirked at the pair of them, nostalgia driven out by a surge of sad sensuality. She was good, he'd discovered that, and he was damned: they were made for each other.

'You leave her alone,' the woman said. 'I know all about you.' It was as if she were in a strange country: the typical Englishwoman abroad. She hadn't even got a phrase book. She was as far from either of them as she was from Hell – or Heaven. Good and evil lived in the same country, spoke the same language, came together like old friends, feeling the same completion, touching hands beside the iron bedstead. 'You want to do what's Right, Rose?' she implored.

Rose whispered again, 'You let us be.'

'You're a Good Girl, Rose. You don't want anything to do with *him*.'

'You don't know a thing.'

There was nothing she could do at the moment but threaten from the door. 'I haven't finished with you yet. I've got friends.'

The Boy watched her go with amazement. He said, 'Who the hell is she?'

'I don't know,' Rose said.

'I never seen her before.' A memory pricked him and passed: it would return. 'What did she want?'

'I don't know.'

'You're a good girl, Rose,' the Boy said, pressing his fingers round the sharp wrist.

She shook her head. 'I'm bad.' She implored him, 'I want to be bad if she's good and you—'

'You'll never be anything but good,' the Boy said. 'There's some wouldn't like you for that, but I don't care.'

'I'll do anything for you. Tell me what to do. I don't want to be like her.'

'It's not what you do,' the Boy said, 'it's what you think.' He boasted. 'It's in the blood. Perhaps when they christened me, the holy water didn't take. I never howled the devil out.'

'Is *she* good?'

'She?' The Boy laughed. 'She's just nothing.'

'We can't stay here,' Rose said. 'I wish we could.' She looked round her at a badly foxed steel engraving of Van Tromp's victory, the three black bedsteads, the two mirrors, the single chest of drawers, the pale mauve knots of flowers on the wallpaper, as if she were safer here than she could ever be in the squally summer night outside. 'It's a nice room.' She wanted to share it with him until it became a home for both of them.

'How'd you like to leave this place?'

'Snow's. Oh no, it's a good place. I wouldn't want to be anywhere else than Snow's.'

'I mean marry me?'

'We aren't old enough.'

'It could be managed. There are ways.' He dropped her wrist and put on a careless air. 'If you wanted. I don't mind.'

'Oh,' she said. 'I want it. But they'll never let us.'

He explained airily, 'It couldn't be in church, not at first. There'd be difficulties. Are you afraid?'

'I'm not afraid,' she said. 'But will they let us?'

'My lawyer'll manage somehow.'

'You got a lawyer?'

'Of course I have.'

'It sounds somehow – grand – and old.'

'A man can't get along without a lawyer.'

She said, 'It's not where I always thought it would be.'

'Where what would be?'

'Someone asking me to marry him. I thought – in the pictures or maybe at night on the front. But this is best,' she said, looking from Van Tromp's victory to the two looking-glasses. She came away from the wall and lifted her face to him. He knew what was expected of him; he regarded her unmade-up mouth with faint nausea. Saturday night, eleven o'clock, the primeval exercise. He pressed his hard puritanical mouth on hers and tasted again the sweetish smell of the human skin. He would have preferred the taste of Coty powder or Kissproof Lipstick or any chemical compound. He shut his eyes and when he opened them again it was to see her waiting like a blind girl, for further alms. It shocked him that she had been unable to detect his repulsion. She said, 'You know what that means?'

'What means?'

'It means I'll never let you down, never, never, never.'

She belonged to him like a room or a chair: the Boy fetched up a smile for the blind lost face, uneasily, with obscure shame.

Chapter One

Everything went well: the inquest never even got on to the newspaper posters: no questions asked. The Boy walked back with Dallow, he should have felt triumphant. He said, 'I wouldn't trust Cubitt if Cubitt knew.'

'Cubitt won't know. Prewitt is scared to say a thing – and you know I don't talk, Pinkie.'

'I've got a feeling we're being followed, Dallow.'

Dallow looked behind. 'No one. I know every bogy in Brighton.'

'No woman?'

'No. Who are you thinking of?'

'I don't know.'

The blind band came up the kerb, scraping the sides of their shoes along the edge, feeling their way in the brilliant light, sweating a little. The Boy walked up the side of the road to meet them. The music they played was plaintive, pitying, something out of a hymn book about burdens: it was like a voice prophesying sorrow at the moment of victory. The Boy met the leader and pushed him out of the way, swearing at him softly, and the whole band hearing their leader move shifted uneasily a foot into the roadway and stood there stranded till the Boy was safely by, like barques becalmed on a huge and landless Atlantic. Then they edged back feeling for the landfall of the pavement.

'What's up with you, Pinkie?' Dallow said. 'They're blind.'

'Why should I get out of my way for a beggar?' but he hadn't realized they were blind, he was shocked by his own action. It was as if he were being driven too far down a road he only wanted to travel a certain distance. He stood and leant on the rail of the front while the mid-week crowd passed and the hard sun flattened.

'What's on your mind, Pinkie?'

'To think of all this trouble over Hale. He deserved what he got, but if I'd known how it would go maybe I'd have let him live. Maybe he wasn't worth killing. A dirty little journalist who played in with Colleoni and got Kite killed. Why should anyone bother about him?' He looked suddenly over his shoulder. 'Have I seen that geezer before?'

'He's only a visitor.'

'I thought I'd seen his tie.'

'Hundreds in the shops. If you were a drinking man I'd say what you needed was a pick-up. Why, Pinkie, everything's going fine. No questions asked.'

'There were only two people could hang us, Spicer and the girl. I've killed Spicer and I'm marrying the girl. Seems to me I'm doing everything.'

'Well, we'll be safe now.'

'Oh yes, *you*'ll be safe. It's me who runs all the risk. *You* know I killed Spicer. Prewitt knows. It only wants Cubitt and I'll need a massacre to put me right this time.'

'You oughtn't to talk that way to me, Pinkie. You've been all bottled up since Kite died. What you want's a bit of fun.'

'I liked Kite,' the Boy said. He stared straight out towards France, an unknown land. At his back beyond the Cosmopolitan, Old Steyne, the Lewes Road, stood the downs, villages, cattle round the dewponds, another unknown land. This was his territory, the populous foreshore, a few thousand acres of houses, a narrow peninsula of electrified track running to London, two or three railway stations with their buffets and buns. It had been Kite's territory, it had been good enough for Kite, and when Kite had died in the waiting-room at St Pancras, it had been as if a father had died, leaving him an inheritance it was his duty never to leave for strange acres. He had inherited even the mannerisms, the bitten thumb nail, the soft drinks. The sun slid off the sea and like a cuttle fish shot into the sky the stain of agonies and endurances.

'Break out, Pinkie. Relax. Give yourself a chance. Come out with me and Cubitt to the Queen of Hearts and celebrate.'

'You know I never touch a drink.'

'You'll have to on your wedding day. Whoever heard of a dry wedding?'

An old man went stooping down the shore, very slowly, turning the stones, picking among the dry seaweed for cigarette ends, scraps of food. The gulls which had stood like candles down the beach rose and cried under the promenade. The old man found a boot and stowed it in his sack and a gull dropped from the parade and swept through the iron nave of the Palace Pier, white and purposeful in the obscurity: half-vulture and half-dove. In the end one always had to learn.

'All right. I'll come,' the Boy said.

'It's the best road-house this side of London,' Dallow encouraged him.

They drove out in the old Morris into the country. 'I like a blow in the country,' Dallow said. It was between lighting-up time and the real dark when the lamps of cars burn in the grey visibility as faintly and unnecessarily as the night lights in nurseries. The advertisements trailed along the arterial road: bungalows and a broken farm, short chalky grass where a hoarding had been pulled down, a windmill offering tea and lemonade, the great ruined sails gaping.

'Poor old Spicer would have liked this ride,' Cubitt said. The Boy sat beside Dallow who drove and Cubitt sat in the dicky. The Boy could see him in the driving mirror bouncing gently up and down on the defective springs.

The Queen of Hearts was floodlit behind the petrol pumps: a Tudor barn converted, a vestige of a farmyard left in the arrangement of the restaurant and bars: a swimming pool where the paddock had been. 'We ought to 'ave brought some girls with us,' Dallow said. 'You can't pick 'em up in this gaff. It's real class.'

'Come in the bar,' Cubitt said and led the way. He stopped on the threshold and nodded towards the girl who sat and drank alone at the long steel bar under the old rafters. 'We better say something, Pinkie. You know the kind of thing – he was a real good old pal, we sympathize with what you feel.'

'What are you clapping about?'

'That's Spicer's girl,' Cubitt said.

The Boy stood in the doorway and took her reluctantly in: hair fair as silver, wide vacuous brow, trim little buttocks shaped by the high seat, alone with her glass and her grief.

'How's things, Sylvie?' Cubitt said.

'Awful.'

'Terrible, wasn't it? He was a good pal. One of the best.'

'You were there, weren't you?' she said to Dallow.

'Frank ought to 'ave mended that stair,' Dallow said. 'Meet Pinkie, Sylvie, the best one in our mob.'

'Were you there, too?'

'He wasn't there,' Dallow said.

'Have another drink?' the Boy said.

Sylvie drained her glass. 'I don't mind if I do. A Sidecar.'

'Two Scotch, a Sidecar, a grape-fruit squash.'

'Why,' Sylvie said, 'don't you drink?'

'No.'

'I bet you don't go with girls either.'

'You got him, Sylvie,' Cubitt said, 'first shot.'

'I admire a man like that,' Sylvie said. 'I think it's wonderful to be fit. Spicie always said you'd break out one day – and then – oh gosh, how wonderful.' She put down her glass, miscalculated, upset the cocktail. She said, 'I'm not drunk. I'm upset about poor Spicie.'

'Go on, Pinkie,' Dallow said, 'have a drink. It'll jerk you up.' He explained to Sylvie, 'He's upset too.' In the dance hall the band was playing, 'Love me to-night, And forget in daylight, All our delight. . . .'

'Have a drink,' Sylvie said. 'I've been awful upset. You can see I've been crying. Aren't my eyes awful. . . . Why, I hardly dared show myself. I can see why people go into monasteries.' The music beat on the Boy's resistance: he watched with a kind of horror and curiosity Spicer's girl friend: she knew the game. He shook his head, speechless in his scared pride. He knew what he was good at: he was the top: there was no limit to his ambition: nothing must lay him open to the mockery of people more experienced than he. To be compared with Spicer and found wanting . . . his eyes shifted miserably and the music wailed its tidings – 'Forget in daylight' – about the game of which they all knew so much more than he did.

'Spicie said he didn't think you'd ever had a girl,' Sylvie said.

'There was plenty Spicer didn't know.'

'You're awful young to be so famous.'

'You and me had better go away,' Cubitt said to Dallow. 'Seems we're not wanted. Come an' lamp the bathing belles.' They moved heavily out of sight. 'Dallie just knows when I like a boy,' Sylvie said.

'Who's Dallie?'

'Your friend, Mr Dallow, silly. Do you dance – why, I don't even know your proper name?' He watched her with scared lust. She had belonged to Spicer: her voice had wailed up the telephone wires making assignations: he had received letters in mauve envelopes, addressed to him: even Spicer had

had something to be proud of, to show to friends – 'my girl'. He remembered some flowers which had come to Frank's labelled 'Broken-hearted'. He was fascinated by her infidelity. She belonged to nobody – unlike a table or a chair. He said slowly, putting his arm round her to take her glass and pressing her breast clumsily, 'I'm going to be married in a day or two.' It was as if he was staking a claim to his share of infidelity: he wasn't to be beaten by experience. He lifted her glass and drank it. The sweetness dripped down his throat, his first alcohol touched the palate like a bad smell: this was what people called pleasure – this and the game. He put his hand on her thigh with a kind of horror: Rose and he: forty-eight hours after Prewitt had arranged things: alone in God knows what apartment – what then, what then? He knew the traditional actions as a man may know the principles of gunnery in chalk on a blackboard, but to translate the knowledge to action, to the smashed village and the ravaged woman, one needed help from the nerves. His own were frozen with repulsion: to be touched, to give oneself away, to lay oneself open – he had held intimacy back as long as he could at the end of a razor blade.

He said, 'Come on. Let's dance.'

They circulated slowly in the dance hall. To be beaten by experience was bad enough, but to be beaten by greenness and innocence, by a girl who carried plates at Snow's, by a little bitch of sixteen years . . .

'Spicie thought a lot of you,' Sylvie said.

'Come out to the cars,' the Boy said.

'I couldn't, not with Spicie dead only yesterday.'

They stood and clapped and then the dance began again. The shaker clacked in the bar, and the leaves of one small tree were pressed against the window beyond the big drum and the saxophone.

'I like the country. It makes me feel romantic. Do you like the country?'

'No.'

'This is *real* country. I saw a hen just now. They use their own eggs in the gin slings.'

'Come out to the cars.'

'I feel that way, too. O gosh, wouldn't it be fine? But I can't, not with poor Spicie . . .'

'You sent flowers, didn't you, you been crying . . .'

'My eyes are awful.'

'What more can you do?'

'It broke my heart. Poor Spicie going off like that.'

'I know. I saw your wreath.'

'It does seem awful, doesn't it? Dancing with you like this and him . . .'

'Come to the cars.'

'Poor Spicie,' but she led the way, and he noticed with uneasiness how she ran – literally ran – across the lit corner of what had once been a farmyard towards the dark car-park and the game. He thought with sickness, 'In three minutes I shall know.'

'Which is your car?' Sylvie asked.

'That Morris.'

'No good to us,' Sylvie said. She darted down the line of cars. 'This Ford.' She pulled the door open, said, 'Oh, pardon me,' and shut it, scrambled into the back of the next car in the line and waited for him. 'Oh,' her voice softly and passionately pronounced from the dim interior, 'I love a Lancia.' He stood in the doorway and the darkness peeled away between him and the fair and vacuous face. Her skirt drawn up above her knees she waited for him with luxurious docility.

He was conscious for a moment of his enormous ambitions under the shadow of the hideous and commonplace act: the suite at the Cosmopolitan, the gold cigar-lighter, chairs stamped with crowns for a foreigner called Eugeen. Hale dropped out of sight, like a stone thrown over a cliff; he was at the beginning of a long polished parquet walk, there were busts of great men and the sound of cheering, Mr Colleoni bowed like a shop-walker, stepping backwards, an army of razors was at his back: a conqueror. Hooves drummed along the straight and a loud-speaker announced the winner: music was playing. His breast ached with the effort to enclose the whole world.

'You've got the doings, haven't you?' Sylvie asked.

With fear and horror he thought: next move, what is it?

'Quick,' Sylvie said, 'before they find us here.'

The parquet floor rolled up like a carpet. The moonlight touched a Woolworth ring and a plump knee. He said in a painful and bitter rage, 'Wait there. I'll get Cubitt for you,' and turned his back on the Lancia and walked back towards the bar. Laughter from the bathing-pool deflected him. He stood in the doorway with the taste of the alcohol on his tongue watching a thin girl in a red rubber cap giggle under the flood lighting. His mind tracked inevitably back and forth to Sylvie like a model engine electrically driven. Fear and curiosity ate at the proud future, he was aware of nausea and retched. Marry, he thought, hell, no; I'd rather hang.

A man in a bathing-slip came running down the highboard, jumped and somersaulted in the pearly brilliant light, struck the dark water; the two bathers swam together, stroke by stroke, towards the shallows, turned and came back, side by side, smooth and unhurried, playing a private game, happy and at ease.

The Boy stood and watched them, and as they came down the pool a second time he saw in the floodlit water his own image shiver at their stroke, the narrow shoulders and the hollow breast, and he felt the brown pointed shoes slip on the splashed and shining tiles.

Chapter Two

Cubitt and Dallow chattered all the way back, a little lit; the Boy stared ahead into the bright core of the darkness. He said suddenly with fury, 'You can laugh.'

'Well, you didn't do so bad,' Cubitt said.

'You can laugh. You think you're safe. But I'm tired of the lot of you. I've a good mind to clear out.'

'Take a long honeymoon,' Cubitt said and grinned, and an owl cried with painful hunger swooping low over a filling station, into the headlights and out again, on furry and predatory wings.

'I'm not going to marry,' the Boy said.

'I knew a geezer once,' Cubitt said, 'was so scared he killed himself. They had to send back the wedding presents.'

'I'm not going to marry.'

'People often feel that way.'

'Nothing's going to make me marry.'

'You've got to marry,' Dallow said. A woman stared from a window of Charlie's Pull-in Café waiting for someone: she didn't look at the car going by, waiting.

'Have a drink,' Cubitt said; he was more drunk than Dallow. 'I brought a flask away. You can't say you don't drink now: we saw you, Dallow and me.'

The Boy said to Dallow, 'I won't marry. Why should I marry?'

'It was your doing,' Dallow said.

'What was his doing?' Cubitt said. Dallow didn't reply, laying his friendly and oppressive hand on the Boy's knee. The Boy took a squint at the stupid devoted face and felt anger at the way another's loyalty could hamper and drive. Dallow was the only man he trusted, and he hated him as if he were his mentor. He said weakly, 'Nothing will make me marry,' watching the long parade of posters going by in the submarine light: Guinness is Good for You, Try a Worthington, Keep that Schoolgirl Complexion: a long series of adjurations, people telling you things: Own Your Own Home, Bennett's for Wedding Rings.

And at Frank's they told him, 'Your girl's here.' He went up the stairs to his room in hopeless rebellion; he would go in and say – I've changed my mind. I can't marry you. Or perhaps – the lawyers say it can't be managed after all. The banisters were still broken and he looked down the long drop to where Spicer's body had lain. Cubitt and Dallow were standing on the exact spot laughing at something: the sharp edge of a broken banister scratched his hand. He put it to his mouth and went in. He thought: I've got to be calm, I've got to keep my wits about me, but he felt his integrity stained by the taste of the spirit at the bar. You could lose vice as easily as you lost virtue, going out of you from a touch.

He took a look at her. She was scared when he said softly, 'What are you doing here?' She had on the hat he disliked and she made a snatch at it as soon as he looked. 'At this time of night,' he said in a shocked way, thinking there was a quarrel to be picked there if he went about it in the right way.

'You've seen this?' Rose implored him. She had the local paper; he hadn't bothered to read it, but there on the front page was the picture of Spicer striding in terror under the iron arches. Rose said, 'It says here – it happened—'

'On the landing,' the boy said. 'I was always telling Frank to mend those banisters.'

'But you said they got him on the course. And he was the one who—'

He faced her with spurious firmness: 'Gave you the ticket? So you said.

Maybe he knew Hale. He knew a lot of geezers I didn't. What of it?' He repeated his question before her dumb stare with confidence: 'What of it?' His mind, he knew, could contemplate any treachery, but she was a good kid, she was bounded by her goodness; there were things she couldn't imagine, and he thought he saw her imagination wilting now in the vast desert of dread.

'I thought,' she said, 'I thought . . .' looking beyond him to the shattered banister on the landing.

'What did you think?'

His fingers curled with passionate hatred round the small bottle in his pocket.

'I don't know. I didn't sleep last night. I had such dreams.'

'What dreams?'

She looked at him with horror, 'I dreamed you were dead.'

He laughed, 'I'm young and spry,' thinking with nausea of the car-park and the invitation in the Lancia.

'You aren't going to stay here, are you?'

'Why not?'

'I'd have thought—' she said, her eyes back again in their gaze at the banisters. She said, 'I'm scared.'

'You've no cause to be,' he said, tickling the vitriol bottle.

'I'm scared for you. Oh,' she said, 'I know I'm no account. I know you've got a lawyer and a car and friends, but this place—' she stumbled hopelessly in an attempt to convey the sense she had of the territory in which he moved: a place of accidents and unexplained events, the stranger with a card, the fight on the course, the headlong fall. A kind of boldness and brazenness came into her face, so that he felt again the faintest stirring of sensuality: 'You've got to come away from here. You've got to marry me like you said.'

'It can't be done after all. I've seen my lawyer. We're too young.'

'I don't mind about that. It's not a *real* marriage, anyway. A registrar doesn't make any difference.'

'You go back where you came from,' he said harshly. 'You little tart.'

'I can't,' she said. 'I'm sacked.'

'What for?' It was as if the handcuffs were meeting. He suspected her.

'I was rude to a customer.'

'Why? What customer?'

'Can't you guess?' she said and went passionately on. 'Who is she, anyway? Interfering . . . pestering . . . *you* must know.'

'I don't know her from Adam,' the Boy said.

She put all her fake experience – drawn from the twopenny library – into the question: 'Is she jealous? Is she someone . . . you know what I mean?' and ready there, masked behind the ingenuous question like the guns in a Q ship, was possessiveness. She was his like a table or a chair, but a table owned you, too – by your finger-prints.

He laughed uneasily. 'What, she? She's old enough to be my mother.'

'Then what does she want?'

'I wish I knew.'

'Do you think,' she said, 'I ought to take this—' she held out the paper to him – 'to the police?'

The ingenuousness – or the shrewdness – of the question shocked him.

Could one ever be safe with someone who realized so little how she had got mixed up in things? He said, 'You got to mind your step,' and thought with dull and tired distaste (it had been the hell of a day): I shall have to marry her after all. He managed a smile: those muscles were beginning to work. He said, 'Listen. You don't need to think about those things. I'm going to marry you. There are ways of getting round the law.'

'Why bother about the law?'

'I don't want any loose talk. Only marriage,' he said with feigned anger, 'will do for me. We got to be married properly.'

'We won't be that whatever we do. The father up at St John's – he says—'

'You don't want to listen too much to priests,' he said. 'They don't know the world like I do. Ideas change, the world moves on ...' His words stumbled before her carved devotion. That face said as clearly as words that ideas never changed, the world never moved: it lay there always, the ravaged and disputed territory between the two eternities. They faced each other as it were from opposing territories, but like troops at Christmas time they fraternized. He said, 'It's the same to you, anyway – and I want to be married – legally.'

'If you want to ...' she said and made a small gesture of complete assent.

'Maybe,' he said, 'we could work it this way. If your father wrote a letter. ...'

'He can't write.'

'Well, he could make his mark, couldn't he, if I got a letter written. ... I don't know how these things work. Maybe he could come to the magistrate's. Mr Prewitt could see about that.'

'Mr Prewitt?' she asked quickly. 'Wasn't he the one – the one at the inquest who was here. ...'

'What of it?'

'Nothing,' she said. 'I just thought ...' but he could see the thoughts going on and on, out of the room to the banisters and the drop, out of that day altogether. ... Somebody turned on the radio down below: some jest of Cubitt's perhaps to represent the right romantic atmosphere. It wailed up the stairs past the telephone and into the room: somebody's band from somebody's hotel, the end of a day's programme. It switched her thoughts away and he wondered for how long it would be necessary for him to sidetrack her mind with the romantic gesture or the loving act: how many weeks and months – his mind wouldn't admit the possibility of years. Some day he would be free again. He put out his hands towards her as if she were the detective with the cuffs and said, 'To-morrow we'll see about things: see your father: why,' the muscles of his mouth faltered at the thought, 'it only takes a couple of days to get married in.'

Chapter Three

He was scared, walking alone back towards the territory he had left – oh, years ago. The pale sea curdled on the shingle and the green tower of the Metropole looked like a dug-up coin verdigrised with age-old mould. The gulls swooped up to the top promenade, screaming and twisting in the sunlight, and a well-known popular author displayed his plump too famous face in the window of the Royal Albion, staring out to sea. It was so clear a day you looked for France.

The Boy crossed over towards Old Steyne walking slowly. The streets narrowed uphill above the Steyne: the shabby secret behind the bright corsage, the deformed breast. Every step was a retreat. He thought he had escaped for ever by the whole length of the parade, and now extreme poverty took him back: a shop where a shingle could be had for two shillings in the same building as a coffin-maker's who worked in oak, elm or lead: no window-dressing but one child's coffin dusty with disuse and the list of hairdressing prices. The Salvation Army Citadel marked with its battlements the very border of his home. He began to fear recognition and feel an obscure shame as if it were his native streets which had the right to forgive and not he to reproach them with the dreary and dingy past. Past the Albert Hostel ('Good Accommodation for Travellers') and there he was, on the top of the hill, in the thick of the bombardment – a flapping gutter, cracked windows, an iron bedstead in a front garden the size of a tabletop. Half Paradise Piece had been torn up as if by bomb bursts; the children played about the steep slope of rubble; a piece of fireplace showed houses had once been there, and a municipal notice announced new flats on a post stuck in the torn gravel and asphalt facing the little dingy damaged row, all that was left of Paradise Piece. His home was gone: a flat place among the rubble may have marked its hearth; the room at the bend of the stairs where the Saturday night exercise had taken place was now just air. He wondered with horror whether it all had to be built again for him; it looked better as air.

He had sent Rose back the night before and now draggingly he rejoined her. It was no good rebelling any more; he had to marry her: he had to be safe. The children were scouting among the rubble with pistols from Woolworth's; a group of girls surlily watched. A child with its leg in an iron brace limped blindly into him; he pushed it off; someone said in a high treble, 'Stick 'em up.' They took his mind back and he hated them for it; it was like the dreadful appeal of innocence, but *there* was not innocence; you had to go back a long way further before you got innocence; innocence was a slobbering mouth, a toothless gum pulling at the teats; perhaps not even that; innocence was the ugly cry of birth.

He found the house in Nelson Place, but before he had time to knock the door opened. Rose had spied him through the broken glass. She said, 'Oh, how glad I am . . . I thought perhaps . . .' In the awful little passage which stank like a lavatory she ran quickly and passionately on, 'It was awful last night . . . you see I've been sending them money . . . they don't understand everyone loses a job some time or another.'

'I'll settle them,' the Boy said. 'Where are they?'

'You got to be careful,' Rose said. 'They get moods.'

'Where are they?'

But there wasn't really much choice of direction: there was only one door and a staircase matted with old newspapers. On the bottom steps between the mud marks stared up the tawny child face of Violet Crow violated and buried under the West Pier in 1936. He opened the door and there beside the black kitchen stove with cold dead charcoal on the floor sat the parents. They had a mood on: they watched him with silent and haughty indifference: a small thin elderly man, his face marked deeply with the hieroglyphics of pain and patience and suspicion: the woman middle-aged, stupid, vindictive. The dishes hadn't been washed and the stove hadn't been lit.

'They got a mood,' Rose said aloud to him. 'They wouldn't let me do a thing. Not even light the fire. I like a clean house, honest I do. Ours wouldn't be like this.'

'Look here, Mr—' the Boy said.

'Wilson,' Rose said.

'Wilson. I want to marry Rose. It seems as she's so young I got to get your permission.'

They wouldn't answer him. They treasured their mood as if it was a bright piece of china only they possessed: something they could show to neighbours as 'mine'.

'It's no use,' Rose said, 'when they got a mood.'

A cat watched them from a wooden box.

'Yes or no,' the Boy said.

'It's no good,' Rose said, 'not when they've got a mood.'

'Answer a plain question,' the Boy said. 'Do I marry Rose or don't I?'

'Come back to-morrow,' Rose said. 'They won't have a mood then.'

'I'm not going to wait on them,' he said. 'They oughter be proud—'

The man suddenly got up and kicked the dead coke furiously across the floor. 'You get out of here,' he said. 'We don't want any truck with you,' he went on, 'never, never, never,' and for a moment in the sunk lost eyes there was a kind of fidelity which reminded the Boy dreadfully of Rose.

'Quiet, father,' the woman said, 'don't talk to them,' treasuring her mood.

'I've come to do business,' the Boy said. 'If you don't want to do business—' He looked round the battered and hopeless room. 'I thought maybe ten pounds would be of use to you,' and he saw swimming up through the blind, vindictive silence incredulity, avarice, suspicion. 'We don't want—' the man began again and then gave out like a gramophone. He began to think: you could see the thoughts bob up one after another.

'We don't want your money,' the woman said. They each had their own kind of fidelity.

Rose said, 'Never mind what they say. I won't stay here.'

'Stop a moment. Stop a moment,' the man said. 'You be quiet, mother.'

He said to the Boy, 'We couldn't let Rose go not for ten nicker – not to a stranger. How do we know you'd treat her right?'

'I'll give you twelve,' the Boy said.

'It's not a question of money,' the man said. 'I like the look of you. We wouldn't want to stand in the way of Rose bettering herself – but you're too young.'

'Fifteen's my limit,' the Boy said, 'take it or leave it.'

'You can't do anything without we say yes,' the man said.

The Boy moved a little away from Rose. 'I'm not all that keen.'

'Make it guineas.'

'You've had my offer.' He looked with horror round the room: nobody could say he hadn't done right to get away from this, to commit any crime . . . When the man opened his mouth he heard his father speaking, that figure in the corner was his mother: he bargained for his sister and felt no desire. . . . He turned to Rose, 'I'm off,' and felt the faintest twinge of pity for goodness which couldn't murder to escape. They said that saints had got – what was the phrase? – 'heroic virtues', heroic patience, heroic endurance, but there was nothing he could see that was heroic in the bony face, protuberant eyes, pallid anxiety, while they bluffed each other and her life was confused in the financial game. 'Well,' he said, 'I'll be seeing you,' and made for the door. At the door he looked back: they were like a family party. Impatiently and contemptuously he gave in to them, 'All right. Guineas. I'll be sending my lawyer,' and as he passed into the evil passage Rose was behind him panting her gratitude.

He played the game to the last card, fetching up a grin and a compliment, 'I'd do more for you.'

'You were wonderful,' she said, loving him among the lavatory smells, but her praise was poison: it marked her possession of him: it led straight to what she expected from him, the horrifying act of a desire he didn't feel. She followed him out into the fresh air of Nelson Place. The children played among the ruins of Paradise Piece, and a wind blew from the sea across the site of his home. A dim desire for annihilation stretched in him: the vast superiority of vacancy.

She said, as she had said once before, 'I always wondered how it'd be.' Her mind moved obscurely among the events of the afternoon, brought out the unexpected discovery. 'I've never known a mood go so quick. They must have liked you.'

Chapter Four

Ida Arnold bit an éclair and the cream spurted between the large front teeth. She laughed a little thickly in the Pompadour Boudoir and said, 'I haven't had as much money to spend since I left Tom.' She took another bite and a wedge of cream settled on the plump tongue. 'I owe it to Fred too. If he hadn't tipped me Black Boy. . . .'

'Why not give everything up,' Mr Corkery said, 'and just have a bit of fun. It's dangerous.'

'Oh, yes it's dangerous,' she admitted, but no real sense of danger could lodge behind those large vivacious eyes. Nothing could ever make her believe that one day she too, like Fred, would be where the worms . . . Her mind couldn't take that track; she could go only a short way before the points automatically shifted and set her vibrating down the accustomed line, the season ticket line marked by desirable residence and advertisements of cruises and small fenced boskages for rural love. She said, eyeing her éclair, 'I never give in. They didn't know what a packet of trouble they were stirring up.'

'Leave it to the police.'

'Oh no. I know what's right. You can't tell me. Who's that, do you think?'

An elderly man in glacé shoes, with a white slip to his waistcoat and a jewelled pin, came padding across the Boudoir. 'Distinguay,' Ida Arnold said.

A secretary trotted a little way behind him, reading out from a list. 'Bananas, oranges, grapes, peaches. . . .'

'Hothouse?'

'Hothouse.'

'Who's that?' Ida Arnold repeated.

'That was all, Mr Colleoni?' the secretary asked.

'What flowers?' Mr Colleoni demanded. 'And could you get any nectarines?'

'No, Mr Colleoni.'

'My dear wife,' Mr Colleoni said, his voice dwindling out of their hearing. They could catch only the word 'passion'. Ida Arnold swivelled her eyes round the elegant furnishing of the Pompadour Boudoir. They picked out like a searchlight a cushion, a couch, the thin clerkly mouth of the man opposite her. She said, 'We could have a fine time here,' watching his mouth.

'Expensive,' Mr Corkery said nervously; a too sensitive hand stroked his thin shanks.

'Black Boy will stand it. And we can't have – you know – fun at the Belvedere. Strait-laced.'

'You wouldn't mind a bit of fun here?' Mr Corkery asked. He blinked. You couldn't tell from his expression whether he desired or dreaded her assent.

'Why should I? It doesn't do anyone any harm that I know of. It's human nature.' She bit at her éclair and repeated the familiar password. 'It's only fun after all.' Fun to be on the right side, fun to be human. . . .

'You go and get my bag,' she said, 'while I book a room. After all – I owe you something. You've worked . . .'

Mr Corkery flushed a little. 'Half and half,' he said.

She grinned at him. 'It's on Black Boy. I pay my debts.'

'A man likes—' Mr Corkery said weakly.

'Trust me, I know what a man likes.' The éclair and the deep couch and the gaudy furnishings were like an aphrodisiac in her tea. She was shaken by a Bacchic and a bawdy mood. In every word either of them uttered she detected the one meaning. Mr Corkery blushed, plunged deeper in his embarrassment. 'A man can't help feeling,' and was shaken by her immense glee.

'You're telling me,' she said, 'you're telling me.'

While Mr Corkery was gone she made her preparations for carnival, the taste of the sweet cake between her teeth. The idea of Fred Hale dodged backwards like a figure on a platform when the train goes out. He belonged to somewhere left behind; the waving hand only contributes to the excitement of the new experience. The new – and yet the immeasurably old. She gazed round the big padded pleasure dome of a bedroom with bloodshot and experienced eyes: the long mirror and the wardrobe and the enormous bed. She settled frankly down on it while the clerk waited. 'It springs,' she said, 'it springs,' and sat there for quite a long while after he'd gone planning the evening's campaign. If somebody had said to her then 'Fred Hale', she would hardly have recognized the name: there was another interest: for the next hour let the police have him.

Then she got up slowly and began to undress. She never believed in wearing much: it wasn't any time at all before she was exposed in the long mirror: a body firm and bulky: a proper handful. She stood on a deep soft rug, surrounded by gilt frames and red velvet hangings, and a dozen common and popular phrases bloomed in her mind – 'A Night of Love', 'You Only Live Once', and the rest. She bore the same relation to passion as a peepshow. She sucked the chocolate between her teeth and smiled, her plump toes working in the rug, waiting for Mr Corkery – just a great big blossoming surprise.

Outside the window the sea ebbed, scraping the shingle, exposing a boot, a piece of rusty iron, and the old man stooped, searching between the stones. The sun dropped behind the Hove houses and dusk came, the shadow of Mr Corkery lengthened, coming slowly up from the Belvedere carrying the suitcases, saving on taxis. A gull swooped screaming down to a dead crab beaten and broken against the iron foundation of the pier. It was the time of near-darkness and of the evening mist from the Channel and of love.

Chapter Five

The Boy closed the door behind him and turned to face the expectant and amused faces.

'Well,' Cubitt said, 'is it all fixed up?'

'Of course it is,' the Boy said, 'when I want a thing—' his voice wavered out unconvincingly. There were half a dozen bottles on his washstand: his room smelt of stale beer.

'Want a thing,' Cubitt said. 'That's good.' He opened another bottle and in the warm stuffy room the froth rose quickly and splashed on the marble top.

'What do you think you're doing?' the Boy said.

'Celebrating,' Cubitt said. 'You're a Roman, aren't you? A betrothal, that's what Romans call it.'

The Boy watched them: Cubitt a little drunk, Dallow preoccupied, two lean hungry faces he hardly knew – hangers-on at the fringes of the great racket who smiled when you smiled and frowned when you frowned. But now they smiled when Cubitt smiled, and suddenly he saw the long way he had slipped since that afternoon on the pier when he arranged the alibi, gave the orders, did what they hadn't got the nerve to do themselves.

Frank's wife Judy put her head in at the door. She was wearing a dressing-gown. Her Titian hair was brown at the roots. 'Good luck, Pinkie,' she said, blinking mascara'd lashes. She had been washing her bra: the little piece of pink silk dripped on the linoleum. Nobody offered her a drink. 'Work, work, work,' she moued at them, going on down the passage to the hot water-pipes.

A long way ... and yet he hadn't made a single false step: if he hadn't gone to Snow's and spoken to the girl, they'd all be in the dock by now. If he hadn't killed Spicer. . . . Not a single false step, but every step conditioned by a pressure he couldn't even place: a woman asking questions, messages on the telephone scaring Spicer. He thought: when I've married the girl, will it stop then? Where else can it drive me, and with a twitch of the mouth, he wondered – what worse—?

'When's the happy day?' Cubitt asked and they all smiled obediently except Dallow.

The Boy's brain began to work again. He moved slowly towards the washstand. He said, 'Haven't you got a glass for me? Don't I do any celebrating?'

He saw Dallow astonished, Cubitt thrown off his mark, the hangers-on doubtful who to follow, and he grinned at them, the one with brains.

'Why, Pinkie . . .' Cubitt said.

'I'm not a drinking man and I'm not a marrying man,' the Boy said. 'So *you* think. But I'm liking one, so why shouldn't I like the other. Give me a glass.'

'Liking,' Cubitt said and grinned uneasily, 'you *liking*. . . .'

'Haven't you seen her?' the Boy said.

'Why, me and Dallow just lamped her. On the stairs. But it was too dark. . . .'

'She's a lovely,' the Boy said, 'she's wasted in a kip. And intelligent. Don't make any mistake. Of course I didn't see any cause to *marry* her, but as it is—' somebody handed him a glass: he took a long draught: the bitter and bubbly fluid revolted him – so this was what they liked – he tightened the muscles of his mouth to hide his revulsion: 'as it is,' he said, 'I'm glad,' and eyed with hidden disgust the pale inch of liquid in the glass before he drained it down.

Dallow watched in silence and the Boy felt more anger against his friend than against his enemy. Like Spicer he knew too much, but what he knew was far more deadly than what Spicer had known. Spicer had known only the kind of thing which brought you to the dock, but Dallow knew what your mirror and your bedsheets knew: the secret fear and the humiliation. He said with hidden fury, 'What's getting you, Dallow?'

The stupid and broken face was hopelessly at a loss.

'Jealous?' the Boy began to boast. 'You've cause when you've seen her. She's not one of your dyed totsies. She's got class. I'm marrying her for your sake, but I'm laying her for my own.' He turned fiendishly on Dallow. 'What's on *your* mind?'

'Well,' Dallow said, 'it's the one you met on the pier, isn't it? I didn't think she was all that good.'

'You,' the Boy said, 'you don't know anything. You're ignorant. You don't know class when you see it.'

'A duchess,' Cubitt said and laughed.

An extraordinary indignation jerked in the Boy's brain and fingers. It was almost as if someone he loved had been insulted. 'Be careful, Cubitt,' he said.

'Don't mind him,' Dallow said. 'We didn't know you'd fallen. . . .'

'We got some presents for you, Pinkie,' Cubitt said, 'furniture for the home,' and indicated two little obscene objects beside the beer on the washstand – the Brighton stationers were full of them – a tiny doll's commode in the shape of a radio set labelled 'The smallest A.1 two-valve receiving set in the world', and a mustard-pot shaped like a lavatory seat with the legend, 'For me and my girl'. It was like a return of all the horror he had ever felt, the hideous loneliness of his innocence. He struck at Cubitt's face and Cubitt dodged, laughing. The two hangers-on slipped out of the room. They hadn't any taste for rough houses. The Boy heard them laugh on the stairs. Cubitt said, 'You'll need 'em in the home. A bed's not the only furniture.' He mocked and backed at the same time.

The Boy said, 'By God, I'll treat you like I treated Spicer.'

No meaning reached Cubitt at once. There was a long time lag. He began to laugh and then saw Dallow's startled face and *heard*. 'What's that?' he said.

'He's crazy,' Dallow intervened.

'You think yourself smart,' the Boy said. 'So did Spicer.'

'It was the banister,' Cubitt said. 'You weren't here. What are you getting at?'

'Of course he wasn't here,' Dallow said.

'You think you know things.' All the Boy's hatred was in the word 'know' and his repulsion: he knew – like Prewitt knew after twenty-five years at the game. 'You don't know everything.' He tried to inject himself with pride, but all the time his eyes went back to the humiliation. 'The smallest A.1. . . .' You could know everything there was in the world and yet if you were ignorant of that one dirty scramble you knew nothing.

'What's he getting at?' Cubitt asked.

'You don't need to listen to him,' Dallow said.

'I mean this,' the Boy said. 'Spicer was milky and I'm the only one in this mob knows how to act.'

'You act too much,' Cubitt said. 'Do you mean – it wasn't the banisters?' The question scared himself: he didn't want an answer. He made uneasily for the door, keeping his eye on the Boy.

Dallow said, 'Of course it was the banisters. I was there, wasn't I?'

'I don't know,' Cubitt said, 'I don't know,' making for the door. 'Brighton's not big enough for him. I'm through.'

'Go on,' the Boy said. 'Clear out. Clear out and starve.'

'I won't starve,' Cubitt said. 'There's others in this town. . . .'

When the door closed the Boy turned on Dallow. 'Go on,' he said 'you go too. You think you can get on without me, but I've only got to whistle. . . .'

'You don't need to talk to me like that,' Dallow said. 'I'm not leaving you. I don't fancy making friends with Crab again so soon.'

But the Boy paid him no attention. He said again, 'I've only got to whistle. . . .' He boasted, 'They'll come tumbling back.' He went over to the brass bed and lay down; he had had a long day. He said, 'Get me Prewitt on the blower. Tell him there's no difficulty at *her* end. Let him fix things quick.'

'The day after to-morrow if he can?' Dallow asked.

'Yes,' the Boy said. He heard the door close and lay with twitching cheek staring at the ceiling. He thought, it's not my fault they get me angry so I want to do things: if people would leave me in peace. . . . His imagination wilted at the word. He tried in a half-hearted way to picture 'peace' – his eyes closed and behind the lids he saw a grey darkness going on and on without end, a country of which he hadn't seen as much as a picture postcard, a place far stranger than the Grand Canyon and the Taj Mahal. He opened them again and immediately poison moved in the veins, for there on the washstand were Cubitt's purchases. He was like a child with haemophilia: every contact drew blood.

Chapter Six

A bell rang muffled in the Cosmopolitan corridor; through the wall against which the bed-end stood Ida Arnold could hear a voice talking on and on: somebody reading a report, perhaps in a conference room or dictating to a dictaphone. Phil lay asleep on the bed in his pants, his mouth a little open showing one yellow tooth and a gob of metal filling. Fun . . . human nature . . . does no one any harm . . . Regular as clockwork the old excuses came back into the alert, sad and dissatisfied brain – nothing ever matched the deep excitement of the regular desire. Men always failed you when it came to the act. She might just as well have been to the pictures.

But it did no one any harm, it was just human nature, no one could call her really bad – a bit free-and-easy perhaps, a bit Bohemian. It wasn't as if she got anything out of it, as if like some people she sucked a man dry and cast him aside like a throw-off – threw him aside like a cast-off glove. She knew what was right and what was wrong. God didn't mind a bit of human nature – what he minded – and her brain switched away from Phil in pants to her mission, to doing good, to seeing that the evil suffered. . . .

She sat up in bed and put her arms round her large naked knees and felt excitement stirring again in the disappointed body. Poor old Fred – the name no longer conveyed any sense of grief or pathos. She couldn't remember anything much about him now but a monocle and a yellow waistcoat and that belonged to poor old Charlie Moyne. The hunt was what mattered. It was like life coming back after a sickness.

Phil opened an eye – yellow with the sexual effort – and watched her apprehensively. She said, 'Awake, Phil?'

'It must be nearly time for dinner,' Phil said. He gave a nervous smile. 'A penny for your thoughts, Ida.'

'I was just thinking,' Ida said, 'that what we really need now is one of Pinkie's men. Somebody scared or angry. They must get scared some time. We've only got to wait.'

She got out of the bed, opened her suitcase and began to lay out the clothes she thought were suitable for dinner in the Cosmopolitan. In the pink, reading-lamp, love-lamp light spangles glittered. She stretched her arms; she no longer felt desire or disappointment: her brain was clear. It was almost dark along the beach; the edge of sea was like a line of writing in whitewash: big sprawling letters. They meant nothing at this distance. A shadow stooped with infinite patience and disinterred some relic from the shingle.

Chapter One

When Cubitt got outside the front door the hangers-on had already vanished. The street was empty. He felt in a dumb, bitter and uncomprehending way like a man who has destroyed his home without having prepared another. The mist was coming up from the sea, and he hadn't got his coat. He was as angry as a child: he wouldn't go back for it: it would be like admitting he was wrong. The only thing to be done now was to drink a strong whisky at the Crown.

At the saloon bar they made way for him with respect. In the mirror marked Booth's Gin he could see his own reflection – the short flaming hair, the blunt and open face, broad shoulders. He stared like Narcissus into his pool and felt better; he wasn't the sort of man to take things lying down; he was valuable. 'Have a whisky?' somebody said. It was the greengrocer's assistant from the corner shop. Cubitt laid a heavy paw across his shoulder, accepting, patronizing: the man who had done a thing or two in his time chummy with the pale ignorant fellow who dreamed from his commercial distance of a man's life. The relationship pleased Cubitt. He had two more whiskies at the grocer's expense.

'Got a tip, Mr Cubitt?'

'I've got other things to think of beside tips,' Cubitt said darkly, adding a splash.

'We were having an argument in here about Gay Parrot for the two-thirty. Seemed to me. . . .'

Gay Parrot . . . the name didn't mean a thing to Cubitt: the drink warmed him: the mist was in his brain: he leant forward towards the mirror and saw 'Booth's Gin . . . Booth's Gin,' haloed above his head. He was involved in high politics: men had been killed: poor old Spicer. Allegiances shifted like heavy balances in his brain: he felt as important as a Prime Minister making treaties.

'There'll be more killing before we're through,' he mysteriously pronounced. He had his wits about him: he wasn't giving anything away; but there was no harm in letting these poor sodden creatures a little way into the secrets of living. He pushed his glass forward and said, 'A drink all round,' but when he looked to either side they'd gone; a face took a backward look through the pane of the saloon door, vanished; they couldn't stand the company of a Man.

'Never mind,' he said, 'never mind,' and drank down his whisky and left. The next thing, of course, was to see Colleoni. He'd say to him, 'Here I am, Mr Colleoni. I'm through with Kite's mob. I won't work under a boy like that. Give me a Man's job and I'll do it.' The mist got at his bones: he shivered involuntarily: a grey goose. . . . He thought: if only Dallow too

. . . and suddenly loneliness took away his confidence; all the heat of the drink seeped out of him, and the mist like seven devils went in. Suppose Colleoni simply wasn't interested. He came down on to the front and saw through the thin fog the high lights of the Cosmopolitan: it was cocktail time.

Cubitt sat down chilled in a glass shelter and stared out towards the sea. The tide was low and the mist hid it: it was just a sliding and a sibilation. He lit a cigarette: the match warmed for a moment the cupped hands. He offered the packet to an elderly gentleman wrapped in a heavy overcoat who shared the shelter. 'I don't smoke,' the old gentleman said sharply and began to cough: a steady hack, hack, hack towards the invisible sea.

'A cold night,' Cubitt said. The old gentleman swivelled his eyes on him like opera glasses and went on coughing: hack, hack, hack: the vocal chords dry as straw. Somewhere out at sea a violin began to play: it was like a sea beast mourning and stretching towards the shore. Cubitt thought of Spicer who'd liked a good tune. Poor old Spicer. The mist blew in, heavy compact drifts of it like ectoplasm. Cubitt had been to a séance once in Brighton: he had wanted to get in touch with his mother, dead twenty years ago. It had come over him quite suddenly – the old girl might have a word for him. She had: she was on the seventh plane where all was very beautiful: her voice had sounded a little boozed, but that wasn't really unnatural. The boys had laughed at him about it, particularly old Spicer. Well, Spicer wouldn't laugh now. He could be summoned himself any time to ring a bell and shake a tambourine. It was a lucky thing he liked music.

Cubitt got up and strolled to the turnpike of the West Pier, which straddled into the mist and vanished towards the violin. He walked up towards the Concert Hall, passing nobody. It wasn't a night for courting couples to sit out. Whatever people there were upon the pier were gathered every one inside the Concert Hall. Cubitt turned round it on the outside looking in: a man in evening dress fiddling to a few rows of people in overcoats, islanded fifty yards out to sea in the middle of the mist. Somewhere in the Channel a boat blew its siren and another answered, and another, like dogs at night waking each other.

Go to Colleoni and say . . . it was all quite easy; the old man ought to be grateful . . . Cubitt looked back towards the shore and saw above the mist the high lights of the Cosmopolitan, and they daunted him. He wasn't used to that sort of company. He went down the iron companionway to the gents and drained the whisky out of him into the movement under the piles and came up on to the deck lonelier than ever. He took a penny out of his pocket and slipped it into an automatic machine: a robot face behind which an electric bulb revolved, iron hands for Cubitt to grip. A little blue card shot out at him: 'Your Character Delineated.' Cubitt read: 'You are mainly influenced by your surroundings and inclined to be capricious and changeful. Your affections are more intense than enduring. You have a free, easy, and genial nature. You make the best of whatever you undertake. A share of the good things of life can always be yours. Your lack of initiative is counter-balanced by your good common sense, and you will succeed where others fail.'

He dragged slowly on past the automatic machines, delaying the moment when there would be nothing for him to do but go to the Cosmopolitan.

'Your lack of initiative . . .' Two leaden football teams waited behind glass for a penny to release them: an old witch with the stuffing coming out of her claw offered to tell his fortune. 'A Love Letter' made him pause. The boards were damp with mist, the long deck was empty, the violin ground on. He felt the need of a deep sentimental affection, orange blossoms and a cuddle in a corner. His great paw yearned for a sticky hand. Somebody who wouldn't mind his jokes, who would laugh with him at the two-valve receiving set. He hadn't meant any harm. The cold reached his stomach, and a little stale whisky returned into his throat. He almost felt inclined to go back to Frank's. But then he remembered Spicer. The boy was mad, killing mad, it wasn't safe. Loneliness dragged him down the solitary boards. He took out his last copper and thrust it in. A little pink card came out with a printed stamp: a girl's head, long hair, the legend 'True Love'. It was addressed to 'My Dear Pet, Spooner's Nook, With Cupid's Love', and there was a picture of a young man in evening dress kneeling on the floor, kissing the hand of a girl carrying a big fur. Up in a corner two hearts were transfixed by an arrow just above Reg. No. 745812. Cubitt thought: it's clever. It's cheap for a penny. He looked quickly over his shoulder: not a soul: and turned it quickly and began to read. The letter was addressed from Cupid's Wings, Amor Lane. 'My dear little girl. So you have discarded me for the Squire's son. You little know how you have ruined my life in breaking faith with me, you have crushed the very soul out of me, as the butterfly on the wheel; but with it all I do not wish anything but your happiness.'

Cubitt grinned uneasily. He was deeply moved. That was what always happened if you took up with anything but a buer; they gave you the air. Grand Renunciations, Tragedies, Beauty moved in Cubitt's brain. If it was a buer of course you took a razor to her, carved her face, but this love printed here was class. He read on: it was literature: it was the way he'd like to write himself. 'After all, when I think of your wondrous, winsome beauty, and culture, I feel what a fool I must have been to dream that you ever really loved me.' Unworthy. Emotion pricked behind his eyelids and he shivered in the mist with cold and beauty. 'But remember, dearest, always, that I love you, and if ever you want a friend just return the little token of love I gave you and I will be your servant and slave. Yours broken-heartedly, John.' It was his own name: an omen.

He moved again past the lighted concert hall and down the deserted deck. Loved and Lost. Tragic griefs flamed under his carrot hair. What can a man do but drink? He got another whisky just opposite the pier head and moved on, planting his feet rather too firmly, towards the Cosmopolitan – plank, plank, plank along the pavement as if he were wearing iron weights under his shoes, like a statue might move, half-flesh, half stone.

'I want to speak to Mr Colleoni.' He said it defiantly. The plush and gilding smoothed away his confidence. He waited uneasily beside the desk while a pageboy searched through the lounges and boudoirs for Mr Colleoni. The clerk turned over the leaves of a big book and then consulted a *Who's Who*. Across the deep carpet the page returned and Crab followed him, sidling and triumphant with his black hair smelling of pomade.

'I said Mr Colleoni,' Cubitt said to the clerk, but the clerk took no notice, wetting his finger, skimming through *Who's Who*.

'You wanted to see Mr Colleoni,' Crab said.

'That's right.'

'You can't. He's occupied.'

'Occupied,' Cubitt said. 'That's a fine word to use. Occupied.'

'Why, if it isn't Cubitt,' Crab said. 'I suppose you want a job.' He looked round in a busy preoccupied way and said to the clerk, 'Isn't that Lord Feversham over there?'

'Yes, sir,' the clerk said.

'I've often seen him at Doncaster,' Crab said, squinting at a nail on his left hand. He swept round on Cubitt. 'Follow me, my man. We can't talk here,' and before Cubitt could reply he was sidling off at a great rate between the gilt chairs.

'It's like this,' Cubitt said, 'Pinkie—'

Half-way across the lounge Crab paused and bowed and moving on became suddenly confidential. 'A fine woman.' He flickered like an early movie. He had picked up between Doncaster and London a hundred different manners; travelling first-class after a successful meeting he had learnt how Lord Feversham spoke to a porter: he had seen old Digby scrutinise a woman.

'Who is she?' Cubitt asked.

But Crab took no notice of the question. 'We can talk here.' It was the Pompadour Boudoir. Through the gilt and glass door beyond the boule tables you could see little signboards pointing down a network of passages – tasteful little chinoiserie signboards with a Tuileries air: 'Ladies'. 'Gentlemen'. 'Ladies' Hairdressing'. 'Gentlemen's Hairdressing'.

'It's Mr Colleoni I want to talk to,' Cubitt said. He breathed whisky over the marquetry, but he was daunted and despairing. He resisted with difficulty the temptation to say 'sir'. Crab had moved on since Kite's day, almost out of sight. He was part of the great racket now – with Lord Feversham and the fine woman. He had grown up.

'Mr Colleoni hasn't time to see everyone,' Crab said. 'He's a busy man.' He took one of Mr Colleoni's cigars out of his pocket and put it in his mouth: he didn't offer one to Cubitt. Cubitt with uncertain hand offered him a match. 'Never mind, never mind,' Crab said, fumbling in his double-breasted waistcoat. He fetched out a gold lighter and flourished it at his cigar. 'What do you want, Cubitt?' he asked.

'I thought maybe,' Cubitt said, but his words wilted among the gilt chairs. 'You know how it is,' he said, staring desperately around. 'What about a drink?'

Crab took him quickly up. 'I wouldn't mind one – just for old time's sake.' He rang for a waiter.

'Old times,' Cubitt said.

'Take a seat,' Crab said, waving a possessive hand at the gilt chairs. Cubitt sat gingerly down. The chairs were small and hard. He saw a waiter watching them and flushed. 'What's yours?' he asked.

'A sherry,' Crab said. 'Dry.'

'Scotch and splash for me' Cubitt said. He sat waiting for his drink, his hands between his knees, silent, his head lowered. He took furtive glances. This was where Pinkie had come to see Colleoni – he had nerve all right.

'They do you pretty well here,' Crab said. 'Of course Mr Colleoni likes nothing but the best.' He took his drink and watched Cubitt pay. 'He likes things smart. Why, he's worth fifty thousand nicker if he's worth a penny. If you ask me what I think,' Crab said, leaning back, puffing at the cigar, watching Cubitt through remote and supercilious eyes, 'he'll go in for politics one day. The Conservatives think a lot of him – he's got contacts.'

'Pinkie—' Cubitt began and Crab laughed. 'Take my advice,' Crab said 'Get out of that mob while there's time. There's no future. . . .' He looked obliquely over Cubitt's head and said, 'See that man going to the gents. That's Mais. The brewer. He's worth a hundred thousand nicker.'

'I was wondering,' Cubitt said, 'if Mr Colleoni. . . .'

'Not a chance,' Crab said. 'Why, ask yourself – what good would you be to Mr Colleoni?'

Cubitt's humility gave way to a dull anger. 'I was good enough for Kite.'

Crab laughed. 'Excuse me,' he said, 'but Kite. . . .' He shook his ash out on to the carpet and said, 'Take my advice. Get out. Mr Colleoni's going to clean up this track. He likes things done properly. No violence. The police have great confidence in Mr Colleoni.' He looked at his watch. 'Well, well, I must be going. I've got a date at the Hippodrome.' He put his hand with patronage on Cubitt's arm. 'There,' he said, 'I'll put in a word for you – for old times' sake. It won't be any good, but I'll do that much. Give my regards to Pinkie and the boys.' He passed – a whiff of pomade and Havana, bowing slightly to a woman at the door, an old man with a monocle on a black ribbon. 'Who the hell—' the old man said.

Cubitt drained his drink and followed. An enormous depression bowed his carrot head, a sense of ill-treatment moved through the whisky fumes – somebody some time had got to pay for something. All that he saw fed the flame: he came out into the entrance hall: a pageboy with a salver infuriated him. Everybody was watching him, waiting for him to go, but he had as much right there as Crab. He glanced round him, and there alone at a little table with a glass of port was the woman Crab knew. He watched her with covetous envy and she smiled at him – 'I think of your wondrous, winsome beauty and culture.' A sense of the immeasurable sadness of injustice took the place of anger. He wanted to confide, to lay down burdens . . . he belched once. . . . 'I will be your loving slave.' The great body turned like a door, the heavy feet altered direction and padded towards the table where Ida Arnold sat.

'I couldn't help hearing,' she said, 'when you went across just now that you knew Pinkie.'

He realised with immense pleasure when she spoke that she wasn't class. It seemed to him like the meeting of two fellow countrymen a long way from home. He said, 'You a friend of Pinkie's?' and felt the whisky in his legs. He asked, 'Mind if I sit down?'

'Tired?'

'That's it,' he said, 'tired.' He sat down with his eyes on her large friendly bosom. He remembered the lines on his character. 'You have a free, easy and genial nature.' By God, he had. He only needed to be treated right.

'Have a drink?'

'No, no,' he said with woolly gallantry, 'it's on me,' but when the drinks came he realized he was out of cash. He had meant to borrow from one of the boys – but then the quarrel. . . . He watched Ida Arnold pay with a five-pound note.

'Know Mr Colleoni?' he asked.

'I wouldn't call it *know*,' she said.

'Crab said you were a fine woman. He's right.'

'Oh – Crab,' she said vaguely, as if she didn't recognize the name.

'You oughter steer clear though,' Cubitt said. 'You've no call to get mixed up in things.' He stared into his glass as into a deep darkness: outside innocence, winsome beauty and culture – unworthy, a tear gathered behind the bloodshot eyeball.

'You a friend of Pinkie's?' Ida Arnold asked.

'Christ, no,' Cubitt said and took some more whisky.

A vague memory of the Bible, where it lay in the cupboard next the Board, the Warwick Deeping, *The Good Companions*, stirred in Ida Arnold's memory. 'I've seen you with him,' she lied: a court-yard, a sewing wench beside the fire, the cock crowing.

'I'm no friend of Pinkie's.'

'It's not safe being friends with Pinkie,' Ida Arnold said. Cubitt stared into his glass like a diviner into his soul, reading the dooms of strangers. 'Fred was a friend of Pinkie's,' she said.

'What you know about Fred?'

'People talk,' Ida Arnold said. 'People talk all the time.'

'You're right,' Cubitt said. The stained eyeballs lifted: they gazed at comfort, understanding. He wasn't good enough for Colleoni: he had broken with Pinkie. Behind her head through the window of the lounge darkness and the retreating sea. 'Christ,' he said, 'you're right.' He had an enormous urge to confession, but the facts were confused. He only knew that these were the times when a man needed a woman's understanding. 'I've never held with it,' he told her. 'Carving's different.'

'Of course, carving's different,' Ida Arnold smoothly and deftly agreed.

'And Kite – that was an accident. They only meant to carve him. Colleoni's no fool. Somebody slipped. There wasn't any cause for bad feeling.'

'Have another drink?'

'It oughter be on me,' Cubitt said. 'But I'm cleaned out. Till I see the boys.'

'It was fine of you – breaking with Pinkie like that. It needed courage after what happened to Fred.'

'Oh, he can't scare me. No broken banisters . . .'

'What do you mean – broken banisters?'

'I wanted to be friendly,' Cubitt said. 'A joke's a joke. When a man's getting married, he oughter take a joke.'

'Married? Who married?'

'Pinkie, of course.'

'Not to the little girl at Snow's?'

'Of course.'

'The little fool,' Ida Arnold said with sharp anger. 'Oh, the little fool.'

'He's not a fool,' Cubitt said. 'He knows what's good for him. If she chose to say a thing or two—'

'You mean, say it wasn't Fred left the ticket?'

'Poor old Spicer,' Cubitt said, watching the bubbles rise in the whisky. A question floated up, 'How did you . . .' but broke in the doped brain. 'I want air,' he said, 'stuffy in here. What say you and I . . .?'

'Just wait awhile,' Ida Arnold said. 'I'm expecting a friend. I'd like you and him to be acquainted.'

'This central heating,' Cubitt said, 'it's not healthy. You go out and catch a chill and the next you know . . .'

'When's the wedding?'

'Whose wedding?'

'Pinkie's.'

'I'm no friend of Pinkie's.'

'You didn't hold with Fred's death, did you?' Ida Arnold softly persisted. 'You understand a man.'

'Carving would have been different.'

Cubitt suddenly, furiously, broke out, 'I can't see a piece of Brighton rock without . . .' He belched and said with tears in his voice, 'Carving's different.'

'The doctors said it was natural causes. He had a weak heart.'

'Come outside,' Cubitt said. 'I got to get some air.'

'Just wait a bit. What do you mean – Brighton rock?'

He stared inertly back at her. He said, 'I got to get some air. Even if it kills me. This central heating . . .' he complained. 'I'm liable to colds.'

'Just wait two minutes.' She put her hand on his arm, feeling an intense excitement, the edge of discovery above the horizon, and was aware herself for the first time of the warm close air welling up round them from hidden gratings, driving them into the open. She said, 'I'll come out with you. We'll take a walk . . .' He watched her with nodding head, with an immense indifference as if he had lost grip on his thought as you loose a dog's lead and it has disappeared, too far to be followed, in what wood . . . He was astonished when she said, 'I'll give you – twenty pounds.' What had he said that was worth that money? She smiled enticingly at him. 'Just let me put on a bit of powder and have a wash.' He didn't respond, he was scared, but she couldn't wait for a reply: she dived for the stairs – no time for the lift. A wash: they were the words she had used to Fred. She ran upstairs, people were coming down, changed, to dinner. She hammered on her door and Phil Corkery let her in. 'Quick,' she said, 'I want a witness.' He was dressed, thank goodness, and she raced him down, but immediately she got into the hall she saw that Cubitt had gone. She ran out on to the steps of the Cosmopolitan, but he wasn't in sight.

'Well,' Mr Corkery said.

'Gone. Never mind,' Ida Arnold said. 'I know now all right. It wasn't suicide. They murdered him.' She said slowly over to herself: '. . . Brighton rock. . . .' The clue would have seemed hopeless to many women, but Ida Arnold had been trained by the Board. Queerer things than that had spidered out under her fingers and Old Crowe's: with complete confidence her mind began to work.

The night air stirred Mr Corkery's thin yellow hair. It may have occurred to him that on an evening like this – after the actions of love – romance was required by any woman. He touched her elbow timidly, 'What a night,' he said. 'I never dreamed – what a night,' but words drained out as she switched towards him her large thoughtful eyes, uncomprehending, full of other ideas. She said slowly, 'The little fool . . . to marry him . . . why, there's no knowing what he'll do.' A kind of righteous mirth moved her to add with excitement, 'We got to save her, Phil.'

Chapter Two

At the bottom of the steps the Boy waited. The big municipal building lay over him like a shadow – departments for births and deaths, for motor licences, for rates and taxes, somewhere in some long corridor the room for marriages. He looked at his watch and said to Mr Prewitt, 'God damn her. She's late.'

Mr Prewitt said, 'It's the privilege of a bride.'

Bride and groom: the mare and the stallion which served her: like a file on metal or the touch of velvet to a sore hand. The Boy said, 'Me and Dallow – we'll walk and meet her.'

Mr Prewitt called after him, 'Suppose she comes another way. Suppose you miss her . . . I'll wait here.'

They turned to the left out of the official street. 'This ain't the way,' Dallow said.

'There's no call on us to wait on her,' the Boy said.

'You can't get out of it now.'

'Who wants to? I can take a bit of exercise, can't I?' He stopped and stared into a small newsagent's window – two-valve receiving sets, the grossness everywhere.

'Seen Cubitt?' he asked, staring in.

'No,' Dallow said. 'None of the boys either.'

The daily and the local papers, a poster packed with news: Scene at Council Meeting. Woman Found Drowned at Black Rock. Collision in Clarence Street: a Wild West magazine, a copy of *Film Fun*; behind the inkpots and the fountain pens and the paper plates for picnics and the little gross toys, the works of wellknown sexologists. The Boy stared in.

'I know how you feel,' Dallow said. 'I was married once myself. It kind of gets you in the stomach. Nerves. Why,' Dallow said, 'I even went and got one of those books, but it didn't tell me anything I didn't know. Except about flowers. The pistills of flowers. You wouldn't believe the funny things that go on among flowers.'

The Boy turned and opened his mouth to speak, but the teeth snapped to again. He watched Dallow with pleading and horror. If Kite had been there, he thought, he could have spoken – but if Kite had been there, he would have had no need to speak . . . he would never have got mixed up.

'These bees . . .' Dallow began to explain and stopped. 'What is it, Pinkie? You don't look too good.'

'I know the rules all right,' the Boy said.

'What rules?'

'You can't teach me the rules,' the Boy went on with gusty anger. 'I watched 'em every Saturday night, didn't I? Bouncing and ploughing.' His eyes flinched as if he were watching some horror. He said in a low voice, 'When I was a kid, I swore I'd be a priest.'

'A priest? You a priest? That's good,' Dallow said. He laughed without conviction, uneasily shifted his foot so that it trod in a dog's ordure.

'What's wrong with being a priest?' the Boy asked. 'They know what's what. They keep away—' his whole mouth and jaw loosened: he might have been going to weep: he beat our wildly with his hands towards the window: Woman Found Drowned, two-valve, *Married Passion*, the horror – 'from this.'

'What's wrong with a bit of fun?' Dallow took him up, scraping his shoe against the pavement edge. The word 'fun' shook the Boy like malaria. He said, 'You wouldn't have known Annie Collins, would you?'

'Never heard of her.'

'She went to the same school I did,' the Boy said. He took a look down the grey street and then the glass before *Married Passion* reflected again his young and hopeless face. 'She put her head on the line,' he said, 'up by Hassocks. She had to wait ten minutes for the seven-five. Fog made it late from Victoria. Cut off her head. She was fifteen. She was going to have a baby and she knew what it was like. She'd had one two years before, and they could 'ave pinned it on twelve boys.'

'It does happen,' Dallow said. 'It's the luck of the game.'

'I've read love stories,' the Boy said. He had never been so vocal before, staring in at the paper plates with frilly edges and the two-valve receiving set: the daintiness and the grossness. 'Frank's wife reads them. You know the sort. Lady Angeline turned her starry eyes towards Sir Mark. They make me sick. Sicker than the other kind' – Dallow watched with astonishment this sudden horrified gift of tongues – 'the kind you buy under the counter. Spicer used to get them. About girls being beaten. Full of shame to expose herself thus before the boys she stooped. . . . It's all the same thing,' he said, turning his poisoned eyes away from the window, from point to point of the long shabby street: a smell of fish, the sawdusted pavement below the carcasses. 'It's fun. It's the game.'

'The world's got to go on,' Dallow said uneasily.

'Why?'

'You don't need to ask me,' Dallow said. 'You know best. You're a Roman, aren't you? You believe . . .'

'Credo in unum Satanum,' the Boy said.

'I don't know Latin. I only know . . .'

'Come on,' the Boy said. 'Let's have it. Dallow's creed.'

'The world's all right if you don't go too far.'

'Is that all?'

'It's time for you to be at the registrar's. Hear the clock. It's striking two now.' A peal of bells stopped their cracked chime and struck – one, two—

The Boy's whole face loosened again: he put his hand on Dallow's arm. 'You're a good sort, Dallow. You know a lot. Tell me—' his hand fell away. He looked beyond Dallow down the street. He said hopelessly, 'Here she is. What's she doing in *this* street?'

'She's not hurrying either,' Dallow commented, watching the thin figure slowly approach. At that distance she didn't even look her age. He said, 'It was clever of Prewitt to get the licence at all considering.'

'Parents' consent,' the Boy said dully. 'Best for morality.' He watched the girl as if she were a stranger he had got to meet. 'And then you see there was a stroke of luck. I wasn't registered. Not anywhere they could find. They added on a year or two. No parents. No guardian. It was a touching story old Prewitt spun.'

She had tricked herself up for the wedding, discarded the hat he hadn't liked: a new mackintosh, a touch of powder and cheap lipstick. She looked like one of the small gaudy statues in an ugly church: a paper crown wouldn't have looked odd on her or a painted heart: you could pray to her but you couldn't expect an answer.

'Where've you been?' the Boy said. 'Don't you know you're late?'

They didn't even touch hands. An awful formality fell between them.

'I'm sorry, Pinkie. You see' – she brought the fact out with shame, as if she were admitting conversation with his enemy – 'I went into the church.'

'What for?' he said.

'I don't know, Pinkie. I got confused. I thought I'd go to confession.'

He grinned at her. 'Confession? That's rich.'

'You see I wanted – I thought—'

'For Christ's sake what?'

'I wanted to be in a state of grace when I married you.' She took no notice at all of Dallow. The theological term lay oddly and pedantically on her tongue. They were two Romans together in the grey street. They understood each other. She used terms common to heaven and hell.

'And did you?' the Boy said.

'No. I went and rang the bell and asked for Father James. But then I remembered. It wasn't any good confessing. I went away.' She said with a mixture of fear and pride. 'We're going to do a mortal sin.'

The Boy said, with bitter and unhappy relish, 'It'll be no good going to confession ever again – as long as we're both alive.' He had graduated in pain: first the school dividers had been left behind, next the razor. He had a sense now that the murders of Hale and Spicer were trivial acts, a boy's game, and he had put away childish things. Murder had only led up to this – this corruption. He was filled with awe at his own powers. 'We'd better be moving,' he said and touched her arm with next to tenderness. As once before he had a sense of needing her.

Mr Prewitt greeted them with official mirth. All his jokes seemed to be spoken in court, with an ulterior motive, to catch a magistrate's ear. In the great institutional hall from which the corridors led off to deaths and births there was a smell of disinfectant. The walls were tiled like a public lavatory. Somebody had dropped a rose. Mr Prewitt quoted promptly, inaccurately, 'Roses, roses all the way, and never a sprig of yew.' A soft hollow hand guided the Boy by the elbow: 'No, no, not that way. That's taxes. That comes later.' He led them up great stone stairs. A clerk passed them carrying printed forms. 'And what is the little lady thinking?' Mr Prewitt said. She didn't answer him.

Only the bride and groom were allowed to mount the sanctuary steps, to kneel down within the sanctuary rails with the priest and the Host.

'Parents coming?' Mr Prewitt asked. She shook her head. 'The great thing is,' Mr Prewitt said, 'it's over quickly. Just sign the names along the dotted line. Sit down here. We've got to wait our turn, you know.'

They sat down. A mop leant in a corner against the tiled wall. The footsteps of a clerk squealed on the icy paving down another passage. Presently a big brown door opened: they saw a row of clerks inside who didn't look up: a man and wife came into the corridor. A woman followed them and took the mop. The man – he was middle-aged – said 'thank you', gave her sixpence. He said, 'We'll catch the three-fifteen after all.' On the woman's face there was a look of faint astonishment, bewilderment, nothing so definite as disappointment. She wore a brown straw and carried an attaché case. She was middle-aged too. She might have been thinking, 'Is that all there is to it – after all these years?' They went down the big stairs walking a little apart, like strangers in a stores.

'Our turn,' Mr Prewitt said, rising briskly. He led the way through the room where the clerks worked. Nobody bothered to look up. Nibs wrote smooth numerals and ran on. In a small inner room with green washed walls like a clinic's the registrar waited: a table, three or four chairs against the wall. It wasn't what she thought a marriage would be like – for a moment she was daunted by the cold poverty of a state-made ceremony.

'Good morning,' the registrar said. 'If the witnesses will just sit down – would you two' – he beckoned them to the table and stared at them with gold-rimmed and glassy importance: it was as if he considered himself on the fringe of the priestly office. The Boy's heart beat: he was sickened by the reality of the moment. He wore a look of sullenness and of stupidity.

'You're both very young,' the registrar said.

'It's fixed,' the Boy said. 'You don't have to talk about it. It's fixed.'

The registrar gave him a glance of intense dislike; he said, 'Repeat after me,' and then ran too quickly on, 'I do solemnly declare that I know not of any lawful impediment,' so that the Boy couldn't follow him. The registrar said sharply, 'It's quite simple. You've only to repeat after me. . . .'

'Go slower,' the Boy said. He wanted to lay his hand on speed and brake it down, but it ran on: it was no time at all, a matter of seconds, before he was repeating the formula 'my lawful wedded wife.' He tried to make it careless, he kept his eyes off Rose, but the words were weighted with shame.

'No ring?' the registrar asked sharply.

'We don't need any ring,' the Boy said. 'This isn't a church,' feeling he could never now rid his memory of the cold green room and the glassy face. He heard Rose repeating by his side: 'I call upon these persons here present to witness . . .' and then the word 'husband', and he looked sharply up at her. If there had been any complacency in her face then he would have struck it. But there was only surprise as if she were reading a book and had come to the last page too soon.

The registrar said, 'You sign here. The charge is seven and sixpence.' He wore an air of official unconcern while Mr Prewitt fumbled.

'These persons,' the Boy said and laughed brokenly. 'That's you, Prewitt and Dallow.' He took the pen and the Government nib scratched into the page, gathering fur; in the old days, it occurred to him, you signed covenants like this in your blood. He stood back and watched Rose awkwardly sign – his temporal safety in return for two immortalities of pain. He had no doubt whatever that this was mortal sin, and he was filled with a kind of gloomy hilarity and pride. He saw himself now as a full grown man for whom the angels wept.

'These persons,' he repeated, ignoring the registrar altogether. 'Come and have a drink.'

'Well,' Mr Prewitt said, 'that's a surprise from you.'

'Oh, Dallow will tell you,' the Boy said, 'I'm a drinking man these days.' He looked across at Rose. 'There's nothing I'm not now,' he said. He took her by the elbow and led the way out to the tiled passage and the big stairs: the mop was gone and somebody had picked up the flower. A couple rose as they came out: the market was firm. He said, 'That was a wedding. Can you beat it? We're' – he meant to say 'husband and wife', but his mind flinched from the defining phrase. 'We got to celebrate,' he said, and like an old relation you can always trust for the tactless word his brain beat on – 'celebrate what?' and he thought of the girl sprawling in the Lancia and the long night coming down.

They went to the pub round the corner. It was nearly closing time, and he stood them pints of bitter and Rose took a port. She hadn't spoken since the registrar had given her the words to say. Mr Prewitt took a quick look round and parked his portfolio. With his dark striped trousers he might really have been at a wedding. 'Here's to the bride,' he said with a jocularity which petered unobtrusively out. It was as if he had tried to crack a joke with a magistrate and scented a rebuff: the old face recomposed itself quickly on serious lines. He said reverently, 'To your happiness, my dear.'

She didn't answer; she was looking at her own face in a glass marked Extra Stout: in the new setting with a foreground of beer handles, it was a strange face. It seemed to carry an enormous weight of responsibility.

'A penny for your thoughts,' Dallow said to her. The Boy put the glass of bitter to his mouth and tasted for the second time – the nausea of other people's pleasures stuck in his throat. He watched her sourly as she gazed wordlessly back at his companions; and again he was sensible of how she completed him. *He* knew her thoughts: they beat unregarded in his own nerves. He said with triumphant venom, 'I can tell you what she's thinking of. Not much of a wedding, she's thinking. She's thinking – it's not what I pictured. That's right, isn't it?'

She nodded, holding the glass of port as if she hadn't learned the way to drink.

'With my body I thee worship,' he began to quote at her, 'with all my worldly goods ... and then,' he said, turning to Mr Prewitt, 'I give her a gold piece.'

'Time, gentlemen,' the barman said, swilling not quite empty glasses into the lead trough, mopping with a yeasty cloth.

'We're up in the sanctuary, do you see, with the priest. ...'

'Drink up, gentlemen.'

Mr Prewitt said uneasily, 'One wedding's as good as another in the eyes of the law.' He nodded encouragingly at the girl who watched them all with famished immature eyes. 'You're married all right. Trust me.'

'Married?' the Boy said. 'Do you call that married?' He screwed up the beery spittle on his tongue.

'Easy on,' Dallow said. 'Give the girl a chance. You don't need to go too far.'

'Come along, gentlemen, empty your glasses.'

'Married?' the Boy repeated. 'Ask her.' The two men drank up in a shocked furtive way and Mr Prewitt said, 'Well, I'll be getting on.' The Boy regarded them with contempt; they didn't understand a thing, and again he was touched by the sense of communion between himself and Rose – she too knew that this evening meant nothing at all, that there hadn't been a wedding. He said with rough kindness, 'Come on. We'll be going,' and raised a hand to put it on her arm – then saw the double image in the mirror (Extra Stout) and let it fall: a married couple the image winked at him.

'Where?' Rose asked.

Where? he hadn't thought of that – you had to take them somewhere – the honeymoon, the week-end at the sea, the present from Margate on the mantelpiece his mother'd had; from one sea to another, a change of pier.

'I'll be seeing you,' Dallow said. He paused a moment at the door, met the Boy's eye, the question, the appeal, understood nothing, and sloped away cheerily waving after Mr Prewitt, leaving them alone.

It was as if they'd never been alone before in spite of the barman drying the glasses: not really alone in the room at Snow's, nor above the sea at Peacehaven – not alone as they were now.

'We'd better be off,' Rose said.

They stood on the pavement and heard the door of the 'Crown' closed and locked behind them – a bolt grind into place; they felt as if they were shut off from an Eden of ignorance. On this side there was nothing to look forward to but experience.

'Are we going to Frank's?' the girl asked. It was one of those moments of sudden silence that falls on the busiest afternoon: not a tram bell, not a cry of steam from the terminus: a flock of birds shot up together into the air above Old Steyne and hovered there as if a crime had been committed on the ground. He thought with nostalgia of the room at Frank's – he knew exactly where to put his hand for money in the soap-dish; everything was familiar; nothing strange there; it shared his bitter virginity.

'No,' he said and again, as noise come back, the clang and crash of afternoon, 'No.'

'Where?'

He smiled with hopeless malice – where did you bring a swell blonde to if not to the Cosmopolitan, coming down by Pullman at the week-end, driving over the downs in a scarlet roadster? Expensive scent and furs, sailing like a new-painted pinnace into the restaurant, something to swank about in return for the nocturnal act. He absorbed Rose's shabbiness like a penance in a long look. 'We'll take a suite,' he said, 'at the Cosmopolitan.'

'No, but where – really?'

'You heard me – the Cosmopolitan.' He flared up. 'Don't you think I'm good enough?'

'You are,' she said, 'but I'm not.'

'We're going there,' he said. 'I can afford it. It's the right place. There was a woman called – Eugeen used to go there. That's why they have crowns on the chairs.'

'Who was she?'

'A foreign polony.'

'Have you been there, then?'

'Of course I've been there.'

Suddenly she put her hands together in an excited gesture. 'I dreamed,' she said and then looked sharply up to see if he was only mocking after all.

He said airily, 'The car's being repaired. We'll walk and send them round for my bag. Where's yours?'

'My what?'

'Your bag.'

'It was so broken, dirty . . .'

'Never mind,' he said with desperate swagger, 'we'll buy you another. Where's your things?'

'Things. . . .'

'Christ, how dumb you are,' he said. 'I mean . . .' but the thought of the night ahead froze his tongue. He drove on down the pavement, the afternoon waning on his face.

She said, 'There was nothing . . . nothing I could marry you in only this. I asked them for a little money. They wouldn't give it me. They'd a right. It was theirs.'

They walked a foot apart along the pavement. Her words scratched tentatively at the barrier like a bird's claws on a window-pane. He could feel her all the time trying to get at him: even her humility seemed to him a trap. The crude quick ceremony was a claim on him. *She* didn't know the reason; she thought – God save the mark – he wanted her. He said roughly, 'You needn't think there's going to be a honeymoon. That nonsense. I'm busy. I've got things to do. I've got . . .' He stopped and turned to her with a kind of scared appeal – let this make no difference, 'I got to be away a lot.'

'I'll wait,' she said. He could already see the patience of the poor and the long-married working up under her skin like a second personality, a modest and shameless figure behind a transparency.

They came out on to the front and evening stood back a pace; the sea dazzled the eyes; she watched it with pleasure as if it was a different sea. He said, 'What did your Dad say to-day?'

'He didn't say a thing. He'd got a mood.'

'And the old woman?'

'She had a mood too.'

'They took the money all right.'

They came to a halt on the front opposite the Cosmopolitan and under its enormous bulk moved a few inches closer. He remembered the pageboy calling a name and Colleoni's gold cigarette case. . . . He said slowly and carefully, shutting uneasiness out, 'Well, we oughter be comfortable there.' He put a hand up to his withered tie, straightened his jacket and set unconvincingly his narrow shoulders. 'Come on.' She followed a pace behind, across the road, up the wide steps. Two old ladies sat on the terrace in wicker chairs in the sun, wrapped round and round with veils. They had an absolute air of security: when they spoke they didn't look at each other, just quietly dropped their remarks into the understanding air. 'Now Willie . . .' 'I always liked Willie.' The Boy made an unnecessary noise coming up the steps.

He walked across the deep pile to the reception desk, Rose just behind him. There was nobody there. He waited furiously – it was a personal insult. A page called 'Mr Pinecoffin. Mr Pinecoffin' across the lounge. The Boy waited. A telephone rang. When the entrance door swung again they could hear one of the old ladies say, 'It was a great blow to Basil.' Then a man in a black coat appeared and said, 'Can I do anything for you?'

The Boy said furiously: 'I've been waiting here . . .'

'You could have touched the bell,' the clerk said coldly and opened a large register.

'I want a room,' the Boy said. 'A double room.'

The clerk stared past him at Rose, then turned a page. 'We haven't a room free,' he said.

'I don't mind what I pay,' the Boy said. 'I'll take a suite.'

'There's nothing vacant,' the clerk said without looking up.

The pageboy, returning with a salver, paused and watched. The Boy said in a low furious voice, 'You can't keep me out of here. My money's as good as anybody else's. . . .'

'No doubt,' the clerk said, 'but there happens to be no room free.' He turned his back and picked up a jar of Stickphast.

'Come on,' the Boy said to Rose, 'this kip stinks.' He strode back down the steps, past the old ladies; tears of humiliation pricked behind his eyes. He had an insane impulse to shout out to them all that they couldn't treat him like that, that he was a killer, he could kill men and not be caught. He wanted to boast. He could afford that place as well as anyone: he had a car, a lawyer, two hundred pounds in the bank . . .

Rose said, 'If I'd had a ring . . .'

He said furiously, 'A ring . . . what sort of a ring? We aren't married. Don't forget that. We aren't married.' But outside on the pavement he restrained himself with immense difficulty and remembered bitterly that he still had a part to play – they couldn't make a wife give evidence, but nothing could prevent a wife except – love, lust he thought with sour horror, and turning back to her he unconvincingly apologised. 'They get me angry,' he said. 'You see I'd promised you—'

'I don't care,' she said. Suddenly with wide astonished eyes she made the foolhardy claim, 'Nothing can spoil to-day.'

'We got to find somewhere,' he said.

'I don't mind where – Frank's?'

'Not to-night,' he said. 'I don't want any of the boys around to-night.'

'We'll think of a place,' she said. 'It's not dark yet.'

These were the hours – when the races were not on, when there was no one to see on business – that he spent stretched on the bed at Frank's. He'd eat a packet of chocolate or a sausage roll, watch the sun shift from the chimney-pots, fall asleep and wake and eat again and sleep with the dark coming in through the window. Then the boys would return with the evening papers and life would start again. Now he was at a loss; he didn't know how to spend so much time when he wasn't alone.

'One day,' she said, 'let's go into the country like we did that time . . .' Staring out to sea she planned ahead . . . he could see the years advancing before her eyes like the line of the tide.

'Anything you say,' he said.

'Let's go on the pier,' she said. 'I haven't been since we went that night – you remember?'

'Nor've I,' he lied quickly and smoothly, thinking of Spicer and the dark and the lightning on the sea – the beginning of something of which he couldn't see the end. They went through the turnstile; there were a lot of people about: a row of anglers watched their floats in the thick green swell: the water moved under their feet.

'Do you know that girl?' Rose asked. The Boy turned his head apathetically. 'Where?' he said. 'I don't know any girls in this place.'

'There,' Rose said. 'I bet she's talking about you.'

The fat stupid spotty face swam back into his memory, nuzzled the glass like some monstrous fish in the Aquarium – dangerous – a sting-ray from another ocean. Fred had spoken to her and he had come up to them upon the front: she'd given evidence – he couldn't remember what she had said – nothing important. Now she watched him, nudged her pasty girl friend, spoke of him, told he didn't know what lies. Christ! he thought, had he got to massacre a world?

'*She* knows you,' Rose said.

'I've never seen her,' he lied, walking on.

Rose said, 'It's wonderful being with you. Everyone knows you. I never thought I'd marry someone famous.'

Who next, he thought, who next? An angler drew back across their path to make his cast, whirling his line, dropped it far out; the float was caught in the cream of a wave and drove a line's length towards the shore. It was cold on the sunless side of the pier; on one side of the glass division it was day: on the other evening advanced. 'Let's cross over,' he said. He began to think again of Spicer's girl: why had he left her in the car? God damn it, after all, she knew the game.

Rose stopped him. 'Look,' she said, 'won't you give me one of those? As a souvenir. They don't cost much,' she said, 'only sixpence.' It was a small glass box like a telephone cabinet. 'Make a record of your own voice,' the legend ran.

'Come on,' he said. 'Don't be soft. What's the good of that?'

For the second time he came up against her sudden irresponsible resentment. She was soft, she was dumb, she was sentimental – and then suddenly she was dangerous. About a hat, about a gramophone record. 'All right,' she said, 'go away. You've never given me a thing. Not even to-day you haven't. If you won't want me why don't you go away? Why don't you leave me alone?' People turned and looked at them – at his acid and angry face, at her hopeless resentment. 'What do you want me for?' she cried at him.

'For Christ's sake . . .' he said.

'I'd rather drown,' she began, but he interrupted her, 'You can have your record.' He smiled nervously. 'I just thought you were crazy,' he said. 'What do you want to hear me on a record for? Aren't you going to hear me every day?' He squeezed her arm. 'You're a good kid. I don't grudge you things. You can have anything you say.' He thought: she's got me where she wants . . . how long? 'You didn't mean those things now, did you?' he wheedled her. His face crinkled in the effort of amiability like an old man's.

'Something came over me,' she said, avoiding his eyes with an expression he couldn't read, obscure and despairing.

He felt relieved, but reluctant. He didn't like the idea of putting anything on a record: it reminded him of finger-prints. 'Do you really,' he said, 'want me to get one of those things? We haven't got a gramophone anyway. You won't be able to hear it. What's the good?'

'I don't want a gramophone,' she said 'I just want to have it there. Perhaps one day you might be away somewhere and I could borrow a gramophone. And you'd speak,' she said with a sudden intensity that scared him.

'What do you want me to say?'

'Just anything,' she said. 'Say something to me. Say Rose and – something.'

He went into the box and closed the door. There was a slot for his sixpence: a mouthpiece: an instruction, 'Speak clearly and close to the instrument'. The scientific paraphernalia made him nervous. He looked over his shoulder and there outside she was watching him, without a smile. He saw her as a stranger: a shabby child from Nelson Place, and he was shaken by an appalling resentment. He put in a sixpence, and, speaking in a low voice for fear it might carry beyond the box, he gave his message up to be graven on vulcanite: 'God damn you, you little bitch, why can't you go back home for ever and let me be?' He heard the needle scratch and the record whirr: then a click and silence.

Carrying the black disc he came out to her. 'Here,' he said, 'take it. I put something on it – loving.'

She took it from him carefully, carried it like something to be defended from the crowd. Even on the sunny side of the pier it was getting cold, and the cold fell between them lika an unanswerable statement – you'd better be getting home now. He had the sense of playing truant from his proper work – he should be at school, but he hadn't learned his lesson. They passed through the turnstile, and he watched her out of the corner of an eye to see what she expected now. If she had shown any excitement he would have slapped her face. But she hugged the record as chilled as he.

'Well,' he said, 'we got to go somewhere.'

She pointed down the steps to the covered walk under the pier. 'Let's go there,' she said, 'it's sheltered there.'

The Boy looked sharply round at her; it was as if deliberately she had offered him an ordeal. For a moment he hesitated: then he grinned at her. 'All right,' he said, 'we'll go *there*.' He was moved by a kind of sensuality: the coupling of good and evil.

In the trees of the Old Steyne the fairy lights were switched on – it was too early, their pale colours didn't show in the last of the day. The long tunnel under the parade was the noisiest, lowest, cheapest section of Brighton's amusements. Children rushed past them in paper sailor-caps marked 'I'm no Angel'; a ghost train rattled by carrying courting couples into a squealing and shrieking darkness. All the way along the landward side of the tunnel were the amusements; on the other little shops: Magpie Ices, Photoweigh, Shellfish, Rocko. The shelves rose to the ceiling: little doors let you in to the obscurity behind, and on the sea side there were no doors at all, no windows, nothing but shelf after shelf from the pebbles to the roof: a breakwater of Brighton rock facing the sea. The lights were always on in the tunnel; the air was warm and thick and poisoned with human breath.

'Well,' the Boy said, 'what's it to be – winkles or Brighton rock?' He watched her as if something important really depended on her answer.

'I'd like a stick of Brighton rock,' she said.

Again he grinned: only the devil, he thought, could have made her answer that. She was good, but he'd got her like you got God in the Eucharist – in the guts. God couldn't escape the evil mouth which chose to eat its own damnation. He padded across to a doorway and looked in. 'Miss,' he said. 'Miss. Two sticks of rock.' He looked around the little pink barred cell as if he owned it; his memory owned it, it was stamped with footmarks, a particular patch of floor had eternal importance: if the cash register had been moved he'd have noticed it. 'What's that?' he asked and nodded at a box, the only unfamiliar object there.

'It's broken rock,' she said, 'going cheap.'

'From the maker's?'

'No. It got broken. Some clumsy fools—' she complained. 'I wish I knew who . . .'

He took the sticks and turned: he knew what he would see – nothing: the promenade was shut out behind the rows of Brighton rock. He had a momentary sense of his own immense cleverness. 'Good-night,' he said, stooped in the little doorway and went out. If only one could boast of one's cleverness, relieve the enormous pressure of pride . . .

They stood side by side sucking their sticks of rock: a woman bustled them to one side. 'Out of the way, you children.' Their glances met: a married couple.

'Where now?' he asked uneasily.

'Perhaps we ought to find – somewhere,' she said.

'There's not all that hurry.' His voice caught a little with anxiety. 'It's early yet. Like a movie?' He wheedled her again. 'I've never took you to a movie.'

But the sense of power left him. Again her passionate assent – 'You're good to me' – repelled him.

Slumped grimly in the three and sixpenny seat, in the half-dark, he asked himself crudely and bitterly what she was hoping for: beside the screen an illuminated clock marked the hour. It was a romantic film: magnificent features, thighs shot with studied care, esoteric beds shaped like winged coracles. A man was killed, but that didn't matter. What mattered was the game. The two main characters made their stately progress towards the bed-sheets: 'I loved you that first time in Santa Monica. . . .' A song under a window, a girl in a nightdress and the clock beside the screen moving on. He whispered suddenly, furiously, to Rose, 'Like cats.' It was the commonest game under the sun – why be scared at what the dogs did in the streets? The music moaned – 'I know in my heart you're divine'. He whispered, 'Maybe we'd better go to Frank's after all,' thinking: we won't be alone there: something may happen: maybe the boys will have drinks: maybe they'll celebrate – there won't be any bed for anyone to-night. The actor with a lick of black hair across a white waste of face said, 'You're mine. All mine.' He sang again under the restless stars in a wash of incredible moonshine, and suddenly, inexplicably, the Boy began to weep. He shut his eyes to hold in his tears, but the music went on – it was like a vision of release to an imprisoned man. He felt constriction and saw – hopelessly out of reach – a limitless freedom: no fear, no hatred, no envy. It was as if he were dead and were remembering the effect of a good confession, the words of absolution: but being dead it was a memory only – he couldn't experience contrition – the ribs of his body were like steel bands which held him down to eternal unrepentance. He said at last, 'Let's go. We'd better go.'

It was quite dark now: the coloured lights were on all down the Hove front. They walked slowly past Snow's, past the Cosmopolitan. An aeroplane flying low burred out to sea, a red light vanishing. In one of the glass shelters an old man struck a match to light his pipe and showed a man and girl cramped in the corner. A wail of music came off the sea. They turned up through Norfolk Square towards Montpellier Road: a blonde with Garbo cheeks paused to powder on the steps up to the Norfolk bar. A bell tolled somewhere for someone dead and a gramophone in a basement played a hymn. 'Maybe,' the Boy said, 'after to-night we'll find some place to go.'

He had his latchkey but he rang the bell. He wanted people, talk . . . but no one answered. He rang again. It was one of those old bells you have to pull: it jangled on the end of its wire: the kind of bell that knows from long experience of dust and spiders and untenanted rooms how to convey that a house is empty. 'They can't 'ave all gone out,' he said, slipped in his latchkey.

A globe had been left burning in the hall. He saw at once the note stuck under the telephone – 'Two's company,' he recognized the drab and sprawling hand of Frank's wife. 'We gone out to celebrate the wedding. Lock your door. Have a good time.' He crumpled the paper up and dropped it on the linoleum. 'Come on,' he said, 'upstairs.' At the top he put his hand on the new banister rail and said, 'You see. We got it mended.' A smell of cabbages and cooking and burnt cloth hung about the dark passage. He nodded – 'That was old Spicer's room. Do you believe in ghosts?'

'I don't know.'

He pushed open his own door and switched on the naked dusty light. 'There,' he said, 'take it or leave it,' and drew aside to expose the big brass bed, the washstand and chipped ewer, the varnished wardrobe with its cheap glass front.

'It's better than a hotel,' she said, 'it's more like home.'

They stood in the middle of the room as if they didn't know what their next move should be. She said, 'Tomorrow I'll tidy up a bit.'

He banged the door to. 'You won't touch a thing,' he said. 'It's my home, do you hear? I won't have you coming in, changing things. . . .' He watched her with fear – to come into your own room, your cave, and find a strange thing there. . . . 'Why don't you take off your hat?' he said. 'You're staying, aren't you?' She took off her hat, her mackintosh – this was the ritual of mortal sin: this, he thought, was what people damned each other for . . . The bell in the hall clanged. He paid it no attention. 'It's Saturday night,' he said with a bitter taste on his tongue, 'it's time for bed.'

'Who is it?' she asked, and the bell jangled again – its unmistakable message to whoever was outside that the house was no longer empty. She came across the room to him, her face was white. 'Is it the police?' she said.

'Why should it be the police? Some friend of Frank's.' But the suggestion startled him. He stood and waited for the clang. It didn't come again. 'Well,' he said, 'we can't stand here all night. We better get to bed.' He felt an appalling emptiness as if he hadn't fed for days. He tried to pretend, taking off his jacket and hanging it over a chair back, that everything was as usual. When he turned she hadn't moved: a thin and half-grown child she trembled between the washstand and the bed. 'Why,' he mocked her with a dry mouth, 'you're scared.' It was as if he had gone back four years and was taunting a schoolfellow into some offence.

'Aren't you scared?' Rose said.

'Me.' He laughed at her unconvincingly and advanced: an embryo of sensuality – he was mocked by the memory of a gown, a back, 'I loved you that first time in Santa Monica. . . .' Shaken by a kind of rage, he took her by the shoulders. He had escaped from Nelson Place to this: he pushed her against the bed. 'It's mortal sin,' he said, getting what savour there was out of innocence, trying to taste God in the mouth: a brass bedball, her dumb, frightened and acquiescent eyes – he blotted everything out in a sad brutal now-or-never embrace: a cry of pain and then the jangling of the bell beginning all over again. 'Christ,' he said, 'can't they let a man alone?' He opened his eyes on the grey room to see what he had done: it seemed to him more like death than when Hale and Spicer had died.

Rose said, 'Don't go. Pinkie, don't go.'

He had an odd sense of triumph: he had graduated in the last human shame – it wasn't so difficult after all. He had exposed himself and nobody had laughed. He didn't need Mr Prewitt or Spicer, only – a faint feeling of tenderness woke for his partner in the act. He put out a hand and pinched the lobe of her ear. The bell clanged in the empty hall. An enormous weight seemed to have lifted. He could face anyone now. He said, 'I'd better see what the bugger wants.'

'Don't go. I'm scared, Pinkie.'

But he had a sense that he would never be scared again. Running down from the track he had been afraid, afraid of pain and more afraid of damnation – of the sudden and unshriven death. Now it was as if he was damned already and there was nothing more to fear ever again. The ugly bell clattered, the long wire humming in the hall, and the bare globe burnt above the bed – the girl, the washstand, the sooty window, the blank shape of a chimney, a voice whispered, 'I love you, Pinkie.' This was hell then; it wasn't anything to worry about: it was just his own familiar room. He said, 'I'll be back. Don't worry. I'll be back.'

At the head of the stairs he put his hand on the new unpainted wood of the mended banister. He pushed it gently and saw how firm it was. He wanted to crow at his own cleverness. The bell shook below him. He looked down: it was a long drop, but you couldn't really be certain that a man from that height would be killed. The thought had never occurred to him before, but men sometimes lived for hours with broken backs, and he knew an old man who went about to this day with a cracked skull which clicked in cold weather when he sneezed. He had a sense of being befriended. The bell jangled: it knew he was at home. He went on down the stairs, his toes catching in the worn linoleum – he was too good for this place. He felt an invincible energy – he hadn't lost vitality upstairs, he'd gained it. What he had lost was a fear. He hadn't an idea who stood outside the door, but he was seized by a sense of wicked amusement. He put up his hand to the old bell and held it silent: he could feel the pull at the wire. An odd tug of war went on with the stranger down the length of the hall, and the Boy won. The pull ceased and a hand beat at the door. The Boy released the bell and moved softly towards the door, but immediately behind his back the bell began to clap again, cracked and hollow and urgent. A ball of paper – 'Lock your door. Have a good time' – scuffled at his toes.

He swung the door boldly open, and there was Cubitt, Cubitt hopelessly and drearily drunk. Somebody had blacked his eye and his breath was sour: drink always upset his digestion.

The Boy's sense of triumph increased: he felt an immeasurable victory. 'Well,' he said, 'what do *you* want?'

'I got my things here,' Cubitt said. 'I want to get my things.'

'Come in and get 'em then,' the Boy said.

Cubitt sidled in. He said, 'I didn't think I'd see you . . .'

'Go on,' the Boy said. 'Get your things and clear out.'

'Where's Dallow?'

The Boy didn't answer.

'Frank?'

Cubitt cleared his throat: his sour breath reached the Boy. 'Look here, Pinkie,' he said, 'you and me – why shouldn't we be friends? Like we always was.'

'*We* were never friends,' the Boy said.

Cubitt took no notice. He got his back to the telephone and watched the Boy with his drunken and cautious eyes. 'You an' me,' he said, the sour phlegm rising in his throat and thickening every word, 'you an' me can't get on separate. Why,' he said, 'we're kind of brothers. We're tied together.'

The Boy watched him, standing against the opposite wall.

'You an' me – it's what I said. We can't get on separate,' Cubitt repeated.

'I suppose,' the Boy said, 'Colleoni wouldn't touch you – not with a stick, but I'm not taking his leavings, Cubitt.'

Cubitt began to weep a little. It was a stage he always reached: the Boy could measure his glasses by his tears: they squeezed reluctantly out, two tears like drops of spirits oozed out of the yellow eyeballs. 'You've no cause to take on like that,' he said, 'Pinkie.'

'You better get your things.'

'Where's Dallow?'

'He's out,' the Boy said. 'They're all out.' The spirit of cruel mischief moved again. 'We're quite alone, Cubitt,' he said. He glanced down the hall at the new patch of linoleum over the place where Spicer had fallen. But it didn't work: the stage of tears was transitory – what came after was sullenness, anger. . . .

Cubitt said, 'You can't treat me like dirt.'

'That how Colleoni treated you?'

'I came here to be friendly,' Cubitt said. 'You can't afford not to be friendly.'

'I can afford more than you'd think,' the Boy said.

Cubitt took him quickly up. 'Lend me five nicker.'

The Boy shook his head. He was shaken by sudden impatience and pride: he was worth more than this – this squabble on worn linoleum under the bare and dusty globe with Cubitt. 'For Christ's sake,' he said, 'get your things and clear out.'

'I've got things I could tell about you . . .'

'Nothing.'

'Fred . . .'

'You'd hang,' the Boy said. He grinned. 'But not me. I'm too young to hang.'

'There's Spicer too.'

'Spicer fell down there.'

'I heard you . . .'

'You heard me? Who's going to believe that?'

'Dallow heard.'

'Dallow's all right,' the Boy said. 'I can trust Dallow. Why, Cubitt,' he went quietly on, 'if you were dangerous, I'd do something about you. But thank your lucky stars you aren't dangerous.' He turned his back on Cubitt and mounted the stairs. He could hear Cubitt behind him – panting; he had no wind.

'I didn't come here to give hard words. Lend me a couple of nicker, Pinkie. I'm broke.'

The Boy didn't answer – 'For the sake of old times' – turned off at the bend of the stairs to his own room.

Cubitt said, 'Wait a moment and I'll tell you a thing or two, you bloody little geezer. There's someone'll give me money – twenty nicker. You – why you – I'll tell you what you are.'

The Boy stopped in front of his door. 'Go on,' he said, 'tell me.'

Cubitt struggled to speak. He hadn't got the right words. He flung his rage and resentment away in phrases light as paper. 'You're mean,' he said, 'you're yellow. You're so yellow you'd kill your best friend to save your own skin. Why' – he laughed thickly – 'you're scared of a girl. Sylvie told me' – but that accusation had come too late. He had graduated now in knowledge of the last human weakness. He listened with amusement, with a kind of infernal pride. The picture Cubitt drew had got nothing to do with him: it was like the pictures men drew of Christ, the image of their own sentimentality. Cubitt couldn't know. He was like a professor describing to a stranger some place he had only read about in books: statistics of imports and exports, tonnage and mineral resources and if the budget balanced, when all the time it was a country the stranger *knew* from thirsting in the desert and being shot at in the foothills. Mean . . . yellow . . . scared: he laughed gently with derision. It was as if he had outsoared the shadow of any night Cubitt could be aware of. He opened his door, went in, closed it and locked it.

Rose sat on the bed with dangling feet like a child in a classroom waiting for a teacher in order to say her lesson. Outside the door Cubitt swore and hacked with his foot, rattled the handle and moved off. She said with immense relief – she was used to drunken men, 'Oh, then it's not the police.'

'Why should it be the police?'

'I don't know,' she said, 'I thought maybe—'

'Maybe what?'

He could only just catch her answer. 'Kolley Kibber.'

For a moment he was amazed. Then he laughed softly with infinite contempt and superiority at a world which used words like innocence. 'Why,' he said, 'that's rich. You knew all along. You guessed. And I thought you were so green you hadn't lost the eggshell. And there you were' – he built her up in the mind's eye that day at Peacehaven, among the harvest wines at Snow's – 'there you were, knowing.'

She didn't deny it: sitting there with her hands locked between her knees she accepted everything. 'It's rich,' he said. 'Why, when you come to think of it – you're as bad as me.' He came across the room and added with a kind of respect, 'There's not a pin to choose between us.'

She looked up with childish devoted eyes and swore solemnly, 'Not a pin.'

He felt desire move again, like nausea in the belly. 'What a wedding night,' he said, 'did you think a wedding night would be like this?' . . . the piece of gold in the palm, the kneeling in the sanctuary, the blessing . . . footsteps in the passage, Cubitt pounded on the door, pounded and lurched away, the stairs creaked, a door slammed. She made her vow again, holding him in her arms, in the attitude of mortal sin, 'Nothing to choose.'

The Boy lay on his back – in his shirt-sleeves – and dreamed. He was in an asphalt playground: one plane tree withered: a cracked bell clanged and the children came out to him. He was new: he knew no one: he was sick with fear – they came towards him with a purpose. Then he felt a cautious hand on his sleeve and in a mirror hanging on the tree he saw the reflection of himself and Kite behind – middle-aged, cheery, bleeding from the mouth. 'Such tits,' Kite said and put a razor in his hand. He knew then what to do: they only needed to be taught once that he would stop at nothing, that there were no rules.

He flung out his arm in a motion of attack, made some indistinguishable comment and turned upon his side. A piece of blanket fell across his mouth; he breathed with difficulty. He was upon the pier and he could see the piles breaking – a black cloud came racing across the channel and the sea rose: the whole pier lurched and settled lower. He tried to scream: no death was so bad as drowning. The deck of the pier lay at a steep angle like that of a liner on the point of its deadly dive; he scrambled up the polished slope away from the sea and slipped again, down and down into his bed in Nelson Place. He lay still thinking, 'What a dream!' and then heard the stealthy movement of his parents in the other bed. It was Saturday night. His father panted like a man at the end of a race and his mother made a horrifying sound of pleasurable pain. He was filled with hatred, disgust, loneliness: he was completely abandoned: he had no share in their thoughts – for the space of a few minutes he was dead, he was like a soul in purgatory watching the shameless act of a beloved person.

Then quite suddenly he opened his eyes, it was as if the nightmare couldn't go further. It was black night, he could see nothing and for a few seconds he believed he was in Nelson Place. Then a clock struck three, clashing close by like the lid of a dustbin in the backyard, and he remembered with immense relief that he was alone. He got out of bed in his half drowse (his mouth was clotted and evil-tasting) and felt his way to the washstand. He took up his tooth-mug, poured out a glass of water and heard a voice say, 'Pinkie? What is it, Pinkie?' He dropped the glass and as the water spilt across his feet he bitterly remembered.

He said cautiously into the dark, 'It's all right. Go to sleep.' He no longer had a sense of triumph or superiority. He looked back on a few hours ago as if he had been drunk then or dreaming – he had been momentarily exhilarated by the strangeness of his experience. Now there would be nothing strange ever again – he was awake. You had to treat these things with commonsense – she knew. The darkness thinned before his wakeful and calculating gaze – he could see the outline of the bedknobs and a chair. He had won a move and lost a move: they couldn't *make* her give evidence, but she knew . . . She loved him whatever that meant, but love was not an eternal thing like hatred and disgust. They saw a better face, a smarter suit . . . The truth came home to him with horror that he had got to keep her love for a lifetime; he would never be able to discard her. If he climbed he had to take Nelson Place with him like a visible scar; the registry office marriage was as irrevocable as a sacrament. Only death could ever set him free.

He was taken by a craving for air, walked softly to the door. In the passage he could see nothing: it was full of the low sound of breathing – from the room he had left, from Dallow's room. He felt like a blind man watched by people he couldn't see. He felt his way to the stairhead and on down to the hall, step by step, creakingly. He put out his hand and touched the telephone, then with his arm outstretched made for the door. In the street the lamps were out, but the darkness no longer enclosed between four walls seemed to thin out across the vast expanse of a city. He could see basement railings, a cat moving, and, reflected on the dark sky, the phosphorescent glow of the sea. It was a strange world: he had never been alone in it before. He had a deceptive sense of freedom as he walked softly down towards the Channel.

The lights were on in Montpellier Road. Nobody was about, and an empty milk bottle stood outside a gramophone shop; far down were the illuminated clock tower and the public lavatories. The air was fresh like country air. He could imagine he had escaped. He put his hands for warmth into his trouser-pockets and felt a scrap of paper which should not have been there. He drew it out – a scrap torn from a notebook – big, unformed, stranger's writing. He held it up into the grey light and read – with difficulty. 'I love you, Pinkie. I don't care what you do. I love you for ever. You've been good to me. Wherever you go, I'll go too.' She must have written it while he talked to Cubitt and slipped it into his pocket while he slept. He crumpled it in his fist: a dustbin stood outside a fishmonger's – then he held his hand. An obscure sense told him you never knew – it might prove useful one day.

He heard a whisper, looked sharply round, and thrust the paper back. In an alley between two shops, an old woman sat upon the ground; he could just see the rotting and discoloured face: it was like the sight of damnation. Then he heard the whisper, 'Blessed art thou among women,' saw the grey fingers fumbling at the beads. This was not one of the damned: he watched with horrified fascination: this was one of the saved.

BOOK SEVEN

Chapter One

It did not seem in the least strange to Rose that she should wake alone – she was a stranger in the country of mortal sin, and she assumed that everything was customary. He was, she supposed, about his business. No alarm-clock dinned her to get up, but the morning light woke her, pouring through the uncurtained glass. Once she heard footsteps in the passage, and once a voice called 'Judy' imperatively. She lay there wondering what a wife had to do – or rather a mistress.

But she didn't lie long – that was frightening, the unusual passivity. It wasn't like life at all – to have nothing to do. Suppose they assumed she knew – about the stove to be lit, the table to be laid, the debris to be cleared away. A clock struck seven; it was an unfamiliar clock (all her life she had lived in hearing of the same one till now), and the strikes seemed to fall more slowly and more sweetly through the early summer air than any she had ever heard before. She felt happy and scared: seven o'clock was a terribly late hour. She scrambled out and was about to mutter her quick 'Our Fathers' and 'Hail Marys' while she dressed, when she remembered again. . . . What was the good of praying now? She'd finished with all that: she had chosen her side: if they damned him they'd got to damn her, too.

In the ewer there was only an inch of water with a grey heavy surface, and when she lifted the lid of the soap-box she found three pound notes wrapped round two half-crowns. She put the lid back: that was just another custom you had to get used to. She took a look round the room, opened a wardrobe and found a tin of biscuits and a pair of boots: some crumbs crunched under her tread. The gramophone record caught her attention on the chair where she'd lain it and she stowed it in the cupboard for greater safety. Then she opened the door: not a sound or sign of life: looked over the banisters, the new wood squeaked under her pressure. Somewhere down below must be the kitchen, the living room, the places where she had to work. She went cautiously down – seven o'clock – what furious faces – in the hall a ball of paper scuffled under her feet. She smoothed it out and read a pencilled message: 'Lock your door. Have a good time.' She didn't understand it: it might as well have been in code – she assumed it must have something to do with this foreign world where you sinned on a bed and people lost their lives suddenly and strange men hacked at your door and cursed you in the night.

She found the basement stairs; they were dark where they dropped under the hall, but she didn't know where to find a switch. Once she nearly tripped and held the wall close with beating heart, remembering the evidence at the inquest, how Spicer had fallen. His death gave the house a feeling of importance: she had never been on the scene of a recent death. At the bottom of the stairs she opened the first door she came to, cautiously, expecting a curse: it was the kitchen all right, but it was empty. It wasn't like either of the kitchens she knew: the one at Snow's clean, polished, busy: the one at home which was just the room where you sat, where people cooked and ate and had moods and warmed themselves on bitter nights and dozed in chairs. This was like the kitchen in a house for sale: the stove was full of cold coke: on the window-sill there were two empty sardine tins: a dirty saucer lay under the table for a cat which wasn't there: a cupboard stood open full of empties.

She went and raked at the dead coke: the stove was cold to the touch: there hadn't been a fire alight there for hours or days. The thought struck her that she'd been deserted: perhaps this was what happened in *this* world, the sudden flight, leaving everything behind, your empty bottles and your girl and the message in code on a scrap of paper. When the door opened she expected a policeman.

It was Dallow in pyjama trousers. He looked in, said, 'Where's Judy?' then seemed to notice her. He said, 'You're up early.'

'Early?' She couldn't understand what he meant.

'I thought it was Judy routing around. You remember me. I'm Dallow.'

She said, 'I thought maybe I'd better light the stove.'

'What for?'

'Breakfast.'

He said, 'If that polony's gone and forgotten—' He went to a dresser and pulled open a drawer. 'Why,' he said, 'what's got you? You don't want a stove. There's plenty here.' Inside the drawer were stacks of tins: sardines, herrings. . . . She said, 'But tea.'

He looked at her oddly. 'Anyone'd think you wanted work. No one here wants any tea. Why take the trouble? There's beer in the cupboard, and Pinkie drinks the milk out of the bottle.' He padded back to the door. 'Help yourself, kid, if you're hungry. Pinkie want anything?'

'He's gone out.'

'Christ's sake, what's come over this house?' He stopped in the doorway and took another look at her as she stood with helpless hands near the dead stove. He said, 'You don't *want* to work, do you?'

'No,' she said doubtfully.

He was puzzled. 'I wouldn't want to stop you,' he said. 'You're Pinkie's girl. You go ahead and light that stove if you want. I'll shut up Judy if she barks, but Christ knows where you'll find the coke. Why, that stove's not been lit since March.'

'I don't want to put anyone out,' Rose said. 'I came down. . . . I thought . . . I'd *got* to light it.'

'You don't need to do a stroke,' Dallow said. 'You take it from me, this is Liberty Hall.' He said, 'You've not seen a bitch with red hair routing around, have you?'

'I haven't seen a soul.'

'Well,' Dallow said, 'I'll be seeing you.' She was alone again in the cold kitchen. Needn't do a stroke . . . Liberty Hall . . . She leant against the whitewashed wall and saw an old flypaper dangling above the dresser; somebody a long time ago had set a mousetrap by a hole, but the bait had been stolen and the trap had snapped on nothing at all. It was a lie when people said that sleeping with a man made no difference: you emerged from pain to this – freedom, liberty, strangeness. A stifled exhilaration moved in her breast, a kind of pride. She opened the kitchen door boldly and there at the head of the basement stairs was Dallow and the red-haired bitch, the woman he'd called Judy. They stood with lips glued together in an attitude of angry passion: they might have been inflicting on each other the greatest injury of which they were either of them capable. The woman wore a mauve dressing-gown with a dusty bunch of paper poppies, the relic of an old November. As they fought mouth to mouth the sweet-toned clock sounded the half-hour. Rose watched them from the foot of the stairs. She had lived years in a night. She knew all about this now.

The woman saw her and took her mouth from Dallow's. 'Well,' she said, 'who's here?'

'It's Pinkie's girl,' Dallow said.

'You're up early. Hungry?'

'No. I just thought – maybe I ought to light the fire.'

'We don't use that fire often,' the woman said. 'Life's too short.' She had little pimples round her mouth and an air of ardent sociability. She stroked her carrot hair and coming down the stairs to Rose fastened a mouth wet and prehensile like a sea anemone upon her cheek. She smelt faintly, stalely, of Californian Poppy. 'Well, dear,' she said, 'you're one of us now,' and she seemed to present to Rose in a generous gesture the half-naked man, the bare dark stairs, the barren kitchen. She whispered softly so that Dallow couldn't hear, 'You won't tell anyone you saw us, dear, will you? Frank gets worked up, an' it don't mean anything, not anything at all.'

Rose dumbly shook her head: this foreign land absorbed her too quickly – no sooner were you past the customs than the naturalization papers were signed, you were conscripted. . . .

'There's a duck,' the woman said. 'Any friend of Pinkie's is a friend of all of us. You'll be meeting the boys before long.'

'I doubt it,' said Dallow from the top of the stairs.

'You mean—'

'We got to talk to Pinkie serious.'

'Did you have Cubitt here last night?' the woman asked.

'I don't know,' Rose said. 'I don't know who anyone is. Someone rang the bell and swore a lot and kicked the door.'

'That was Cubitt,' the woman gently explained.

'We got to talk to Pinkie serious. It's not safe,' Dallow said.

'Well, dear, I'd better be getting back to Frank.' She paused on a step just above Rose. 'If you ever want a dress cleaned, dear, you couldn't do better than give it to Frank. Though I say it who shouldn't. There's no one like Frank for getting out grease marks. An' he hardly charges a thing to lodgers.' She bent down and laid a freckled finger on Rose's shoulder. 'It could do with a sponge now.'

'But I haven't got anything to wear, only this.'

'Oh well, dear, in that case. . . .' She bent and whispered confidentially, 'Make your hubby buy you one,' then gathered the faded dressing-gown around her and loped up the stairs. Rose could see a dead white leg, like something which has lived underground, covered with russet hairs, a dingy slipper flapped a loose heel. It seemed to her that everyone was very kind: there seemed to be a companionship in mortal sin.

Pride swelled in her breast as she came up from the basement. She was accepted. She had experienced as much as any woman. Back in the bedroom she sat on the bed and waited and heard the clock strike eight. She wasn't hungry; she was sensible of an immense freedom – no time-table to keep, no work which had got to be done. You suffered a little pain and then came out on the other side to this amazing liberty. There was only one thing she wanted now – to let others see her happiness. She could walk into Snow's now like any other customer, rap the table with a spoon and demand service. She could boast . . . It was a fantasy, but sitting on the bed while time drifted by it became an idea, something she was really able to do. In less than half an hour they would be opening for breakfast. If she had the money . . . She brooded with her eyes on the soap-dish. She thought: after all we are married – in a way; he's given me nothing but that record: he wouldn't grudge me half a crown. She stood up and listened, then walked softly over to the washstand. With her fingers on the lid of the soap-dish she waited – somebody was coming down the passage: it wasn't Judy and it wasn't Dallow – perhaps it was the man they called Frank. The footsteps passed; she lifted the lid and unwrapped the half-crown. She had stolen biscuits, she had never stolen money before. She expected to feel shame, but it didn't come – only again the odd swell of pride. She was like a child in a new school who finds she can pick up the esoteric games and passwords in the cement playground, at once, by instinct.

In the world outside it was Sunday – she'd forgotten that: the church bells reminded her, shaking over Brighton. Freedom again in the early sun, freedom from the silent prayers at the altar, from the awful demands made on you at the sanctuary rail. She had joined the other side now for ever. The half-crown was like a medal for services rendered. People coming back from seven-thirty Mass, people on the way to eight-thirty Matins – she watched them in their dark clothes like a spy. She didn't envy them and she didn't despise them: they had their salvation and she had Pinkie and damnation.

At Snow's the blinds had just gone up; a girl she knew called Maisie was laying a few tables – the only girl she cared about, a new girl like herself and not much older. She watched her from the pavement – and Doris, the senior waitress with her habitual sneer, doing nothing at all except flick a duster where Maisie had already been. Rose clutched the half-crown closer; well, she had only got to go in, sit down, tell Doris to fetch her a cup of coffee and a roll, tip her a couple of coppers – she could patronize the whole lot of them. She was married. She was a woman. She was happy. What would they feel like when they saw her coming through the door?

And she didn't go in. That was the trouble. How would she feel, flaunting her freedom? Then through the pane she caught Maisie's eye; she stood there with a duster staring back, bony, immature, like her own image in a mirror. And *she* stood now where Pinkie had stood – outside, looking in. This was what the priests meant by one flesh. And just as she days ago had motioned, Maisie motioned – a slant of the eyes, an imperceptible nod towards the side door. There was no reason at all why she shouldn't go in at the front, but she obeyed Maisie. It was like doing something you'd done before.

The door opened and Maisie was there. 'Rose, what's wrong?' She ought to have had wounds to show: she felt guilty at having only happiness. 'I thought I'd come,' she said, 'and see you. I'm married.'

'Married?'

'Kind of.'

'Oh, Rose, what's it like?'

'Lovely.'

'You got rooms?'

'Yes.'

'What do you do all day?'

'Nothing at all. Just lie about.'

The childish face in front of her took on the wrinkled expression of grief. 'God, Rosie, you're lucky. Where did you meet him?'

'Here.'

A hand bonier than her own seized her by the wrist: 'Oh, Rosie, ain't he got a friend?'

She said lightly, 'He's not got friends.'

'Maisie,' a voice called shrilly from the café, 'Maisie.' Tears lay ready in the eyes: in Maisie's eyes not Rose's: she hadn't meant to hurt her friend. An impulse of pity made her say, 'It's not all that good, Maisie.' She tried to destroy the appearance of her own happiness. 'Sometimes he's bad to me. Oh, I can tell you,' she urged, 'it's not all roses.'

But 'not roses,' she thought as she turned back to the parade, 'if it's not all roses, what is it?' And mechanically, walking back towards Frank's without her breakfast, she began to think – what have I done to deserve to be so happy? She'd committed a sin: that was the answer: she was having her cake in this world, not in the next, and she didn't care. She was stamped with him, as his voice was stamped on the vulcanite.

A few doors from Frank's, from a shop where they sold the Sunday papers, Dallow called to her. 'Hi, kid.' She stopped. 'You got a visitor.'

'Who?'

'Your mother.'

She was stirred by a feeling of gratitude and pity: her mother hadn't been happy like this. She said, 'Give me a *News of the World*. Mum likes a Sunday paper.' In the back room somebody was playing a gramophone. She said to the man who kept the shop, 'Sometime would you let me come here – and play a record I got?'

'O' course he will,' Dallow said.

She crossed the road and rang at Frank's door. Judy opened it; she was still in her dressing-gown, but underneath she now had on her corsets. 'You got a visitor,' she said.

'I know.' Rose ran upstairs: it was the biggest triumph you could ever expect – to greet your mother for the first time in your own house – ask her to sit down on your own chair: to look at one another with an equal experience. There was nothing now, Rose felt, her mother knew about men she didn't know: that was the reward for the painful ritual upon the bed. She flung the door gladly open and there was the woman.

'What are you—?' she began, and said, 'They told me it was my mother.'

'I had to tell them something,' the woman gently explained. She said, 'Come in, dear, and shut the door behind you,' as if it were *her* room.

'I'll call Pinkie.'

'I'd like a word with your Pinkie.' You couldn't get round her; she stood there like the wall at the end of an alley scrawled with the obscene chalk messages of an enemy. She was the explanation – it seemed to Rose – of sudden harshnesses, of the nails pressing her wrist. She said, 'You'll not see Pinkie. I won't have anyone worry Pinkie.'

'He's going to have plenty to worry him soon.'

'Who are you?' Rose implored her. 'Why do you interfere with us? You're not the police.'

'I'm like everyone else. I want justice,' the woman cheerfully remarked, as if she were ordering a pound of tea. Her big prosperous carnal face hung itself with smiles. She said, 'I want to see *you're* safe.'

'I don't want any help,' Rose said.

'You ought to go home.'

Rose clenched her hands in defence of the brass bed, the ewer of dusty water: 'This is home.'

'It's no good your getting angry, dear,' the woman continued. 'I'm not going to lose my temper with you again. It's not your fault. You don't understand how things are. Why, you poor little thing, I pity you,' and she advanced across the linoleum as if she intended to take Rose in her arms.

Rose backed against the bed, 'You keep your distance.'

'Now don't get agitated, dear. It won't help. You see – I'm determined.'

'I don't know what you mean. Why can't you talk straight?'

'There's things I've got to break – gently.'

'Keep away from me. Or I'll scream.'

The woman stopped. 'Now let's talk sensible, dear. I'm here for your own good. You got to be saved. Why—' she seemed for a moment at a loss for words. She said in a hushed voice, 'Your life's in danger.'

'You go away if that's all—'

'All,' the woman was shocked. 'What do you mean, all?' Then she laughed resolutely. 'Why, dear, for a moment you had me rattled. All, indeed. It's enough, isn't it? I'm not joking now. If you don't know it, you got to know it. There's nothing he wouldn't stop at.'

'Well?' Rose said, giving nothing away.

The woman whispered softly across the few feet between them, 'He's a murderer.'

'Do you think I don't know *that*?' Rose said.

'God's sake,' the woman said, 'do you mean—'

'There's nothing *you* can tell me.'

'You crazy little fool – to marry him knowing that. I got a good mind to let you be.'

'I won't complain,' Rose said.

The woman hooked on another smile, as you hook on a wreath. 'I'm not going to lose my temper, dear. Why if I let you be, I wouldn't sleep at nights. It wouldn't be Right. Listen to me; maybe you don't know what happened. I got it all figured out now. They took Fred down under the parade, into one of those little shops and strangled him – least they would have strangled him, but his heart gave out first.' She said in an awe-struck voice, 'They strangled a dead man,' then added sharply, 'you aren't listening.'

'I know it all,' Rose lied. She was thinking hard – she was remembering

Pinkie's warning – 'Don't get mixed up.' She thought wildly and vaguely: he did his best for me; I got to help him now. She watched the woman closely; she would never forget that plump, good-natured, ageing face: it stared out at her like an idiot's from the ruins of a bombed home. She said, 'Well, if you think that's how it was, why don't you go to the police?'

'Now you're talking sense,' the woman said. 'I only want to make things clear. This is the way it is, dear. There's a certain person I've paid money to who's told me things. And there's things I've figured out for myself. But that person – he won't give evidence. For reasons. And you need a lot of evidence – seeing how the doctors made it natural death. Now if you—'

'Why don't you give it up?' Rose said. 'It's over and done, isn't it? Why not let us all be?'

'It wouldn't be right. Besides – he's dangerous. Look what happened here the other day. You don't tell *me* that was an accident.'

'You haven't thought, have you,' Rose said, 'why he did it? You don't kill a man for no reason.'

'Well, why did he?'

'I don't know.'

'Ask him.'

'I don't need to know.'

'You think he's in love with you,' the woman said, 'he's not.'

'He married me.'

'And why? because they can't make a wife give evidence. You're just a witness like that other man was. My dear,' she again tried to close the gap between them, 'I only want to save you. He'd kill *you* as soon as look at you if he thought he wasn't safe.'

With her back to the bed Rose watched her approach. She let her put her large cool pastry-making hands upon her shoulders. 'People change,' she said.

'Oh, no they don't. Look at me. I've never changed. It's like those sticks of rock: bite it all the way down, you'll still read Brighton. That's human nature.' She breathed mournfully over Rose's face – a sweet and winey breath.

'Confession . . . repentance,' Rose whispered.

'That's just religion,' the woman said. 'Believe me, it's the world we got to deal with.' She went pat pat on Rose's shoulder, her breath whistling in her throat. 'You pack a bag and come away with me. I'll look after you. You won't have any cause to fear.'

'Pinkie . . .'

'I'll look after Pinkie.'

Rose said, 'I'll do anything – anything you want . . .'

'That's the way to talk, dear.'

'If you'll let us alone.'

The woman backed away. A momentary look of fury was hung up among the wreaths discordantly. 'Obstinate,' she said. 'If I was your mother . . . a good hiding.' The bony and determined face stared back at her: all the fight there was in the world lay there – warships cleared for action and bombing fleets took flight between the set eyes and the stubborn mouth. It was like the map of a campaign marked with flags.

'Another thing,' the woman bluffed. 'They can send you to gaol. Because you know. You told me so. An accomplice, that's what you are. After the fact.'

'If they took Pinkie, do you think,' she asked with astonishment, 'I'd mind?'

'Gracious,' the woman said, 'I only came here for your sake. I wouldn't have troubled to see you first, only I don't want to let the Innocent suffer' – the aphorism came clicking out like a ticket from a slot machine. 'Why, won't you lift a finger to stop him killing you?'

'He wouldn't do me any harm.'

'You're young. You don't know things like I do.'

'There's things *you* don't know.' She brooded darkly by the bed, while the women argued on: a God wept in a garden and cried out upon a cross; Molly Carthew went to everlasting fire.

'I know one thing you don't. I know the difference between Right and Wrong. They didn't teach you *that* at school.'

Rose didn't answer; the woman was quite right: the two words meant nothing to her. Their taste was extinguished by stronger foods – Good and Evil. The woman could tell her nothing she didn't know about these – she knew by tests as clear as mathematics that Pinkie was evil – what did it matter in that case whether he was right or wong?

'You're crazy,' the woman said. 'I don't believe you'd lift a finger if he was killing you.'

Rose came slowly back to the outer world. She said, 'Maybe I wouldn't.'

'If I wasn't a kind woman I'd give you up. But I've got a sense of responsibility.' Her smiles hung very insecurely when she paused at the door. 'You can warn that young husband of yours,' she said, 'I'm getting warm to him. I got my plans.' She went out and closed the door, then flung it open again for a last attack. 'You be careful, dear,' she said. 'You don't want a murderer's baby,' and grinned mercilessly across the bare bedroom floor. 'You better take precautions.'

Precautions. . . . Rose stood at the bed-end and pressed a hand against her body, as if under that pressure she could discover. . . . *That* had never entered her mind; and she thought of what she might have let herself in for came like a sense of glory. A child . . . and that child would have a child . . . it was like raising an army of friends for Pinkie. If They damned him and her, They'd have to deal with them, too. There was no end to what the two of them had done last night upon the bed: it was an eternal act.

Chapter Two

The Boy stood back in the doorway of the newspaper shop and saw Ida Arnold come out. She looked a little flushed, a little haughty sailing down the street; she paused and gave a small boy a penny. He was so surprised he dropped it, staring after her heavy careful retreat.

The Boy gave a sudden laugh, rusty and half-hearted. He thought: she's drunk. . . . Dallow said, 'That was a narrow squeak.'

'What was?'

'Your mother-in-law.'

'Her . . . how did *you* know?'

'She asked for Rose.'

The Boy put down the *News of the World* upon the counter – a headline stood up – 'Assault on Schoolgirl in Epping Forest'. He walked across to Frank's thinking hard, and up the stairs. Half-way he stopped: she'd dropped an artificial violet from a spray. He picked it off the stair: it smelt of California Poppy. Then he went in, holding the flower concealed in his palm, and Rose came across to him, welcoming. He avoided her mouth. 'Well,' he said and tried to express in his face a kind of rough and friendly jocularity, 'I hear your Mum's been visiting you,' and waited anxiously for her reply.

'Oh, yes,' Rose said doubtfully, 'she did look in.'

'Not one of her moody days?'

'No.'

He kneaded the violet furiously in his palm. 'Well, did she think it suited you – being married?'

'Oh, yes, I think she did. . . . She didn't say much.'

The Boy went across to the bed and slipped on his coat. He said, 'You been out too I hear?'

'I thought I'd go and see friends.'

'What friends?'

'Oh – at Snow's.'

'You call *them* friends?' he asked with contempt. 'Well, did you see them?'

'Not really. Only one – Maisie. For a minute.'

'And then you got back here in time to catch your Mum. Don't you want to know what I've been up to?'

She stared stupidly at him: his manner scared her. 'If you like.'

'What do you mean, if I like? You aren't as dumb as that.' The wire anatomy of the flower pricked his palm. He said, 'I got to have a word with Dallow. Wait here,' and left her.

He called to Dallow across the street, and when Dallow joined him, he said, 'Where's Judy?'

'Upstairs.'

'Frank working?'

'Yes.'

'Come down to the kitchen then.' He led the way down the stairs; in the basement dusk his feet crunched on dead coke. He sat down on the edge of the kitchen table and said, 'Have a drink.'

'Too early,' Dallow said.

'Listen,' the Boy said. An expression of pain crossed his face as if he were about to wring out an appalling confession. 'I trust you,' he said.

'Well,' Dallow said, 'what's getting you?'

'Things aren't too good,' the Boy said. 'People are getting wise to a lot of things. Christ,' he said, 'I killed Spicer and I married the girl. Have I got to have that massacre?'

'Was Cubitt here last night?'

'He was and I sent him away. He begged – he wanted a fiver.'

'Did you give it him?'

'Of course I didn't. D'you think I'd let myself be blackmailed by a thing like him?'

'You oughter have given him something.'

'It's not him I'm worried about.'

'You ought to be.'

'Be quiet, can't you,' the Boy suddenly and shrilly squealed at him. He jerked his thumb towards the ceiling. 'It's *her* I'm worried about.' He opened his hand and said, 'God damn it I dropped that flower.'

'Flower . . .?'

'Be quiet, can't you, and listen,' he said low and furiously. 'That wasn't her Mum.'

'Who was it?' Dallow asked.

'The buer who's been asking questions . . . the one who was with Fred in the taxi the day . . .' He put his head for a moment between his hands in an attitude of grief or desperation – but it wasn't either: it was the rush of memories. He said, 'I got a headache. I got to think clear. Rose told me it was her Mum. What's she after?'

'You don't think,' Dallow said, 'she's talked?'

'I got to find out,' the Boy said.

'I'd have trusted her,' Dallow said, 'all the way.'

'I wouldn't trust anyone that far. Not you, Dallow.'

'But if she's talking, why does she talk to *her* – why not to the police?'

'Why don't any of them talk to the police?' He stared with troubled eyes at the cold stove. He was haunted by his ignorance. 'I don't know what they're getting at.' Other people's feelings bored at his brain: he had never before felt this desire to understand. He said passionately, 'I'd like to carve the whole bloody boiling.'

'After all,' Dallow said, 'she don't know much. She only knows it wasn't Fred left the card. If you ask me she's a dumb little piece. Affectionate, I daresay, but dumb.'

'You're the dumb one, Dallow. She knows a lot. She knows I killed Fred.'

'You sure?'

'She told me so.'

'An' she married you?' Dallow said. 'I'm damned if I understand what they *want*.'

'If we don't do something quick it looks to me as if all Brighton'll know we killed Fred. All England. The whole God-damned world.'

'What can *we* do?'

The Boy went over to the basement window crunching on the coke: a tiny asphalt yard with an old dustbin which hadn't been used for weeks: a blocked grating, and a sour smell. He said, 'It's no good stopping now. We got to go on.' People passed overhead, invisible from the waist upwards: a shabby shoe scuffled the pavement wearing out the toecap; a bearded face stooped suddenly into sight looking for a cigarette-end. He said slowly, 'It ought to be easy to quiet her. We quieted Fred an' Spicer, an' she's only a kid. . . .'

'Don't be crazy,' Dallow said. 'You can't go on like that.'

'Maybe I got to. No choice. Maybe it's always that way – you start and then you go on going on.'

'We're making a mistake,' Dallow said. 'I'd stake you a fiver she's straight. Why – you told me yourself – she's stuck on you.'

'Why did she say it was her Mum then?' He watched a woman go by: young as far as the thighs: you couldn't see further up than that. A spasm of disgust shook him. He's given way: he had even been proud of *that* – what he could have done with Spicer's girl, Sylvie, in a Lancia. Oh, it was all right, he supposed, to take every drink once – if you could stop at that, say 'never again', not go on – going on.

'I can tell it myself,' Dallow said. 'Clear as clear. She's stuck on you all right.'

Stuck: high heels trodden over, bare legs moving out of sight. 'If she's stuck,' he said, 'it makes it easier – she'll do what I say.' A piece of newspaper blew along the street: the wind was from the sea.

Dallow said, 'Pinkie, I won't stand for any more killing.'

The Boy turned his back to the window and his mouth made a bad replica of mirth. He said, 'But suppose she killed herself?' An insane pride bobbed in his breast; he felt inspired: it was like a love of life returning to the blank heart: the empty tenement and then the seven devils worse than the first. . . .

Dallow said, 'For Christ's sake, Pinkie. You're imagining things.'

'We'll soon see,' the Boy said.

He came up the stairs from the basement, looking this way and that for the scented flower of cloth and wire. He could see it nowhere. Rose's voice said, 'Pinkie,' over the new banister: she was waiting there for him anxiously on the landing. She said, 'Pinkie, I got to tell you. I wanted to keep you from worrying – but there's got to be someone I don't have to lie to. That wasn't Mum, Pinkie.'

He came slowly up, watching her closely, judging. 'Who was it?'

'It was that woman. The one who used to come to Snow's asking questions.'

'What did she want?'

'She wanted me to go away from here.'

'Why?'

'Pinkie, she *knows*.'

'Why did you say it was your Mum?'

'I told you – I didn't want you to worry.'

He was beside her, watching her. She faced him back with a worried candour, and he found that he believed her as much as he believed anyone: his restless cocky pride subsided: he felt an odd sense of peace, as if – for a while – he hadn't got to plan.

'But then,' Rose went anxiously on, 'I thought – perhaps you ought to worry.'

'That's all right,' he said and put his hand on her shoulder in an awkward embrace.

'She said something about paying money to someone. She said she was getting warm to you.'

'I don't worry,' he said and pressed her back. Then he stopped, looking over her shoulder. In the doorway of the room the flower lay. He had dropped it when he closed the door – and then – he began at once to calculate – she followed me, of course she saw the flower, she knew I *knew*. That explains everything, the confession. . . . All the while he was down there below with Dallow she had been wondering what she had to do to cover her mistake. A clean breast – the phrase made him laugh – a clean tart's breast, the kind of breast Sylvie sported – cleaned up for use. He laughed again: the horror of the world lay like infection in his throat.

'What is it, Pinkie?'

'That flower,' he said.

'What flower?'

'The one *she* brought.'

'What . . . where . . .?'

Perhaps she hadn't seen it then . . . maybe she was straight after all . . . who knows? Who, he thought, will ever know? And with a kind of sad excitement – what did it matter anyway? He had been a fool to think it made any difference; he couldn't afford to take risks. If she were straight and loved him it would be just so much easier, that was all. He repeated, 'I don't worry. I don't need to worry. I know what to do. Even if she got to know everything I know what to do.' He watched her shrewdly. He brought his hand round and pressed her breast. 'It won't hurt,' he said.

'What won't hurt, Pinkie?'

'The way I'll manage things—' he started agilely away from his dark suggestion. 'You don't want to leave me, do you?'

'Never,' Rose said.

'That's what I mean,' he said. 'You wrote it, didn't you. Trust me, I'll manage things if the worst comes to the worst – so it won't hurt either of us. You can trust me,' he went smoothly and rapidly on, while she watched him with the tricked expression of someone who has promised too much, too quickly. 'I knew,' he said, 'you'd feel like that. About us never parting. What you wrote.'

She whispered with dread. 'It's a mortal . . .'

'Just one more,' he said. 'What difference does it make? You can't be damned twice over, and we're damned already – so they say. And anyway it's only if the worst . . . if she finds out about Spicer.'

'Spicer,' Rose moaned, 'you don't mean Spicer too. . . .'

'I only mean,' he said, 'if she finds out that I was here – in the house – but we don't need to worry till she does.'

'But Spicer . . .' Rose said.

'I was here,' he said, 'when it happened, that's all. I didn't even see him fall, but my solicitor . . .'

'He was here too?' Rose said.

'Oh, yes.'

'I remember now,' Rose said. 'Of course I read the paper. They couldn't believe, could they, that he'd cover up anything really wrong. A solicitor.'

'Old Prewitt,' the Boy said, 'why—' again the unused laugh came into rusty play. 'He's the Soul of Honour.' He pressed her breast again and uttered his qualified encouragement. 'Oh no, there's no cause to worry till *she* finds out. Even then you see there's *that* escape. But perhaps she never will. And if she doesn't, why,' – his fingers touched her with secret revulsion – 'we'll just go on, won't we,' and he tried to make the horror sound like love, 'the way we are.'

Chapter Three

But it was the Soul of Honour none the less who really worried him. If Cubitt had given that woman the idea that there was something wrong about Spicer's death as well, who could she go to now but Mr Prewitt? She wouldn't attempt anything with Dallow; but a man of law – when he was as clever as Prewitt was – was always frightened of the law. Prewitt was like a man who keeps a tame lion cub in his house. He could never be quite certain that the lion to whom he had taught so many tricks, to beg and eat out of his hand, might not one day unexpectedly mature and turn on him. Perhaps he might cut his cheek shaving – and the law would smell the blood.

In the early afternoon he couldn't wait any longer; he set out for Prewitt's house. First he told Dallow to keep an eye on the girl in case. . . . More than ever yet he had the sense that he was being driven further and deeper than he'd ever meant to go. A curious and cruel pleasure touched him – he didn't really care so very much – it was being decided for him, and all he had to do was to let himself easily go. He knew what the end might be – it didn't horrify him: it was easier than life.

Mr Prewitt's house was in a street parallel to the railway, beyond the terminus: it was shaken by shunting engines; the soot settled continuously on the glass and the brass plate. From the basement window a woman with tousled hair stared suspiciously up at him – she was always there watching visitors from a hard and bitter face. She was never explained: he had always thought she was the cook, but it appeared now she was the 'spouse' – twenty-five years at the game. The door was opened by a girl with grey underground skin – an unfamiliar face. 'Where's Tilly?' the Boy said.

'She's left.'

'Tell Prewitt, Pinkie's here.'

'He's not seeing anyone,' the girl said. 'This is a Sunday, ain't it?'

'He'll see me.' The Boy walked into the hall, opened a door, sat down in a room lined with filing boxes: he knew the way. 'Go on,' he said, 'tell him. I know he's asleep. You wake him up.'

'You seem to be at home here,' the girl said.

'I am.' He knew what those filing boxes contained marked Rex *v.* Innes, Rex *v.* T. Collins – they contained just air. A train shunted and the empty boxes quivered on the shelves: the window was open only a crack, but the radio from next door came in – Radio Luxembourg.

'Shut the window,' he said. She shut it sullenly. It made no difference, the walls were so thin you could hear the neighbour move behind the shelves like a rat. He said, 'Does that music always play?'

'Unless it's a talk,' she said.

'What are you waiting for? Go and wake him.'

'He told me not to. He's got indigestion.'

Again the room vibrated and the music wailed through the wall.

'He's always got it after lunch. Go on and wake him.'

'It's a Sunday.'

'You'd better go quick.' He obscurely threatened her, and she slammed the door on him – a little plaster fell.

Under his feet in the basement someone was moving the furniture about – the spouse, he thought. A train hooted and a smother of smoke fell into the street. Over his head Mr Prewitt began to speak – there was nothing anywhere to keep out sound. Then footsteps across the ceiling and on the stairs.

Mr Prewitt's smile went on as the door opened. 'What brings our young cavalier?'

'I just wanted to see you,' the Boy said. 'See how you were getting along.' A spasm of pain drove the smile from Mr Prewitt's face. 'You ought to eat more careful,' the Boy said.

'Nothing does it any good,' Mr Prewitt said.

'You drink too much.'

'Eat, drink, for to-morrow . . .' Mr Prewitt writhed with his hand on his stomach.

'You got an ulcer?' the Boy said.

'No, no, nothing like that.'

'You ought to have your inside photographed.'

'I don't believe in the knife,' Mr Prewitt said quickly and nervously, as if it were a suggestion constantly made for which he had to have the answer on the tongue.

'Don't that music ever stop?'

'When I get tired of it,' Mr Prewitt said, 'I beat on the wall.' He took a paper-weight off his desk and struck the wall twice: the music broke into a high oscillating wail and ceased. They could hear the neighbour move furiously behind the shelves. 'How now? A rat?' Mr Prewitt quoted. The house shook as a heavy engine pulled out. 'Polonius,' Mr Prewitt explained.

'Polony? What polony?'

'No, no,' Mr Prewitt said. 'The rank intruding fool, I mean. In Hamlet.'

'Listen,' the Boy said impatiently, 'has a woman been round here asking questions?'

'What sort of questions?'

'About Spicer.'

Mr Prewitt said with sickly despair, 'Are people asking questions?' He sat down quickly and bent with indigestion. 'I've just been waiting for this.'

'There's no need to get scared,' the Boy said. 'They can't prove anything. You just stick to your story.' He sat down opposite Mr Prewitt and regarded him with grim contempt. 'You don't want to ruin yourself,' he said.

Mr Prewitt looked sharply up. 'Ruin?' he said. 'I'm ruined now.' He vibrated with the engines on his chair, and somebody in the basement slammed the floor beneath their feet. 'What-ho! old mole,' Mr Prewitt said. 'The spouse – you've never met the spouse.'

'I've seen her,' the Boy said.

'Twenty-five years. Then this.' The smoke came down outside the window like a blind. 'Has it ever occurred to you,' Mr Prewitt said, 'that you're lucky? The worst that can happen to you is you'll hang. But I can rot.'

'What's upsetting you?' the Boy said. He was confused – as if a weak man had struck him back. He wasn't used to this – the infringement of other people's lives. Confession was an act one did – or didn't do – oneself.

'When I took on your work,' Mr Prewitt said, 'I lost the only other job I had. The Bakely Trust. And now I've lost you.'

'You got everything there is of mine.'

'There won't be any more soon. Colleoni's going to take over this place from you, and he's got his lawyer. A man in London. A swell.'

'I haven't thrown my sponge in yet.' He sniffed the air tainted with gasometers and said, 'I know what's wong with you. You're drunk.'

'On Empire burgundy,' Mr Prewitt said. 'I want to tell you things. Pinkie, I want—' the literary phrase came glibly out – 'to unburden myself.'

'I don't want to hear them. I'm not interest in *your* troubles.'

'I married beneath me,' Mr Prewitt said. 'It was my tragic mistake. I was young. An affair of uncontrollable passion. I was a passionate man,' he said wriggling with indigestion. 'You should see her,' he said, 'now. My God.' He leant forward and said in a whisper – 'I watch the little typists go by carrying their little cases. I'm quite harmless. A man may watch. My God, how neat and trim.' He broke off, his hand vibrating on the chair arm. 'Listen to the old mole down there. She's ruined me.' His old lined face had taken a holiday – from bonhomie, from cunning, from the legal jest. It was a Sunday and it was itself. Mr Prewitt said, 'You know what Mephistopheles said to Faustus when he asked where Hell was? He said, "Why, this is Hell, nor are we out of it".' The Boy watched him with fascination and fear.

'She's cleaning in the kitchen,' Mr Prewitt said, 'but she'll be coming up later. You ought to meet her – it'd be a treat. The old hag. What a joke it would be, wouldn't it, to tell her – everything. That I'm concerned in a murder. That people are asking questions. To pull down the whole damned house like Samson.' He stretched his arms wide and contracted them in the pain of indigestion. 'You're right,' he said, 'I've got an ulcer. But I won't have the knife. I'd rather die. I'm drunk, too. On Empire burgundy. Do you see that photo there – by the door? A school group. Lancaster College. Not one of the great schools perhaps, but you'll find it in the Public Schools Year Book. You'll see me there – cross-legged in the bottom row. In a straw hat.'

He said softly, 'We had field days with Harrow. A rotten set they were. No *esprit de corps.*'

The Boy didn't so much as turn his head to look. He had never known Prewitt like this before: it was a frightening and an entrancing exhibition. A man was coming alive before his eyes: he could see the nerves set to work in the agonised flesh, thought bloom in the transparent brain.

'To think,' Mr Prewitt said, 'an old Lancaster boy – to be married to that mole in the cellarage down there and to have as only client—' he gave his mouth an expression of fastidious disgust – 'you. What would old Manders say? A great Head.'

He had the bit between his teeth: he was like a man determined to live before he died; all the insults he had swallowed from police witnesses, the criticisms of magistrates, regurgitated from his tormented stomach. There was nothing he wouldn't tell to anybody. An enormous self-importance was blossoming out of his humiliation; his wife, the Empire burgundy, the empty files and the vibration of locomotives on the line, they were the important landscape of his great drama.

'You talk too easily,' the Boy said.

'Talk?' Mr Prewitt said. 'I could shake the world. Let them put me in the dock if they like. I'll give them – revelation. I've sunk so deep I carry—' he was shaken by an enormous windy self-esteem – he hiccupped twice – 'the secrets of the sewer.'

'If I'd known you drank,' the Boy said, 'I wouldn't have touched you.'

'I drink – on Sundays. It's the day of rest.' He suddenly beat his foot upon the floor and screamed furiously, 'Be quiet down there.'

'You need a holiday,' the Boy said.

'I sit here and sit here – the bell rings, but it's only the groceries – tinned salmon, she has a passion for tinned salmon. Then I ring the bell – and in comes that pasty stupid – I watch the typists going by. I could embrace their little portable machines.'

'You'd be all right,' the Boy said – nervous and shaken with the conception of another life growing in the brain – 'if you took a holiday.'

'Sometimes,' Mr Prewitt said, 'I have an urge to expose myself – shamefully – in a park.'

'I'll give you money.'

'No money can heal a mind diseased. This is Hell nor are we out of it. How much could you spare?'

'Twenty nicker.'

'It would go only a little way.'

'Boulogne – why not slip across the Channel?' the Boy asked with horrified disgust, 'enjoy yourself,' watching the grubby and bitten nails, the shaky hands which were the instruments of pleasure.

'Could you spare some small sum like that, my boy? Don't let me rob you. Though, of course, "I have done the state some service".'

'You can have it to-morrow – on conditions. You got to leave by the morning boat – stay away as long as you can. Maybe I'll send you more.' It was like fastening a leech on to the flesh – he felt weakness and disgust. 'Let me know when it's finished and I'll see.'

'I'll go, Pinkie – when you say. And – you won't tell my spouse?'

'I keep *my* mouth shut.'

'Of course. I trust you, Pinkie, and you can trust me. Recuperated by this holiday I shall return—'

'Take a long one.'

'Bullying police sergeants shall recognise my renewed astuteness. Defending the outcast.'

'I'll send the money first thing. Till then you don't see anyone. You go back to bed. Your indigestion's cruel. If anyone comes round you're not in.'

'As you say, Pinkie, as you say.'

It was the best he could do. He let himself out of the house and looking down met in the basement the hard suspicious gaze of Mr Prewitt's spouse; she had a duster in her hand and she watched him like a bitter enemy from her cave, under the foundations. He crossed the road and took one more look at the villa, and there in an upper window half-concealed by the curtains stood Mr Prewitt. He wasn't watching the Boy – he was just looking out – hopelessly, for what might turn up. But it was a Sunday and there weren't any typists.

Chapter Four

He said to Dallow. 'You got to watch the place. I don't trust him a yard. I can just see him looking out there, waiting for something, and seeing *her*. . . .'

'He wouldn't be such a fool.'

'He's drunk. He says he's in Hell.'

Dallow laughed. 'Hell. That's good.'

'You're a fool, Dallow.'

'I don't believe in what my eyes don't see.'

'They don't see much then,' the Boy said. He left Dallow and went upstairs. But oh, if this was Hell, he thought, it wasn't so bad: the old-fashioned telephone, the narrow stairs, the snug and dusty darkness – it wasn't like Prewitt's house, comfortless, shaken, with the old bitch in the basement. He opened the door of his room and there, he thought, was *his* enemy – he looked round with angry disappointment at his changed room – the position of everything a little altered and the whole place swept and clean and tidied. He condemned her, 'I told you not to.'

'I've only cleared up, Pinkie.'

'It was her room now, not his: the wardrobe and the washstand shifted, and the bed – of course she hadn't forgotten the bed. It was her Hell now if it was anybody's – he disowned it. He felt driven out, but any change must be for the worse. He watched her, disguising his hatred, trying to read age into her face, how she would look one day staring up from his basement. He had come back wrapped in another person's fate – a doubled darkness.

'Don't you like it, Pinkie?'

He wasn't Prewitt: he'd got guts: he hadn't lost his fight. He said, 'Oh, this – it's fine. It was just I wasn't expecting it.'

She misread his constraint. 'Bad news?'

'Not yet. We got to be prepared, of course. I *am* prepared.' He went to the window and stared out through a forest of wireless masts towards a cloudy peaceful Sunday sky, then back at the changed room. This was how it might look if he had gone away and other tenants. . . . He watched her closely while he did his sleight of hand, passing off his idea as hers. 'I got the car all ready. We could go out into the country where no one would hear. . . .' He measured her terror carefully and before she could pass the card back to him, he changed his tone. 'That's only if the worst comes to the worst.' The phrase intrigued him: he repeated it: the worst – that was the stout woman with her glassy righteous eye coming up the smoky road – to the worst – and that was drunken ruined Mr Prewitt watching from behind the curtains for just one typist. 'It won't happen,' he encouraged her.

'No,' she passionately agreed. 'It won't, it can't.' Her enormous certainty had a curious effect on him – it was as if that plan of his too were being tidied, shifted, swept until he couldn't recognize his own. He wanted to argue that it *might* happen: he discovered in himself an odd nostalgia for the darkest act of all.

She said, 'I'm so happy. It can't be so bad after all.'

'What do you mean?' he said. 'Not bad? It's mortal sin.' He glanced with furious disgust at the made bed as if he contemplated a repetition of the act there and then – to thrust the lesson home.

'I know,' she said. 'I know, but still—'

'There's only one thing worse,' he said. It was as if she were escaping him: already she was domesticating their black alliance.

'I'm happy,' she argued bewilderedly. 'You're good to me.'

'That doesn't mean a thing.'

'Listen,' she said, 'what's that?' A thin wailing came through the window.

'The kid next door.'

'Why doesn't somebody quiet it?'

'It's a Sunday. Maybe they're out,' he said. 'You want to do anything? The flickers?'

She wasn't listening to him: the unhappy continuous cry absorbed her: she wore a look of responsibility and maturity. 'Somebody ought to see what it wants,' she said.

'It's just hungry or something.'

'Maybe it's ill.' She listened with a kind of vicarious agony. 'Things happen to babies suddenly. You don't know what it mightn't be.'

'It isn't yours.'

She turned bemused eyes towards him. 'No,' she said, 'but I was thinking – it might be.' She said with passion, 'I wouldn't leave it all an afternoon.'

He said uneasily, 'They haven't either. It's stopped. What did I tell you?' But her words lodged in his brain – 'It might be.' He had never thought of that. He watched her with terror and disgust as if he were watching the ugly birth itself, the rivet of another life already pinning him down, and she stood there listening – with relief and patience, as if already she had passed through years of this anxiety and knew that the relief never lasted long and that the anxiety always began again.

Chapter Five

Nine o'clock in the morning: he came furiously out into the passage; the morning sun trickled in over the top of the door below, staining the telephone. He called, 'Dallow, Dallow.'

Dallow came slowly up from the basement in his shirt-sleeves. He said, 'Hallo, Pinkie. You look as if you hadn't slept.'

The Boy said, 'You keeping away from me?'

'Of course I'm not, Pinkie. Only – you being married – I thought you'd want to be alone.'

'You call it,' the Boy said, 'being alone?' He came down the stairs; he carried in his hand the mauve scented envelope Judy had thrust under the door. He hadn't opened it. His eyes were bloodshot. He carried down with him the marks of a fever – the beating pulse and the hot forehead and the restless brain.

'Johnnie phoned me early,' Dallow said. 'He's been watching since yesterday. No one's been to see Prewitt. We got scared for nothing.'

The Boy paid him no attention. He said, 'I want to be alone, Dallow. Really alone.'

'You been taking on too much at your age,' Dallow said and began to laugh. 'Two nights . . .'

The Boy said, 'She's got to go before she—' He couldn't express the magnitude of his fear or its nature to anyone.

'It's not safe to quarrel,' Dallow said quickly and cautiously.

'No,' the Boy said, 'it won't ever be safe again. I know that. No divorce. Nothing at all except dying. All the same,' he put his hand on the vulcanite for coolness, 'I told you – I had a plan.'

'It was crazy. Why should that poor kid want to die?'

He said with bitterness, 'She loves me. She says she wants to be with me always. And if I don't want to live. . . .'

'Dally,' a voice called, 'Dally.' The Boy looked sharply and guiltily round; he hadn't heard Judy moving silently above in her naked feet and her corsets. He was absorbed, trying to get the plan straight, tied up in its complexity, uncertain who it was who had to die . . . himself or her or both. . . .

'What you want, Judy?' Dallow said.

'Frank's finished your coat.'

'Let it be,' Dallow said. 'I'll fetch it in a shake.'

She blew him an avaricious unsatisfied kiss and padded back to her room.

'I started something there all right,' Dallow said. 'Sometimes I wish I hadn't. I don't want trouble with poor old Frank, an' she's so careless.'

The Boy looked at Dallow broodingly, as if perhaps he knew from his long service what one did.

'Suppose,' he said, 'you had a child?'

'Oh,' Dallow said, 'I leave that to her. It's *her* funeral.' He said, 'You got a letter there from Colleoni?'

'But what does she do?'

'The usual, I suppose.'

'And if she doesn't,' the Boy persisted, 'an' she began a child?'

'There's pills.'

'They don't always work, do they?' the Boy said. He had thought he'd learned everything, but he was back now in his state of appalled ignorance.

'They never work, if you ask me,' Dallow said. 'Colleoni written?'

'If Prewitt grassed, there wouldn't be a hope, would there?' the Boy brooded.

'He won't grass. And anyway he'll be in Boulogne to-night.'

'But *if* he did . . . or say I thought he had . . . there'd be nothing to do then, would there, but kill myself. And she – she wouldn't want to live without me. If she thought. . . . And all the time perhaps it wouldn't be true. They call it – don't they? – a suicide pact.'

'What's got you, Pinkie? You're not giving in?'

'I mightn't die.'

'That's murder, too.'

'They don't hang you for it.'

'You're crazy, Pinkïe. Why, I wouldn't stand for a thing like that.' He gave the Boy a shocked and friendly blow. 'You're joking, Pinkie – there's nothing wrong with the poor kid – except for liking you.' The Boy said not a thing; he had an air of removing his thoughts, like heavy bales and stacking them inside, turning the key on all the world. 'You want to lie down a bit and rest,' Dallow said uneasily.

'I want to lie down alone,' the Boy said. He went slowly upstairs. When he opened the door he knew what he would see: he looked away as if to shut out temptation from the ascetic and the poisoned brain. He heard her say: 'I was just going out for a while, Pinkie. Is there anything I can do for you?'

Anything. . . . His brain staggered with the immensity of its demands. He said gently, 'Nothing,' and schooled his voice to softness. 'Come back soon. We got things to talk about.'

'Worried?'

'Not worried. I got things straight,' he gestured with deadly humour at his head, 'in the box here.'

He was aware of her fear and tension – the sharp breath and the silence and then the voice steeled for despair. 'Not bad news, Pinkie?'

He flew out at her. 'For Christ's sake go.'

He heard her coming back across the room to him, but he wouldn't look up: this was his room, his life. He felt that if he could concentrate enough, it would be possible to eliminate every sign of her . . . everything would be just the same as before . . . before he entered Snow's and felt under that cloth for a ticket which wasn't there and began the deception and shame. The whole origin of the thing was lost; he could hardly remember Hale as a person or his murder as a crime – it was all now him and her.

'If anything's happened . . . you can tell me . . . I'm not scared. There must be some way, Pinkie, not to . . .' She implored him, 'Let's talk about it first.'

He said, 'You're fussed about nothing, I want you to go all right, you can go,' he went savagely on, 'to . . .' But he stopped in time, raked up a smile, 'Go and enjoy yourself.'

'I won't be gone long, Pinkie.' He heard the door close, but he knew she was lingering in the passage – the whole house was hers now. He put his hand in his pocket and pulled out the paper – 'I don't care what you do . . . wherever you go, I'll go too.' It sounded like a letter read in court and printed in the newspapers. He heard her feet upon the stairs going down.

Dallow looked in and said, 'Prewitt should be starting now. I'll feel better when he's on that boat. You don't think, do you, she'd get the police to hunt him out?'

'She hasn't got the evidence,' the Boy said. 'You're safe enough when he's out of the way.' He spoke dully as if he'd lost all interest in whether Prewitt went or stayed – it was something which concerned other people. He'd gone beyond that.

'You too,' Dallow said. 'You'll be safe.'

The Boy didn't answer.

'I told Johnnie to see he got on the boat safe and then phone us. He'll be ringing up now almost any time. We oughter have a party to celebrate, Pinkie. My God, how sunk she'll feel when she turns up there and finds him gone.' He went to the window and looked out. 'Maybe we'll have some peace then. We'll have got out of it easy. When you come to think. Hale and poor old Spicer. I wonder where he is now.' He stared sentimentally out through the thin chimney smoke and the wireless masts. 'What about you an' me – an' the girl, of course – shifting off to some new place? It's not going to be so good here now with Colleoni butting in.' He turned back into the room. 'That letter' – and the telephone began to ring. He said, 'That'll be Johnnie,' and hurried out.

It occurred to the Boy that it wasn't the sound of feet on the stairs he recognized, it was the sound of the stairs themselves – he could tell those particular stairs even under a stranger's weight: there was always a creak at the third and seventh step down. This was the place he had come to after Kite had picked him up – he had been coughing on the Palace pier in the bitter cold, listening to the violin wailing behind the glass. Kite had given him a cup of hot coffee and brought him here – God knows why – perhaps because he was out and wasn't down, perhaps because a man like Kite needed a little sentiment like a tart who keeps a Pekinese. Kite had opened the door of No. 63 and the first thing he'd seen was Dallow embracing Judy on the stairs and the first thing he had smelt was Frank's iron in the basement. Everything had been of a piece: nothing had really changed: Kite had died, but he had prolonged Kite's existence – not touching liquor, biting his nails in the Kite way, until *she* came and altered everything.

Dallow's voice drifted up the stairs. 'Oh, I dunno. Send some pork sausages. Or a tin of beans.'

He came back into the room. 'It wasn't Johnnie,' he said. 'Just the International. We oughter be hearing from Johnnie.' He sat anxiously down on the bed and said, 'That letter from Colleoni. What does it say?'

The Boy tossed it across to him. 'Why,' Dallow said, 'you haven't opened it.' He began to read: 'Well,' he said, 'it's bad, of course. It's what I thought. And yet it's not so bad either. Not when you come to look at it.' He glanced cautiously up over the mauve notepaper at the Boy, sitting there by the washstand, thinking. 'We're played out here, that's what it comes to. He's got most of our boys and all the bookies. But he doesn't want trouble. He's a business man – he says a fight like you had the other day brings a track into – disrepute. Disrepute,' Dallow repeated thoughtfully.

'He means,' the Boy said, 'the suckers stay away.'

'Well, that's sense. He says he'll pay you three hundred nicker for the goodwill. Goodwill?'

'He means not carving his geezers.'

'It's a good offer,' Dallow said. 'It's what I was saying just now – we could clear out right away from this damned town and this phoney buer asking questions, start again on a good line – or maybe retire altogether, buy a pub, you an' me – an' the girl, of course.' He said, 'When the hell's Johnnie going to phone. It makes me nervous.'

The Boy said nothing for a while, looking at his bitten nails. Then he said, 'Of course – you know the world, Dallow. You've travelled.'

'There's not many places I don't know,' Dallow agreed, 'between here and Leicester.'

'I was born here,' the Boy said. 'I know Goodwood and Hurst Park. I've been to Newmarket. But I'd feel a stranger away from here.' He claimed with dreary pride, 'I suppose I'm real Brighton', as if his single heart contained all the cheap amusements, the Pullman cars, the unloving week-ends in gaudy hotels, and the sadness after coition.

A bell rang. 'Listen,' Dallow said. 'Is that Johnnie?'

But it was only the front door. Dallow looked at his watch. 'I can't think what's keeping him,' he said. 'Prewitt oughter be on board by now.'

'Well,' the Boy said with gloom, 'we change, don't we? It's as you say. We got to see the world. . . . After all I took to drink, didn't I? I can take to other things.'

'An' you got a girl,' Dallow said with hollow cheeriness. 'You're growing up, Pinkie – like your father.'

Like my father. . . . The Boy was shaken again with his nocturnal Saturday disgust. He couldn't blame his father now . . . it was what you came to . . . you got mixed up, and then, he supposed, the habit grew . . . you gave yourself away weakly. You couldn't even blame the girl. It was life getting at you . . . there were the blind seconds when you thought it fine. 'We'd be safer,' he said, 'without her,' touching the loving message in the trouser-pocket.

'She's safe enough now. She's crazy about you.'

'The trouble with you is,' the Boy said, 'you don't look ahead. There's years. . . . And any day she might fall for a new face or get vexed or something . . . if I don't keep her smooth . . . there's no security,' he said. The door opened and there she was back again: he bit his words short and smirked a welcome. But it wasn't hard – she took deception with such hopeless ease that he could feel a sort of tenderness for her stupidity and a companionship in her goodness – they were both doomed in their own way. Again he got the sense that she completed him.

She said, 'I hadn't got a key. I had to ring. I felt afraid soon as I'd gone out that something might be wrong. I wanted to be here, Pinkie.'

'There's nothing wrong,' he said. The telephone began to ring. 'There, you see, there's Johnnie now.' He said to Dallow joylessly, 'You got your wish.'

They heard his voice at the phone shrill with suspense. 'That you, Johnnie? Yes? What was that? You don't mean. . . . Oh yes, we'll see you later. Of course you'll get your money.' He came back up and at the right place the stairs creaked – his broad, brutal and innocent face bore good news like a boar's head at a feast. 'That's fine,' he said, 'fine. I was getting anxious. I don't mind telling you. But he's on the boat now an' she left the pier ten minutes ago. We got to celebrate this. By God, you're clever, Pinkie. You think of everything.'

Chapter Six

Ida Arnold had had more than a couple. She sang softly to herself over the Guinness – 'One night in an alley Lord Rothschild said to me . . .' The heavy motion of the waves under the pier was like the sound of bath water; it set her going. She sat there massively alone – no harm in her for anybody in the world – minus one. The world was a good place if you didn't weaken; she was like the chariot in a triumph – behind her were all the big battalions – right's right, an eye for an eye, when you want to do a thing well, do it yourself. Phil Corkery made his way towards her – behind him through the long glass windows of the tea-room you could see the lights of Hove; green copper Metropole domes swam in the layer of last light under the heavy nocturnal clouds slumping down. The spray tossed up like fine rain against the windows. Ida Arnold stopped singing and said, 'Do you see what I see?'

Phil Corkery sat down; it wasn't like summer at all in this glass breakwater: he looked cold in his grey flannel trousers and his blazer with the old something-or-other arms on the pocket: a little pinched, all passion spent. 'It's them,' he said wearily. 'How did *you* know they'd be here?'

'I didn't,' Ida said. 'It's fate.'

'I'm tired of the sight of them.'

'But think *how* tired,' she said with cheery relish, '*they* are.' They looked across a waste of empty tables towards France, towards the Boy and Rose – and a man and woman they didn't recognize. If the party had come there to celebrate or something, she had spoiled their fun. The Guinness welled warmly up into her throat. She had an enormous sense of well-being; she belched and said, 'Pardon me,' lifting a black-gloved hand. She said, 'I suppose he's gone, too?'

'He's gone.'

'We aren't lucky with our witnesses,' she said. 'First Spicer, then the girl, then Prewitt and now Cubitt.'

'He took the first morning train – with your money.'

'Never mind,' she said. 'They're alive. They'll come back. An' I can wait
– thanks to Black Boy.'

Phil Corkery looked at her askance; it was astonishing that he had ever
had the nerve to send her, to send that power and purpose, postcards from
seaside resorts – from Hastings a crab from whose stomach you could wind
out a series of views, from Eastbourne a baby sitting upon a rock which
lifted to disclose the High Street and Boots' Library and a fernery, from
Bournemouth (was it?) a bottle containing photographs of the promenade,
the rock garden, the new swimming pool. . . . It was like offering a bun to
an elephant in Africa. He was shaken by a sense of terrific force . . .
When she wanted a good time nothing would stop her, and when she
wanted justice. . . . He said nervously, 'Don't you think, Ida, we've done
enough. . . .'

She said, 'I haven't finished yet,' with her eyes on the little doomed party.
'You never know. They think they're safe: they'll do something crazy now.'
The Boy sat there silent beside Rose. He had a glass of drink but he hadn't
tasted it; only the man and the woman chattered about this and that.

'We've done our best. It's a matter for the police or no one,' Phil said.

'You heard them that first time.' She began to sing again, 'One night in
an alley . . .'

'It's not our business now.'

'Lord Rothschild said to me . . .' She broke off to set him gently right.
You couldn't let a friend have wrong ideas. 'It's the business of anyone who
knows the difference between right and wrong.'

'But you're so terribly certain about things, Ida. You go busting in. . . .
Oh, you mean weil, but how do we know the reasons he may have had.
. . . And besides,' he accused her, 'you're only doing it because it's fun. Fred
wasn't anyone you cared about.'

She switched towards him her large and lit-up eyes. 'Why,' she said, 'I
don't say it hasn't been – exciting.' She felt quite sorry it was all over now.
'What's the harm in that? I like doing what's right, that's all.'

Rebellion bobbed weakly up – 'And what's wrong, too, Ida.'

She smiled at him with enormous and remote tenderness. 'Oh, that. That's
not wrong. That does no one any harm. That's not like murder.'

'Priests say it is.'

'Priests,' she exclaimed with scorn. 'Why, even Romans don't believe in
that. Or that girl wouldn't be living with him now.' She said, 'You can trust
me. I've seen the world. I know people,' and she turned her attention heavily
back on Rose. 'You wouldn't let me leave a little girl like that – to him?
She's vexing, of course, she's stupid, but she don't deserve that.'

'How do you know she doesn't *want* to be left?'

'You aren't telling me, are you, that she wants to die? Nobody wants that.
Oh, no. I don't give up until she's safe. Get me another Guinness.' A long
way out beyond the West Pier you could see the lights of Worthing – a sign
of bad weather, and the tide rolled regularly in, a gigantic white splash in
the dark against the breakwaters nearer shore. You could hear it pounding
at the piles, like a boxer's fist against a punchball in training for the human
jaw, and softly and just a little tipsily Ida Arnold began to recall the people
she had saved: a man she had once pulled out of the sea when she was a

young woman, the money to a blind beggar, and the kind word in season to the despairing schoolgirl in the Strand.

Chapter Seven

'Poor old Spicer too,' Dallow said, 'he got the same idea – he thought he'd have a pub somewhere some day.' He slapped Judy's thigh and said, 'What about me an' you settling in with the young people.' He said, 'I can see it now. Right out in the country. On one of those arterials with the charabancs stopping: the Great North Road: "Pull in here". I wouldn't be surprised if there wasn't more money in the long run . . .' He stopped and said to the Boy, 'What's up? Take a drink. There's nothing to worry about now.'

The Boy looked across the tea-room and the empty tables to where the woman sat. How she hung on. Like a ferret he'd seen on the Down, among the chalky holes, fastened to a hare's throat. All the same *this* hare escaped. He had no cause to fear her now. He said in a dull voice, 'The country. I don't know much about the country.'

'It's healthy,' Dallow said. 'Why, you'll live to eighty with your missus.'

'Sixty-odd years,' the Boy said, 'it's a long time.' Behind the woman's head the Brighton lamps beaded out towards Worthing. The last sunset light slid lower in the sky and the heavy indigo clouds came down over the Grand, the Metropole, the Cosmopolitan, over the towers and domes. Sixty years: it was like a prophecy – a certain future: a horror without end.

'You two,' Dallow said. 'What's got you both?'

This was the tea-room to which they had all come after Fred's death – Spicer and Dallow and Cubitt. Dallow was right, of course: they were safe – Spicer dead and Prewitt out of the way and Cubitt God knows where. (They'd never get *him* into a witness box: he knew too well he'd hang – he'd played too big a part – and the prison record of 1923 lay behind him.) And Rose was his wife. As safe as they could ever be. They'd won out – finally. He had – Dallow right again – sixty years ahead. His thoughts came to pieces in his hand: Saturday nights: and then the birth, the child, habit and hate. He looked across the tables; the woman's laughter was like defeat.

He said, 'This place is stuffy. I got to have some air.' He turned slowly to Rose. 'Come for a stroll,' he said. Between the table and the door he picked the right thought out of all the pieces, and when they came out on the windy side of the pier he shouted to her, 'I got to go away from here.' He put his hand on her arm and guided her with terrible tenderness into shelter. The waves came breaking up from France, pounding under their feet. A spirit of recklessness took him: it was like the moment when he had seen Spicer bending by his suitcase, Cubitt begging for money in the passage. Through the glass panes Dallow sat with Judy by the drinks. It was like the first week of the sixty years – the contact and the sensual tremble and the stained sleep and waking not alone; in the wild and noisy darkness he had the whole future in his brain. It was like a slot machine: you put in a penny and the light goes on and the doors open and the figures move. He said with agile tenderness, 'This was where we met that night. Remember?'

'Yes,' she said and watched him with fear.

'We don't want *them* with us,' he said. 'Let's get into the car an' drive' – he watched her closely – 'into the country.'

'It's cold.'

'It won't be in the car.' He dropped her arm and said, 'Of course – if you don't want to come – I'll go alone.'

'But where?'

He said with studied lightness, 'I told you. In the country.' He took a penny out of his pocket and slammed it home in the nearest slot-machine. He pulled a handle, didn't look at what he did, and with a rattle the packets of fruit gums came dropping out – a bonus – lemon and grape-fruit and liquorice all-sorts. He said, 'I've got a lucky hand.'

'Is something wrong?' Rose said.

He said, 'You saw her, didn't you? Believe me – she's never going to leave go. I saw a ferret once – out by the track.' As he turned one of the pier lights caught his eyes: a gleam: an exhilaration. He said, 'I'm going for a ride. You stay here if you want to.'

'I'll come,' she said.

'You needn't.'

'I'll come.'

At the shooting range he paused. He was taken with a kind of wild humour. 'Got the time?' he asked the man.

'You know what the time is. I've told you before how I won't stand . . .'

'You needn't get your rag out,' the Boy said. 'Give me a gun.' He lifted it, got the sight firmly on the bull, then deliberately shifted it and fired. He thought: 'Something had agitated him', the witness said.

'What's up with you to-day?' the man exclaimed. 'You only got an outer.'

He laid the rifle down. 'We need a freshner. We're going for a ride in the country. Good night.' He planted his information pedantically, as carefully as he had had them lay Fred's cards along the route – for later use. He even turned back and said, 'We're going Hastings way.'

'I don't want to know,' the man said, 'where you're going.'

The old Morris was parked near the pier. The self-starter wouldn't work: he had to turn the handle. He stood a moment looking at the old car with an expression of disgust: as if this was all you got out of a racket. . . . He said, 'We'll go the way we went that day. Remember. In the bus.' Again he planted his information for the attendant to hear. 'Peacehaven. We'll get a drink.'

They swung out round by the Aquarium and ground up hill in second gear. He had one hand in his pocket feeling for the scrap of paper on which she had written her message. The hood flapped and the split discoloured glass of the windscreen confined his view. He said, 'It's going to rain like hell soon.'

'Will this hood keep it out?'

'It doesn't matter,' he said, staring ahead. '*We* won't get wet.'

She didn't dare ask him what he meant – she wasn't sure, and as long as she wasn't sure she could believe that they were happy, that they were lovers taking a drive in the dark with all the trouble over. She put a hand on him and felt his instinctive withdrawal: for a moment she was shaken by an awful doubt – if this was the darkest nightmare of all, if he didn't love her, as the woman said . . . The wet windy air flapped her face through the rent. It didn't matter: she loved him: she had her responsibility. The buses passed them going downhill to the town: little bright domestic cages in which people sat with baskets and books: a child pressed her face to the glass and for a moment at a traffic light they were so close the face might have been held against her breast. 'A penny for your thoughts,' he said and caught her unawares – 'Life's not so bad.'

'Don't you believe it,' he said. 'I'll tell you what it is. It's gaol, it's not knowing where to get some money. Worms and cataract, cancer. You hear 'em shrieking from the upper windows – children being born. It's dying slowly.'

It was coming now – she knew it: the dashboard light lit the bony mind-made-up fingers: the face was in darkness, but she could imagine the exhilaration, the bitter excitement, the anarchy in the eyes. A rich man's private car – Daimler or Bentley she didn't know the makes – rolled smoothly past them. He said, 'What's the hurry?' He took his hand out of his pocket and laid on his knee a paper she recognised. He said, 'You mean that – don't you?' He had to repeat it – 'Don't you?' She felt as if she were signing away more than her life – heaven, whatever that was, and the child in the bus, and the baby crying in the neighbour's house. 'Yes,' she said.

'We'll go and have a drink,' he said, 'and then – you'll see. I got everything settled.' He said with hideous ease, 'It won't take a minute.' He put his arm round her waist and his face was close to hers: she could see him now, considering and considering; his skin smelt of petrol: everything smelt of petrol in the little leaking out-dated car. She said, 'Are you sure . . . can't we wait . . . one day?'

'What's the good? You saw her there to-night. She's hanging on. One day she'll get her evidence. What's the use?'

'Why not *then*?'

'It might be too late *then*'. He said disjointedly through the flapping hood, 'A knock and the next thing you know . . . the cuffs . . . too late. . . .' He said with cunning, 'We wouldn't be together then.' He put down his foot and the needle quivered up to thirty-five – the old car wouldn't do more than forty, but it gave an immense impression of reckless speed: the wind battered on the glass and tore through the rent. He began softly to intone – 'Dona nobis pacem.'

'He won't.'

'What do you mean?'

'Give us peace.'

He thought: there'll be time enough in the years ahead – sixty years – to repent of this. Go to a priest. Say: 'Father, I've committed murder twice. And there was a girl – she killed herself.' Even if death came suddenly, driving home to-night, the smash on the lamp-post – there was still 'between the stirrup and the ground'. The houses on one side ceased altogether, and the sea came back to them, beating at the undercliff drive, a darkness and deep sound. He wasn't really deceiving himself – he'd learnt the other day that when the time was short there were other things than contrition to think about. It didn't matter anyway … he wasn't made for peace, he couldn't believe in it. Heaven was a word: hell was something he could trust. A brain was only capable of what it could conceive, and it couldn't conceive what it had never experienced; his cells were formed of the cement school-playground, the dead fire and the dying man in the St Pancras waiting-room, his bed at Frank's and his parents' bed. An awful resentment stirred in him – why shouldn't he have had his chance like all the rest, seen his glimpse of heaven if it was only a crack between the Brighton walls … He turned as they went down to Rottingdean and took a long look at her as if she might be it – but the brain couldn't conceive – he saw a mouth which wanted the sexual embrace, the shape of breasts demanding a child. Oh, she was good all right, he supposed, but she wasn't good enough: he'd got her down.

Above Rottingdean the new villas began: pipe-dream architecture: up on the downs the obscure skeleton of a nursing home, winged like an aeroplane. He said, 'They won't hear us in the country.' The lights petered out along the road to Peacehaven: the chalk of a new cutting flapped like white sheets in the headlight: cars came down on them blinding them. He said, 'The battery's low.'

She had the sense that he was a thousand miles away – his thoughts had gone on beyond the act she couldn't tell where. He was wise; he was foreseeing, she thought, things she couldn't conceive – eternal punishment, the flames … She felt terror, the idea of pain shook her, their purpose drove up in a flurry of rain against the old stained windscreen. This road led nowhere else. It was said to be the worst act of all, the act of despair, the sin without forgiveness; sitting there in the smell of petrol she tried to realise despair, the mortal sin, but she couldn't; it didn't feel like despair. He was going to damn himself, but she was going to show them that they couldn't damn him without damning her too. There was nothing he could do, she wouldn't do: she felt capable of sharing any murder. A light lit his face and left it; a frown, a thought, a child's face. She felt responsibility move in her breasts; she wouldn't let him go into that darkness alone.

The Peacehaven streets began, running out towards the cliffs and the downs: thorn-bushes grew up round the To Let boards; streets ended in obscurity, in a pool of water and in salty grass. It was like the last effort of despairing pioneers to break new country. The country had broken them. He said, 'We'll go to the hotel and have a drink and then – I know the right place.'

The rain was coming tentatively down; it beat on the faded scarlet doors of Lureland, the poster of next week's Whist Drive and last week's Dance. They ran for it to the hotel door. In the lounge there was nobody at all – white marble statuettes and on the green dado above the panelled walls Tudor roses and lilies picked out in gold. Siphons stood about on blue-topped tables, and on the stained-glass windows medieval ships tossed on cold curling waves. Somebody had broken the hands off one of the statuettes – or perhaps it was made like that, something classical in white drapery, a symbol of victory or despair. The Boy rang a bell and a boy of his own age came out of the public bar to take his order: they were oddly alike and allusively different – narrow shoulders, thin face, they bristled like dogs at the sight of each other.

'Piker,' the Boy said.

'What of it?'

'Give us service,' the Boy said. He took a step forward and the other backed and Pinkie grinned at him. 'Bring us two double brandies,' he said, 'and quick.' He said softly, 'Who would have thought I'd find Piker here?' She watched him with amazement that he could find any distraction from their purpose. She could hear the wind on upstair windows; where the steps curved another tombstone statuette raised its ruined limbs. He said, 'We were at the school together. I used to give him hell in the breaks.' The other returned with the brandies and brought, sidelong and scared and cautious, a whole smoky childhood with him. She felt a pang of jealousy against him because to-night she should have had all there was of Pinkie.

'You a servant?' the Boy said.

'I'm not a servant, I'm a waiter.'

'You want me to tip you?'

'I don't want your tips.'

The Boy took his brandy and drank it down; he coughed when it took him by the throat. It was like the stain of the world in his stomach. He said, 'Here's courage.' He said to Piker, 'What's the time?'

'You can read it on the clock,' Piker said, 'if you can read.'

'Haven't you any music?' the Boy said. 'God damn it, we want to celebrate.'

'There's the piano. An' the wireless.'

'Turn it on.'

The wireless was hidden behind a potted plant: a violin came wailing out, the notes shaken by atmospherics. The Boy said, 'He hates me. He hates my guts,' and turned to mock at Piker, but he'd gone. He said to Rose, 'You'd better drink that brandy.'

'I don't need it,' she said.

'Have it your own way.'

He stood by the wireless and she by the empty fire-place: three tables and three siphons and a Moorish-Tudor-God-knows-what-of-a-lamp were between them: they were gripped by an awful unreality, the need to make conversation, to say 'What a night!' or 'It's cold for the time of year'. She said, 'So he was at your school.'

'That's right.' They both looked at the clock: it was almost nine, and behind the violin the rain tapped against the seaward windows. He said awkwardly, 'We'd better be moving soon.'

She began to pray to herself, 'Holy Mary, Mother of God,' but then she stopped – she was in mortal sin: it was no good praying. Her prayers stayed here below with the siphons and the statuettes: they had no wings. She waited by the fireplace in terrified patience. He said uneasily, 'We ought to write – something, so people will know.'

'It doesn't matter, does it?' she said.

'Oh yes,' he said quickly, 'it does. We got to do things right. This is a pact. You read about them in the newspapers.'

'Do lots of people – do it?'

'It's always happening,' he said; an awful and airy confidence momentarily possessed him: the violin faded out and the time signal pinged through the rain. A voice behind the plant gave them the weather report – storms coming up from the Continent, a depression in the Atlantic, to-morrow's forecast. She began to listen and then remembered that to-morrow's weather didn't matter at all.

He said, 'Like another drink – or something?' He looked round for a Gents sign – 'I just got to go – an' wash.' She noticed the weight in his pocket – it was going to be that way. He said, 'Just add a piece on that note while I'm gone. Here's a pencil. Say you couldn't live without me, something like that. We got to do this right, as it's always done.' He went out into the passage and called to Piker and got his direction, then went up the stairs. At the statuette he turned and looked down into the panelled lounge. This was the kind of moment one kept for memory – the wind at the pier end, Sherry's and the men singing, lamplight on the harvest Burgundy, the crisis as Cubitt battered at the door. He found that he remembered it all without repulsion; he had a sense that somewhere, like a beggar outside a shuttered house, tenderness stirred, but he was bound in a habit of hate. He turned his back and went on up the stairs. He told himself that soon he would be free again – they'd see the note. He hadn't known she was all that unhappy, he would say, because they'd got to part: she must have found the gun in Dallow's room and brought it with her. They'd test it for finger-prints, of course, and then – he stared out throught the lavatory window: invisible rollers beat under the cliff. Life would go on. No more human contacts, other people's emotions washing at the brain – he would be free again: nothing to think about but himself. Myself: the word echoed hygienically on among the porcelain basins, the taps and plugs and wastes. He took the revolver out of his pocket and loaded it – two chambers. In the mirror above the wash-basin he could see his hand move round the metal death, adjusting the safety-catch. Down below the news was over and the music had begun again – it wailed upwards like a dog over a grave, and the huge darkness pressed a wet mouth against the panes. He put the revolver back and went out into the passage. That was the next move. Another statuette pointed an obscure moral with cemetery hands and a chaplet of marble flowers, and again he felt the prowling presence of pity.

Chapter Eight

'They've been gone a long while,' Dallow said. 'What are they up to?'

'Who cares?' Judy said. 'They want to be' – she pressed her plump lips against Dallow's cheek – 'alone' – her red hair caught in his mouth – a sour taste. 'You know what love is,' she said.

'He doesn't.' He was uneasy – conversations came back to him. He said, 'He hates her guts.' He put his arm half-heartedly round Judy – it was no good spoiling a party, but he wished he knew what Pinkie had in mind. He took a long drink out of Judy's glass, and somewhere Worthing way a siren wailed. Through the window he could see a couple mooning at the pier end, and an old man got his fortune card from the witch behind glass.

'Why don't he get clear of her then?' Judy asked. Her mouth looked for his mouth down the line of his jaw. She drew herself indignantly up and said, 'Who's that polony over there? What does she want lamping us all the time? This is a free country.'

Dallow turned and looked. His brain worked very slowly, first the statement – 'I never seen her,' and then the memory. 'Why,' he said, 'it's that damned buer who's been getting Pinkie rattled.' He got cumbrously to his feet and stumbled a little between the tables. 'Who are you?' he asked. 'Who are you?'

'Ida Arnold,' she said, 'for what it's worth. My friends call me Ida.'

'I'm not your friend.'

'You better be,' she said gently. 'Have a drink. Where's Pinkie gone – and Rose? You ought to 'ave brought them along. This is Phil. Introduce the lady friend.' She ran softly on, 'It's time we all got together. What's your name?'

'Don't you know what people get who poke their noses . . .'

'Oh, I know,' she said. 'I know all right. I was with Fred the day you finished him.'

'Talk sense,' Dallow said. 'Who the hell are you?'

'You ought to know. You followed us all the way up the front in that old Morris of yours.' She smiled quite amiably at him. He wasn't her game. 'It seems an age ago now, doesn't it?'

It was true all right – it seemed an age.

'Have a drink,' Ida said, 'you may as well. An' where's Pinkie? He didn't seem to like the look of me to-night. What were you celebrating? Not what's happened to Mr Prewitt? You won't have heard that.'

'What do you mean?' Dallow said. The wind got up against the glass and the waitresses yawned.

'You'll see it in the morning papers. I don't want to spoil your fun. And of course you'll know it sooner than that if he talks.'

'He's gone abroad.'

'He's at the police-station now,' she said with complete confidence. 'They brought him right back,' she went elaborately on. 'You ought to choose your solicitors better, men who can afford to take a holiday. They've got him for swindling. Arrested on the quay.'

He watched her uneasily. He didn't believe her – but all the same . . . 'You know an awful lot,' he said. 'Do you sleep at nights?'

'Do you?'

The big broken face had a kind of innocence about it. 'Me?' he said. 'I don't know a thing.'

'It was a waste giving him all that money. He'd have run anyway – and it didn't look good. When I got hold of Johnnie at the pier—'

He stared at her with hopeless amazement. 'You got hold of Johnnie? How the hell . . . ?'

She said simply, 'People like me.' She took a drink and said, 'His mother treated him shameful when he was a kid.'

'Whose mother?'

'Johnnie's.'

Dallow was impatient, puzzled, scared. 'What the hell,' he said, 'do you know about Johnnie's mother?'

'What he told me,' she said. She sat there completely at her ease, her big breasts ready for any secrets. She carried her air of compassion and comprehension about her like a rank cheap perfume. She said gently, 'I got nothing against you. I like to be friendly. Bring over your lady friend.'

He glanced quickly over his shoulder and back again. 'I better not,' he said. His voice fell. He too began automatically to confide. 'Truth is, she's a jealous bitch.'

'You don't say. And her old man . . .'

'Oh, her old man,' he said, 'he's all right. What Frank doesn't see, he doesn't mind.' He dropped his voice still lower. 'And he can't see much – he's blind.'

'I didn't know that,' she said.

'You wouldn't,' he said. 'Not from his pressing and ironing. He's got a wonderful hand with an iron.' He broke suddenly off. 'What the hell,' he said, 'did you mean – you didn't know *that*? What did you know?'

'There isn't much,' she said, 'I've not picked up – here and there. The neighbours always talk.' She was barnacled with pieces of popular wisdom.

'Who's talking?' It was Judy now. She'd come across to them. 'An' what 'ave they got to talk about? Why, if I chose to put my tongue round some of their doings. But I wouldn't like to,' Judy said. 'I wouldn't like to.' She looked vaguely round. 'What *has* happened to those two?'

'Perhaps I scared them,' Ida Arnold said.

'*You* scared them?' Dallow said. 'That's rich. Pinkie's not scared that easy.'

'What I want to know is,' Judy said, 'what neighbour's said what?'

Somebody was shooting at the range: when the door opened and a couple came in they could hear the shots – one, two, three. 'That'll be Pinkie,' Dallow said. 'He was always good with a gun.'

'You better go an' see,' Ida gently remarked, 'that he doesn't do something desperate – with his gun – when he gets to know.'

Dallow said, 'You jump to things. We got no cause to be afraid of Mr Prewitt.'

'You gave him money, I suppose, for something.'

'Aw,' he said, 'Johnnie's been joking.'

'Your friend Cubitt seemed to think . . .'

'Cubitt doesn't know a thing.'

'Of course,' she admitted, 'he wasn't there, was he? That time, I mean. But you . . .' she said. 'Wouldn't twenty pounds be of use to you? After all you don't want to get into trouble . . . Let Pinkie carry his own crimes.'

'You make me sick,' he said. 'You think you know a lot and you don't know a thing.' He said to Judy, 'I'm goin' to have a drain. You want to keep your mouth shut or this polony . . .' He stretched a gesture, hopelessly – he couldn't express what she mightn't put over on you. He went uneasily out, and the wind caught him, so that he had to grab at his old greasy hat and hold it on. Going down the steps to the gents was like going down into a ship's engine-room in a storm. The whole place shook a little under his feet as the swell came up against the piles and drove on to break against the beach. He thought: I oughter warn Pinkie about Prewitt if it's true . . . He *had* things on his mind, other things besides old Spicer. He came up the ladder and looked down the deck – Pinkie wasn't to be seen. He went on past the peep machines – not in sight. It was someone else shooting at the booth.

He asked the man, 'Seen Pinkie?'

'What's the game?' the man said. 'You know I seen him. *An'* he's gone for a ride in the country – with his girl – for a freshener – Hastings way. *An'* I suppose you want to know the time too. Well,' the man said, 'I'm swearing nothing. You can pitch on someone else for your phoney alibis.'

'You're crackers,' Dallow said. He moved away. Across the noisy sea the hour began to strike in Brighton churches: he counted one, two, three, four, and stopped. He was scared – suppose it *was* true, suppose Pinkie knew, and it was that mad scheme . . . What the hell was he taking anyone for a ride in the country at this hour, except to a roadhouse, and Pinkie didn't go to roadhouses? He said softly, 'I won't stand for it,' aloud. He was confused, he wished he hadn't drunk all that beer. She was a good kid. He remembered her in the kitchen, going to light the stove. And why not? he thought, staring gloomily out to sea; he was shaken by a sudden sentimental desire which Judy couldn't satisfy: for a paper with your breakfast and warm fires. He began to walk rapidly down the pier towards the turnstiles. There were things he wouldn't stand for.

He knew the Morris wouldn't be on the rank, but all the same he had to go and see for himself. Its absence was like a voice speaking quite plainly in his ear. 'Suppose she kills herself . . . a pact may be murder, but they don't hang you for it.' He stood there hopelessly, not knowing what to do. Beer clouded his brain: he passed a harassed hand across his face. He said to the attendant, 'You see that Morris go out?'

'Your friend and his girl took it,' the man said, hobbling between a Talbot and an Austin. One leg was gammy, he moved it with a mechanism worked from his pocket, lurching with an air of enormous strain to pocket sixpence, to say 'It's a fine night'; he looked worn with the awful labour of the trivial act. He said, 'They're goin' up to Peacehaven for a drink. Don't ask me why.' Hand in pocket he pulled the hidden wire and made his unsteady and diagonal way towards a Ford. 'The rain won't hold off long,' his voice came back, and 'Thank you, sir,' and then again the labour of movement as a Morris Oxford backed in, the pulling at the wire.

Dallow stood there hopelessly at a loss. There were buses . . . but everything would be over long before a bus got in. Better to wash his hands of the whole thing . . . after all he didn't *know*; in half an hour he might see the old car coming back past the Aquarium, Pinkie driving and the girl beside him, but he knew very well in his heart that it would never come, not with both of them, that way. The Boy had left too many signs behind him – the message at the shooting-range, at the car-park: he wanted to be followed in good time, in his own time, to fit in with his story. The man came lurching back. He said, 'I thought your friend seemed queer to-night. Sort of lit up.' It was as if he were talking in the witness box, giving the evidence he was meant to give.

Dallow turned hopelessly away . . . fetch Judy, go home, wait . . . and there was the woman standing a few feet away. She'd followed him and listened. He said, 'God's sakes, this is your doing. You made him marry her, you made him . . .'

'Get a car,' she said, 'quick.'

'I've not got the money for a car.'

'I have. You better hurry.'

'There's no cause to hurry,' he said weakly. 'They've just gone for a drink.'

'You know what they've gone for,' she said. 'I don't. But if *you* want to keep out of this, you'd better get that car.'

The first rain began to blow up the parade as he weakly argued. 'I don't know a thing.'

'That's right,' she said. 'You're just taking me for a drive, that's all.' She burst suddenly out at him: 'Don't be a fool. You better have me for a friend. . . .' She said, 'You see what's come to Pinkie.'

All the same he didn't hurry. What was the good? Pinkie had laid *this* trail. Pinkie thought of everything, they were meant to follow in due course, and find . . . He hadn't got the imagination to see what they'd find.

Chapter Nine

The Boy stopped at the head of the stairs and looked down. Two men had come into the lounge: hearty and damp in camel-hair coats they shook out their moisture like dogs and were noisy over their drinks. 'Two pints,' they ordered, 'in tankards,' and fell suddenly silent scenting a girl in the lounge. They were upper-class, they'd learned that tankard trick in class hotels: he watched their gambits with hatred from the stairs. Anything female was better than nothing, even Rose; but he could sense their half-heartedness. She wasn't worth more than a little sidelong swagger. 'I think we touched eighty.'

'I made it eighty-two.'

'She's a good bus.'

'How much did they sting you?'

'A couple of hundred. She's cheap at the price.'

Then they both stopped and took an arrogant look at the girl by the statuette. She wasn't worth bothering about, but if she absolutely fell, without trouble . . . One of them said something in a low voice and the other laughed. They took long swills of bitter from the tankards.

Tenderness came up to the very window and looked in. What the hell right had they got to swagger and laugh . . . if she was good enough for him. He came down the stairs into the hall; they looked up and moued to each other, as much as to say – 'Oh well, she wasn't really worth the trouble.'

One of them said, 'Drink up. We better get on with the good work. You don't think Zoe'll be out?'

'Oh no. I said I might drop in.'

'Her friend all right?'

'She's hot.'

'Let's get on then.'

They drained their beer and moved arrogantly to the door, taking a passing look at Rose as they went. He could hear them laugh outside the door. They were laughing at him. He came a few steps into the lounge: again they were bound in an icy constraint. He had a sudden inclination to throw up the whole thing, to get into the car and drive home, and let her live. It was less a motion of pity than of weariness – there was such a hell of a lot to do and think of, there were going to be so many questions to be answered. He could hardly believe in the freedom at the end of it, and even that freedom was to be in a strange place. He said, 'The rain's worse.' She stood there waiting; she couldn't answer: she was breathing hard as if she'd run a long way – and she looked old. She was sixteen, but this was how she might have looked after years of marriage, of the childbirth and the daily quarrel: they had reached death and it affected them like age.

She said, 'I wrote what you wanted.' She waited for him to take the scrap of paper and write his own message to the coroner, to *Daily Express* readers, to what one called the world. The other boy came cautiously into the lounge and said, 'You haven't paid.' While Pinkie found the money, she was visited by an almost overwhelming rebellion – she had only to go out, leave him, refuse to play. He couldn't make her kill herself: life wasn't as bad as that. It came like a revelation, as if someone had whispered to her that she was someone, a separate creature – not just one flesh with him. She could always escape – if he didn't change his mind. Nothing was decided. They could go in the car wherever he wanted them to go; she could take the gun from his hand, and even then – at the last moment of all – she needn't shoot. Nothing was decided – there was always hope.

'That's your tip,' the Boy said. 'I always tip a waiter.' Hate came back. He said, 'You a good Roman, Piker? Do you go to Mass on Sundays like they tell you?'

Piker said with weak defiance, 'Why not, Pinkie?'

'You're afraid,' the Boy said. 'You're afraid of burning.'

'Who wouldn't be?'

'I'm not.' He looked with loathing into the past – a cracked bell ringing, a child weeping under the cane – and repeated, 'I'm not afraid.' He said to Rose, 'We'll be going.' He came tentatively across and put a nail against her cheek – half caress, half threat – and said, 'You'd love me always, wouldn't you?'

'Yes.'

He gave her one more chance: 'You'd always have stuck to me,' and when she nodded her agreement, he began wearily the long course of action which one day would let him be free again.

Outside in the rain the self-starter wouldn't work again: he stood with his coat-collar turned up and pulled the handle. She wanted to tell him he mustn't stand there, getting wet, because she'd changed her mind: they were going to live – by hook or by crook, but she didn't dare. She pushed hope back – to the last possible moment. When they drove off she said, 'Last night . . . the night before . . . you didn't hate me, did you, for what we did?'

He said, 'No, I didn't hate you.'

'Even though it was a mortal sin.'

It was quite true – he hadn't hated her; he hadn't even hated the act. There had been a kind of pleasure, a kind of pride, a kind of – something else. The car lurched back on to the main road; he turned the bonnet to Brighton. An enormous emotion beat on him; it was like something trying to get in; the pressure of gigantic wings against the glass. Dona nobis pacem. He withstood it, with all the bitter force of the school bench, the cement playground, the St Pancras waiting-room, Dallow's and Judy's secret lust, and the cold unhappy moment on the pier. If the glass broke, if the beast – whatever it was – got in, God knows what it would do. He had a sense of huge havoc – the confession, the penance and the sacrament – and awful distraction, and he drove blind into the rain. He could see nothing through the cracked stained windscreen. A bus came upon them and pulled out just in time – he was on the wrong side. He said, suddenly at random, 'We pull in here.'

An ill-made street petered out towards the cliff – bungalows of every shape and kind, a vacant plot full of salt grass and wet thorn bushes like bedraggled fowls, no lights except in three windows. A radio played, and in a garage a man was doing something to his motor-bike which roared and spluttered in the darkness. He drove a few yards in, turned out his headlights, switched off his engine. The rain came noisily in through the rent in the hood and they could hear the sea battering the cliff. He said, 'Well, take a look. It's the world.' Another light went on behind a stained-glass door (the laughing Cavalier between Tudor roses) and looking out as if it was he who'd got to take some sort of farewell of the bike and the bungalows and the rainy street, he thought of the words in the Mass – 'He was in the world and the world was made by Him and the world knew Him not.'

It was about as far as hope could be stretched; she had to say now or never – 'I won't do it. I never meant to do it.' It was like some romantic adventure – you plan to fight in Spain, and then before you know the tickets are taken for you, the introductions are pressed into your hand, somebody has come to see you off, everything is real. He put his hand in his pocket and pulled out the gun. He said, 'I got it out of Dallow's room.' She wanted to say she didn't know how to use it, to make any excuse, but he seemed to have thought of everything. He explained, 'I've put up the safety-catch. All you need do is pull on this. It isn't hard. Put it in your ear – that'll hold it steady.' His youth came out in the crudity of his instruction: he was like a boy playing on an ash-heap. 'Go on,' he said, 'take it.'

It was amazing how far hope could stretch. She thought: I needn't say anything yet. I can take the gun and then – throw it out of the car, run away, do something to stop everything. But all the time she felt the steady pressure of his will. *His* mind was made up. She took the gun; it was like a treachery. What will he do, she thought, if I don't . . . shoot. Would he shoot himself alone, without her? Then he would be damned, and she wouldn't have her chance of being damned too, of showing Them they couldn't pick and choose. To go on living for years . . . you couldn't tell what life would do to you in making you meek, good, repentant. Belief in her mind had the bright clarity of images, of the crib at Christmas: here goodness ended, past the cow and the sheep, and there evil began – Herod seeking the child's birthplace from his turreted keep. She wanted to be with Herod – if *he* were there. You could win to the evil side suddenly, in a moment of despair or passion, but through a long life the guardian good drove you remorselessly towards the crib, the 'happy death'.

He said, 'We don't want to wait any longer. Do you want me to do it first?'

'No,' she said, 'no.'

'All right then. You take a walk – or better still I'll take a walk an' you stay here. When it's over, I'll come back an' do it too.' Again he gave the sense that he was a boy playing a game, a game in which you could take in the coldest detail of the scalping knife or the bayonet wound and then go home to tea. He said, 'It'll be too dark for me to see much.'

He opened the door of the car. She sat motionless with the gun on her lap. Behind them on the main road a car went slowly past towards Peacehaven. He said awkwardly, 'You know what to do?' He seemed to think that some motion of tenderness was expected of him. He put out his mouth and kissed her on the cheek; he was afraid of the mouth – thoughts travel too easily from lip to lip. He said, 'It won't hurt,' and began to walk back a little way towards the main road. Hope was stretched now as far as it would go. The radio had stopped; the motor-bicycle exploded twice in the garage, feet moved on gravel and on the main road she could hear a car reversing.

If it was a guardian angel speaking to her now, he spoke like a devil – he tempted her to virtue like a sin. To throw away the gun was a betrayal; it would be an act of cowardice: it would mean that she chose never to see him again for ever. Moral maxims dressed in pedantic priestly tones remembered from old sermons, instructions, confessions – 'you can plead for him at the throne of Grace' – came to her like unconvincing insinuations. The evil act was the honest act, the bold and the faithful – it was only lack of courage, it seemed to her, that spoke so virtuously. She put the gun up to her ear and put it down again with a feeling of sickness – it was a poor love that was afraid to die. She hadn't been afraid to commit mortal sin – it was death not damnation which was scaring her. Pinkie said it wouldn't hurt. She felt his will moving her hand – she could trust him. She put up the gun again.

A voice called sharply 'Pinkie' and she heard somebody splashing in the puddles. Footsteps ran . . . she couldn't tell where. It seemed to her that this must be news, that this must make a difference. She couldn't kill herself when this might mean good news. It was as if somewhere in the darkness the will which had governed her hand relaxed, and all the hideous forces of self-preservation came flooding back. It didn't seem real – that she had really intended to sit there and press the trigger. 'Pinkie,' the voice called again, and the splashing steps came nearer. She pulled the car door open and flung the revolver far away from her towards the damp scrub.

In the light from the stained glass she saw Dallow and the woman – and a policeman who looked confused as if he didn't quite know what was happening. Somebody came softly round the car behind her and said, 'Where's that gun? Why don't you shoot? Give it me.'

She said, 'I threw it away.'

The others approached cautiously like a deputation. Pinkie called out suddenly in a breaking childish voice, 'You bloody squealer, Dallow.'

'Pinkie,' Dallow said, 'it's no use. They got Prewitt.' The policeman looked ill-at-ease like a stranger at a party.

'Where's that gun?' Pinkie said again. He screamed with hate and fear, 'My God, have I got to have a massacre?'

She said, 'I threw it away.'

She could see his face indistinctly as it leant in over the little dashboard light. It was like a child's, badgered, confused, betrayed: fake years slipped away – he was whisked back towards the unhappy playground. He said, 'You little . . .' he didn't finish – the deputation approached, he left her, diving into his pocket for something. 'Come on, Dallow,' he said, 'you bloody squealer,' and put his hand up. Then she couldn't tell what happened: glass – somewhere – broke, he screamed and she saw his face – steam. He screamed and screamed, with his hands up to his eyes; he turned and ran; she saw a police baton at his feet and broken glass. He looked half his size, doubled up in appalling agony: it was as if the flames had literally got him and he shrank – shrank into a schoolboy flying in panic and pain, scrambling over a fence, running on.

'Stop him,' Dallow cried: it wasn't any good: he was at the edge, he was over: they couldn't even hear a splash. It was as if he'd been withdrawn suddenly by a hand out of any existence – past or present, whipped away into zero – nothing.

Chapter Ten

'It shows,' Ida Arnold said. 'you only have to hold on.' She emptied her glass of stout and laid it down on Henekey's upturned barrel.

'And Prewitt?' Clarence asked.

'How slow you are, you old ghost. I just made that up. I couldn't chase over France for him, and the police – you know what police are – they always want evidence.'

'They had Cubitt?'

'Cubitt wouldn't talk when he was sober. And you'd never get him drunk enough to talk to them. Why, this is slander what I've been telling you. Or it would be slander – if *he* were alive.'

'I wonder you don't feel bad about that, Ida.'

'Somebody else would have been dead if we hadn't turned up.'

'It was her own choice.'

But Ida Arnold had an answer to everything. 'She didn't understand. She was only a kid. She thought he was in love with her.'

'An' what does she think now?'

'Don't ask me. I've done my best. I took her home. What a girl needs at
a time like that is her mother and dad. Anyway she's got me to thank she
isn't dead.'

'How did you get the policeman to go with you?'

'We told him they'd stolen the car. The poor man didn't know what it
was all about, but he acted quick when Pinkie pulled out the vitriol.'

'And Phil Corkery?'

'He's talking of Hastings,' she said, 'next year, but I have a sort of feeling
there won't be any postcards for me after this.'

'You're a terrible woman, Ida,' Clarence said. He sighed deeply and
stared into his glass. 'Have another?'

'No thank you, Clarence. I got to be getting home.'

'You're a terrible woman,' Clarence repeated; he was a little drunk, 'but
I got to give you credit. You act for the best.'

'He's not on my conscience anyway.'

'As you say it was him or her.'

'There wasn't any choice,' Ida Arnold said. She got up; she was like a
figurehead of Victory. She nodded to Harry at the bar.

'You've been away, Ida?'

'Just a week or two.'

'It doesn't seem so long,' Harry said.

'Well, good night all.'

'Good night. Good night.'

She took the tube to Russell Square and walked, carrying her suitcase: let
herself in and looked in the hall for letters. There was only one – from Tom.
She knew what that would be about, and her great warm heart softened as
she thought: After all, when all's said, Tom an' I know what Love is. She
opened the door on to the basement stairs and called, 'Crowe. Old Crowe.'

'You, Ida?'

'Come up for a chat an' we'll have a turn with the Board.'

The curtains were drawn as she had left them – nobody had touched the
china on the mantelpiece, but Warwick Deeping wasn't in the bookshelf
and *The Good Companions* was on its side. The char had been in – she
could see that – borrowing. She got out a box of chocolate biscuits for Old
Crowe; the lid had not been left properly on and they were a little soft and
stale. Then carefully she lifted out the Board, cleared the table and laid it
in the centre. SUIKILLEYE, she thought. I know what that means now. The
Board had forseen it all – Sui, its own word for the scream, the agony, the
leap. She brooded gently with her fingers on the Board. When you came to
think of it, the Board had saved Rose, and a multitude of popular sayings
began to pass together into her mind. It was like when the points shift and
the signal goes down and the red lamp changes to green and the great engine
takes the accustomed rails. It's a strange world, there's more things in heaven
and earth . . .

Old Crowe came peering in. 'What's it to be, Ida?'

'I want to ask advice,' Ida said. 'I want to ask whether maybe I ought to
go back to Tom.'

Chapter Eleven

Rose could just see the old head bent towards the grill. The priest had a whistle in his breath. He listened – patiently – whistling, while she painfully brought out her whole agony. She could hear the exasperated women creak their chairs outside waiting for confession. She said, 'It's *that* I repent. Not going with him.' She was defiant and tearless in the stuffy box; the old priest had a cold and smelt of eucalyptus. He said gently and nasally, 'Go on, my child.'

She said, 'I wish I'd killed myself. I ought to 'ave killed myself.' The old man began to say something, but she interrupted him. 'I'm not asking for absolution. I don't want absolution. I want to be like him – damned.'

The old man whistled as he drew in his breath. She felt certain he understood nothing. She repeated monotonously, 'I wish I'd killed myself.' She pressed her hands against her breasts in the passion of misery. She hadn't come to confess, she had come to think; she couldn't think at home where the stove hadn't been lit and her father had got a mood and her mother – she could tell it in her sidelong questions – was wondering how much money Pinkie ... She would have found the courage now to kill herself if she hadn't been afraid that somewhere in that obscure countryside of death they might miss each other – mercy operating somehow for one and not for the other. She said with breaking voice, 'That woman. *She* ought to be damned. Saying he wanted to get rid of me. She doesn't know about love.'

'Perhaps she was right,' the old priest murmured.

'And you don't either,' she said furiously, pressing her childish face against the grill.

The old man suddenly began to talk, whistling every now and then and blowing eucalyptus through the grill. He said, 'There was a man, a Frenchman, you wouldn't know about him, my child, who had the same idea as you. He was a good man, a holy man, and he lived in sin all through his life, because he couldn't bear the idea that any soul could suffer damnation.' She listened with astonishment. He said, 'This man decided that if any soul was going to be damned, he would be damned too. He never took the sacraments, he never married his wife in church. I don't know, my child, but some people think he was – well, a saint. I think he died in what we are told is mortal sin – I'm not sure: it was in the war: perhaps ...' He sighed and whistled, bending his old head. He said, 'You can't conceive, my child, nor can I or anyone the ... appalling ... strangeness of the mercy of God.'

Outside the chairs creaked again and again – people impatient to get their own repentance, absolution, penance finished for the week. He said, 'It was a case of greater love hath no man than this that he lay down his soul for his friend.'

He shivered and sneezed. 'We must hope and pray,' he said, 'hope and pray. The Church does not demand that we believe any soul is cut off from mercy.'

She said with sad conviction, 'He's damned. He knew what he was about. He was a Catholic too.'

He said gently, 'Corruptio optimi est pessima.'

'Yes, father?'

'I mean – a Catholic is more capable of evil than anyone. I think perhaps – because we believe in Him – we are more in touch with the devil than other people. But we must hope,' he said mechanically, 'hope and pray.'

'I want to hope,' she said, 'but I don't know how.'

'If he loved you, surely,' the old man said, 'that shows there was some good . . .'

'Even love like that?'

'Yes.'

She brooded on the idea in the little dark box. He said, 'And come back soon – I can't give you absolution now – but come back – to-morrow.'

She said weakly, 'Yes, father. . . . And if there's a baby . . .'

He said, 'With your simplicity and his force . . . Make him a saint – to pray for his father.'

A sudden feeling of immense gratitude broke through the pain – it was as if she had been given the sight a long way off of life going on again. He said, 'Pray for me, my child.'

She said, 'Yes, oh yes.'

Outside she looked up at the name on the confessional box – it wasn't any name she remembered. Priests come and go.

She went out into the street – the pain was still there, you couldn't shake it off with a word; but the worst horror she thought was over – the horror of the complete circle – to be back at home, back at Snow's – they'd take her back – just as if the Boy had never existed at all. He had existed and would always exist. She had a sudden conviction that she carried life, and she thought proudly: Let them get over that if they can; let them get over that. She turned out on to the front opposite the Palace Pier and began to walk firmly away from the direction of her home towards Frank's. There was something to salvaged from that house and room, something else they wouldn't be able to get over – his voice speaking a message to her: if there was a child, speaking to the child. 'If he loved you,' the priest had said, 'that shows . . .' She walked rapidly in the thin June sunlight towards the worst horror of all.

THE END OF
THE AFFAIR

The End of the Affair
To C

'Man has places in his heart which do not yet exist,
and into them enters suffering in order that they
may have existence.'

LÉON BLOY

Chapter One

A story has no beginning or end: arbitrarily one chooses that moment of experience from which to look back or from which to look ahead. I say 'one chooses' with the inaccurate pride of a professional writer who – when he has been seriously noted at all – has been praised for his technical ability, but do I in fact of my own will *choose* that black wet January night on the Common, in 1946, the sight of Henry Miles slanting across the wide river of rain, or did these images choose me? It is convenient, it is correct according to the rules of my craft to begin just there, but if I had believed then in a God, I could also have believed in a hand, plucking at my elbow, a suggestion, 'Speak to him: he hasn't seen you yet.'

For why should I have spoken to him? If hate is not too large a term to use in relation to any human being, I hated Henry – I hated his wife Sarah too. And he, I suppose, came soon after the events of that evening to hate me: as he surely at times must have hated his wife and that other, in whom in those days we were lucky enough not to believe. So this is a record of hate far more than of love, and if I come to say anything in favour of Henry and Sarah I can be trusted: I am writing against the bias because it is my professional pride to prefer the near-truth, even to the expression of my near-hate.

It was strange to see Henry out on such a night: he liked his comfort and after all – or so I thought – he had Sarah. To me comfort is like the wrong memory at the wrong place or time: if one is lonely one prefers discomfort. There was too much comfort even in the bed-sitting-room I had at the wrong – the south – side of the Common, in the relics of other people's furniture. I thought I would go for a walk through the rain and have a drink at the local. The little crowded hall was full of strangers' hats and coats and I took somebody else's umbrella by accident – the man on the second floor had friends in. Then I closed the stained-glass door behind me and made my way carefully down the steps that had been blasted in 1944 and never repaired. I had reason to remember the occasion and how the stained glass, tough and ugly and Victorian, stood up to the shock as our grandfathers themselves would have done.

Directly I began to cross the Common I realized I had the wrong umbrella, for it sprang a leak and the rain ran down under my macintosh collar, and then it was I saw Henry. I could so easily have avoided him; he had no umbrella and in the light of the lamp I could see his eyes were blinded with the rain. The black leafless trees gave no protection: they stood around like broken waterpipes, and the rain dripped off his stiff dark hat and ran in streams down his black civil servant's overcoat. If I had walked straight by him, he wouldn't have seen me, and I could have made certain by stepping two feet off the pavement, but I said, 'Henry, you are almost a stranger,' and saw his eyes light up as though we were old friends.

'Bendrix,' he said with affection, and yet the world would have said *he* had the reasons for hate, not me.

'What are you up to, Henry, in the rain?' There are men whom one has an irresistible desire to tease: men whose virtues one doesn't share. He said evasively, 'Oh, I wanted a bit of air,' and during a sudden blast of wind and rain he just caught his hat in time from being whirled away towards the north side.

'How's Sarah?' I asked because it might have seemed odd if I hadn't, though nothing would have delighted me more than to have heard that she was sick, unhappy, dying. I imagined in those days that any suffering she underwent would lighten mine, and if she were dead I could be free: I would no longer imagine all the things one does imagine under my ignoble circumstances. I could even like poor silly Henry, I thought, if Sarah were dead.

He said, 'Oh, she's out for the evening somewhere,' and set that devil in my mind at work again, remembering other days when Henry must have replied just like that to other inquirers, while I alone knew where Sarah was. 'A drink?' I asked, and to my surprise he put himself in step beside me. We had never before drunk together outside his home.

'It's a long time since we've seen you, Bendrix.' For some reason I am a man known by his surname – I might never have been christened for all the use my friends make of the rather affected Maurice my literary parents gave me.

'A long time.'

'Why, it must be – more than a year.'

'June 1944,' I said.

'As long as that – well, well.' The fool, I thought, the fool to see nothing strange in a year and a half's interval. Less than five hundred yards of flat grass separated our two 'sides'. Had it never occurred to him to say to Sarah, 'How's Bendrix doing? What about asking Bendrix in?' and hadn't her replies ever seemed to him . . . odd, evasive, suspicious? I had fallen out of their sight as completely as a stone in a pond. I suppose the ripples may have disturbed Sarah for a week, a month, but Henry's blinkers were firmly tied. I had hated his blinkers even when I had benefited from them, knowing that others could benefit too.

'Is she at the cinema?' I asked.

'Oh no, she hardly ever goes.'

'She used to.'

The 'Pontefract Arms' was still decorated for Christmas with paper streamers and paper bells, the relics of commercial gaiety, mauve and orange, and the young landlady leant her breasts against the bar with a look of contempt for her customers.

'Pretty,' Henry said, without meaning it, and stared around with a certain lost air, a shyness, for somewhere to hang his hat. I got the impression that the nearest he had ever before been to a public bar was the chophouse off Northumberland Avenue where he ate lunch with his colleagues from the Ministry.

'What will you have?'

'I wouldn't mind a whisky.'

'Nor would I, but you'll have to make do with rum.'

We sat at a table and fingered our glasses: I had never had much to say to Henry. I doubt whether I should ever have troubled to know Henry or Sarah well if I had not begun in 1939 to write a story with a senior civil servant as the main character. Henry James once, in a discussion with Walter Besant, said that a young woman with sufficient talent need only pass the mess-room windows of a Guards' barracks and look inside in order to write a novel about the Brigade, but I think at some stage of her book she would have found it necessary to go to bed with a Guardsman if only in order to check on the details. I didn't exactly go to bed with Henry, but I did the next best thing, and the first night I took Sarah out to dinner I had the cold-blooded intention of picking the brain of a civil servant's wife. She didn't know what I was at; she thought, I am sure, I was genuinely interested in her family life, and perhaps that first awakened her liking for me. What time did Henry have breakfast? I asked her. Did he go to the office by tube, bus or taxi? Did he bring his work home at night? Did he have a brief-case with the royal arms on it? Our friendship blossomed under my interest: she was so pleased that anybody should take Henry seriously. Henry was important, but important rather as an elephant is important, from the size of his department; there are some kinds of importance that remain hopelessly damned to unseriousness. Henry was an important assistant secretary in the Ministry of Pensions – later it was to be the Ministry of Home Security. Home Security – I used to laugh at that later in those moments when you hate your companion and look for any weapon. ... A time came when I deliberately told Sarah that I had only taken Henry up for the purpose of copy, copy too for a character who was the ridiculous, the comic element in my book. It was then she began to dislike my novel. She had an enormous loyalty to Henry (I could never deny that), and in those clouded hours when the demon took charge of my brain and I resented even harmless Henry, I would use the novel and invent episodes too crude to write. ... Once when Sarah had spent a whole night with me (I had looked forward to it as a writer looks forward to the last word of his book) I had spoilt the occasion suddenly by a chance word which broke the mood of what sometimes seemed for hours at a time a complete love. I had fallen sullenly asleep about two and woke at three, and putting my hand on her arm woke Sarah. I think I had meant to make everything well again, until my victim turned her face, bleary and beautiful with sleep and full of trust, towards me. She had forgotten the quarrel, and I found even in her forgetfulness a new cause. How twisted we humans are, and yet they say a God made us; but I find it hard to conceive of any God who is not as simple as a perfect equation, as clear as air. I said to her, 'I've lain awake thinking of Chapter Five. Does Henry ever eat coffee beans to clear his breath before an important conference?' She shook her head and began to cry silently, and I of course pretended not to understand the reason – a simple question, it had been worrying me about my character, this was not an attack on Henry, the nicest people sometimes eat coffee beans. ... So I went on. She wept awhile and went to sleep. She was a good sleeper, and I took even her power to sleep as an added offence.

Henry drank his rum quickly, his gaze wandering miserably among the mauve and orange streamers. I asked, 'Had a good Christmas?'

'Very nice. Very nice,' he said.

'At home?' Henry looked up at me as though my inflection of the word sounded strange.

'Home? Yes, of course.'

'And Sarah's well?'

'Yes.'

'Have another rum?'

'It's my turn.'

While Henry fetched the drinks I went into the lavatory. The walls were scrawled with phrases: 'Damn you, landlord, and your breasty wife.' 'To all pimps and whores a merry syphilis and a happy gonorrhea.' I went quickly out again to the cheery paper streamers and the clink of glass. Sometimes I see myself reflected too closely in other men for comfort, and then I have an enormous wish to believe in the saints, in heroic virtue.

I repeated to Henry the two lines I had seen. I wanted to shock him, and it surprised me when he said simply, 'Jealousy's an awful thing.'

'You mean the bit about the breasty wife?'

'Both of them. When you are miserable, you envy other people's happiness.' It wasn't what I had ever expected him to learn in the Ministry of Home Security. And there – in that phrase – the bitterness leaks again out of my pen. What a dull lifeless quality this bitterness is. If I could I would write with love, but if I could write with love, I would be another man: I would never have lost love. Yet suddenly across the shiny tiled surface of the bar-table I felt something, nothing so extreme as love, perhaps nothing more than a companionship in misfortune. I said to Henry, 'Are *you* miserable?'

'Bendrix, I'm worried.'

'Tell me.'

I expect it was the rum that made him speak, or was he partly aware of how much I knew about him? Sarah was loyal, but in a relationship such as ours had been you can't help picking up a thing or two. . . . I knew he had a mole on the left of his navel because a birthmark of my own had once reminded Sarah of it: I knew he suffered from short sight, but wouldn't wear glasses with strangers (and I was still enough of a stranger never to have seen him in them): I knew his liking for tea at ten: I even knew his sleeping habits. Was he conscious that I knew so much already, that one more fact would not alter our relation? He said, 'I'm worried about Sarah, Bendrix.'

The door of the bar opened and I could see the rain lashing down against the light. A little hilarious man darted in and called out, 'Wot cher, everybody,' and nobody answered.

'Is she ill? I thought you said . . .'

'No. Not ill. I don't think so.' He looked miserably around – this was not his *milieu*. I noticed that the whites of his eyes were bloodshot; perhaps he hadn't been wearing his glasses enough – there are always so many strangers, or it might have been the after-effect of tears. He said, 'Bendrix, I can't talk here,' as though he had once been in the habit of talking somewhere. 'Come home with me.'

'Will Sarah be back?'

'I don't expect so.'

I paid for the drinks, and that again was a symptom of Henry's disturbance – he never took other people's hospitality easily. He was always the one in a taxi to have the money ready in the palm of his hand, while we others fumbled. The avenues of the Common still ran with rain, but it wasn't far to Henry's. He let himself in with a latch-key under the Queen Anne fanlight and called, 'Sarah. Sarah.' I longed for a reply and dreaded a reply, but nobody answered. He said, 'She's out still. Come into the study.'

I had never been in his study before: I had always been Sarah's friend, and when I met Henry it was on Sarah's territory, her haphazard living-room where nothing matched, nothing was period or planned, where everything seemed to belong to that very week because nothing was ever allowed to remain as a token of past taste or past sentiment. Everything was used there; just as in Henry's study I now felt that very little had ever been used. I doubted whether the set of Gibbon had once been opened, and the set of Scott was only there because it had – probably – belonged to his father, like the bronze copy of the Discus Thrower. And yet he was happier in his unused room simply because it was his: his possession. I thought with bitterness and envy: if one possesses a thing securely, one need never use it.

'A whisky?' Henry asked. I remembered his eyes and wondered if he were drinking more than he had done in the old days. Certainly the whiskies he poured out were generous doubles.

'What's troubling you, Henry?' I had long abandoned that novel about the senior civil servant: I wasn't looking for copy any longer.

'Sarah,' he said.

Would I have been frightened if he had said that, in just that way, two years ago? No, I think I should have been overjoyed – one gets so hopelessly tired of deception. I would have welcomed the open fight if only because there might have been a chance, however small, that through some error of tactics on his side I might have won. And there has never been a time in my life before or since when I have so much wanted to win. I have never had so strong a desire even to write a good book.

He looked up at me with those red-rimmed eyes and said, 'Bendrix, I'm afraid.' I could no longer patronize him: he was one of misery's graduates: he had passed in the same school, and for the first time I thought of him as an equal. I remember there was one of those early brown photographs in an Oxford frame on his desk, the photograph of his father, and looking at it I thought how like the photograph was to Henry (it had been taken at about the same age, the middle forties) and how unlike. It wasn't the moustache that made it different – it was the Victorian look of confidence, of being at home in the world and knowing the way around, and suddenly I felt again that friendly sense of companionship. I liked him better than I would have liked his father (who had been in the Treasury). We were fellow strangers.

'What is it you're afraid of, Henry?'

He sat down in an easy chair as though somebody had pushed him and said with disgust, 'Bendrix, I've always thought the worst thing, the very worst, a man could do . . .' I should certainly have been on tenterhooks in those other days: strange to me, and how infinitely dreary, the serenity of innocence.

'You know you can trust me, Henry.' It was possible, I thought, that she had kept a letter, though I had written so few. It is a professional risk that authors run. Women are apt to exaggerate the importance of their lovers and they never foresee the disappointing day when an indiscreet letter will appear marked 'Interesting' in an autograph catalogue priced at five shillings.

'Take a look at this then,' Henry said.

He held a letter out to me: it was not in my handwriting. 'Go on. Read it,' Henry said. It was from some friend of Henry's and he wrote, 'I suggest the man you want to help should apply to a fellow called Savage, 159 Vigo Street. I found him able and discreet, and his employees seemed less nauseous than those chaps usually are.'

'I don't understand, Henry.'

'I wrote to this man and said that an acquaintance of mine had asked my advice about private detective agencies. It's terrible, Bendrix. He must have seen through the pretence.'

'You really mean . . .?'

'I haven't done anything about it, but there the letter sits on my desk reminding me. . . . It seems so silly, doesn't it, that I can trust her absolutely not to read it though she comes in here a dozen times a day. I don't even put it away in a drawer. And yet I can't trust . . . she's out for a walk now. A *walk*, Bendrix.' The rain had penetrated his guard also and he held the edge of his sleeve towards the gas fire.

'I'm sorry.'

'You were always a special friend of hers, Bendrix. They always say, don't they, that a husband is the last person really to know the kind of woman. . . . I thought tonight, when I saw you on the Common, that if I told you, and you laughed at me, I might be able to burn the letter.'

He sat there with his damp arm extended, looking away from me. I had never felt less like laughing, and yet I would have liked to laugh if I had been able.

I said, 'It's not the sort of situation one laughs at, even if it *is* fantastic to think . . .'

He asked me longingly, 'It *is* fantastic. You do think that I'm a fool, don't you . . .?'

I would willingly have laughed a moment before, and yet now, when I only had to lie, all the old jealousies returned. Are husband and wife so much one flesh that if one hates the wife one has to hate the husband too? His question reminded me of how easy he had been to deceive: so easy that he seemed to me almost a conniver at his wife's unfaithfulness, like the man who leaves loose notes in a hotel bedroom connives at theft, and I hated him for the very quality which had once helped my love.

The sleeve of his jacket steamed away in front of the gas and he repeated, still looking away from me, 'Of course, I can tell you think me a fool.'

Then the demon spoke, 'Oh no, I don't think you a fool, Henry.'

'You mean, you really think it's . . . possible?'

'Of course it's possible. Sarah's human.'

He said indignantly, 'And I always thought you were her friend,' as though it was I who had written the letter.

'Of course,' I said, 'you know her so much better than I ever did.'

'In some ways,' he said gloomily, and I knew he was thinking of the very ways in which I had known her the best.

'You asked me, Henry, if I thought you were a fool. I only said there was nothing foolish in the idea. I said nothing against Sarah.'

'I know, Bendrix. I'm sorry. I haven't been sleeping well lately. I wake up in the night wondering what to do about this wretched letter.'

'Burn it.'

'I wish I could.' He still had it in his hand and for a moment I really thought he was going to set it alight.

'Or go and see Mr Savage,' I said.

'But I can't pretend to *him* that I'm not her husband. Just think, Bendrix, of sitting there in front of a desk in a chair all the other jealous husbands have sat in, telling the same story. . . . Do you think there's a waiting-room, so that we see each other's faces as we pass through?' Strange, I thought, you would almost have taken Henry for an imaginative man. I felt my superiority shaken and the old desire to tease awoke in me again. I said, 'Why not let me go, Henry?'

'You?' I wondered for a moment if I had gone too far, if even Henry might begin to suspect.

'Yes,' I said, playing with the danger, for what did it matter now if Henry learnt a little about the past? It would be good for him and perhaps teach him to control his wife better. 'I could pretend to be a jealous lover,' I went on. 'Jealous lovers are more respectable, less ridiculous, than jealous husbands. They are supported by the weight of literature. Betrayed lovers are tragic, never comic. Think of Troilus. I shan't lose my *amour propre* when I interview Mr Savage.' Henry's sleeve had dried, but he still held it towards the fire and now the cloth began to scorch. He said, 'Would you really do that for me, Bendrix?' and there were tears in his eyes, as though he had never expected or deserved this supreme mark of friendship.

'Of course I would. Your sleeve's burning, Henry.'

He looked at it as though it belonged to someone else.

'But this is fantastic,' he said. 'I don't know what I've been thinking about. First to tell you and then to ask you – this. One can't spy on one's wife through a friend – and that friend pretend to be her lover.'

'Oh, it's not done,' I said, 'but neither is adultery or theft or running away from the enemy's fire. The not done things are done every day, Henry. It's part of modern life. I've done most of them myself.'

He said, 'You're a good chap, Bendrix. All I needed was a proper talk – to clear my head,' and this time he really did hold the letter to the gas flame. When he had laid the last scrap in the ash-tray, I said, 'The name was Savage and the address either 159 or 169 Vigo Street.'

'Forget it,' Henry said. 'Forget what I've told you. It doesn't make sense. I've been getting bad headaches lately. I'll see a doctor.'

'That was the door,' I said. 'Sarah's come in.'

'Oh,' he said, 'that will be the maid. She's been to the pictures.'

'No, it was Sarah's step.'

He went to the door and opened it, and automatically his face fell into the absurd lines of gentleness and affection. I had always been irritated by that mechanical response to her presence because it meant nothing – one cannot always welcome a woman's presence, even if one is in love, and I believed

Sarah when she told me they had never been in love. There was more genuine welcome, I believe, in my moments of hate and distrust. At least to me she was a person in her own right – not part of a house like a bit of porcelain, to be handled with care.

'Sar-ah,' he called. 'Sar-ah', spacing the syllables with an unbearable falsity.

How can I make a stranger see her as she stopped in the hall at the foot of the stairs and turned to us? I have never been able to describe even my fictitious characters except by their actions. It has always seemed to me that in a novel the reader should be allowed to imagine a character in any way he chooses: I do not want to supply him with ready-made illustrations. Now I am betrayed by my own technique, for I do not want any other woman substituted for Sarah, I want the reader to see the one broad forehead and bold mouth, the conformation of the skull, but all I can convey is an indeterminate figure turning in the dripping macintosh, saying, 'Yes, Henry?' and then 'You?' She had always called me 'you'. 'Is that you?' on the telephone, 'Can you? Will you? Do you?' so that I imagined, like a fool, for a few minutes at a time, there was only one 'you' in the world and that was me.

'It's nice to see you,' I said – this was one of the moments of hate. 'Been out for a walk?'

'Yes.'

'It's a filthy night,' I said accusingly, and Henry added with apparent anxiety, 'You're wet through, Sarah. One day you'll catch your death of cold.'

A *cliché* with its popular wisdom can sometimes fall through a conversation like a note of doom, yet even if we had known he spoke the truth, I wonder if either of us would have felt any genuine anxiety for her break through our nerves, distrust, and hate.

Chapter Two

I cannot say how many days passed. The old disturbance had returned and in that state of blackness one can no more tell the days than a blind man can notice the changes of light. Was it the seventh day or the twenty-first that I decided on my course of action? I have a vague memory now, after three years have passed, of vigils along the edge of the Common, watching their house from a distance, by the pond or under the portico of the eighteenth-century church, on the off-chance that the door would open and Sarah come down those unblasted and well-scoured steps. The right hour never struck. The rainy days were over and the nights were fine with frost, but like a ruined weather-house neither the man nor the woman came out; never again did I see Henry making across the Common after dusk. Perhaps he was ashamed at what he had told me, for he was a very conventional man. I write the adjective with a sneer, and yet if I examine myself I find only admiration and trust for the conventional, like the villages one sees from the high road where the cars pass, looking so peaceful in their thatch and stone, suggesting rest.

I remember I dreamed a lot of Sarah in those obscure days or weeks. Sometimes I would wake with a sense of pain, sometimes with pleasure. If a woman is in one's thoughts all day, one should not have to dream of her at night. I was trying to write a book that simply would not come. I did my daily five hundred words, but the characters never began to live. So much in writing depends on the superficiality of one's days. One may be preoccupied with shopping and income tax returns and chance conversations, but the stream of the unconscious continues to flow undisturbed, solving problems, planning ahead: one sits down sterile and dispirited at the desk, and suddenly the words come as though from the air: the situations that seemed blocked in a hopeless impasse move forward: the work has been done while one slept or shopped or talked with friends. But this hate and suspicion, this passion to destroy went deeper than the book – the unconscious worked on it instead, until one morning I woke up and knew, as though I had planned it overnight, that this day I was going to visit Mr Savage.

What an odd collection the trusted professions are. One trusts one's lawyer, one's doctor, one's priest, I suppose, if one is a Catholic, and now I added to the list one's private detective. Henry's idea of being scrutinized by the other clients was quite wrong. The office had two waiting-rooms, and I was admitted alone into one. It was curiously unlike what you would expect in Vigo Street – it had something of the musty air in the outer office of a solicitor's, combined with a voguish choice of reading matter in the waiting-room which was more like a dentist's – there were *Harper's Bazaar* and *Life* and a number of French fashion periodicals, and the man who showed me in was a little too attentive and well-dressed. He pulled me a chair to the fire and closed the door with great care. I felt like a patient and I suppose I was a patient, sick enough to try the famous shock treatment for jealousy.

The first thing I noticed about Mr Savage was his tie: I suppose it represented some old boys' association: next how well his face was shaved under the faint brush of powder, and then his forehead, where the pale hair receded, which glistened, a beacon-light of understanding, sympathy, anxiety to be of service. I noticed that when he shook hands he gave my fingers an odd twist. I think he must have been a freemason, and if I had been able to return the pressure, I would probably have received special terms.

'Mr Bendrix?' he said. 'Sit down. I think that is the most comfortable chair.' He patted a cushion for me and stood solicitously beside me until I had successfully lowered myself into it. Then he drew a straight chair up beside me as though he were going to listen to my pulse. 'Now just tell me everything in your own words,' he said. I can't imagine what other words I could have used but my own. I felt embarrassed and bitter: I had not come here for sympathy, but to pay, if I could afford it, for some practical assistance.

I began, 'I don't know what your charges are for watching?'

Mr Savage gently stroked his striped tie. He said, 'Don't worry about that now, Mr Bendrix. I charge three guineas for this preliminary consultation, but if you don't wish to proceed any further I make no charge at all, none at all. The best advertisement, you know,' – he slid the *cliché* in like a thermometer – 'is a satisfied client.'

In a common situation, I suppose, we all behave much alike and use the same words. I said, 'This is a very simple case,' and I was aware with anger that Mr Savage really knew all about it before I began to speak. Nothing that I had to say would be strange to Mr Savage, nothing that he could unearth would not have been dug up so many dozens of times already that year. Even a doctor is sometimes disconcerted by a patient, but Mr Savage was a specialist who dealt in only one disease of which he knew every symptom.

He said with a horrible gentleness, 'Take your time, Mr Bendrix.'

I was becoming confused like all his other patients. 'There's really nothing to go on,' I explained.

'Ah, that's my job,' Mr Savage said. 'You just give me the mood, the atmosphere. I assume we are discussing Mrs Bendrix?'

'Not exactly.'

'But she passes under that name?'

'No, you are getting this quite wrong. She's the wife of a friend of mine.'

'And he's sent you?'

'No.'

'Perhaps you and the lady are – intimate?'

'No. I've only seen her once since 1944.'

'I'm afraid I don't quite understand. This is a watching case, you said.'

I hadn't realized till then that he had angered me so much. 'Can't one love or hate,' I broke out at him, 'as long as that? Don't make any mistkae. I'm just another of your jealous clients, I don't claim to be any different from the rest, but there's been a time-lag in my case.'

Mr Savage laid his hand on my sleeve as though I were a fretful child. 'There's nothing discreditable about jealousy, Mr Bendrix. I always salute it as the mark of true love. Now this lady we are discussing, you have reason to suppose that she is now – intimate with another?'

'Her husband thinks that she's deceiving him. She has private meetings. She lies about where she's been. She has – secrets.'

'Ah, secrets, yes.'

'There may be nothing in it, of course.'

'In my long experience, Mr Bendrix, there almost invariably is.' As though he had sufficiently reassured me now to go ahead with the treatment, Mr Savage returned to his desk and prepared to write. Name. Address. Husband's occupation. With his pencil poised for a note, Mr Savage asked, 'Does Mr Miles know of this interview?'

'No.'

'Our man mustn't be observed by Mr Miles?'

'Certainly not.'

'It adds a complication.'

'I may show him your reports later. I don't know.'

'Can you give me any facts about the household? Is there a maid?'

'Yes.'

'Her age?'

'I wouldn't know. Thirty-eight?'

'You don't know if she has any followers?'

'No. And I don't know her grandmother's name.'

Mr Savage gave me a patient smile: I thought for a moment that he planned to leave his desk and pat me down again. 'I can see, Mr Bendrix, that you haven't had experience of inquiries. A maid's very relevant. She can tell us so much about her mistress's habits – if she is willing. You'd be surprised what a lot *is* relevant to even the simplest inquiry.' He certainly that morning proved his point: he covered pages with his small scratchy handwriting. Once he broke off his questions to ask me, 'Would you object, if it was urgently necessary, to my man coming to your house?' I told him I didn't mind and immediately felt as though I were admitting some infection to my own room. 'If it could be avoided . . .'

'Of course. Of course. I understand,' and I really believe he did understand. I could have told him that his man's presence would be like dust over the furniture and stain my books like soot, and he would have felt no surprise or irritation. I have a passion for writing on clean single-lined foolscap: a smear, a tea-mark, on a page makes it unusable, and a fantastic notion took me that I must keep my paper locked up in case of an unsavoury visitor. I said, 'It would be easier if he gave me warning. . . .'

'Certainly, but it's not always possible. Your address, Mr Bendrix, and your telephone number?'

'It's not a private line. My landlady has an extension.'

'All my men use great discretion. Would you want the reports weekly or would you prefer only to receive the finished inquiry?'

'Weekly. It may never be finished. There's probably nothing to find out.'

'Have you often been to your doctor and found nothing wrong? You know, Mr Bendrix, the fact that a man feels the need of our services almost invariably means that there is something to report.'

I suppose I was lucky to have Mr Savage to deal with. He had been recommended as being less disagreeable than men of his profession usually are, but nevertheless I found his assurance detestable. It isn't, when you come to think of it, a quite respectable trade, the detection of the innocent, for aren't lovers nearly always innocent? They have committed no crime, they are certain in their own minds that they have done no wrong, 'as long as no one but myself is hurt', the old tag is ready on their lips, and love, of course, excuses everything – so they believe, and so I used to believe in the days when I loved.

And when we came to the charges, Mr Savage was surprisingly moderate: three guineas a day, and expenses, 'which must be approved of course'. He explained them to me as 'the odd coffee, you know, and sometimes our man has to stand a drink.' I made a feeble joke about not approving whisky, but Mr Savage didn't detect the humour. 'I knew a case,' he told me, 'when a month's inquiry was saved by a double at the proper time – the cheapest whisky my client ever paid for.' He explained that some of his clients liked to have a daily account, but I told him I would be satisfied with a weekly one.

The whole affair had gone very briskly: he had almost convinced me by the time I came out into Vigo Street that this was the kind of interview which happened to all men sooner or later.

Chapter Three

'And if there's anything more you could tell me that would be relevant?'
I remember Mr Savage had said – a detective must find it as important as
a novelist to amass his trivial material before picking out the right clue. But
how difficult that picking out is – the release of the real subject. The
enormous pressure of the outside world weighs on us like a *peine forte et
dure*. Now that I come to write my own story the problem is still the same,
but worse – there are so many more facts, now that I have not to invent
them. How can I disinter the human character from the heavy scene – the
daily newspaper, the daily meal, the traffic grinding towards Battersea, the
gulls coming up from the Thames looking for bread, and the early summer
of 1939 glinting on the park where the children sailed their boats – one of
those bright condemned pre-war summers? I wondered whether, if I thought
long enough, I could detect, at the party Henry had given, her future lover.
We saw each other for the first time, drinking bad South African sherry
because of the war in Spain. I noticed Sarah, I think, because she was happy:
in those years the sense of happiness had been a long while dying under the
coming storm. One detected it in drunken people, in children, seldom
elsewhere. I liked her at once because she said she had read my books and
left the subject there – I found myself treated at once as a human being
rather than as an author. I had no idea whatever of falling in love with her.
For one thing, she was beautiful, and beautiful women, especially if they
are intelligent also, stir some deep feeling of inferiority in me. I don't know
whether psychologists have yet named the Cophetua complex, but I have
always found it hard to feel sexual desire without some sense of superiority,
mental or physical. All I noticed about her that first time was her beauty
and her happiness and her way of touching people with her hands, as though
she loved them. I can only recall one thing she said to me, apart from that
statement with which she began – 'You do seem to dislike a lot of people.'
Perhaps I had been talking smartly about my fellow writers. I don't
remember.

What a summer it was. I am not going to try and name the month exactly
– I should have to go back to it through so much pain, but I remember
leaving the hot and crowded room, after drinking too much bad sherry, and
walking on the Common with Henry. The sun was falling flat across the
Common and the grass was pale with it. In the distance the houses were the
houses in a Victorian print, small and precisely drawn and quiet: only one
child cried a long way off. The eighteenth-century church stood like a toy
in an island of grass – the toy could be left outside in the dark, in the dry
unbreakable weather. It was the hour when you make confidences to a
stranger.

Henry said, 'How happy we could all be.'

'Yes.'

I felt an enormous liking for him, standing there on the Common, away from his own party, with tears in his eyes. I said, 'You've got a lovely house.'

'My wife found it.'

I had met him only a week ago – at another party: he was in the Ministry of Pensions in those days, and I had buttonholed him for the sake of my material. Two days later came the card. I learned later that Sarah had got him to send it. 'Have you been married long?' I asked him.

'Ten years.'

'I thought your wife was charming.'

'She's a great help to me,' he said. Poor Henry. But why should I say poor Henry? Didn't he possess in the end the winning cards – the cards of gentleness, humility and trust?

'I must be going back,' he said. 'I mustn't leave it all to her, Bendrix,' and he laid his hand on my arm as though we'd known each other a year. Had he learnt the gesture from her? Married people grow like each other. We walked back side by side, and as we opened the hall-door, I saw reflected in a mirror from an alcove two people separating as though from a kiss – one was Sarah. I looked at Henry. Either he had not seen or he did not care – or else, I thought, what an unhappy man he must be.

Would Mr Savage have considered that scene relevant? It was not, I learnt later, a lover who was kissing her; it was one of Henry's colleagues at the Ministry of Pensions whose wife had run away with an able seaman a week before. She had met him for the first time that day, and it seems unlikely that he would still be part of the scene from which I had been so firmly excluded. Love doesn't take as long as that to work itself out.

I would have liked to have left that past time alone, for as I write of 1939 I feel all my hatred returning. Hatred seems to operate the same glands as love: it even produces the same actions. If we had not been taught how to interpret the story of the Passion, would we have been able to say from their actions alone whether it was the jealous Judas or the cowardly Peter who loved Christ?

Chapter Four

When I got home from Mr Savage's and my landlady told me that Mrs Miles had been on the telephone, I felt the elation I used to feel when I heard the front door close and her step in the hall. I had a wild hope that the sight of me a few days before had woken not love, of course, but a sentiment, a memory which I might work on. At the time it seemed to me that if I could have her once more – however quickly and crudely and unsatisfactorily – I would be at peace again: I would have washed her out of my system, and afterwards I would leave her, not she me.

It was odd after eighteen months' silence dialling that number: Macaulay 7753, and odder still that I had to look it up in my address book because I was uncertain of the last digit. I sat listening to the ringing tone, and I wondered whether Henry was back yet from the Ministry and what I should say if he answered. Then I realized that there was nothing wrong any more with the truth. Lies had deserted me, and I felt as lonely as though they had been my only friends.

The voice of a highly-trained maid repeated the number into my ear-drum. I said, 'Is Mrs Miles in?'

'Mrs Miles?'

'Isn't that Macaulay 7753?'

'Yes.'

'I want to speak to Mrs Miles.'

'You've got the wrong number,' and she rang off. It had never occurred to me that the small things alter too with time.

I looked Miles up in the directory, but the old number was still there: the directory was more than a year out of date. I was just going to dial Inquiries when the telephone rang again, and it was Sarah herself. She said with some embarrassment, 'Is that you?' She had never called me by any name, and now without her old terms of affection she was at a loss. I said, 'Bendrix speaking.'

'This is Sarah. Didn't you get my message?'

'Oh, I was going to ring you, but I had to finish an article. By the way, I don't think I've got your number now. It's in the book, I suppose?'

'No. Not yet. We've changed. It's Macaulay 6204. I wanted to ask you something.'

'Yes?'

'Nothing very dreadful. I wanted to have lunch with you, that's all.'

'Of course. I'd be delighted. When?'

'You couldn't manage tomorrow?'

'No. Not tomorrow. You see, I've simply got to get this article . . .'

'Wednesday?'

'Would Thursday do?'

'Yes,' she said, and I could almost imagine disappointment in a mono-syllable – so our pride deceives us.

'Then I'll meet you at the Café Royal at one.'

'It's good of you,' she said, and I could tell from her voice that she meant it. 'Until Thursday.'

'Until Thursday.'

I sat with the telephone receiver in my hand and I looked at hate like an ugly and foolish man whom one did not want to know. I dialled her number, I must have caught her before she had time to leave the telephone, and said, 'Sarah. Tomorrow's all right. I'd forgotten something. Same place. Same time,' and sitting there, my fingers on the quiet instrument, with something to look forward to, I thought to myself: I remember. This is what hope feels like.

Chapter Five

I laid the newspaper flat on the table and read the same page over and over again because I wouldn't look at the doorway. People were continually coming in, and I wouldn't be one of those who by moving their heads up and down betray a foolish expectation. What have we all got to expect that we allow ourselves to be so lined with disappointment? There was the usual murder in the evening paper and a Parliamentary squabble about sweet-rationing, and she was now five minutes late. It was my bad luck that she caught me looking at my watch. I heard her voice say, 'I'm sorry. I came by bus and the traffic was bad.'

I said, 'The tube's quicker.'

'I know, but I didn't want to be quick.'

She had often disconcerted me by the truth. In the days when we were in love, I would try to get her to say more than the truth – that our affair would never end, that one day we should marry. I wouldn't have believed her, but I would have liked to hear the words on her tongue, perhaps only to give me the satisfaction of rejecting them myself. But she never played that game of make-believe, and then suddenly, unexpectedly, she would shatter my reserve with a statement of such sweetness and amplitude. . . . I remember one when I was miserable at her calm assumption that one day our relations would be over, hearing with incredulous happiness, 'I have never, never loved a man as I love you, and I never shall again.' Well, she hadn't known it, I thought, but she too played the same game of make-believe.

She sat down beside me and asked for a glass of lager. 'I've booked a table at Rules,' I said.

'Can't we stay here?'

'It's where we always used to go.'

'Yes.'

Perhaps we were looking strained in our manner, because I noticed we had attracted the attention of a little man who sat on a sofa not far off. I tried to outstare him and that was easy. He had a long moustache and fawn-like eyes and he looked hurriedly away: his elbow caught his glass of beer and spun it on to the floor, so that he was overcome with confusion. I was sorry then because it occurred to me that he might have recognized me from my photographs: he might even be one of my few readers. He had a small boy sitting with him, and what a cruel thing it is to humiliate a father in the presence of his son. The boy blushed scarlet when the waiter hurried forward, and his father began to apologize with unnecessary vehemence.

I said to Sarah, 'Of course you must lunch wherever you like.'

'You see, I've never been back there.'

'Well, it was never your restaurant, was it?'

'Do you go there often?'

'It's convenient for me. Two or three times a week.'

She stood up abruptly and said, 'Let's go,' and was suddenly taken with a fit of coughing. It seemed too big a cough for her small body: her forehead sweated with its expulsion.

'That's nasty.'

'Oh, it's nothing. I'm sorry.'

'Taxi?'

'I'd rather walk.'

As you go up Maiden Lane on the left-hand side there is a doorway and a grating that we passed without a word to each other. After the first dinner, when I had questioned her about Henry's habits and she had warmed to my interest, I had kissed her there rather fumblingly on the way to the tube. I don't know why I did it, unless perhaps that image in the mirror had come into my mind, for I had no intention of making love to her: I had no particular intention even of looking her up again. She was too beautiful to excite me with the idea of accessibility.

When we sat down, one of the old waiters said to me, 'It's a very long time since you've been here, sir,' and I wished I hadn't made my false claim to Sarah.

'Oh,' I said, 'I lunch upstairs nowadays.'

'And you, Ma'am, it's a long time too. . . .'

'Nearly two years,' she said with the accuracy I sometimes hated.

'But I remember it was a big lager you used to like.'

'You've got a good memory, Alfred,' and he beamed with pleasure at the memory. She had always had the trick of getting on well with waiters.

Food interrupted our dreary small-talk, and only when we had finished the meal did she give any indication of why she was there. 'I wanted you to lunch with me,' she said, 'I wanted to ask you about Henry.'

'Henry?' I repeated, trying to keep disappointment out of my voice.

'I'm worried about him. How did you find him the other night? Was he strange at all?'

'I didn't notice anything wrong,' I said.

'I wanted to ask you – oh, I know you're very busy – whether you could look him up occasionally. I think he's lonely.'

'With you?'

'You know he's never really noticed me. Not for years.'

'Perhaps he's begun to notice you when you aren't there.'

'I'm not out much,' she said, 'nowadays,' and her cough conveniently broke that line of talk. By the time the fit was over, she had thought out her gambits, though it wasn't like her to avoid the truth. 'Are you on a new book?' she asked. It was like a stranger speaking, the kind of stranger one meets at a cocktail party. She hadn't committed that remark, even the first time, over the South African sherry.

'Of course.'

'I didn't like the last one much.'

'It was a struggle to write at all just then – Peace coming . . .' And I might just as well have said peace going.

'I sometimes was afraid you'd go back to that old idea – the one I hated. Some men would have done.'

'A book takes me a year to write. It's too hard work for a revenge.'

'If you knew how little you had to revenge . . .'

'Of course I'm joking. We had a good time together; we're adults, we knew it had to end some time. Now, you see, we can meet like friends and talk about Henry.'

I paid the bill and we went out, and twenty yards down the street was the doorway and the grating. I stopped on the pavement and said, 'I suppose you're going to the Strand?'

'No, Leicester Square.'

'I'm going to the Strand.' She stood in the doorway and the street was empty. 'I'll say good-bye here. It was nice seeing you.'

'Yes.'

'Call me up any time you are free.'

I moved towards her: I could feel the grating under my feet. 'Sarah,' I said. She turned her head sharply away, as though she were looking to see if anyone were coming, to see if there was time . . . but when she turned again the cough took her. She doubled up in the doorway and coughed and coughed. Her eyes were red with it. In her fur coat she looked like a small animal cornered.

'I'm sorry.'

I said with bitterness, as though I had been robbed of something, 'That needs attending to.'

'It's only a cough.' She held her hand out and said, 'Good-by – Maurice.' The name was like an insult. I said 'Good-bye', but didn't take her hand: I walked quickly away without looking round, trying to give the appearance of being busy and relieved to be gone, and when I heard the cough begin again, I wished I had been able to whistle a tune, something jaunty, adventurous, happy, but I have no ear for music.

Chapter Six

When young one builds up habits of work that one believes will last a lifetime and withstand any catastrophe. Over twenty years I have probably averaged five hundred words a day for five days a week. I can produce a novel in a year, and that allows time for revision and the correction of the typescript. I have always been very methodical and when my quota of work is done, I break off even in the middle of a scene. Every now and then during the morning's work I count what I have done and mark off the hundreds on my manuscript. No printer need make a careful cast-off of my work, for there on the front page of my typescript is marked the figure – 83,764. When I was young not even a love affair would alter my schedule.

A love affair had to begin after lunch, and however late I might be in getting to bed – so long as I slept in my own bed – I would read the morning's work over and sleep on it. Even the war hardly affected me. A lame leg kept me out of the Army, and as I was in Civil Defence, my fellow workers were only too glad that I never wanted the quiet morning turns of duty. I got, as a result, a quite false reputation for keenness, but I was keen only for my desk, my sheet of paper, that quota of words dripping slowly, methodically, from the pen. It needed Sarah to upset my self-imposed discipline. The bombs between those first daylight raids and the V1s of 1944 kept their own convenient nocturnal habits, but so often it was only in the mornings that I could see Sarah, for in the afternoon she was never quite secure from friends, who, their shopping done, would want company and gossip before the evening siren. Sometimes she would come in between two queues, and we would make love between the greengrocer's and the butcher's.

But it was quite easy to return to work even under those conditions. So long as one is happy one can endure any discipline: it was unhappiness that broke down the habits of work. When I began to realize how often we quarrelled, how often I picked on her with nervous irritation, I became aware that our love was doomed: love had turned into a love-affair with a beginning and an end. I could name the very moment when it had begun, and one day I knew I should be able to name the final hour. When she left the house I couldn't settle to work: I would reconstruct what we had said to each other: I would fan myself into anger or remorse. And all the time I knew I was forcing the pace. I was pushing, pushing the only thing I loved out of my life. As long as I could make-believe that love lasted, I was happy – I think I was even good to live with, and so love did last. But if love had to die, I wanted it to die quickly. It was as though our love were a small creature caught in a trap and bleeding to death: I had to shut my eyes and wring its neck.

And all that time I couldn't work. So much of a novelist's writing, as I have said, takes place in the unconscious: in those depths the last word is written before the first word appears on paper. We remember the details of our story, we do not invent them. War didn't trouble those deep sea-caves, but now there was something of infinitely greater importance to me than war, than my novel – the end of love. That was being worked out now, like a story: the pointed word that set her crying, that seemed to have come so spontaneously to the lips, had been sharpened in those underwater caverns. My novel lagged, but my love hurried like inspiration to the end.

I don't wonder that she hadn't liked my last book. It was written all the time against the grain, without help, for no reason but that one had to go on living. The reviewers said it was the work of a craftsman: that was all that was left me of what had been a passion. I thought perhaps with the next novel the passion would return, the excitement would wake again of remembering what one had never consciously known, but for a week after lunching with Sarah at Rules I could do no work at all. There it goes again – the I, I, I, as though this were my story, and not the story of Sarah, Henry, and of course, that third, whom I hated without yet knowing him, or even believing in him.

I had tried to work in the morning and failed: I drank too much with my lunch so the afternoon was wasted: after dark I stood at the window with the lights turned off and could see across the flat dark Common the lit windows of the north side. It was very cold and my gas fire only warmed me if I huddled close, and then it scorched. A few flakes of snow drifted across the lamps of the south side and touched the pane with thick damp fingers. I didn't hear the bell ring. My landlady knocked on the door and said, 'A Mr Parkis to see you,' thus indicating by a grammatical article the social status of my caller. I had never heard the name, but I told her to show him in.

I wondered where I had seen before those gentle apologetic eyes, that long outdated moustache damp with the climate? I had only turned on my reading lamp and he came towards it, peering short-sightedly; he couldn't make me out in the shadows. He said, 'Mr Bendrix, sir?'

'Yes.'

He said, 'The name's Parkis,' as though that might mean something to me. He added, 'Mr Savage's man, sir.'

'Oh yes. Sit down. Have a cigarette.'

'Oh no, sir,' he said, 'not on duty – except of course, for purposes of concealment.'

'But you aren't on duty now?'

'In a manner, sir, yes. I've just been relieved, sir, for half an hour while I make my report. Mr Savage said as how you'd like it weekly – with expenses.'

'There is something to report?' I wasn't sure whether it was disappointment I felt or excitement.

'It's not quite a blank sheet, sir,' he remarked complacently, and took an extraordinary number of papers and envelopes from his pocket in searching for the right one.

'Do sit down. You make me uncomfortable.'

'As you please, sir.' Sitting down he could see me a little more closely. 'Haven't I met you somewhere before, sir?'

I had taken the first sheet out of the envelope: it was the expenses account, written in a very neat script as though by a schoolboy. I said, 'You write very clearly.'

'That's my boy. I'm training him in the business.' He added hastily, 'I don't put anything down for him, sir, unless I leave him in charge, like now.'

'He's in charge, is he?'

'Only while I make my report, sir.'

'How old is he?'

'Gone twelve,' he said as though his boy were a clock. 'A youngster can be useful and costs nothing except a comic now and then. And nobody notices him. Boys are born lingerers.'

'It seems odd work for a boy.'

'Well, sir, he doesn't understand the real significance. If it came to breaking into a bedroom, I'd leave him behind.'

I read:

January 18.	Two evening papers	2d.
	Tube return	1/8d.
	Coffee. Gunters	2/-

He was watching me closely as I read. 'The coffee place was more expensive than I cared for,' he said, 'but it was the least I could take without drawing attention.'

January 19.	Tubes	2/4d.
	Bottled Beers	3/-
	Cocktail	2/6d.
	Pint of Bitter	1/6d.

He interrupted my reading again. 'The beer's a bit on my conscience, sir, because I upset a glass owing to carelessness. But I was a little on edge, there being something to report. You know, sir, there's sometimes weeks of disappointment, but this time on the second day. . . .'

Of course I remembered him, and his embarrassed boy. I read under January 19 (I could see at a glance that on January 18 there was only a record of insignificant movements): 'The party in question went by bus to Piccadilly Circus. She seemed agitated. She proceeded up Air Street to the Café Royal where a gentleman was waiting for her. Me and my boy . . .'

He wouldn't leave me alone. 'You'll notice, sir, it's in a different hand. I never let my boy write the reports in case there's anything of an intimate character.'

'You take good care of him,' I said.

'Me and my boy sat down on a proximate couch,' I read. 'The party and the gentleman were obviously very close, treating each other with affectionate lack of ceremony, and I think on one occasion holding hands below the table. I could not be certain of this, but the party's left hand was out of sight and the gentleman's right hand too which generally indicates a squeeze of that nature. After a short and intimate conversation they proceeded on foot to a quiet and secluded restaurant known to its customers as Rules and choosing a couch rather than a table they ordered two pork chops.'

'Are the pork chops important?'

'They might be marks of identification, sir, if frequently indulged in.'

'You didn't identify the man, then?'

'You will see, sir, if you read on.'

'I drank a cocktail at the bar when I observed this order of the pork chops, but I was unable to elicit from any of the waiters or from the lady behind the bar the identity of the gentleman. Although I couched my questions in a vague and nonchalant manner they obviously aroused curiosity, and I thought it better to leave. However by striking up an acquaintance with the stage doorkeeper of the Vaudeville Theatre I was able to keep the restaurant under observation.'

'How,' I asked, 'did you strike up the acquaintance?'

'At the bar of the "Bedford Head", sir, seeing as the parties were safely occupied with the order for chops, and afterwards accompanied him back to the theatre, where the stage door . . .'

'I know the place.'

'I have tried to compress my report, sir, to essentials.'

'Quite right.'

The report continued: 'After lunch the parties proceeded together up Maiden Lane and parted outside a general grocery. I had the impression they were labouring under great emotion, and it occurred to me that they might be parting for good, a happy ending if I may say so to this investigation.'

Again he interrupted me anxiously, 'You'll forgive the personal touch?'

'Of course.'

'Even in my profession, sir, we sometimes find our emotions touched, and I *liked* the lady – the party in question, that is.'

'I hesitated whether to follow the gentleman or the party in question, but I decided my instructions would not permit the former. I followed the latter therefore. She walked a little way towards Charing Cross Road, appearing much agitated. Then she turned into the National Portrait Gallery but only stayed a few minutes. . . .'

'Is there anything more of importance?'

'No, sir. I think really she was just looking for a place to sit down because next thing she turned into a church.'

'A church?'

'A Roman church, sir, in Maiden Lane. You'll find it all there. But not to pray, sir. Just to sit.'

'You know even that much, do you?'

'Naturally I followed the party in. I knelt down a few pews behind so as to appear a *bona fide* worshipper, and I can assure you, sir, she didn't pray. She's not a Roman, is she, sir?'

'No.'

'It was to sit in the dark, sir, till she calmed down.'

'Perhaps she was meeting someone?'

'No, sir. She only stayed three minutes and she didn't speak to anyone. If you ask me, she wanted a good cry.'

'Possibly. But you are wrong about the hands, Mr Parkis.'

'The hands, sir?'

I moved so that the light caught my face more fully.

'We never so much as touched hands.'

I felt sorry for him now that I had had my joke – I felt sorry to have scared yet further someone already so timid. He watched me with his mouth a little open, as though he had received a sudden hurt and was now waiting paralysed for the next stab. I said, 'I expect that sort of mistake often happens, Mr Parkis. Mr Savage ought to have introduced us.'

'Oh no, sir,' he said miserably, 'it was up to me.' Then he bent his head and sat there, looking into his hat that lay on his knees. I tried to cheer him up. 'It's not serious,' I said. 'If you look at it from the outside, it's really quite funny.'

'But I'm on the inside, sir,' he said. He turned his hat round and went on in a voice as damp and dreary as the Common outside, 'It's not Mr Savage I mind about, sir. He's as understanding a man as you'll meet in the profession – it's my boy. He started with great ideas about me.' He fished from the depths of his misery a deprecating and frightened smile. 'You know the kind of reading they do, sir. Nick Carters and the like.'

'Why should he ever know about this?'

'You've got to play straight with a child, sir, and he's sure to ask questions. He'll want to know how I followed up – that's the thing he's learning, to follow up.'

'Couldn't you tell him that I'd been able to identify the man – just that, and I wasn't interested?'

'It's kind of you to suggest it, sir, but you have to look at this all round. I don't say I wouldn't do it even to my boy, but what's he going to think if he ever comes across you – in the course of the investigation?'

'That's not necessary.'

'But it might well happen, sir.'

'Why not leave him at home this time?'

'It's just making matters worse, sir. He hasn't got a mother, and it's his school holidays and I've always gone on the lines of educating him in his holidays – with Mr Savage's full approval. No. I made a fool of myself that time, and I've got to face it. If only he weren't quite so serious, sir, but he does take it to heart when I make a floater. One day Mr Prentice – that's Mr Savage's assistant, a rather hard man, sir – said, "Another of your floaters, Parkis," in the boy's hearing. That's what opened his eyes first.' He stood up with an air of enormous resolution (who are we to measure another man's courage?) and said, 'I've been keeping you, sir, talking about *my* problems.'

'I've enjoyed it, Mr Parkis,' I said without irony. 'Try not to worry. Your boy must take after you.'

'He has his mother's brains, sir,' he said sadly. 'I must hurry. It's cold out, though I found him a nice sheltered spot before I came away. But he's so keen I don't trust him to keep dry. Would you mind initialling the expenses, sir, if you approve them?'

I watched him from my window with his thin macintosh turned up and his old hat turned down; the snow had increased and already under the third lamp he looked like a small snowman with the mud showing through. It occurred to me with amazement that for ten minutes I had not thought of Sarah or of my jealousy; I had become nearly human enough to think of another person's trouble.

Chapter Seven

Jealousy, or so I have always believed, exists only with desire. The Old Testament writers were fond of using the words 'a jealous God', and perhaps it was their rough and oblique way of expressing belief in the love of God for man. But I suppose there are different kinds of desire. My desire now was nearer hatred than love, and Henry I had reason to believe, from what Sarah once told me, had long ceased to feel any physical desire for her. And yet, I think, in those days he was as jealous as I was. His desire was simply for companionship: he felt for the first time excluded from Sarah's confidence: he was worried and despairing – he didn't know what was going on or what was going to happen. He was living in a terrible insecurity. To that extent his plight was worse than mine. I had the security of possessing nothing. I could have no more than I had lost, while he still owned her presence at the table, the sound of her feet on the stairs, the opening and closing of doors, the kiss on the cheek – I doubt if there was much else now, but what a lot to a starving man is just that much. And perhaps what made it worse, he had once enjoyed the sense of security as I never had. Why, at the moment when Mr Parkis returned across the Common, he didn't even know that Sarah and I had once been lovers. And when I write that word my brain against my will travels irresistibly back to the point where pain began.

A whole week went by after the fumbling kiss in Maiden Lane before I rang Sarah up. She had mentioned at dinner that Henry didn't like the cinema and so she rarely went. They were showing a film of one of my books at Warner's and so, partly to 'show off', partly because I felt that kiss must somehow be followed up for courtesy's sake, partly too because I was still interested in the married life of a civil servant, I asked Sarah to come with me. 'I suppose it's no good asking Henry?'

'Not a bit,' she said.

'He could join us for dinner afterwards?'

'He's bringing a lot of work back with him. Some wretched Liberal is asking a question next week in the House about widows.' So you might say that the Liberal – I believe he was a Welshman called Lewis – made our bed for us that night.

The film was not a good film, and at moments it was acutely painful to see situations that had been so real to me twisted into the stock *clichés* of the screen. I wished I had gone to something else with Sarah. At first I had said to her, 'That's not what I wrote, you know,' but I couldn't keep on saying that. She touched me sympathetically with her hand, and from then on we sat there with our hands in the innocent embrace that children and lovers use. Suddenly and unexpectedly, for a few minutes only, the film came to life. I forgot that this was my story, and that for once this was my dialogue, and was genuinely moved by a small scene in a cheap restaurant. The lover had ordered steak and onions, the girl hesitated for a moment to take the onions because her husband didn't like the smell, the lover was hurt and angry because he realized what was behind her hesitation, which brought to his mind the inevitable embrace on her return home. The scene was a success: I had wanted to convey the sense of passion through some common simple episode without any rhetoric in words or action, and it worked. For a few seconds I was happy – this was writing: I wasn't interested in anything else in the world. I wanted to go home and read the scene over: I wanted to work at something new: I wished, how I wished, that I hadn't invited Sarah Miles to dinner.

Afterwards – we were back at Rules and they had just fetched our steaks – she said, 'There was one scene you *did* write.'

'About the onions?'

'Yes.' And at that very moment a dish of onions was put on the table. I said to her – it hadn't even crossed my mind that evening to desire her – 'And does Henry mind onions?'

'Yes. He can't bear them. Do you like them?'

'Yes.' She helped me to them and then helped herself.

Is it possible to fall in love over a dish of onions? It seems improbable and yet I could swear it was just then that I fell in love. It wasn't, of course, simply the onions – it was that sudden sense of an individual woman, of a frankness that was so often later to make me happy and miserable. I put my hand under the cloth and laid it on her knee, and her hand came down and held mine in place. I said, 'It's a good steak,' and heard like poetry her reply, 'It's the best I've ever eaten.'

There was no pursuit and no seduction. We left half the good steak on our plates and a third of the bottle of claret and came out into Maiden Lane with the same intention in both our minds. At exactly the same spot as before, by the doorway and the grill, we kissed. I said, 'I'm in love.'

'Me too.'

'We can't go home.'

'No.'

We caught a taxi by Charing Cross station and I told the driver to take us to Arbuckle Avenue – that was the name they had given among themselves to Eastbourne Terrace, the row of hotels that used to stand along the side of Paddington Station with luxury names, Ritz, Carlton, and the like. The doors of these hotels were always open and you could get a room any time of day for an hour or two. A week ago I revisited the terrace. Half of it was gone – the half where the hotels used to stand had been blasted to bits, and the place where we made love that night was a patch of air. It had been the Bristol; there was a potted fern in the hall and we were shown the best room by a manageress with blue hair: a real Edwardian room with a great gilt double bed and red velvet curtains and a full-length mirror. (People who came to Arbuckle Avenue never required twin beds.) I remember the trivial details very well: how the manageress asked me whether we wanted to stay the night: how the room cost fifteen shillings for a short stay: how the electric meter only took shillings and we hadn't one between us, but I remember nothing else – how Sarah looked the first time or what we did, except that we were both nervous and made love badly. It didn't matter. We had started – that was the point. There was the whole of life to look forward to then. Oh, and there's one other thing I always remember. At the door of our room ('our room' after half an hour), when I kissed her again and said how I hated the thought of her going home to Henry, she said, 'Don't worry. He's busy on the widows.'

'I hate even the idea of his kissing you,' I said.

'He won't. There's nothing he dislikes more than onions.'

I saw her home to her side of the Common. Henry's light shone below the door of his study, and we went upstairs. In the living-room we held our hands against each other's bodies, unable to let go. 'He'll be coming up,' I said, 'any moment.'

'We can hear him,' she said, and she added with horrifying lucidity, 'There's one stair that always squeaks.'

I hadn't time to take off my coat. We kissed and heard the squeak of the stair, and I watched sadly the calmness of her face when Henry came in. She said, 'We were hoping you'd come up and offer us a drink.'

Henry said, 'Of course. What will you have, Bendrix?' I said I wouldn't have a drink; I had work to do.

'I thought you said you never worked at night.'

'Oh, this doesn't count. A review.'

'Interesting book?'

'Not very.'

'I wish I had your power of – putting things down.'

Sarah saw me to the door and we kissed again. At that moment it was Henry I liked, not Sarah. It was as though all the men in the past and all the men in the future cast their shade over the present. 'What's the matter?' she asked me. She was always quick to read the meaning behind a kiss, the whisper in the brain.

'Nothing,' I said. 'I'll call you in the morning.'

'It would be better if I called you,' she told me, and caution, I thought, caution, how well she knows how to conduct an affair like this, and I remembered again the stair that always – 'always' was the phrase she had used – squeaked.

BOOK TWO

Chapter One

The sense of unhappiness is so much easier to convey than that of happiness. In misery we seem aware of our own existence, even though it may be in the form of a monstrous egotism: this pain of mine is individual, this nerve that winces belongs to me and to no other. But happiness annihilates us: we lose our identity. The words of human love have been used by the saints to describe their vision of God, and so, I suppose, we might use the terms of prayer, meditation, contemplation to explain the intensity of the love we feel for a woman. We too surrender memory, intellect, intelligence, and we too experience the deprivation, the *noche oscura*, and sometimes as a reward a kind of peace. The act of love itself has been described as the little death, and lovers sometimes experience too the little peace. It is odd to find myself writing these phrases as though I loved what in fact I hate. Sometimes I don't recognize my own thoughts. What do I know of phrases like 'the dark night' or of prayer, who have only one prayer? I have inherited them, that is all, like a husband who is left by death in the useless possession of a woman's clothes, scents, pots of cream. ... And yet there *was* this peace. ...

That is how I think of those first months of war – was it a phoney peace as well as a phoney war? It seems now to have stretched arms of comfort and reassurance all over those months of dubiety and waiting, but the peace must, I suppose, even at that time have been punctuated by misunderstanding and suspicion. Just as I went home that first evening with no exhilaration but only a sense of sadness and resignation, so again and again I returned home on other days with the certainty that I was only one of many men – the favourite lover for the moment. This woman, whom I loved so obsessively that if I woke in the night I immediately found the thought of her in my brain and abandoned sleep, seemed to give up all her time to me. And yet I could feel no trust: in the act of love I could be arrogant, but alone I had only to look in the mirror to see doubt, in the shape of a lined face and a lame leg – why me? There were always occasions when we couldn't meet – appointments with a dentist or a hairdresser, occasions when Henry entertained, when they were alone together. It was no good telling myself that in her own home she would have no opportunity to betray me (with the egotism of a lover I was already using that word with its suggestion of a non-existent duty) while Henry worked on the widows' pensions or – for he was soon shifted from that job – on the distribution of gas-masks and the design of approved cardboard cases, for didn't I know it was possible to make love in the most dangerous circumstances, if the desire were there? Distrust grows with a lover's success. Why, the very next time we saw each other it happened in just the way that I should have called impossible.

I woke with the sadness of her last cautious advice still resting on my mind, and within three minutes of waking her voice on the telephone dispelled it. I have never known a woman before or since so able to alter a whole mood by simply speaking on the telephone, and when she came into a room or put her hand on my side she created at once the absolute trust I lost with every separation.

'Hello,' she said, 'are you asleep?'

'No. When can I see you? This morning?'

'Henry's got a cold. He's staying at home.'

'If only you could come here. . . .'

'I've got to stay in to answer the telephone.'

'Just because he's got a cold?'

Last night I had felt friendship and sympathy for Henry, but already he had become an enemy, to be mocked and resented and covertly run down.

'He's lost his voice completely.'

I felt a malicious delight at the absurdity of his sickness: a civil servant without a voice whispering hoarsely and ineffectively about widows' pensions. I said, 'Isn't there any way to see you?'

'But of course.'

There was silence for a moment on the line and I thought we had been cut off. I said, 'Hello. Hello.' But she had been thinking, that was all, carefully, collectedly, quickly, so that she could give me straight-away the correct answer. 'I'm giving Henry a tray in bed at one. We could have sandwiches ourselves in the living-room. I'll tell him you want to talk over the film – or that story of yours', and immediately she rang off the sense of trust was disconnected and I thought, how many times before has she planned in just this way? When I went to her house and rang the bell, I felt like an enemy – or a detective, watching her words as Parkis and his son were to watch her movements a few years later. And then the door opened and trust came back.

There was never any question in those days of who wanted whom – we were together in desire. Henry had his tray, sitting up against two pillows in his green woollen dressing-gown, and in the room below, on the hardwood floor, with a single cushion for support and the door ajar, we made love. When the moment came, I had to put my hand gently over her mouth to deaden that strange sad angry cry of abandonment, for fear Henry should hear it overhead.

To think I had intended just to pick her brain. I crouched on the floor beside her and watched and watched, as though I might never see this again – the brown indeterminate-coloured hair like a pool of liquor on the parquet, the sweat on her forehead, the heavy breathing as though she had run a race and now like a young athlete lay in the exhaustion of victory.

And then the stair squeaked. For a moment we neither of us moved. The sandwiches were stacked uneaten on the table, the glasses had not been filled. She said in a whisper, 'He went downstairs.' She sat in a chair and put a plate in her lap and a glass beside her.

'Suppose he heard,' I said, 'as he passed.'

'He wouldn't have known what it was.'

I must have looked incredulous, for she explained with dreary tenderness, 'Poor Henry. It's never happened – not in the whole ten years,' but all the same we weren't so sure of our safety: we sat there silently listening until the stair squeaked again. My voice sounded to myself cracked and false as I said rather too loudly, 'I'm glad you like that scene with the onions,' and Henry pushed open the door and looked in. He was carrying a hot-water-bottle in a grey flannel cover. 'Hello, Bendrix,' he whispered.

'You shouldn't have fetched that yourself,' she said.

'Didn't want to disturb you.'

'We were talking about the film last night.'

'Hope you've got everything you want,' he whispered to me. He took a look at the claret Sarah had put out for me. 'Should have given him the '29,' he breathed in his undimensional voice and drifted out again, clasping the hot-water-bottle in its flannel cover, and again we were alone.

'Do you mind?' I asked her, and she shook her head. I didn't really know what I meant – I think I had an idea that the sight of Henry might have roused remorse, but she had a wonderful way of eliminating remorse. Unlike the rest of us she was unhaunted by guilt. In her view when a thing was done, it was done: remorse died with the act. She would have thought it unreasonable of Henry, if he had caught us, to be angry for more than a moment. Catholics are always said to be freed in the confessional from the mortmain of the past – certainly in that respect you could have called her a born Catholic, although she believed in God as little as I did. Or so I thought then and wonder now.

If this book of mine fails to take a straight course, it is because I am lost in a strange region: I have no map. I sometimes wonder whether anything that I am putting down here is true. I felt that afternoon such complete trust when she said to me suddenly, without being questioned, 'I've never loved anybody or anything as I do you.' It was as if, sitting there in the chair with a half-eaten sandwich in her hand, she was abandoning herself as completely as she had done, five minutes back, on the hardwood floor. We most of us hesitate to make so complete a statement – we remember and we foresee and we doubt. She had no doubts. The moment only mattered. Eternity is said not to be an extension of time but an absence of time, and sometimes it seemed to me that her abandonment touched that strange mathematical point of endlessness, a point with no width, occupying no space. What did time matter – all the past and the other men she may from time to time (there is that word again) have known, or all the future in which she might be making the same statement with the same sense of truth? When I replied that I loved her too in that way, I was the liar, not she, for I never lose the consciousness of time: to me the present is never here: it is always last year or next week.

She wasn't lying even when she said, 'Nobody else. Ever again.' There are contradictions in time, that's all, that don't exist on the mathematical point. She had so much more capacity for love than I had – I couldn't bring down that curtain round the moment, I couldn't forget and I couldn't *not* fear. Even in the moment of love, I was like a police officer gathering evidence of a crime that hadn't yet been committed, and when more than seven years later I opened Parkis's letter the evidence was all there in my memory to add to my bitterness.

Chapter Two

'Dear sir,' the letter said, 'I am glad to be able to report that me and my boy have made friendly contact with the domestic at Number 17. This has enabled the investigation to proceed with greater speed because I am sometimes able to take a squint at the party's engagement book and thus obtain movements, also inspect from day to day the contents of the party's waste-paper basket, from which I include herewith an interesting exhibit, which please return with observations. The party in question also keeps a diary and has kept one for some years, but so far the domestic who in future I shall refer to for greater security as my friend has not been able to lay hand on it, being as how the party keeps the same under lock and key, which may or may not be a suspicious circumstance. Apart from the important exhibit attached hereto, the party seems to spend a great deal of time in not keeping the appointments arranged as per her engagement book which has to be regarded as a blind, however personally unwilling to take a low view or cast a bias in an investigation of this order where exact truth is desired for the sake of all parties.'

We are not hurt only by tragedy: the grotesque too carries weapons, undignified, ridiculous weapons. There were times when I wanted to crush Mr Parkis's rambling evasive inefficient reports into his mouth in the presence of that boy of his. It was as if in my attempt to trap Sarah (but for what purpose? To hurt Henry or to hurt myself?) I had let a clown come tumbling into our intimacy. Intimacy. Even that word smacks of Mr Parkis's reports. Didn't he write once, 'Though I have no direct evidence of intimacy having taken place at 16 Cedar Road, the party certainly showed an intent to deceive.'? But that was later. In this report of his I learned only that on two occasions when Sarah had written down engagements to visit her dentist and her dressmaker, she had not turned up at her appointments if they had ever existed; she had evaded pursuit. And then turning over Mr Parkis's crude document, written in mauve ink on cheap notepaper in his thin Waverley handwriting, I saw the bold clean writing of Sarah herself. I had not realized I would recognize it after nearly two years.

It was only a scrap of paper pinned to the back of the report, and it was marked with a big A in red pencil. Under the A, Mr Parkis had written, 'Important in view of possible proceedings that all documentary evidence should be returned for filing.' The scrap had been salvaged from the waste-paper basket and smoothed carefully out as it might have been by a lover's hand. And certainly it must have been addressed to a lover: 'I have no need to write to you or talk to you, you know everything before I can speak, but when one loves, one feels the need to use the same old ways one has always used. I know I am only beginning to love, but already I want to abandon

everything, everybody but you: only fear and habit prevent me. Dear ...'
There was no more. It stared boldly up to me, and I couldn't help thinking
how I had forgotten every line of all the notes she had once addressed to me.
Wouldn't I have kept them if they had ever confessed so completely to her
love, and for fear of my keeping them hadn't she always in those days been
careful to write to me, as she put it, 'between the lines'? But this latest love
had burst the cage of lines. It had refused to be kept between them out of
sight. There was one code word I did remember – 'onions'. That word had
been allowed in our correspondence to represent discreetly our passion. Love
became 'onions', even the act itself 'onions'. 'Already I want to abandon
everything, everybody, but you,' and onions I thought, with hatred, onions
– that was the way in my time.

I wrote 'No comment' under the scrap of letter, put it back in an envelope
and addressed it to Mr Parkis, but when I woke in the night I could recite
the whole thing over to myself, and the word 'abandon' took on many kinds
of physical image. I lay there unable to sleep, one memory after another
pricking me with hatred and desire: her hair fanning out on the parquet
floor and the stair squeaking, a day in the country when we had lain down
in a ditch out of view of the road and I could see the sparkle of frost between
the fronds of hair on the hard ground and a tractor came pushing by at the
moment of crisis and the man never turned his head. Why doesn't hatred
kill desire? I would have given anything to sleep. I would have behaved like
a schoolboy if I had believed in the possibility of a substitute. But there was
a time when I had tried to find a substitute, and it hadn't worked.

I am a jealous man – it seems stupid to write these words in what is, I
suppose, a long record of jealousy, jealousy of Henry, jealousy of Sarah and
jealousy of that other whom Mr Parkis was so maladroitly pursuing. Now
that all this belongs to the past, I feel my jealousy of Henry only when
memories become particularly vivid (because I swear that if we had been
married, with her loyalty and my desire, we could have been happy for a
lifetime), but there still remains jealousy of my rival – a melodramatic word
painfully inadequate to express the unbearable complacency, confidence and
success he always enjoys. Sometimes I think he wouldn't even recognize me
as part of the picture, and I feel an enormous desire to draw attention to
myself, to shout in his ear, 'You can't ignore me. Here I am. Whatever
happened later, Sarah loved me then.'

Sarah and I used to have long arguments on jealousy. I was jealous even
of the past, of which she spoke to me frankly as it came up – the affairs that
meant nothing at all (except possibly the unconscious desire to find that
final spasm Henry had so woefully failed to evoke). She was as loyal to her
lovers as she was to Henry, but what should have provided me with some
comfort (for undoubtedly she would be loyal to me too) angered me. There
was a time when she would laugh at my anger, simply refusing to believe
that it was genuine, just as she refused to believe in her own beauty, and I
would be just as angry because she refused to be jealous of my past or my
possible future. I refused to believe that love could take any other form
than mine: I measured love by the extent of my jealousy, and by that standard
of course she could not love me at all.

The arguments always took the same form and I only describe one
particular occasion because on that occasion the argument ended in action

– a stupid action leading nowhere, unless eventually to this doubt that always comes when I begin to write, the feeling that after all perhaps she was right and I was wrong.

I remember saying angrily, 'This is just a hang-over from your old frigidity. A frigid woman is never jealous, you simply haven't caught up yet on ordinary human emotions.'

It angered me that she didn't make any claim. 'You may be right. I'm only saying I want you to be happy. I hate your being unhappy. I don't mind anything you do that makes you happy.'

'You just want an excuse. If I sleep with somebody else, you feel you can do the same – any time.'

'That's neither here nor there. I want you to be happy, that's all.'

'You'd make my bed for me?'

'Perhaps.'

Insecurity is the worst sense that lovers feel: sometimes the most humdrum desireless marriage seems better. Insecurity twists meanings and poisons trust. In a closely beleaguered city every sentry is a potential traitor. Even before the days of Mr Parkis I was trying to check on her: I would catch her out in small lies, evasions that meant nothing except her fear of me. For every lie I would magnify into a betrayal, and even in the most open statement I would read hidden meanings. Because I couldn't bear the thought of her so much as touching another man, I feared it all the time, and I saw intimacy in the most casual movement of the hand.

'Wouldn't you want me to be happy, rather than miserable?' she asked with unbearable logic.

'I'd rather be dead or see you dead,' I said, 'than with another man. I'm not eccentric. That's ordinary human love. Ask anybody. They'd all say the same – if they loved at all.' I jibed at her. 'Anyone who loves is jealous.'

We were in my room. We had come there at a safe time of day, the late spring afternoon, in order to make love; for once we had hours of time ahead of us and so I squandered it all in a quarrel and there was no love to make. She sat down on the bed and said, 'I'm sorry. I didn't mean to make you angry. I expect you're right.' But I wouldn't let her alone. I hated her because I wished to think she didn't love me: I wanted to get her out of my system. What grievance, I wonder now, had I got against her, whether she loved me or not? She had been loyal to me for nearly a year, she had given me a great deal of pleasure, she had put up with my moods, and what had I given her in return apart from the momentary pleasure? I had come into this affair with my eyes open, knowing that one day this must end, and yet, when the sense of insecurity, the logical belief in the hopeless future descended like melancholia, I would badger her and badger her, as though I wanted to bring the future in now at the door, an unwanted and premature guest. My love and fear acted like conscience. If we had believed in sin, our behaviour would hardly have differed.

'You'd be jealous of Henry,' I said.

'No. I couldn't be. It's absurd.'

'If you saw your marriage threatened . . .'

'It never would be,' she said drearily, and I took her words as an insult and walked straight out and down the stairs and into the street. Is this the end, I wondered, play-acting to myself? There's no need ever to go back. If

I can get her out of my system, can't I find somewhere a quiet friendly marriage that would go on and on? Then perhaps I wouldn't feel jealous because I wouldn't love enough: I would just be secure, and my self-pity and hatred walked hand in hand across the darkening Common like idiots without a keeper.

When I began to write I said this was a story of hatred, but I am not convinced. Perhaps my hatred is really as deficient as my love. I looked up just now from writing and caught sight of my own face in a mirror close to my desk, and I thought, does hatred really look like that? For I was reminded of that face we have all of us seen in childhood, looking back at us from the shop-window, the features blurred with our breath, as we stare with such longing at the bright unobtainable objects within.

It must have been some time in May 1940 when this argument broke out. War had helped us in a good many ways, and that was how I had almost come to regard war as a rather disreputable and unreliable accomplice in my affair. (Deliberately I would put the caustic soda of that word 'affair', with its suggestion of a beginning and an end, upon my tongue.) I suppose Germany by this time had invaded the Low Countries: the spring like a corpse was sweet with the smell of doom, but nothing mattered to me but two practical facts – Henry had been shifted to Home Security and worked late, my landlady had removed to the basement for fear of air-raids, and no longer lurked upon the floor above watching over the banisters for undesirable visitors. My own life had altered not at all, because of my lameness (I have one leg a little shorter than the other, the result of an accident in childhood); only when the air-raids started did I feel it necessary to become a warden. It was for the time being as though I had signed out of the war.

That evening I was still full of my hatred and distrust when I reached Piccadilly. More than anything in the world I wanted to hurt Sarah. I wanted to take a woman back with me and lie with her upon the same bed in which I made love to Sarah; it was as though I knew that the only way to hurt her was to hurt myself. It was dark and quiet by this time in the streets, though up in the moonless sky moved the blobs and beams of the searchlights. You couldn't see faces where the women stood in doorways and at the entrances of the unused shelters. They had to signal with their torches like glow-worms. All the way up Sackville Street the little lights went on and off. I found myself wondering what Sarah was doing now. Had she gone home or was she waiting on the chance of my return?

A woman flashed on her light and said, 'Like to come home with me, dear?' I shook my head and walked on. Further up the street a girl was talking to a man: as she lit up her face for him, I got a glimpse of something young, dark and happy and not yet spoiled: an animal that didn't yet recognize her captivity. I passed and then came back up the road towards them; as I approached the man left her and I spoke. 'Like a drink?' I said.

'Coming home with me afterwards?'

'Yes.'

'I'll be glad of a quick one.'

We went into the pub at the top of the street and I ordered two whiskies, but as she drank I couldn't see her face for Sarah's. She was younger than Sarah, she couldn't have been more than nineteen, more beautiful, one might even have said less spoiled, but only because there was so much less to spoil:

I found I no more wanted her than I wanted the company of a dog or a cat. She was telling me that she had a nice flat on the top floor only a few houses down: she told me what rent she had to pay and what her age was and where she was born and how she had worked for a year in a café. She told me she didn't go home with anybody who spoke to her, but she could see at once I was a gentleman. She said she had a canary called Jones named after the gentleman who had given it her. She began to talk of the difficulty of getting groundsel in London. I thought: if Sarah is still in my room I can ring up. I heard the girl asking me whether if I had a garden I would sometimes remember her canary. She said, 'You don't mind me asking, do you?'

Looking at her over my whisky I thought how odd it was that I felt no desire for her at all. It was as if quite suddenly after all the promiscuous years I had grown up. My passion for Sarah had killed simple lust for ever. Never again would I be able to enjoy a woman without love.

And yet surely it was not love that had brought me into this pub; I had told myself all the way from the Common that it was hate, as I tell myself still, writing this account of her, trying to get her out of my system for ever, for I have always told myself that if she died, I could forget her.

I went out of the pub, leaving the girl with her whisky to finish and a pound-note as a salve to her pride, and walked up New Burlington Street as far as a telephone-box. I had no torch with me and I was forced to strike match after match before I could complete the dialling of my number. Then I heard the ringing tone and I could imagine the telephone where it stood on my desk and I knew exactly how many steps Sarah would have to take to reach it if she were sitting in a chair or lying on the bed. And yet I let it go on ringing in the empty room for half a minute. Then I telephoned to her home and the maid told me she had not yet come in. I thought of her walking about on the Common in the black-out – it wasn't a very safe place in those days, and looking at my watch I thought, if I hadn't been a fool we should still have had three hours together. I went back home alone and tried to read a book, but all the time I was listening for the telephone which never rang. My pride prevented me telephoning her again. At last I went to bed and took a double dose of sleeping-draught, so that the first I knew in the morning was Sarah's voice on the telephone, speaking to me as if nothing had happened. It was like perfect peace again until I put the receiver down, when immediately that devil in my brain prompted the thought that the waste of those three hours meant nothing at all to her.

I have never understood why people who can swallow the enormous improbability of a personal God boggle at a personal Devil. I have known so intimately the way that demon works in my imagination. No statement that Sarah ever made was proof against his cunning doubts, though he would usually wait till she had gone to utter them. He would prompt our quarrels long before they occurred: he was not Sarah's enemy so much as the enemy of love, and isn't that what the devil is supposed to be? I can imagine that if there existed a God who loved, the devil would be driven to destroy even the weakest, the most faulty imitation of that love. Wouldn't he be afraid that the habit of love might grow, and wouldn't he try to trap us all into being traitors, into helping him extinguish love? If there is a God who uses us and makes his saints out of such material as we are, the devil too may have his ambitions; he may dream of training even such a person as myself, even poor Parkis, into being his saints, ready with borrowed fanaticism to destroy love wherever we find it.

Chapter Three

For I thought I could detect in Parkis's next report a genuine enthusiasm for the devil's game. At last he had really scented love and now he stalked it, his boy at his heels like a retriever. He had discovered where Sarah was spending so much of her time: more than that, he knew for certain that the visits were surreptitious. I had to admit that Mr Parkis had proved himself an astute detective. He had arranged with the help of his boy to get the Miles's maid outside the house just at the moment when the 'party in question' walked down Cedar Road toward No. 16. Sarah stopped and spoke to the maid, whose day off it was, and the maid introduced her to young Parkis. Then Sarah went on and turned the next corner, where Parkis himself was waiting. He saw her walk a little way and then return. When she found the maid and young Parkis were out of sight she rang the bell at No. 16. Mr Parkis then set to work to check on the inhabitants of No. 16. This was not so easy, as the house was divided into flats and he had no means yet of knowing which of the three bells Sarah rang. He promised a final report in a few days. All he had to do, when next Sarah started out in this direction, was to get ahead of her and dust the three bells with powder. 'There is, of course, apart from exhibit A, no proof of misconduct by the party in question. If on the strength of these reports such proofs are required with a view to legal proceedings, it may be necessary after a suitable interval to follow the party into the flat. A second witness, who can identify the party, would be required. It is not necessary to catch the party in the act; a certain disarrangement of clothes and agitation might be held sufficient by the Courts.'

Hatred is very like physical love: it has its crisis and then its periods of calm. Poor Sarah, I could think, reading Mr Parkis's report, for this moment had been the orgasm of my hatred, and now I was satisfied. I could feel sorry for her, hemmed in as she was. She had committed nothing but love, and here were Parkis and his boy watching every movement, plotting with her maid, putting powder on bells, planning violent eruptions into what perhaps was the only peace that nowadays she enjoyed. I had half a mind to tear up the report and call the spies off her. Perhaps I would have done so if I had not, at the seedy club to which I belonged, opened a *Tatler* and seen Henry's photograph. Henry was successful now: in the last Birthday Honours he had received a CBE for his services at the Ministry: he had been appointed Chairman of a Royal Commission: and here he was at the gala night of a British film called *The Last Siren*, pallid and pop-eyed in the flashlight with Sarah on his arm. She had lowered her head to escape the flash, but I would have recognized that close knotty hair which trapped or resisted the fingers. Suddenly I wanted to put out my hand and touch her, the hair of her head and her secret hair, I wanted her lying beside me, I wanted to be able to turn my head on the pillow and speak to her, I wanted the almost imperceptible smell and taste of her skin, and there was Henry facing the pressman's camera with the complacency and assurance of a Departmental head.

I sat down under a staghead presented by Sir Walter Besant in 1898 and wrote to Henry. I wrote that I had something of importance to discuss with him and would he lunch with me – he could choose any day during the next week. It was typical of Henry that he rang up with great promptitude and at the same time suggested I should lunch with him – never have I known a man who was a more uneasy guest. I can't remember exactly what the excuse was, but it angered me. I think he said his own club had some particularly good port, but the real reason was that the sense of obligation irked him – even the small obligation of a free meal. He little guessed how small his obligation was going to be. He had chosen a Saturday and on that day my club is almost empty. The daily journalists have no paper to produce, the school inspectors have gone home to Bromley and Streatham, I never know quite what happens on that day to the clergy – perhaps they stay indoors to prepare their sermons. As for the authors (for whom the club had been founded), nearly all of them are hanging on the wall – Conan Doyle, Charles Garvice, Stanley Weyman, Nat Gould, with an occasional more illustrious and familiar face: the living you can count on the fingers of one hand. I have always felt at home in the club because there is so little likelihood of meeting a fellow writer.

I remember Henry chose a Vienna steak – it was a mark of his innocence. I really believe that he had no idea what he was ordering and expected something like a Wiener Schnitzel. Playing as he was away from the home ground, he was too ill at ease to comment on the dish and somehow he managed to ram the pink soggy mixture down. I remembered that pompous appearance before the flashlights and made no attempt to warn him when he chose Cabinet Pudding. During the hideous meal (the club that day surpassed itself) we talked elaborately about nothing. Henry did his best to lend an appearance of Cabinet secrecy to the proceedings of a Royal Commission that were reported daily in the Press. We went into the lounge for coffee and found ourselves entirely alone beside the fire in a waste of black horsehair sofas. I thought how suitable the horns along the walls were to the situation, and putting my feet up on the old-fashioned fender shut Henry firmly into his corner. I stirred my coffee and said, 'How's Sarah?'

'Pretty well,' Henry said evasively. He tasted his port with care and suspicion: he hadn't forgotten, I suppose, the Vienna steak.

'Are you still worried?' I asked him.

He shifted his gaze unhappily. 'Worried?'

'You *were* worried. You told me so.'

'I don't remember. She's pretty well,' he explained weakly, as though I had been referring to her health.

'Did you ever consult that detective?'

'I hoped you'd forgotten it. I wasn't well – you see, there was this Royal Commission brewing. I was overworked.'

'Do you remember I offered to see him for you?'

'We must both have been a bit overwrought.' He stared up at the old horns overhead, screwing up his eyes in his attempt to read the name of the donor. He said stupidly, 'You seem to have a lot of heads.' I wasn't going to let him off. I said, 'I went to see him a few days later.'

He put down his glass and said, 'Bendrix, you have absolutely no right . . .'

'I'm paying all the charges.'

'It's infernal cheek.' He stood up, but I had him penned in where he couldn't get past without an act of violence, and violence wasn't in Henry's character.

'Surely you'd have liked her cleared?' I said.

'There was nothing to clear. I want to go, please.'

'I think you ought to read the reports.'

'I've no intention . . .'

'Then I think I shall have to read you the bit about the surreptitious visits. Her love letter I returned to the detectives for filing. My dear Henry, you've been properly led up the garden.'

I really thought that he was going to hit me. If he had, I would have struck back with pleasure, struck back at this oaf to whom Sarah had remained in her way so stupidly loyal for so many years, but at that moment the secretary of the club came in. He was a man with a long grey beard and a soup-stained waistcoat, who looked like a Victorian poet but in fact wrote little sad reminiscences of the dogs he had once known. (*For Ever Fido* had been a great success in 1912.) 'Ah, Bendrix,' he said, 'I haven't seen you here in a long while.' I introduced him to Henry and he said with the quickness of a hairdresser, 'I've been following the reports every day.'

'What reports?' For once Henry's work had not come first to his mind when that word was uttered.

'The Royal Commission.'

When at last he had gone, Henry said, 'Now will you please give me the reports and let me pass.'

I imagined that he had been thinking things over while the secretary was with us, so I handed him the last report. He put it straight into the fire and rammed it home with the poker. I couldn't help thinking that the gesture had dignity. 'What are you going to do?' I asked.

'Nothing.'

'You haven't got rid of the facts.'

'To hell with the facts,' Henry said. I had never heard him swear before.

'I can always let you have a carbon copy.'

'Will you let me go now?' Henry said. The demon had done its work, I felt drained of venom. I took my legs off the fender and let Henry pass. He walked straight out of the club, forgetting his hat, that black superior hat that I had seen come dripping across the Common – it seemed an age and not a matter of weeks ago.

Chapter Four

I had expected to overtake him, or at least to come in sight of him ahead up the long reach of Whitehall, and so I carried his hat with me, but he was nowhere to be seen. I turned back not knowing where to go. That is the worst of time nowadays – there is so much of it. I looked in the small bookshop near Charing Cross Underground and wondered whether Sarah at this moment might have laid her hand on the powdered bell in Cedar Road with Mr Parkis waiting round the corner. If I could have turned back time I think I would have done so: I would have let Henry go walking by, blinded by the rain. But I am beginning to doubt whether anything I can do will ever alter the course of events. Henry and I are allies now, in our fashion, but are we allies against an infinite tide?

I went across the road, past the fruit-hawkers, and into the Victoria Gardens. Not many people were sitting on the benches in the grey windy air, and almost at once I saw Henry, but it took me a moment to recognize him. Out of doors, without a hat, he seemed to have joined the anonymous and the dispossessed, the people who come up from the poorer suburbs and nobody knows – the old man feeding sparrows, the woman with a brown-paper parcel marked Swan & Edgar's. He sat there with his head bent, looking at his shoes. I have been sorry for myself for so long, so exclusively, that it seemed strange to me to feel sorry for my enemy. I put the hat quietly down on the seat beside him and would have walked away, but he looked up and I could see that he had been crying. He must have travelled a very long way. Tears belong to a different world from Royal Commissions.

'I'm sorry, Henry,' I said. How easily we believe we can slide out of our guilt by a motion of contrition.

'Sit down,' Henry commanded with the authority of his tears, and I obeyed him. He said, 'I've been thinking. Were you two lovers, Bendrix?'

'Why should you imagine . . .?'

'It's the only explanation.'

'I don't know what you are talking about.'

'It's the only excuse too, Bendrix. Can't you see that what you've done is – monstrous?' As he spoke he turned his hat over and checked the maker's name.

'I suppose you think I'm an awful fool, Bendrix, not to have guessed. Why didn't she leave me?'

Had I got to instruct him about the character of his own wife? The poison was beginning to work in me again. I said, 'You have a good safe income. You're a habit she's formed. You're security.' He listened seriously and attentively as though I were a witness before the Commission giving evidence on oath. I went sourly on, 'You were no more trouble to us than you'd been to the others.'

'There were others too?'

'Sometimes I thought you knew all about it and didn't care. Sometimes I longed to have it out with you – like we are doing now when it's too late. I wanted to tell you what I thought of you.'

'What did you think?'

'That you were her pimp. You pimped for me and you pimped for them, and now you are pimping for the latest one. The eternal pimp. Why don't you get angry, Henry?'

'I never knew.'

'You pimped with your ignorance. You pimped by never learning how to make love with her, so she had to look elsewhere. You pimped by giving opportunities ... You pimped by being a bore and a fool, so now somebody who isn't a bore and fool is playing about with her in Cedar Road.'

'Why did she leave you?'

'Because I became a bore and a fool too. But I wasn't born one, Henry. You created me. She wouldn't leave you, so I became a bore, boring her with complaints and jealousy.'

He said, 'People have a great opinion of your books.'

'And they say you're a first-class chairman. What the hell does our work matter?'

He said sadly, 'I don't know anything else that does,' looking up at the grey cumulus passing above the south bank. The gulls flew low over the barges and the shot-tower stood black in the winter light among the ruined warehouses. The man who fed the sparrows had gone and the woman with the brown-paper parcel, the fruitsellers cried like animals in the dusk outside the station. It was as if the shutters were going up on the whole world; soon we should all of us be abandoned to our own devices. 'I wondered why you hadn't been to see us all that time,' Henry said.

'I suppose – in a way – we'd got to the end of love. There was nothing else we could do together. She could shop and cook and fall asleep with you, but she could only make love with me.'

'She's very fond of you,' he said as though it were his job to comfort *me*, as though my eyes were the ones bruised with tears.

'One isn't satisfied with fondness.'

'I was.'

'I wanted love to go on and on, never to get less. ....' I had never spoken to anyone like this, except Sarah, but Henry's reply was not Sarah's. He said, 'It's not in human nature. One has to be satisfied ...' but that wasn't what Sarah had said, and sitting there beside Henry in the Victoria Gardens, watching the day die, I remembered the end of the whole 'affair'.

Chapter Five

She had said to me – they were nearly the last words I heard from her before she came dripping into the hall from her assignation – 'You needn't be so scared. Love doesn't end. Just because we don't see each other. . . .' She had already made her decision, though I didn't know it till next day, when the telephone presented nothing but the silent open mouth of somebody found dead. She said, 'My dear, my dear. People go on loving God, don't they, all their lives without seeing Him?'

'That's not our kind of love.'

'I sometimes don't believe there's any other kind.' I suppose I should have recognized that she was already under a stranger's influence – she had never spoken like that when we were first together. We had agreed so happily to eliminate God from our world. As I shone the torch carefully to light her way across the devastated hall, she said again, 'Everything must be all right. If we love enough.'

'I can't turn on any more,' I said. 'You've got everything.'

'You don't know,' she said. 'You don't know.'

The glass from the windows crumbled under our feet. Only the old Victorian stained glass above the door had stood firm. The glass turned white where it powdered like the ice children have broken in wet fields or along the side of roads. She told me again, 'Don't be scared.' I knew she wasn't referring to those strange new weapons that still, after five hours, droned steadily up from the south like bees.

It was the first night of what were later called the V1s in June 1944. We had become unused to air-raids. Apart from the short spell in February 1944, there had been nothing since the blitz petered out with the great final raids of 1941. When the sirens went and the first robots came over, we assumed that a few planes had broken through our night defence. One felt a sense of grievance when the All Clear had still not sounded after an hour. I remember saying to Sarah, 'They must have got slack. Too little to do,' and at that moment, lying in the dark on my bed, we saw our first robot. It passed low across the Common and we took it for a plane on fire and its odd deep bumble for the sound of an engine out of control. A second came and then a third. We changed our minds then about our defences. 'They are shooting them like pigeons,' I said, 'they must be crazy to go on.' But go on they did, hour after hour, even after the dawn had begun to break, until even we realized that this was something new.

We had only just lain down on the bed when the raid started. It made no difference. Death never mattered at those times – in the early days I even used to pray for it: the shattering annihilation that would prevent for ever the getting up, the putting on of clothes, the watching her torch trail across to the opposite side of the Common like the tail-light of a slow car driving away. I have wondered sometimes whether eternity might not after all exist as the endless prolongation of the moment of death, and that was the moment I would have chosen, that I would still choose if she were alive, the moment of absolute trust and absolute pleasure, the moment when it was impossible to quarrel because it was impossible to think. I have complained of her caution, and bitterly compared our use of the word 'onions' with the scrap of her writing Mr Parkis had salvaged, but reading her message to my unknown successor would have hurt less if I hadn't known how capable she was of abandonment. No, the V1s didn't affect us until the act of love was over. I had spent everything I had, and was lying back with my head on her stomach and her taste – as thin and elusive as water – in my mouth, when one of the robots crashed down on to the Common and we could hear the glass breaking further down the south side.

'I suppose we ought to go to the basement,' I said.

'Your landlady will be there. I can't face other people.'

After possession comes the tenderness of responsibility when one forgets one is only a lover, responsible for nothing. I said, 'She may be away. I'll go down and see.'

'Don't go. Please don't go.'

'I won't be a moment.' It was a phrase one continued to use, although one knew in those days that a moment might well be eternity long. I put on my dressing-gown and found my torch. I hardly needed it: the sky was grey now and in the unlit room I could see the outline of her face.

She said, 'Be quick.'

As I ran down the stairs I heard the next robot coming over, and then the sudden waiting silence when the engine cut out. We hadn't yet had time to learn that that was the moment of risk, to get out of the line of glass, to lie flat. I never heard the explosion, and I woke after five seconds or five minutes in a changed world. I thought I was still on my feet and I was puzzled by the darkness: somebody seemed to be pressing a cold fist into my cheek and my mouth was salty with blood. My mind for a few moments was clear of everything except a sense of tiredness as though I had been on a long journey. I had no memory at all of Sarah and I was completely free from anxiety, jealousy, insecurity, hate: my mind was a blank sheet on which somebody had just been on the point of writing a message of happiness. I felt sure that when my memory came back, the writing would continue and that I should be happy.

But when memory did return it was not in that way. I realized first that I was lying on my back and that what balanced over me, shutting out the light, was the front door: some other débris had caught it and suspended it a few inches over my body, though the odd thing was that later I found myself bruised from the shoulders to the knees as if by its shadow. The fist that fitted into my cheek was the china handle of the door, and it had knocked out a couple of my teeth. After that, of course, I remembered Sarah and Henry and the dread of love ending.

I got out from under the door and dusted myself down. I called to the basement but there was nobody there. Through the blasted doorway I could see the grey morning light and I had a sense of great emptiness stretching out from the ruined hall: I realized that a tree which had blocked the light had simply ceased to exist – there was no sign of even a fallen trunk. A long way off wardens were blowing whistles. I went upstairs. The first flight had lost its banisters and was a foot deep in plaster, but the house hadn't really, by the standard of those days, suffered badly: it was our neighbours who had caught the full blast. The door of my room was open and coming along the passage I could see Sarah; she had got off the bed and was crouched on the floor – from fear, I supposed. She looked absurdly young, like a naked child. I said, 'That was a close one.'

She turned quickly and stared at me with fear. I hadn't realized that my dressing-gown was torn and dusted all over with plaster; my hair was white with it, and there was blood on my mouth and cheeks. 'Oh, God,' she said, 'you're alive.'

'You sound disappointed.'

She got up from the floor and reached for her clothes. I told her, 'There's no point in your going yet. There must be an All Clear soon.'

'I've got to go,' she said.

'Two bombs don't fall in one place,' I said, but automatically, for that was a piece of folklore that had often proved false.

'You're hurt.'

'I've lost two teeth, that's all.'

'Come over here, let me wash your face.' She had finished dressing before I had time to make another protest – no woman I have ever known could dress as quickly. She bathed my face very slowly and carefully.

'What were you doing on the floor?' I asked.

'Praying.'

'Who to?'

'To anything that might exist.'

'It would have been more practical to come downstairs.' Her seriousness frightened me. I wanted to tease her out of it.

'I did,' she said.

'I didn't hear you.'

'There was nobody there. I couldn't see you, until I saw your arm stretching out from under the door. I thought you were dead.'

'You might have come and tried.'

'I did. I couldn't lift the door.'

'There was room to move me. The door wasn't holding me. I'd have woken up.'

'I don't understand. I knew for certain you were dead.'

'There wasn't much to pray for then, was there?' I teased her. 'Except a miracle.'

'When you are hopeless enough,' she said, 'you can pray for miracles. They happen, don't they, to the poor, and I was poor.'

'Stay till the All Clear.' She shook her head and walked straight out of the room. I followed her down the stairs and began against my will to badger her. 'Shall I see you this afternoon?'

'No. I can't.'

'Some time tomorrow . . .'

'Henry's coming back.'

Henry. Henry. Henry – that name tolled through our relationship, damping every mood of happiness or fun or exhilaration with its reminder that love dies, affection and habit win the day. 'You needn't be so scared,' she said, 'love doesn't end . . .' and nearly two years passed before that meeting in the hall and, 'You?'

Chapter Six

For days after that, of course, I had hope. It was only a coincidence, I thought, that the telephone wasn't answered, and when after a week I met the maid and inquired about the Mileses and learnt that she was away in the country, I told myself that in war-time letters are lost. Morning after morning I would hear the rattle in the post-box and deliberately I would remain upstairs until my landlady fetched my mail. I wouldn't look through the letters – disappointment had to be postponed, hope kept alive as long as possible; I would read each letter in turn and only when I reached the bottom of the pile could I be certain that there was nothing from Sarah. Then life withered until the four o'clock post, and after that one had to get through the night again.

For nearly a week I didn't write to her: pride prevented me, until one morning I abandoned it completely, writing anxiously and bitterly, marking the envelope addressed to the north side, 'Urgent' and 'Please forward'. I got no reply and then I gave up hope and remembered exactly what she had said. 'People go on loving God, don't they, all their lives without seeing Him?' I thought with hatred, she always has to show up well in her own mirror: she mixes religion with desertion to make it sound noble to herself. She won't admit that now she prefers to go to bed with X.

That was the worst period of all: it is my profession to imagine, to think in images: fifty times through the day, and immediately I woke during the night, a curtain would rise and the play would begin: always the same play, Sarah making love, Sarah with X, doing the same things that we had done together, Sarah kissing in her own particular way, arching herself in the act of sex and uttering that cry like pain, Sarah in abandonment. I would take pills at night to make me sleep quickly, but I never found any pills that would keep me asleep till daylight. Only the robots were a distraction during the day: for a few seconds between the silence and the crash my mind would be clear of Sarah. Three weeks passed and the images were as clear and frequent as at first and there seemed no reason why they should ever end, and I began quite seriously to think of suicide. I even set a date, and I saved up my sleeping pills with what was almost a sense of hope. I needn't after all go on like this indefinitely, I told myself. Then the date came and the play went on and on and I didn't kill myself. It wasn't cowardice: it was a memory that stopped me – the memory of the look of disappointment on Sarah's face when I came into the room after the V1 had fallen. Hadn't she, at heart, hoped for my death, so that her new affair with X would hurt her conscience less, for she had a kind of elementary conscience? If I killed myself now, she wouldn't have to worry about me at all, and surely after our four years together there would be moments of worry even with X. I wasn't going to give her that satisfaction. If I had known a way I would have increased her worries to breaking point and my impotence angered me. How I hated her.

Of course there is an end of hate as there is an end of love. After six months I realized that I had not thought of Sarah all one day and that I had been happy. It couldn't have been quite the end of hate because at once I went into a stationer's to buy a picture postcard and write a jubilant message on it that might – who knows? – cause a momentary pain, but by the time I had written her address I had lost the desire to hurt and dropped the card into the road. It was strange that hate should have been revived again by that meeting with Henry. I remember thinking, as I opened Mr Parkis's next report, if only love could revive like that too.

Mr Parkis had done his work well: the powder had worked and the flat had been located – the top flat in 16 Cedar Road: the occupant, a Miss Smythe and her brother, Richard. I wondered whether Miss Smythe was as convenient a sister as Henry was a husband, and all my latent snobbery was aroused by the name – that y, and final e. I thought, has she fallen as low as a Smythe in Cedar Road? Was he the end of a long chain of lovers in the last two years, or when I saw him (and I was determined to see him less obscurely than in Mr Parkis's reports) would I be looking at the man for whom she had deserted me in June 1944?

'Shall I ring the bell and walk right in and confront him like an injured husband?' I asked Mr Parkis (who had met me by appointment in an A.B.C. – it was his own suggestion as he had the boy with him and couldn't take him into a bar).

'I'm against it, sir,' Mr Parkis said, adding a third spoonful of sugar to his tea. His son sat at a table out of earshot with a glass of orangeade and a bun. He observed everybody who came in, as they shook the thin watery snow from their hats and coats, watched with his alert brown beady eyes as though he had to make a report later – perhaps he had, part of the Parkis training. 'You see, sir,' Mr Parkis said, 'unless you were willing to give evidence, it complicates things in the Courts.'

'It will never reach the Courts.'

'An amicable settlement?'

'A lack of interest,' I said. 'One can't really make a fuss about a man called Smythe. I'd just like to see him – that's all.'

'The safest thing, sir, would be a meter inspector.'

'I can't dress up in a peaked cap.'

'I share your feelings, sir. It's a thing I try to avoid. And I'd like the boy to avoid it too when the time comes.' His sad eyes followed every movement his boy made. 'He wanted an ice, sir, but I said no, not in this weather,' and he shivered a little as though the thought of the ice had chilled him. For a moment I had no idea of his meaning when he said, 'Every profession has its dignity, sir.'

I said, 'Would you lend me your boy?'

'If you assure me there'll be nothing unpleasant, sir,' he said doubtfully.

'I don't want to call when Mrs Miles is there. This scene will have a Universal certificate.'

'But why the boy, sir?'

'I'll say he's feeling ill. We've come to the wrong address. They couldn't help letting him sit down for a while.'

'It's in the boy's capacity,' Mr Parkis said with pride 'and nobody can resist Lance.'

'He's called Lance, is he?'

'After Sir Lancelot, sir. Of the Round Table.'

'I'm surprised. That was a rather unpleasant episode, surely.'

'He found the Holy Grail,' Mr Parkis said.

'That was Galahad. Lancelot was found in bed with Guinevere.' Why do we have this desire to tease the innocent? Is it envy? Mr Parkis said sadly, looking across at his boy as though he had betrayed him, 'I hadn't heard.'

Chapter Seven

Next day – to spite his father – I gave the boy an ice in the High Street before we went to Cedar Road. Henry Miles was holding a cocktail party – so Mr Parkis had reported, and the coast was clear. He handed the boy over to me, after twitching his clothes straight. The boy was wearing his best things in honour of his first stage appearance with a client, while I was wearing my worst. Some of the strawberry ice fell from his spoon and made a splash upon his suit. I sat in silence till the last drop was drained. Then I said, 'Another?' He nodded. 'Strawberry again?'

He said, 'Vanilla,' and added a long while after, 'Please.'

He ate the second ice with great deliberation, carefully licking the spoon as though he were removing fingerprints. Then we went hand in hand across the Common to Cedar Road like a father and son. Sarah and I are both childless, I thought. Wouldn't there have been more sense in marrying and having children and living quietly together in a sweet and dull peace than in this furtive business of lust and jealousy and the reports of Parkis?

I rang the bell on the top floor of Cedar Road. I said to the boy, 'Remember. You're feeling ill.'

'If they give me an ice ...' he began: Parkis had trained him to be prepared.

'They won't.'

I assumed it was Miss Smythe who opened the door – a middle-aged woman with the grey tired hair of charity-bazaars. I said, 'Does Mr Wilson live here?'

'No. I'm afraid ...'

'You don't happen to know if he's in the flat below?'

'There's nobody called Wilson in this house.'

'Oh dear,' I said. 'I've brought the boy all this way, and now he's feeling ill. . . .'

I dared not look at the boy, but from the way in which Miss Smythe gazed at him, I felt sure he was silently and efficiently carrying out his part: Mr Savage would have been proud to acknowledge him as a member of his team.

'Do let him come in and sit down,' Miss Smythe said.

'It's very kind of you.'

I wondered how often Sarah had passed through this door into the little cluttered hall. Here I was in the home of X. Presumably the brown soft hat on the hook belonged to him. The fingers of my successor – the fingers that touched Sarah – daily turned the handle of the door which opened now on the yellow flame of the gas-fire, pink-shaded lamps burning through the snow-grey afternoon, a waste of cretonne loosecovers. 'Can I fetch your little boy a glass of water?'

'It's very kind of you.' I remembered I had said that before.

'Or some orange-squash.'

'You mustn't bother.'

'Orange-squash,' the boy said firmly: again the long pause and 'Please' as she went through the door. Now we were alone I looked at him: he really did look ill, crouching back on the cretonne. If he had not winked at me, I would have wondered whether perhaps . . . Miss Smythe returned, carrying the orange-squash, and I said, 'Say thank you, Arthur.'

'Is his name Arthur?'

'Arthur James,' I said.

'It's quite an old-fashioned name.'

'We're an old-fashioned family. His mother was fond of Tennyson.'

'She's . . .?'

'Yes,' I said and she looked at the child with commiseration.

'He must be a comfort to you.'

'And an anxiety,' I said. I began to feel shame: she was so unsuspicious, and what good was I doing here? I was no nearer meeting X, and would I be any happier for giving a face to the man upon the bed? I altered my tactics. I said, 'I ought to introduce myself. My name is Bridges.'

'And mine is Smythe.'

'I have a strong feeling I have met you somewhere before.'

'I don't think so. I have a very good memory for faces.'

'Perhaps I have seen you on the Common.'

'I go there sometimes with my brother.'

'Not by any chance a John Smythe?'

'No,' she said, 'Richard. How is the little boy feeling?'

'Worse,' said Parkis's son.

'Do you think we ought to take his temperature?'

'Can I have some more orange-squash?'

'It can do no harm, can it?' Miss Smythe wondered. 'Poor child. Perhaps he has a fever.'

'We've trespassed on you enough.'

'My brother would never forgive me if I didn't make you stay. He's very fond of children.'

'Is your brother in?'

'I'm expecting him any moment.'

'Home from work?'

'Well, his working day is really Sunday.'

'A clergyman?' I asked with secret malice and received the puzzling answer, 'Not exactly.' A look of worry came down like a curtain between us and she retired behind it with her private troubles. As she got up the hall door opened and there was X. I had an impression, in the dusk of the hall, of a man with a handsome actor's face – a face that looked at itself too often in mirrors, a taint of vulgarity, and I thought sadly and without satisfaction, I wish she had better taste. Then he came through into the light of the lamps. The gross livid spots which covered his left cheek were almost like marks of distinction – I had maligned him, he could have no satisfaction in looking at himself in any glass.

Miss Smythe said, 'My brother Richard. Mr Bridges. Mr Bridges's little boy is not feeling well. I asked them in.'

He shook hands with his eye on the boy: I noticed the dryness and heat of his hands. He said, 'I've seen your boy before.'

'On the Common?'

'Perhaps.'

He was too powerful for the room: he didn't go with the cretonne. Did his sister sit here, while they, in another room . . . or did they send her out on errands while they made love?

Well, I had seen the man; there wasn't anything to stay for – except all the other questions that now were released by the sight of him – where had they met? Had she made the first move? What had she seen in him? How long, how often had they been lovers? There were words she had written that I knew by heart: 'I have no need to write to you or talk to you . . . I know I am only beginning to love, but already I want to abandon everything, everybody but you,' and I stared up at the raw spots on his cheek and thought, there is no safety anywhere: a humpback, a cripple – they all have the trigger that sets love off.

'What was the real purpose of your coming?' he suddenly broke into my thoughts.

'I told Miss Smythe – a man called Wilson. . . .'

'I don't remember your face, but I remember your son's.' He made a short frustrated gesture as though he wanted to touch the boy's hand: his eyes had a kind of abstract tenderness. He said, 'You don't have to be afraid of me. I am used to people coming here. I assure you I only want to be of use.'

Miss Smythe explained, 'People are often so shy.' I couldn't for the life of me think what it was all about.

'I was just looking for a man called Wilson.'

'You know that *I* know there's no such man.'

'If you would lend me a telephone directory I could check his address. . . .'

'Sit down again,' he said and brooded gloomily over the boy.

'I must be going. Arthur's feeling better and Wilson . .' His ambiguity made me ill at ease.

'You can go if you want to, of course, but can't you leave the boy here – if only for half an hour? I want to talk to him.' It occurred to me that he had recognized Parkis's assistant and was going to cross-question him. I said, 'Anything you want to ask him you can ask me.' Every time he turned his unmarked cheek towards me my anger grew: every time I saw the ugly flavid cheek it died away and I couldn't believe – any more than I could believe that lust existed here among the flowered cretonnes, with Miss Smythe getting tea. But despair can always produce an answer and despair asked me now: Would you so much rather it was love and not lust?

'You and I are too old,' he said. 'But the schoolmasters and the priests – they've only just begun to corrupt *him* with their lies.'

'I don't know what the hell you mean,' I said, and added quickly, 'I'm sorry,' to Miss Smythe.

'There you are, you see,' he said. 'Hell, and if I angered you, as like as not you'd say My God.'

It seemed to me that I had shocked him: he might be a Nonconformist minister: Miss Smythe had said he worked on Sundays, but how horribly bizarre that a man like that should be Sarah's lover. Suddenly it diminished her importance: her love affair became a joke: she herself might be used as a comic anecdote at my next dinner party. For a moment I was free of her. The boy said, 'I feel sick. Can I have some more orangeade?'

Miss Smythe said, 'My dear, I think you'd better not.'

'Really I must be taking him away. It's been very good of you.' I tried to keep the spots well in view. I said, 'I'm very sorry if I offended you at all. It was quite by accident. I don't happen to share your religious beliefs.'

He looked at me with surprise. 'But I have none. I believe in nothing.'

'I thought you objected . . .'

'I hate the trappings that are left over. Forgive me. I go too far, Mr Bridges, I know, but I'm sometimes afraid that people will be reminded even by conventional words – good-bye for instance. If only I could believe that my grandson would not even know what a word like god had meant to us any more than a word in Swahili.'

'Have you a grandson?'

He said gloomily, 'I have no children. I envy you your boy. It's a great duty and a great responsibility.'

'What did you want to ask him?'

'I wanted him to feel at home here because then he might return. There are so many things one wants to tell a child. How the world came into existence. I wanted to tell him about death. I wanted to rid him of all the lies they inject at school.'

'Rather a lot to do in half an hour.'

'One can sow a seed.'

I said maliciously, 'That comes out of the Gospels.'

'Oh, I've been corrupted too. You don't need to tell me that.'

'Do people really come to you – on the quiet?'

'You'd be surprised,' Miss Smythe said. 'People are longing for a message of hope.'

'Hope?'

'Yes, hope,' Smythe said. 'Can't you see what hope there'd be, if everybody in the world knew that there was nothing else but what we have here? No future compensation, rewards, punishments.' His face had a crazy nobility when one cheek was hidden. 'Then we'd begin to make this world like heaven.'

'There's a terrible lot to be explained first,' I said.

'Can I show you my library?'

'It's the best rationalist library in South London,' Miss Smythe explained.

'I don't need to be converted, Mr Smythe. I believe in nothing as it is. Except now and then.'

'It's the now and thens we have to deal with.'

'The odd thing is that those are the moments of hope.'

'Pride can masquerade as hope. Or selfishness.'

'I don't think that has anything to do with it at all. It happens suddenly, for no reason, a scent . . .'

'Ah,' Smythe said, 'the construction of a flower, the argument from design, all that business about a watch requiring a watchmaker. It's old-fashioned. Schwenigen answered all that twenty-five years ago. Let me show you. . . .'

'Not today. I must really take the boy home.'

Again he made that gesture of frustrated tenderness, like a lover who has been rejected. I wondered suddenly from how many death-beds he had been excluded. I found I wanted to give him some message of hope too, but then the cheek turned and I saw only the arrogant actor's face. I preferred him when he was pitiable, inadequate, out of date. Ayer, Russell – they were the fashion today, but I doubted whether there were many logical positivists in his library. He only had the crusaders, not the detached.

At the door – I noticed that he didn't use that dangerous term good-bye – I shot directly at his handsome cheek, 'You should meet a friend of mine, Mrs Miles. She's interested . . .' and then I stopped. The shot had gone home. The spots seemed to flush a deeper red and I heard Miss Smythe say, 'Oh, my dear,' as he turned abruptly away. There was no doubt that I had given him pain, but the pain was mine as well as his. How I wished my shot had gone astray.

In the gutter outside Parkis's boy was sick. I let him vomit, standing there wondering, has he lost her too? Is there no end to this? Have I now got to discover Y?

Chapter Eight

Parkis said, 'It was really very easy, sir. There was such a crush, and Mrs Miles thought I was one of his friends from the Ministry, and Mr Miles thought I was one of *her* friends.'

'Was it a good cocktail party?' I asked, remembering again that first meeting and the sight of Sarah with the stranger.

'Highly successful I should say, sir, but Mrs Miles seemed a bit out of sorts. A very nasty cough, she's got.' I heard him with pleasure: perhaps at this party there had been no alcove-kissing or touching. He laid a brown-paper parcel on my desk and said with pride, 'I knew the way to her room from the maid. If anyone had taken notice of me, I should have been looking for the toilet, but nobody did. There it was, out on her desk; she must have worked on it that day. Of course, she may be very cautious, but my experience of diaries is they always give things away. People invent their little codes, but you soon see through them, sir. Or they leave out things, but you soon learn what they leave out.' While he spoke I unwrapped the book and opened it. 'It's human nature, sir, that if you keep a diary, you want to remember things. Why keep it otherwise?'

'Did you look at this?' I asked.

'I ascertained its nature, sir, and from one entry judged she wasn't of the cautious type.'

'It's not this year's,' I said. 'It's two years old.'

For a moment he was dashed.

'It will serve my purpose,' I said.

'It would do the trick as well, sir – if nothing's been condoned.'

The journal was written in a big account book, the familiar bold hand-writing crossed by the red and blue lines. There were not daily entries and I was able to reassure Parkis – 'It covers several years.'

'I suppose something must have made her take it out to read.' Is it possible, I wondered, that some memory of me, of our affair, had crossed her mind this very day, that something may have troubled her peace? I said to Parkis, 'I'm glad to have this, very glad. You know, I really think we can close our account now.'

'I hope you feel satisfied, sir.'

'Quite satisfied.'

'And that you'll so write to Mr Savage, sir. He gets the bad reports from clients, but the good ones never get written. The more a client's satisfied, the more he wants to forget; to put us right out of mind. You can hardly blame them.'

'I'll write.'

'And thank you, sir, for being kind to the boy. He was a bit upset, but I know how it is – it's difficult to draw the line over ices with a boy like Lance. He gets them out of you with hardly a word said.' I longed to read, but Parkis lingered. Perhaps he didn't really trust me to remember him and wanted to impress more firmly on my memory those hang-dog eyes, that penurious moustache. 'I've enjoyed our association, sir – if one can talk of enjoying under the sad circumstances. We don't always work for real gentlemen even when they have titles. I had a peer of the realm once, sir, who flew into a rage when I gave him my report as though I were the guilty party myself. It's a discouraging thing, sir. The more you succeed the more glad they are to see the last of you.'

I was very conscious of wanting to see the last of Parkis and his words woke my sense of guilt. I couldn't hurry the man away. He said, 'I've been thinking, sir, I'd like to give you a little memento – but then that's just what you wouldn't want to receive.' How strange it is to be liked. It automatically awakens a certain loyalty. So I lied to Parkis, 'I've always enjoyed our talks.'

'Which started, sir, so inauspiciously. With that silly mistake.'

'Did you ever tell your boy?'

'Yes, sir, but only after some days, after the success with the waste-paper basket. That took away the sting.'

I looked down at the book and read: 'So happy. M. returns tomorrow.' I wondered for a moment who M. was. How strange too and unfamiliar to think that one had been loved, that one's presence had once had the power to make a difference between happiness and dullness in another's day.

'But if you really wouldn't resent a memento, sir . . .'

'Of course I wouldn't, Parkis.'

'I have something here, sir, that might be of interest and use.' He took out of his pocket an object wrapped in tissue paper and slid it shyly across the desk towards me. I unwrapped it. It was a cheap ash-tray marked Hotel Metropole, Brightlingsea. 'There's quite a history, sir, with that. You remember the Bolton case.'

'I can't say I do.'

'It made a great stir, sir, at the time. Lady Bolton, her maid and the man, sir. All discovered together. That ash-tray stood beside the bed. On the lady's side.'

'You must have collected quite a little museum.'

'I should have given it to Mr Savage – he took a particular interest – but I'm glad now, sir, I didn't. I think you'll find the inscription will evoke comment when your friends put out their cigarettes, and there's your answer pat – the Bolton Case. They'll all want to hear more of that.'

'It sounds sensational.'

'It's all human nature, sir, isn't it, and human love. Though I *was* surprised. Not having expected the third. And the room not large or fashionable. Mrs Parkis was alive then, but I didn't like to tell her the details. She got disturbed by things.'

'I'll certainly treasure the memento,' I said.

'If ash-trays could speak, sir.'

'Indeed, yes.'

But even Parkis with that profound thought had finished up his words. A last pressure of the hand, a little sticky (perhaps it had been in contact with Lance's), and he was gone. He was not one of those whom one expects to see again. Then I opened Sarah's journal. I thought first I would look for that day in June 1944 when everything ended, and after I had discovered the reason for that there were many other dates from which I could learn exactly, checking them with my diary, how it was that her love had petered out. I wanted to treat this as a document in a case – one of Parkis's cases – should be treated, but I hadn't that degree of calmness, for what I found when I opened the journal was not what I was expecting. Hate and suspicion and envy had driven me so far away that I read her words like a declaration of love from a stranger. I had expected plenty of evidence against her – hadn't I so often caught her out in lies? – and now here in writing that I could believe, as I couldn't believe her voice, was the complete answer. For it was the last couple of pages I read first, and I read them again at the end to make sure. It's a strange thing to discover and to believe that you are loved, when you know that there is nothing in you for anybody but a parent or a God to love.

Chapter One

... anything left, when we'd finished, but You. For either of us. I might have taken a lifetime spending a little love at a time, eking it out here and there, on this man and that. But even the first time, in the hotel near Paddington, we spent all we had. You were there, teaching us to squander, like you taught the rich man, so that one day we might have nothing left except this love of You. But You are too good to me. When I ask You for pain, You give me peace. Give it him too. Give him my peace – he needs it more.

February 12, 1946.
Two days ago I had such a sense of peace and quiet and love. Life was going to be happy again, but last night I dreamed I was walking up a long staircase to meet Maurice at the top. I was still happy because when I reached the top of the staircase we were going to make love. I called to him that I was coming, but it wasn't Maurice's voice that answered; it was a stranger's that boomed like a fog-horn warning lost ships, and scared me. I thought, he's let his flat and gone away and I don't know where he is, and going down the stairs again the water rose beyond my waist and the hall was thick with mist. Then I woke up. I'm not at peace any more. I just want him like I used to in the old days. I want to be eating sandwiches with him. I want to be drinking with him in a bar. I'm tired and I don't want any more pain. I want Maurice. I want ordinary corrupt human love. Dear God, you know I want to want Your pain, but I don't want it now. Take it away for a while and give it me another time.

After that I started the book from the beginning. She hadn't entered the journal every day, and I had no wish to read every entry. The theatres she had been to with Henry, the restaurants, the parties – all that life of which I knew nothing had still the power to hurt.

Chapter Two

June 12, 1944.

Sometimes I get so tired of trying to convince him that I love him and shall love him for ever. He pounces on my words like a barrister and twists them. I know he is afraid of that desert which would be around him if our love were to end, but he can't realize that I feel exactly the same. What he says aloud, I say to myself silently and write it here. What can one build in the desert? Sometimes after a day when we have made love many times, I wonder whether it isn't possible to come to an end of sex, and I know that he is wondering too and is afraid of that point where the desert begins. What do we do in the desert if we lose each other? How does one go on living after that?

He is jealous of the past and the present and the future. His love is like a medieval chastity belt: only when he is there, with me, in me, does he feel safe. If only I could make him feel secure, then we could love peacefully, happily, not savagely, inordinately, and the desert would recede out of sight. For a lifetime perhaps.

If one could believe in God, would he fill the desert?

I have always wanted to be liked or admired. I feel a terrible insecurity if a man turns on me, if I lose a friend. I don't even want to lose a husband. I want everything, all the time, everywhere. I'm afraid of the desert. God loves you, they say in the churches, God is everything. People who believe that don't need admiration, they don't need to sleep with a man, they feel safe. But I can't invent a belief.

All today Maurice has been sweet to me. He tells me often that he has never loved another woman so much. He thinks that by saying it often, he will make me believe it. But I believe it simply because I love him in exactly the same way. If I stopped loving him, I would cease to believe in his love. If I loved God, then I would believe in His love for me. It's not enough to need it. We have to love first, and I don't know how. But I need it, how I need it.

All day he was sweet. Only once, when a man's name was mentioned, I saw his eyes move away. He thinks I still sleep with other men, and if I did, would it matter so much? If sometimes he has a woman, do I complain? I wouldn't rob him of some small companionship in the desert if we can't have each other there. Sometimes I think that if the time came he would refuse me even a glass of water; he would drive me into such complete isolation that I would be alone with nothing and nobody – like a hermit, but they were never alone, or so they say. I am so muddled. What are we doing to each other? Because I know that I am doing to him exactly what he is doing to me. We are sometimes so happy, and never in our lives have we known more unhappiness. It's as if we were working together on the same statue, cutting it out of each other's misery. But I don't even know the design.

June 17, 1944.

Yesterday I went home with him and we did the usual things. I haven't the nerve to put them down, but I'd like to, because now when I'm writing it's already tomorrow and I'm afraid of getting to the end of yesterday. As long as I go on writing, yesterday is today and we are still together.

While I waited for him yesterday there were speakers out on the Common: the I.L.P. and the Communist Party, and the man who just tells jokes, and there was a man attacking Christianity. The Rationalist Society of South London or some name like that. He would have been good-looking if it hadn't been for the spots which covered one cheek. There were very few people in his audience and no hecklers. He was attacking something dead already, and I wondered why he took the trouble. I stayed and listened for a few minutes: he was arguing against the arguments for a God. I hadn't really known there were any - except this cowardly need I feel of not being alone.

I had a sudden fear that Henry might have changed his mind and sent a telegram to say that he would be home. I never know what I fear most - my disappointment or Maurice's disappointment. It works the same way with both of us: we pick quarrels. I am angry with myself and he is angry with me. I went home and there was no telegram, and I was ten minutes late in meeting Maurice and began to be angry so as to meet his anger and then unexpectedly he was sweet to me.

We had never before had quite so long a day, and there was all the night to follow. We bought lettuce and rolls and the butter-ration - we didn't want much to eat and it was very warm. It's warm now too: everybody will say, what a lovely summer, and I'm in a train going into the country to join Henry, and everything's over for ever. I'm scared: this *is* the desert, and there's nobody, nothing, for miles and miles around. If I were in London, I might be killed quickly, but if I were in London I'd go to the telephone and ring the only number I know by heart. I often forget my own: I suppose Freud would say that I want to forget it because it's Henry's number too. But I love Henry: I want him to be happy. I only hate him today because he *is* happy, and I am not and Maurice is not, and he won't know a thing. He'll say I look tired and think it's the curse - he no longer bothers to keep the count of those days.

This evening the sirens went - I mean last evening of course, but what does it matter? In the desert there's no time. But I can come out of the desert when I want to. I can catch a train home tomorrow and ring him up on the telephone. Henry will be still in the country perhaps, and we can spend the night together. A vow's not all that important - a vow to somebody I've never known, to somebody I don't really believe in. Nobody will know that I've broken a vow, except me and Him - and He doesn't exist, does he? He can't exist. You can't have a merciful God and this despair.

If I went back, where would we be? Where we were yesterday before the sirens went, and the year before that. Angry with each other for fear of the end, wondering what we should do with life when there was nothing left.

I needn't wonder any more – there's nothing to fear any more. This is the end. But, dear God, what shall I do with this desire to love?

Why do I write 'dear God'? He isn't dear – not to me he isn't. If he exists, then he put the thought of this vow into my mind and I hate him for it. I hate. Every few minutes a grey stone church and a public-house run backwards down the line: the desert is full of churches and public-houses. And multiple stores, and men on bicycles, and grass and cows, and factory chimneys. You see them through the sand like fish through the water in a tank. And Henry waits too in the tank, raising his muzzle for my kiss.

We paid no attention to the sirens. They didn't matter. We weren't afraid of dying that way. But then the raid went on and on. It wasn't an ordinary raid: the papers aren't allowed to say yet, but everybody knows. This was the new thing we had been warned about. Maurice went downstairs to see if there was anyone in the basement – he was afraid about me and I was afraid about him. I knew something was going to happen.

He hadn't been gone two minutes when there was an explosion in the street. His room was at the back and nothing happened except that the door was sucked open and some plaster fell, but I knew that he was at the front of the house when the bomb fell. I went down the stairs: they were cluttered with rubbish and broken banisters, and the hall was in an awful mess. I didn't see Maurice at first, and then I saw his arm coming out from under the door. I touched his hand: I could have sworn it was a dead hand. When two people have loved each other, they can't disguise a lack of tenderness in a kiss, and wouldn't I have recognized life if there was any of it left in touching his hand? I knew that if I took his hand and pulled it towards me, it would come away, all by itself, from under the door. Now, of course, I know that this was hysteria. I was cheated. He wasn't dead. Is one responsible for what one promises in hysteria? Or what promises one breaks? I'm hysterical now, writing all this down. But there's not a single person anywhere to whom I can even say I'm unhappy because they would ask me why and the questions would begin and I would break down. I mustn't break down because I must protect Henry. Oh, to hell with Henry, to hell with Henry. I want somebody who'll accept the truth about me and doesn't need protection. If I'm a bitch and a fake, is there nobody who will love a bitch and a fake?

I knelt down on the floor: I was mad to do such a thing: I never even had to do it as a child – my parents never believed in prayer, any more than I do. I hadn't any idea what to say. Maurice was dead. Extinct. There wasn't such a thing as a soul. Even the half-happiness I gave him was drained out of him like blood. He would never have the chance to be happy again. With anybody I thought: somebody else could have loved him and made him happier than I could, but now he won't have that chance. I knelt and put my head on the bed and wished I could believe. Dear God, I said – why dear, why dear? – make me believe. I can't believe. Make me. I said, I'm a bitch and a fake and I hate myself. I can't do anything of myself. *Make* me believe. I shut my eyes tight, and I pressed my nails into the palms of my hands until I could feel nothing but the pain, and I said, I will believe. Let him be alive, and I *will* believe. Give him a chance. Let him have his happiness. Do this and I'll believe. But that wasn't enough. It doesn't hurt to believe. So I said, I love him and I'll do anything if you'll make him alive.

I said very slowly, I'll give him up for ever, only let him be alive with a chance, and I pressed and pressed and I could feel the skin break, and I said, People can love without seeing each other, can't they, they love You all their lives without seeing You, and then he came in at the door, and he was alive, and I thought now the agony of being without him starts, and I wished he was safely back dead again under the door.

July 9, 1944.

Caught the 8.30 with Henry. Empty first-class carriage. Henry read aloud the Proceedings of the Royal Commission. Caught taxi at Paddington and dropped Henry at the Ministry. Made him promise to be home tonight. Taximan made mistake and drove me to the south side, past Number 14. Door mended and front windows boarded. It is horrible feeling dead. One wants to feel alive again in any way. When I got to the north side there were old letters that hadn't been forwarded because I told them 'forward nothing'. Old book catalogues, old bills, a letter marked 'Urgent. Please forward'. I wanted to open it and see if I were alive still, but I tore it up with the catalogues.

Chapter Three

July 10, 1944.

I thought, I shall not be breaking my promise if accidentally on the Common I run into Maurice, and so I went out after breakfast and again after lunch and again in the early evening, walking about and never seeing him. I couldn't stay out after six because Henry had guests for dinner. The speakers were there again as they were in June, and the man with the spots was still attacking Christianity and nobody was caring. I thought, if only he could convince me that you don't have to keep a promise to someone you don't believe in, that miracles don't happen, and I went and listened to him for a while, but all the time I was looking round in case Maurice might come in sight. He talked about the date of the Gospels and how the earliest one wasn't written within a hundred years of Christ being born. I had never realized they were as early as that, but I couldn't see that it mattered much when the legend began. And then he told us that Christ never claimed to be God in the Gospels, but was there such a man as Christ at all and what do the Gospels matter anyway, compared with this pain of waiting around and not seeing Maurice? A woman with grey hair distributed little cards on which his name was printed, Richard Smythe, and his address in Cedar Road, and there was an invitation to anybody to come and talk to him in private. Some people refused to take the cards and walked away as though the woman was asking for a subscription and others dropped them on the grass (I saw her pick some up, for economy's sake I suppose). It seemed very sad – the horrible spots, and talking about something nobody was interested in, and the cards dropped were like offers of friendship turned down. I put the card in my pocket and hoped he saw me do it.

Sir William Mallock came to dinner. He was one of Lloyd George's advisers on National Insurance, very old and important. Henry of course has nothing to do with pensions any longer, but he keeps an interest in the subject and likes to recall those days. Wasn't it widows' pensions he was working on when Maurice and I had dinner for the first time and everything started? Henry began a long argument with Mallock full of statistics about whether if widows' pensions were raised another shilling they would reach the same height as ten years ago. They disagreed about the cost of living, and it was a very academic argument because they both said the country couldn't afford to raise them anyway. I had to talk to Henry's chief in the Ministry of Home Security, and I couldn't think of anything to talk about but the V1s, and I longed suddenly to tell everybody about coming downstairs and finding Maurice buried. I wanted to say, I was naked, of course, because I hadn't had time to dress. Would Sir William Mallock have even turned his head, or would Henry have heard? He has a wonderful knack of hearing nothing but the subject in hand and the subject in hand at that moment was the cost-of-living index for 1943. I was naked, I wanted to say, because Maurice and I had been making love all the evening.

I looked at Henry's chief. He was a man called Dunstan. He had a broken nose and his battered face looked like a potter's error – a rejected-for-export face. All he would do, I thought, was smile: he wouldn't be cross or indifferent – he would accept it as something that human beings did. I had a sense that I had only to make a move and he would reply to it. I wondered, why shouldn't I? Why shouldn't I escape from this desert if only for half an hour? I haven't promised anything about strangers, only about Maurice. I can't be alone for the rest of my life with Henry, nobody admiring me, nobody excited by me, listening to Henry talking to other people, fossilizing under the drip of conversation like that bowler hat in the Cheddar Caves.

July 15, 1944.

Had lunch with Dunstant at the Jardin des Gourmets. He said ...

July 21, 1944.

Had drinks with Dunstan at home, while he waited for Henry. All went on to ...

July 22, 1944.

Had dinner with D. He came home afterwards for another drink. But it didn't work, it didn't work.

July 23–July 30, 1944.

D. telephoned. Said I was out. Started on tour with Henry. Civil Defence in Southern England. Conferences with Chief Wardens and Borough Engineers. Blast problems. Deep shelter problems. The problem of pretending to be alive. Henry and I sleeping side by side night after night like figures on tombs. In the new reinforced shelter at Bigwell-on-Sea the Chief Warden kissed me. Henry had gone ahead into the second chamber with the mayor and the engineer, and I stopped the Warden, touching his arm and asking him a question about the steel bunks, something stupid about why there weren't double bunks for the married. I meant him to want to kiss me. He twisted me round against a bunk, so that the metal made a line of pain across my back and kissed me . Then he looked so astonished that I laughed and kissed him back. But nothing worked. Will it never work again? The mayor came back with Henry. He was saying, 'At a pinch we can find room for two hundred.' That night, when Henry was at an official dinner, I asked trunks to get me Maurice's number. I lay on my bed, waiting for it to come through. I said to God, I've kept my promise for six weeks. I can't believe in you, I can't love you, but I've kept my promise. If I don't come alive again, I'm going to be a slut, just a slut. I'm going to destroy myself quite deliberately. Every year I'll be more used. Will you like that any better than if I break my promise? I'll be like those women in bars who laugh too much and have three men with them, touching them without intimacy. I'm falling in pieces already.

I kept the receiver tucked in my shoulder, and the Exchange said, 'We are ringing your number now.' I said to God, If he answers, I'll go back to-morrow. I knew exactly where the telephone stood beside his bed. Once I had knocked it down in my sleep, hitting out with my fist. A girl's voice said, 'Hello,' and I nearly rang off. I had wanted Maurice to be happy, but had I wanted him to find happiness quite so quickly? I felt a bit sick in the stomach until logic came to my aid, and I made my brain argue with me – why shouldn't he? You left him: you want him to be happy. I said, 'Could I speak to Mr Bendrix?' But everything had gone flat. Perhaps he wouldn't even want me to break my promise now: perhaps he had found somebody who would stay with him, have meals with him, go with him to places, sleep with him night after night till it was sweet and customary, answer his telephone for him. Then the voice said, 'Mr Bendrix isn't here. He's gone away for a few weeks: I've borrowed the flat.'

I rang off. At first I was happy, and then I was miserable again. I didn't know where he was. We were not in touch. In the same desert, seeking the same water-holes perhaps, but out of sight, always alone. For it wouldn't be a desert if we were together. I said to God, 'So that's it. I begin to believe in you, and if I believe in you I shall hate you. I have free will to break my promise, haven't I, but I haven't the power to gain anything from breaking it. You let me telephone, but then you close the door in my face. You let me sin, but you take away the fruits of my sin. You let me try to escape with D., but you don't allow me to enjoy it. You make me drive love out, and then you say there's no lust for you either. What do you expect me to do now, God? Where do I go from here?'

When I was at school I learnt about a King – one of the Henrys, the one who had Becket murdered – and he swore when he saw his birthplace burnt by his enemies that because God had done that to him, 'because You have robbed me of the town I love most, the place where I was born and bred, I will rob You of that which You love most in me.' Odd how I've remembered that prayer after sixteen years. A King swore it on his horse seven hundred years ago, and I pray it now, in a hotel room at Bigwell-on-Sea – Bigwell Regis. I'm going to rob you, God, of what you love most in me. I've never known the Lord's Prayer by heart, but I remember that one – is it a prayer? Of what you love most in me.

What do you love most? If I believed in you, I suppose I'd believe in the immortal soul, but is that what you love? Can you really see it there under the skin? Even a God can't love something that doesn't exist, he can't love something he cannot see. When he looks at me, does he see something I can't see? It must be lovely if he is able to love it. That's asking me to believe too much, that there's anything lovely in me. I want men to admire me, but that's a trick you learn at school – a movement of the eyes, a tone of voice, a touch of the hand on the shoulder or the head. If they think you admire them, they will admire you because of your good taste, and when they admire you, you have an illusion for a moment that there's something to admire. All my life I've tried to live in that illusion – a soothing drug that allows me to forget that I'm a bitch and a fake. But what are you supposed to love then in the bitch and the fake? Where do you find that immortal soul they talked about? Where do you see this lovely thing in me – in me, of all people? I can understand you can find it in Henry – my Henry, I mean. He's gentle and good and patient. You can find it in Maurice who thinks he hates, and loves, loves all the time. Even his enemies. But in this bitch and fake where do you find anything to love?

Tell me that, God, and I'll set about robbing you of it for ever.

How did the King keep his promise? I wish I could remember. I can remember nothing more about him than that he let the monks scourge him over the tomb of Becket. That doesn't sound like the answer. It must have happened before.

Henry's away again tonight. If I go down into the bar and pick a man up and take him on to the beach and lie with him among the sand-dunes, won't I be robbing you of what you love most? But it doesn't work. It doesn't work any longer. I can't hurt you if I don't get any pleasure from it. I might as well stick pins in myself like those people in the desert. The desert. I want to do something that I enjoy and that will hurt you. Otherwise what is it but mortification and that's like an expression of belief. And believe me, God, I don't believe in you yet, I don't believe in you yet.

Chapter Four

September 12, 1944.

Lunched at Peter Jones and bought new lamp for Henry's study. A prim lunch surrounded by other women. Not a man anywhere. It was like being part of a regiment. Almost a sense of peace. Afterwards went to a news cinema in Piccadilly and saw ruins in Normandy and the arrival of an American politician. Nothing to do till seven when Henry would be back. Had a couple of drinks by myself. It was a mistake. Have I got to give up drinking too? If I eliminate everything, how will I exist? I was somebody who loved Maurice and went with men and enjoyed my drinks. What happens if you drop all the things that make you I? Henry came in. I could tell he was very pleased about something: he obviously wanted me to ask him what it was, but I wouldn't. So in the end he had to tell me. 'They are recommending me for an OBE.'

'What's that?' I asked.

He was rather dashed that I didn't know. He explained that the next stage in a year or two when he was head of his department would be a CBE, 'and after that,' he said, 'when I retire they'll probably give me a KBE'

'It's confusing,' I said, 'couldn't you stick to the same letters?'

'Wouldn't you like to be Lady Miles?' Henry said, and I thought angrily, all I want in the word is to be Mrs Bendrix and I have given up that hope for ever. Lady Miles – who doesn't have a lover and doesn't drink but talks to Sir William Mallock about pensions. Where would *I* be all that time?

Last night I looked at Henry when he was asleep. So long as I was what the law considers the guilty party, I could watch him with affection, as though he were a child who needed my protection. Now I was what they called innocent, I was maddened continually by him. He had a secretary who sometimes rang him up at home. She would say, 'Oh, Mrs Miles, is H.M. in?' All the secretaries used those unbearable initials, not intimate but companionable. H.M. I thought, looking at him asleep, H.M. His Majesty and His Majesty's consort. Sometimes in his sleep he smiled, a moderate brief civil servant smile, as much as to say, yes, very amusing, but now we'd better get on with the job, hadn't we?

I said to him once, 'Have you ever had an affair with a secretary?'

'Affair?'

'Love affair.'

'No, of course not. What makes you think such a thing?'

'I don't know. I just wondered.'

'I've never loved any other woman,' he said and began to read the evening paper. I couldn't help wondering, is my husband so unattractive that no woman has ever wanted him? Except me, of course. I must have wanted him, in a way, once, but I've forgotten why, and I was too young to know what I was choosing. It's so unfair. While I loved Maurice, I loved Hnery, and now I'm what they call good, I don't love anyone at all. And You least of all.

Chapter Five

May 8, 1945.

Went down to St James's Park in the evening to watch them celebrate V.E. day. It was very quiet beside the floodlit water between the Horse Guards and the palace. Nobody shouted or sang or got drunk. People sat on the grass in twos, holding hands. I suppose they were happy because this was peace and there were no more bombs. I said to Henry, 'I don't like the peace.'

'I'm wondering where I shall be drafted from the Ministry of Home Security.'

'Ministry of Information?' I asked, trying to be interested.

'No, no, I wouldn't take it. It's full of temporary civil servants. How would you like the Home Office?'

'Anything, Henry, that pleased you,' I said. Then the Royal Family came out on the balcony and the crowd sang very decorously. They weren't leaders like Hitler, Stalin, Churchill, Roosevelt: they were just a family who hadn't done any harm to anybody. I wanted Maurice beside me. I wanted to begin again. I wanted to be one of a family too.

'Very moving, isn't it,' Henry said. 'Well, we can all sleep quiet at night now,' as though we ever did anything else at night but just sleep quiet.

September 10, 1945.

I have got to be sensible. Two days ago when I was clearing out my old bag – Henry suddenly gave me a new one as a 'peace present' – it must have cost him a lot of money – I found a card saying 'Richard Smythe 16 Cedar Road 4–6 daily for private advice. Anyone welcome.' I thought, I have been pulled about long enough. Now I'll take a different medicine. If he can persuade me that nothing happened, that my promise doesn't count, I'll write to Maurice and ask him if he wants to go on again. Perhaps I'll even leave Henry. I don't know. But first I've got to be sensible. I won't be hysterical any more. I'll be reasonable. So I went and rang the bell in Cedar Road.

Now I'm trying to remember what happened. Miss Smythe made tea and after tea she went and left me alone with her brother. He asked me what my difficulties were. I sat on a chintz sofa and he sat on a rather hard chair with a cat on his lap. He stroked the cat and he had beautiful hands and I didn't like them. I almost liked the spots better, but he chose to sit showing me only his good cheek.

I said, 'Will you tell me why you are so certain there isn't a God?'

He watched his own hands stroking the cat, and I felt sorry for him because he was proud of his hands. If his face hadn't been marked, perhaps he would have had no pride.

'You've listened to me speaking on the Common?'

'Yes,' I said.

'I have to put things very simply there. To sting people into thinking for themselves. You've started thinking for yourself?'

'I suppose so.'

'What church have you been brought up in?'

'None.'

'So you aren't a Christian?'

'I may have been christened – it's a social convention, isn't it?'

'If you haven't any faith, why do you want my help?'

Why indeed? I couldn't tell him about Maurice under the door and my promise. Not yet I couldn't. And that wasn't the whole point, for how many promises I've made and broken in a lifetime. Why did this promise stay, like an ugly vase a friend has given and one waits for a maid to break it, and year after year she breaks the things one values and the ugly vase remains? I had never really faced his question, and now he had to repeat it.

I said, 'I'm not sure that I don't believe. But I don't want to.'

'Tell me,' he said and because he forgot the beauty of his own hands and turned towards me his ugly cheek, forgetting himself in the desire to help, I found myself talking – about that night and the bomb falling and the stupid vow.

'And you really believe,' he said, 'that perhaps . . .'

'Yes.'

'Think of the thousands of people all over the world praying now, and their prayers aren't answered.'

'There were thousands of people dying in Palestine when Lazarus . . .'

'We don't believe that story, do we, you and I?' he said with a kind of complicity.

'Of course not, but millions of people have. They must have thought it reasonable . . .'

'People don't demand that a thing be reasonable if their emotions are touched. Lovers aren't reasonable, are they?'

'Can you explain away love too?' I asked.

'Oh yes,' he said. 'The desire to possess in some, like avarice: in others the desire to surrender, to lose the sense of responsibility, the wish to be admired. Sometimes just the wish to be able to talk, to unburden yourself to someone who won't be bored. The desire to find again a father or a mother. And of course under it all the biological motive.'

I thought, it's all true, but isn't there something over? I've dug up all that in myself, in Maurice too, but still the spade hasn't touched rock. 'And the love of God?' I asked him.

'It's all the same. Man made God in his own image, so it's natural he should love him. You know those distorting mirrors at fairs. Man's made a beautifying mirror too in which he sees himself lovely and powerful and just and wise. It's his idea of himself. He recognizes himself easier than in the distorting mirror which only makes him laugh, but how he loves himself in the other.'

When he spoke of distorting and beautifying mirrors, I couldn't remember what we were talking about for the thought of all those times since adolescence when he had looked in mirrors and tried to make them beautifying and not distorting simply by the way he held his head. I wondered why he hadn't grown a beard long enough to hide the spots; wouldn't the hair grow there or was it because he hated deception? I had an idea that he was a man who really loved the truth, but there was that word love again, and it was only too obvious into how many desires his love of truth could be split. A compensation for the injury of his birth, the desire for power, the wish to be admired all the more because the poor haunted face would never cause physical desire. I had an enormous wish to touch it with my hand, to comfort it with words of love as permanent as the wound. It was like when I saw Maurice under the door. I wanted to pray: to offer up some inordinate sacrifice if only he could be healed, but now there was no sacrifice left for me to offer.

'My dear,' he said, 'leave the idea of God out of this. It's just a question of your lover and your husband. Don't confuse the thing with phantoms.'

'But how do I decide – if there's no such thing as love?'

'You have to decide what will be the happiest in the long run.'

'Do you believe in happiness?'

'I don't believe in any absolute.'

I thought the only happiness he ever gets is this: the idea that he can comfort, advise, help, the idea that he can be of use. It drives him every week on to the Common, to talk to people who move away, never asking questions, dropping his cards on the turf. How often does anybody really come as I have come today? I asked him, 'Do you have many callers?'

'No,' he said. His love of truth was greater than his pride. He said, 'You are the first – for a very long time.'

'It's been good to talk to you,' I said. 'You've cleared my mind quite a lot.' It was the only comfort one could give him – to feed his illusion.

He said shyly, 'If you could spare the time, we could really start at the beginning and go to the root of things. I mean, the philosophical arguments and the historical evidence.'

I suppose I must have made some evasive reply for he went on, 'It's really important. We mustn't despise our enemies. They have a case.'

'They have?'

'It's not a sound one, except superficially. It's specious.'

He watched me with anxiety. I think he was wondering whether I was one of those who walked away. It seemed a little thing to ask when he said nervously, 'An hour a week. It would help you a great deal,' and I thought, haven't I all of time now? I can read a book or go to a cinema, and I don't read the words or remember the pictures. Myself and my own misery drum in my ear and fill my eyes. For a minute this afternoon I forgot them. 'Yes,' I said, 'I'll come. It's good of you to spare the time,' I said, shovelling all the hope I could into his lap, praying to the God he was promising to cure me of, 'Let me be of use to him.'

October 2, 1945.

It was very hot today and it dripped with rain. So I went into the dark church at the corner of Park Road to sit down for a while. Henry was at home and I didn't want to see him. I try to remember to be kind at breakfast, kind at lunch when he's home, kind at dinner, and sometimes I forget and he's kind back. Two people being kind to each other for a lifetime. When I came in and sat down and looked round I realized it was a Roman church, full of plaster statues and bad art, realistic art. I hated the statues, the crucifix, all the emphasis on the human body. I was trying to escape from the human body and all it needed. I thought I could believe in some kind of a God that bore no relation to ourselves, something vague, amorphous, cosmic, to which I had promised something and which had given me something in return – stretching out of the vague into the concrete human life, like a powerful vapour moving among the chairs and walls. One day I too would become part of that vapour – I would escape myself for ever. And then I came into that dark church in Park Road and saw the bodies standing around me on all the altars – the hideous plaster statues with their complacent faces, and I remembered that they believed in the resurrection of the body, the body I wanted destroyed for ever. I had done so much injury with this body. How could I want to preserve any of it for eternity, and suddenly I remembered a phrase of Richard's – about human beings inventing doctrines to satisfy their desires, and I thought how wrong he is. If I were to invent a doctrine it would be that the body was never born again, that it rotted with last year's vermin. It's strange how the human mind swings back and forth, from one extreme to another. Does truth lie at some point of the pendulum's swing, at a point where it never rests, not in the dull perpendicular mean where it dangles in the end like a windless flag, but at an angle, nearer one extreme than another? If only a miracle could stop the pendulum at an angle of sixty degrees, one would believe the truth was there. Well, the pendulum swung today and I thought, instead of my own body, of Maurice's. I thought of certain lines life had put on his face as personal as a line of his writing: I thought of a new scar on his shoulder that wouldn't have been there if once he hadn't tried to protect another man's body from a falling wall. He didn't tell me why he was in hospital those three days: Henry told me. That scar was part of his character as much as his jealousy. And so I thought, do I want that body to be vapour (mine yes, but his?), and I knew I wanted that scar to exist through all eternity. But could my vapour love that scar? Then I began to want my body that I hated, but only because it could love that scar. We can love with our minds, but can we love only with our minds? Love extends itself all the time, so that we can even love with our senseless nails: we love even with our clothes, so that a sleeve can feel a sleeve.

Richard's right, I thought, we have invented the resurrection of the body because we do need our own bodies, and immediately I admitted that he was right and that this was a fairy-tale we tell each other for comfort, I no longer felt any hate of those statues. They were like bad coloured pictures in Hans Andersen: they were like bad poetry, but somebody had needed to write them, somebody who wasn't so proud that he hid them rather than expose his foolishness. I walked up the church, looking at them one after the other: in front of the worst of all – I don't know who she was – a middle-aged man was praying. He had put his bowler hat beside him and in the bowler hat, wrapped in newspaper, were some sticks of celery.

And of course on the altar there was a body too – such a familiar body, more familiar than Maurice's, that it had never struck me before as a body with all the parts of a body, even the parts the loin-cloth concealed. I remembered one in a Spanish church I had visited with Henry, where the blood ran down in scarlet paint from the eyes and the hands. It had sickened me. Henry wanted me to admire the twelfth-century pillars, but I was sick and I wanted to get out into the open air. I thought, these people love cruelty. A vapour couldn't shock you with blood and cries.

When I came out into the plaza I said to Henry, 'I can't bear all these painted wounds.' Henry was very reasonable – he's always reasonable. He said, 'Of course it's a very materialistic faith. A lot of magic. . . .'

'Is magic materialistic?' I asked.

'Yes. Eye of newt and toe of frog, finger of birth-strangled babe. You can't have anything more materialistic than that. In the Mass they still believe in transubstantiation.'

I knew all about that, but I had an idea that it had more or less died out at the Reformation, except for the poor of course. Henry put me right (how often has Henry rearranged my muddled thoughts). 'Materialism isn't only an attitude for the poor,' he said. 'Some of the finest brains have been materialist, Pascal, Newman. So subtle in some directions: so crudely superstitious in others. One day we may know why: it may be a glandular deficiency.'

So today I looked at that material body on that material cross, and I wondered, how could the world have nailed a vapour there? A vapour of course felt no pain and no pleasure. It was only my superstition that imagined it could answer my prayers. Dear God, I had said. I should have said, Dear Vapour. I had said I hate you, but can one hate a vapour? I could hate that figure on the Cross with its claim to my gratitude – 'I've suffered this for you', but a vapour . . . And yet Richard believed in less even than a vapour. He hated a fable, he fought against a fable, he took a fable seriously. I couldn't hate Hansel and Gretel, I couldn't hate their sugar house as he hated the legend of heaven. When I was a child I could hate the wicked queen in Snow White, but Richard didn't hate his fairy-tale Devil. The Devil didn't exist and God didn't exist, but all his hatred was for the good fairy-tale, not for the wicked one. Why? I looked up at that over-familiar body, stretched in imaginary pain, the head drooping like a man asleep. I thought, sometimes I've hated Maurice, but would I have hated him if I hadn't loved him too? Oh God, if I could really hate you, what would that mean?

Am I a materialist after all, I wondered? Have I some glandular deficiency that I am so uninterested in the really important unsuperstitious things and causes – like the Charity Commission and the index of living and better calories for the working class? Am I a materialist because I believe in the independent existence of that man with the bowler, the metal of the cross, these hands I can't pray with? Suppose God did exist, suppose he was a body like that, what's wrong in believing that his body existed as much as mine? Could anybody love him or hate him if he hadn't got a body? I can't love a vapour that was Maurice. That's coarse, that's beastly, that's materialist, I know, but why shouldn't I be beastly and coarse and materialist. I walked out of the church in a flaming rage, and in defiance of Henry and all the reasonable and the detached I did what I had seen people do in Spanish churches: I dipped my finger in the so-called holy water and made a kind of cross on my forehead.

Chapter Six

January 10, 1946.

I couldn't stand the house tonight, so I walked out into the rain. I remembered the time when I had stuck my nails into my palms, and I didn't know it but You moved in the pain. I said, 'Let him be alive,' not believing in You, and my disbelief made no difference to You. You took it into Your love and accepted it like an offering, and to-night the rain soaked through my coat and my clothes and into my skin, and I shivered with the cold, and it was for the first time as though I nearly loved You. I walked under Your windows in the rain and I wanted to wait under them all night only to show that after all I might learn to love and I wasn't afraid of the desert any longer because You were there. I came back into the house and there was Maurice with Henry. It was the second time You had given him back: the first time I had hated You for it and You'd taken my hate like You'd taken my disbelief into Your love, keeping them to show me later, so that we could both laugh – as I have sometimes laughed at Maurice, saying, 'Do you remember how stupid we were . . .?'

Chapter Seven

January 18, 1946.

I was having lunch with Maurice for the first time for two years – I had telephoned and asked him to meet me – and my bus got held up in the traffic at Stockwell and I was ten minutes late. I felt the fear for a moment I always felt in the old days, that something would happen to spoil the day, that he would be angry with me. But I had no desire to get in first now with my anger. Like a lot of other things the capacity for anger seems dead in me. I wanted to see him and ask him about Henry. Henry's been odd lately. It was strange of him to go out and drink in a pub with Maurice. Henry only drinks at home or at his club. I thought he might have talked to Maurice. Strange if he's worried about me. There's never been less cause for worry since we married first. But when I was with Maurice there didn't seem any other reason to be with him except to be with him. I found out nothing about Henry. Every now and then he tried to hurt me and he succeeded because he was really hurting himself, and I can't bear to watch him hurting himself.

Have I broken that old promise, lunching with Maurice? A year ago I would have thought so, but I don't think so now. I was very literal in those days because I was afraid, because I didn't know what it was all about, because I had no trust in love. We lunched at Rules and I was happy just being with him. Only for a little I was unhappy, saying good-bye above the grating I thought he was going to kiss me again, and I longed for it, and then a fit of coughing took me and the moment passed. I knew, as he walked away, he was thinking all kinds of untrue things and he was hurt by them, and I was hurt because he was hurt.

I wanted to cry unobserved, and I went to the National Portrait Gallery, but it was students' day – there were too many people, so I went back to Maiden Lane and into the church that's always too dark to look at your neighbour. I sat there. It was quite empty except for me and for a little man who came in and prayed quietly in a pew behind. I remembered the first time I had been in one of those churches and how I had hated it. I didn't pray. I had prayed once too often. I said to God, as I might have said to my father, if I could ever have remembered having one, Dear God, I'm tired.

February 3, 1946.

Today I saw Maurice but he didn't see me. He was on his way to the 'Pontefract Arms', and I trailed behind him. I had spent an hour in Cedar Road – a long dragging hour trying to follow poor Richard's arguments and only getting from them a sense of inverted belief. Could anyone be so serious, so argumentative about a legend? When I understood anything at all, it was some strange fact I didn't know that hardly seemed to me to help his case. Like the evidence that there had been a man called Christ. I came out feeling tired and hopeless. I had gone to him to rid me of a superstition, but every time I went his fanaticism fixed the superstition deeper. I was helping him, but he wasn't helping me. Or was he? For an hour I had hardly thought of Maurice, but then suddenly there he was, crossing the end of the street.

I followed him all the way, keeping him in sight. So many times we had been together to the 'Pontefract Arms'. I knew which bar he'd go to, what he'd order. Should I go in after him, I wondered, and order mine and see him turn and everything would start over again? The mornings would be full of hope because I could telephone him as soon as Henry left, and there would be evenings to look forward to when Henry warned me that he would be home late. And perhaps now I would leave Henry. I'd done my best. I had no money to bring Maurice and his books brought in little more than enough to keep himself, but on typing alone, with me to help, we should save fifty pounds a year. I don't fear poverty. Sometimes it's easier to cut your coat to fit the cloth than lie on the bed you've made.

I stood at the door and watched him go up to the bar. If he turns round and sees me, I told God, I'll go in, but he didn't turn round. I began to walk home, but I couldn't keep him out of my mind. For nearly two years we had been strangers. I hadn't known what he was doing at any particular hour of the day, but now he was a stranger no longer because I knew as in the old days where he was. He would have one more beer and then he would go back to the familiar room to write. The habits of his day were still the same and I loved them as one loves an old coat. I felt protected by his habits. I never want strangeness.

And I thought, how happy I can make him and how easily. I longed again to see him laugh with happiness. Henry was out. He had had a lunch engagement after the office, and he had telephoned to say that he wouldn't be in till seven. I would wait till half-past six and then I would telephone Maurice. I would say, I am coming for tonight and all the other nights. I'm tired of being without you. I would pack the large blue suitcase and the small brown one. I would take enough clothes for a month's holiday. Henry was civilized and by the end of a month the legal aspects would have been settled, the immediate bitterness would be over, and anything else I needed from the house could be fetched at leisure. There wouldn't be much bitterness: it wasn't as though we were still lovers. Marriage had become friendship, and the friendship after a little could go on the same as before.

Suddenly I felt free and happy. I'm not going to worry about you any more, I said to God as I walked across the Common, whether you exist or whether you don't exist, whether you gave Maurice a second chance or whether I imagined everything. Perhaps this is the second chance I asked for him. I'm going to make him happy, that's my second vow, God, and stop me if you can, stop me if you can.

I went upstairs to my room and I began to write to Henry. Darling Henry, I wrote, but that sounded hypocritical. Dearest was a lie, and so it had to be like an acquaintance, 'Dear Henry.' So 'Dear Henry,' I wrote, 'I'm afraid this will be rather a shock to you, but for the last five years I've been in love with Maurice Bendrix. For two years nearly we haven't seen each other or written but it doesn't work. I can't live happily without him, so I've gone away. I know I haven't been much of a wife for a long time, and I haven't been a mistress at all since June 1944, so everybody's the worse off all round. I thought once I could just have this love affair and it would peter slowly and contentedly out, but it hasn't worked that way. I love Maurice more than I did in 1939. I've been childish, I suppose, but now I realize that sooner or later one has to choose or one makes a mess in all directions. Good-bye. God bless you.' I crossed out 'God bless you' very deeply so that it couldn't be read. It sounded smug, and anyway Henry doesn't believe in God. Then I wanted to put Love, but the word sounded unsuitable although I knew it was true. I do love Henry in my shabby way.

I put the letter in an envelope and marked it Very Personal. I thought that would warn Henry not to open it in anybody's presence – for he might bring home a friend, and I didn't want his pride hurt. I pulled out the suitcase and began to pack and then I suddenly thought, where did I put the letter? I found it at once, but then I thought, suppose in my hurry I forget to put it in the hall and Henry waits and waits for me to come home. So I carried it downstairs to put it in the hall. My packing was nearly done – only an evening dress to fold, and Henry wasn't due for another half an hour.

I had just put the letter on the hall table on top of the afternoon's post when I heard a key in the door. I snatched it up again, I don't know why, and then Henry came in. He looked ill and harassed. He said, 'Oh, you're here?' and walked straight by me and into his study. I waited a moment and then I followed. I thought, I'll have to give him the letter now: it's going to need more courage. When I opened the door I saw him sitting in his chair by the fire he hadn't bothered to light, and he was crying.

'What is it, Henry?' I asked him. He said, 'Nothing. I've got a bad headache, that's all.'

I lit the fire for him. I said, 'I'll get you some veganin.'

'Don't bother,' he said. 'It's better already.'

'What sort of day have you had?'

'Oh, much the same as usual. A bit tiresome.'

'Who was your lunch date?'

'Bendrix.'

'Bendrix?' I said.

'Why not Bendrix? He gave me lunch at his club. A horrible lunch.'

I came behind him and put my hand on his forehead. It was an odd thing to be doing just before leaving him for ever. He used to do that to me when we were first married and I had terrible nervous headaches because nothing was going right. I forgot for a moment that I would only *pretend* to be cured that way. He put up his own hand and pressed mine harder against his forehead. 'I love you,' he said. 'Do you know that?'

'Yes,' I said. I could have hated him for saying it: it was like a claim. If you really loved me, I thought, you'd behave like any other injured husband. You'd get angry and your anger would set me free.

'I can't do without you,' he said. Oh yes, you can, I wanted to protest. It will be inconvenient, but you can. You changed your newspaper once and you soon got used to it. These are words, conventional words of a conventional husband, and they don't mean anything at all: then I looked up at his face in the mirror and he was crying still.

'Henry,' I said, 'what's wrong?'

'Nothing. I told you.'

'I don't believe you. Has something happened at the office?'

He said with unfamiliar bitterness, 'What could happen there?'

'Did Bendrix upset you in some way?'

'Of course not. How could he?'

I wanted to take away his hand, but he held it there. I was afraid of what he'd say next: of the unbearable burdens he was laying on my conscience. Maurice would be home by now: if Henry hadn't come in, I would have been with him in five minutes. I would have seen happiness instead of misery. If you don't see misery you don't believe in it. You can give anyone pain from a distance. Henry said, 'My dear, I haven't been much of a husband.'

'I don't know what you mean,' I said.

'I'm dull for you. My friends are dull. We no longer – you know – do anything together.'

'It has to stop sometime,' I said, 'in any marriage. We are good friends.' That was to be my escape line. When he agreed I would give him the letter, I would tell him what I was going to do, I would walk out of the house. But he missed his cue, and I'm still here, and the door has closed again against Maurice. Only I can't put the blame on God this time. I closed the door myself. Henry said, 'I can never think of you as a friend. You can do without a friend,' and he looked back at me from the mirror and he said, 'Don't leave me, Sarah. Stick it a few more years. I'll try . . .' but he couldn't think himself what he'd try. Oh, it would have been better for both of us if I'd left him years ago, but I can't hit him when he's there and now he'll always be there because I've seen what his misery looks like.

I said, 'I won't leave you. I promise.' Another promise to keep, and when I had made it I couldn't bear to be with him any more. He'd won and Maurice had lost, and I hated him for his victory. Would I have hated Maurice for his? I went upstairs and tore up the letter so small nobody could put it together again, and I kicked the suitcase under the bed because I was too tired to start unpacking, and I started writing this down. Maurice's pain goes into his writing: you can hear the nerves twitch through his sentences. Well, if pain can make a writer, I'm learning, Maurice, too. I wish I could talk to you just once. I can't talk to Henry. I can't talk to anyone. Dear God, let me talk.

Yesterday I bought a crucifix, a cheap ugly one because I had to do it quickly. I blushed when I asked for it. Somebody might have seen me in the shop. They ought to have opaque glass in their doors like rubber-goods shops. When I lock the door of my room, I can take it out from the bottom of my jewel-case. I wish I knew a prayer that wasn't me, me, me. Help *me*. Let *me* be happier. Let *me* die soon. Me, me, me.

Let me think of those awful spots on Richard's cheek. Let me see Henry's face with the tears falling. Let me forget me. Dear God, I've tried to love and I've made such a hash of it. If I could love you, I'd know how to love them. I believe the legend. I believe you were born. I believe you died for us. I believe you are God. Teach me to love. I don't mind my pain. It's their pain I can't stand. Let my pain go on and on, but stop theirs. Dear God, if only you could come down from your Cross for a while and let me get up there instead. If I could suffer like you, I could heal like you.

February 4, 1946.

Henry took a day off work. I don't know why. He gave me lunch and we went to the National Gallery and we had an early dinner and went to the theatre. He was like a parent coming down to the school and taking the child out. But he's the child.

February 5, 1946.

Henry's planning a holiday abroad for us in the spring. He can't make up his mind between the châteaux of the Loire or Germany where he could make a report on the morale of the Germans under bombing. I never want the spring to come. There I go again. I want. I don't want. If I could love You, I could love Henry. God was made man. He was Henry with his astigmatism, Richard with his spots, not only Maurice. If I could love a leper's sores, couldn't I love the boringness of Henry? But I'd turn from the leper if he were here, I suppose, as I shut myself away from Henry. I want the dramatic always. I imagine I'm ready for the pain of your nails, and I can't stand twenty-four hours of maps and Michelin guides. Dear God, I'm no use. I'm still the same bitch and fake. Clear me out of the way.

February 6, 1946.

Today I had a terrible scene with Richard. He was telling me of the contradictions in the Christian churches, and I was trying to listen, but I wasn't succeeding very well, and he noticed it. He said to me suddenly, 'What do you come here for?' and before I could catch myself, I said, 'To see you.'

'I thought you came to learn,' he said, and I told him that's what I meant.

I knew he didn't believe me, and I thought his pride would be hurt, and he'd be angry, but he wasn't angry at all. He got up from his chintzy chair and came and sat with me on the chintzy sofa on the side where his cheek wouldn't show. He said, 'It's meant a lot to me, seeing you every week,' and then I knew that he was going to make love to me. He put his hand on my wrist and asked, 'Do you like me?'

'Yes, Richard, of course,' I said, 'or I wouldn't be here.'

'Will you marry me?' he asked, and his pride made him ask it as though he were asking whether I'd take another cup of tea.

'Henry might object,' I said, trying to laugh it off.

'Nothing will make you leave Henry?' and I thought angrily, if I haven't left him for Maurice, why the hell should I be expected to leave him for you?'

'I'm married.'

'That doesn't mean anything to me or you.'

'Oh yes, it does,' I said. I had to tell him some time. 'I believe in God,' I said, 'and all the rest. You've taught me to. You and Maurice.'

'I don't understand.'

'You've always said the priests taught you to disbelieve. Well, it can work the other way too.'

He looked at his beautiful hands – he had those left. He said very slowly, 'I don't care what you believe. You can believe the whole silly bag of tricks for all I care. I love you, Sarah.'

'I'm sorry,' I said.

'I love you more than I hate all that. If I had children by you, I'd let you pervert them.'

'You shouldn't say that.'

'I'm not a rich man. It's the only bribe I can offer, giving up my faith.'

'I'm in love with somebody else, Richard.'

'You can't love him much if you feel bound by that silly vow.'

I said drearily, 'I've done my best to break it, but it didn't work.'

'Do you think me a fool?'

'Why should I?'

'To expect you to love a man with this.' He turned his bad cheek towards me. 'You believe in God,' he said. 'That's easy. You are beautiful. You have no complaint, but why should I love a God who gave a child this?'

'Dear Richard,' I said, 'there's nothing so very bad ...' I shut my eyes and put my mouth against the cheek. I felt sick for a moment because I fear deformity, and he sat quiet and let me kiss him, and I thought I am kissing pain and pain belongs to You as happiness never does. I love You in Your pain. I could almost taste metal and salt in the skin, and I thought, How good You are. You might have killed us with happiness, but You let us be with You in pain.

I felt him move abruptly away and I opened my eyes. He said, 'Good-bye.'

'Good-bye, Richard.'

'Don't come back,' he said, 'I can't bear your pity.'

'It's not pity.'

'I've made a fool of myself.'

I went away. It wasn't any good staying. I couldn't tell him I envied him, carrying the mark of pain around with him like that, seeing You in the glass every day instead of this dull human thing we call beauty.

February 10, 1946.

I have no need to write to You or talk to You, that's how I began a letter to You a little time ago, and I was ashamed of myself and I tore it up because it seemed such a silly thing to write a letter to You who know everything before it comes into my mind. Did I ever love Maurice as much before I loved You? Or was it really You I loved all the time? Did I touch You when I touched him? Could I have touched You if I hadn't touched him first, touched him as I never touched Henry, anybody? And he loved me and touched me as he never did any other woman. But was it me he loved, or You? For he hated in me the things You hate. He was on Your side all the time without knowing it. You willed our separation, but he willed it too. He worked for it with his anger and his jealousy, and he worked for it with his love. For he gave me so much love, and I gave him so much love that soon there wasn't anything left, when we'd finished, but You. For either of us. I might have taken a lifetime spending a little love at a time, eking it out here and there, on this man and that. But even the first time, in the hotel near Paddington, we spent all we had. You were there, teaching us to squander, like you taught the rich man, so that one day we might have nothing left except this love of You. But You are too good to me. When I ask You for pain, You give me peace. Give it him too. Give him my peace – he needs it more.

February 12, 1946.

Two days ago I had such a sense of peace and quiet and love. Life was going to be happy again, but last night I dreamed I was walking up a long staircase to meet Maurice at the top. I was still happy because when I reached the top of the staircase we were going to make love. I called to him that I was coming, but it wasn't Maurice's voice that answered; it was a stranger's that boomed like a fog-horn warning lost ships, and scared me. I thought, he's let his flat and gone away and I don't know where he is, and going down the stairs again the water rose beyond my waist and the hall was thick with mist. Then I woke up. I'm not at peace any more. I just want him like I used to in the old days. I want to be eating sandwiches with him. I want to be drinking with him in a bar. I'm tired and I don't want any more pain. I want Maurice. I want ordinary corrupt human love. Dear God, you know I want to want Your pain, but I don't want it now. Take it away for a while and give it me another time.

Chapter One

I couldn't read any more. Over and over again I had skipped when a passage hurt me too much. I had wanted to discover about Dunstan, though I hadn't wanted to discover that much, but now I had read on, it slipped far back in time, like a dull date in history. It wasn't of present importance. The entry I was left with was an entry only one week old. 'I want Maurice. I want ordinary corrupt human love.'

It's all I can give you, I thought. I don't know about any other kind of love, but if you think I've squandered all of that you're wrong. There's enough left for our two lives, and I thought of that day when she had packed her suitcase and I sat working here, not knowing that happiness was so close. I was glad that I hadn't known and I was glad that I knew. I could act now. Dunstan didn't matter. The air-raid warden didn't matter. I went to the telephone and dialled her number.

The maid answered. I said, 'This is Mr Bendrix. I want to speak to Mrs Miles.' She told me to hold on. I felt breathless as though I were at the end of a long race as I waited for Sarah's voice, but the voice that came was the maid's telling me that Mrs Miles was out. I don't know why I didn't believe her. I waited five minutes and then with my handkerchief stretched tight over the mouthpiece I rang again.

'Is Mr Miles in?'

'No, sir.'

'Could I speak to Mrs Miles then? This is Sir William Mallock.'

There was only a very short pause before Sarah replied. 'Good evening. This is Mrs Miles.'

'I know,' I said, 'I know your voice, Sarah.'

'You . . . I thought . . .'

'Sarah,' I said, 'I'm coming to see you.'

'No, please no. Listen, Maurice. I'm in bed. I'm speaking from there now.'

'All the better.'

'Don't be a fool, Maurice. I mean I'm ill.'

'Then you'll have to see me. What's the matter, Sarah?'

'Oh, nothing. A bad cold. Listen, Maurice.' She spaced her words slowly like a governess and it angered me. 'Please don't come I can't see you.'

'I love you, Sarah, and I'm coming.'

'I won't be here. I'll get up.' I thought, if I run, it will only take me four minutes across the Common; she can't dress in that time. 'I'll tell the maid not to let anybody in.'

'She's not got the build of a chucker-out. And I'd have to be chucked out, Sarah.'

'Please, Maurice . . . I'm asking you. I haven't asked anything of you for a long time.'

'Except one lunch.'

'Maurice, I'm not awfully fit. I just can't see you today. Next week . . .'

'There've been a terrible lot of weeks. I want to see you now. This evening.'

'Why, Maurice?'

'You love me.'

'How do you know?'

'Never mind. I want to ask you to come away with me.'

'But Maurice, I can answer you on the phone just as well. The answer's no.'

'I can't touch you by telephone, Sarah.'

'Maurice, my dear, please. Promise you won't come.'

'I'm coming.'

'Listen, Maurice. I'm feeling awfully sick. And the pain's bad tonight. I don't want to get up.'

'You don't have to.'

'I swear I'll get up and dress and leave the house, unless you promise. . . .'

'This is more important to both of us, Sarah, than a cold.'

'Please, Maurice, please. Henry will be home soon.'

'Let him be.' I rang off.

It was a worse night than the one when I met Henry a month before. This time it was sleet instead of rain: it was half-way to snow and the edged drops seemed to slash their way in through the buttonholes of one's raincoat: they obscured the lamps on the Common, so that it was impossible to run, and I can't run fast anyway because of my leg. I wished I had brought my war-time torch with me, for it must have taken eight minutes for me to reach the house on north side. I was just stepping off the pavement to cross when the door opened and Sarah came out. I thought with happiness, I have her now. I knew with absolute certainty that before the night was out we should have slept together again. And once that had been renewed, anything might happen. I had never known her before and I had never loved her so much. The more we know the more we love, I thought. I was back in the territory of trust.

She was in too much of a hurry to see me across the wide roadway through the sleet. She turned to the left and walked rapidly away. I thought, she will need somewhere to sit down and then I have her trapped. I followed twenty yards behind, but she never looked back. She skirted the Common, past the pond and the bombed bookshop, as though she were making for the tube. Well, if it were necessary, I was prepared to talk to her even in a crowded train. She went down the tube-stairs and up to the booking-office, but she had no bag with her and when she felt in her pockets no loose money either – not even the three halfpence that would have enabled her to travel up and down till midnight. Up the stairs again, and across the road where the trams run. One earth had been stopped, but another had obviously come to mind. I was triumphant. She was afraid, but she wasn't afraid of me, she was afraid of herself and what was going to happen when we met. I felt I had won the game already, and I could afford to feel a certain pity for my victim.

I wanted to say to her, Don't worry, there's nothing to fear, we'll both be happy soon, the nightmare's nearly over.

And then I lost her. I had been too confident and I had allowed her too big a start. She had crossed the road twenty yards ahead of me (I was delayed again by my bad leg coming up the stairs), a tram ran between, and she was gone. She might have turned left down the High Street or gone straight ahead down Park Road, but I couldn't see her. I wasn't very worried – if I didn't find her today, I would the next. Now I knew the whole absurd story of the vow, now I was certain of her love, I was assured of her. If two people loved, they slept together; it was a mathematical formula, tested and proved by human experience.

There was an A.B.C. in the High Street and I tried that. She wasn't there. Then I remembered the church at the corner of Park Road, and I knew at once that she had gone there. I followed, and sure enough there she was sitting in one of the side aisles close to a pillar and a hideous statue of the virgin. She wasn't praying. She was just sitting there with her eyes closed. I only saw her by the light of the candles before the statue, for the whole place was very dark. I sat down behind her like Mr Parkis and waited. I could have waited years now that I knew the end of the story. I was cold and wet and very happy. I could even look with charity towards the altar and the figure dangling there. She loves us both, I thought, but if there is to be a conflict between an image and a man, I know who will win. I could put my hand on her thigh or my mouth on her breast: he was imprisoned behind the altar and couldn't move to plead *his* cause.

Suddenly she began to cough with her hand pressed to her side. I knew she was in pain and I couldn't leave her alone in pain. I came and sat beside her and put my hand on her knee while she coughed. I thought, If only one had a touch that could heal. When the fit was over, she said, 'Please won't you let me be.'

'I'll never let you be,' I said.

'What's come over you, Maurice? You weren't like that the other day at lunch.'

'I was bitter. I didn't know you loved me.'

'Why do you think I do?' she asked, but she let my hand rest on her knee. I told her then how Mr Parkis had stolen her diary – I didn't want any lies between us now.

'It wasn't a good thing to do,' she said.

'No.' She began to cough again and afterwards in her exhaustion she leant her shoulder against me.

'My dear,' I said, 'it's all over now. The waiting, I mean. We're going away together.'

'No,' she said.

I put my arm round her and touched her breast. 'This is where we begin again,' I said. 'I've been a bad lover, Sarah. It was the insecurity that did it. I didn't trust you. I didn't know enough about you. But I'm secure now.'

She said nothing, but she still leant against me. It was like an assent. I said, 'I'll tell you how it had better be. Go back home and lie in bed for a couple of days – you don't want to travel with a cold like that. I'll ring up every day and see how you are. When you are well enough, I'll come over and help you pack. We won't stay here. I have a cousin in Dorset who has an empty cottage I can use. We'll stay there a few weeks and rest. I'll be able to finish my book. We can face the lawyers afterwards. We need a rest, both of us. I'm tired and I'm sick to death of being without you, Sarah.'

'Me too.' She spoke so low that I wouldn't have heard the phrase if I had been a stranger to it, but it was like a signature tune that had echoed through all our relationship, from the first love-making in the Paddington hotel. 'Me too' for loneliness, griefs, disappointments, pleasures and despairs, the claim to share everything.

'Money's going to be short,' I said, 'but not too short. I've been commissioned to do a Life of General Gordon and the advance is enough to keep us for three months comfortably. By that time I can hand in the novel and get an advance on that. Both books will be out this year, and they should keep us till another's ready. I can work, with you there. You know, any moment now I'm going to come through. I'll be a vulgar success yet, and you'll hate it and I'll hate it, but we'll buy things and be extravagant and it will be fun, because we'll be together.'

Suddenly I realized she was asleep. Exhausted by her flight she had fallen asleep against my shoulder as so many times, in taxis, in buses, on a park-seat. I sat still and let her be. There was nothing to disturb her in the dark church. The candles flapped around the virgin, and there was nobody else there. The slowly growing pain in my upper arm where her weight lay was the greatest pleasure I had ever known.

Children are supposed to be influenced by what you whisper to them in sleep, and I began to whisper to Sarah, not loud enough to wake her, hoping that the words would drop hypnotically into her unconscious mind. 'I love you, Sarah,' I whispered. 'Nobody has ever loved you as much before. We are going to be happy. Henry won't mind except his pride, and pride soon heals. He'll find himself a new habit to take your place – perhaps he'll collect Greek coins. We are going away, Sarah, we are going away. Nobody can stop it now. You love me, Sarah,' and I fell silent as I began to wonder whether I ought to buy a new suitcase. Then she woke coughing.

'I've been asleep,' she said.

'You must go home now, Sarah. You're cold.'

'It isn't home, Maurice,' she said. 'I don't want to go away from here.'

'It's cold.'

'I don't mind the cold. And it's dark. I can believe anything in the dark.'

'Just believe in us.'

'That's what I meant.' She shut her eyes again, and looking up at the altar I thought with triumph, almost as though he were a living rival, You see – these are the arguments that win, and gently moved my fingers across her breast.

'You're tired, aren't you?' I asked.

'Very tired.'

'You shouldn't have run away from me like that.'

'It wasn't you I was running from.' She moved her shoulder. 'Please Maurice, go now.'

'You ought to be in bed.'

'I will be soon. I don't want to go back with you. I just want to say good-bye here.'

'Promise you won't stay long.'

'I promise.'

'And you'll telephone to me?'

She nodded, but looking down at her hand where it lay in her lap like something thrown away, I saw that she had her fingers crossed. I asked with suspicion, 'You are telling me the truth?' I uncrossed her fingers with mine and said, 'You aren't planning to escape me again?'

'Maurice, dear Maurice,' she said, 'I haven't got the strength.' She began to cry, thrusting her fists into her eyes as a child does.

'I'm sorry,' she said. 'Just go away. Please, Maurice, have a bit of mercy.'

One gets to the end of badgering and contriving: I couldn't go on with that appeal in my ears. I kissed her on the tough and knotty hair, and coming away I found her lips, smudgy and salt, on the corner of my mouth. 'God bless you,' she said, and I thought, That's what she crossed out in her letter to Henry. One says good-bye to another's good-bye unless one is Smythe and it was an involuntary act when I repeated her blessing back to her, but turning as I left the church and seeing her huddled there at the edge of the candle-light, like a beggar come in for warmth, I could imagine a God blessing her: or a God loving her. When I began to write our story down, I thought I was writing a record of hate, but somehow the hate has got mislaid and all I know is that in spite of her mistakes and her unreliability, she was better than most. It's just as well that one of us should believe in her: she never did in herself.

Chapter Two

The next few days I had to make a great effort to be sensible. I was working for both of us now. In the morning I set myself a minimum of seven hundred and fifty words on the novel, but usually I managed to get a thousand done by eleven o'clock. It's astonishing the effect of hope: the novel that had dragged all through the last year ran towards its end. I knew that Henry left for work around nine-thirty, and the most likely hour for her to telephone was between then and twelve-thirty. Henry had started coming home for lunch (so Parkis had told me); there was no chance of her telephoning again before three. I would revise my day's work and do my letters until twelve-thirty, and then I was released however gloomily from expectation. Until two-thirty I could put in time at the British Museum Reading Room, making notes for the life of General Gordon. I couldn't absorb myself in reading and note-taking as I could in writing the novel, and the thought of Sarah came between me and the missionary life in China. Why had I been invited to write this biography? I often wondered. They would have done better to have chosen an author who believed in Gordon's God. I could appreciate the obstinate stand at Khartoum – the hatred of the safe politicians at home, but the Bible on the desk belonged to another world of thought from mine. Perhaps the publisher half hoped that my cynical treatment of Gordon's Christianity would cause a *succès de scandale*. I had no intention of pleasing him: this God was also Sarah's God, and I was going to throw no stones at any phantom she believed she loved. I hadn't during that period any hatred of her God, for hadn't I in the end proved stronger?

One day as I ate my sandwiches, on to which my indelible pencil somehow always got transferred, a familiar voice greeted me from the desk opposite in a tone hushed out of respect for our fellow workers. 'I hope all goes well now, sir, if you'll forgive the personal intrusion.'

I looked over the back of my desk at the unforgettable moustache. 'Very well, Parkis, thank you. Have an illicit sandwich?'

'Oh no, sir, I couldn't possibly . . .'

'Come now. Imagine it's on expenses.' Reluctantly he took one and opening it up remarked with a kind of horror, as though he had accepted a coin and found it gold, 'It's real ham.'

'My publisher sent me a tin from America.'

'It's too good of you, sir.'

'I still have your ash-tray, Parkis,' I whispered, because my neighbour had looked angrily up at me.

'It's of sentimental value only,' he whispered back.

'How's your boy?'

'A little bilious, sir.'

'I'm surprised to find you here. Work? You aren't watching one of us, surely?' I couldn't imagine that any of the dusty inmates of the reading-room – the men who wore hats and scarves indoors for warmth, the Indian who was painfully studying the complete works of George Eliot, or the man who slept every day with his head laid beside the same pile of books – could be concerned in any drama of sexual jealousy.

'Oh no, sir. This isn't work. It's my day off, and the boy's back at school today.'

'What are you reading?'

'The Times Law Reports, sir. Today I'm on the Russell case. They give a kind of background to one's work, sir. Open up vistas. They take one away from the daily petty detail. I knew one of the witnesses in this case, sir. We were in the same office once. Well, he's gone down to history as I never shall now.'

'Oh, you never know, Parkis.'

'One does know, sir. That's the discouraging thing. The Bolton case was as far as I'll ever get. The law that forbade the evidence in divorce cases being published was a blow to men of my calling. The judge, sir, never mentions us by name, and he's very often prejudiced against the profession.'

'It had never struck me,' I said with sympathy.

Even Parkis could awake a longing. I could never see him without the thought of Sarah. I went home in the tube with hope for company, and sitting at home, in dying expectation of the telephone-bell ringing, I saw my companion depart again: it wouldn't be today. At five o'clock I dialled the number, but as soon as I heard the ringing-tone I replaced the receiver: perhaps Henry was back early and I couldn't speak to Henry now, for I was the victor, since Sarah loved me and Sarah wanted to leave him. But a delayed victory can strain the nerves as much as a prolonged defeat.

Eight days passed before the telephone rang. It wasn't the time of day I expected, for it was before nine o'clock in the morning, and when I said, 'Hullo,' it was Henry who answered.

'Is that Bendrix?' he asked. There was something very queer about his voice, and I wondered, has she told him?

'Yes. Speaking.'

'An awful thing's happened. You ought to know. Sarah's dead.'

How conventionally we behave at such moments. I said, 'I'm terribly sorry, Henry.'

'Are you doing anything tonight?'

'No.'

'I wish you'd come over for a drink. I don't fancy being alone.

Chapter One

I stayed the night with Henry. It was the first time I had slept in Henry's house. They had only one guest-room and Sarah was there (she had moved into it a week before so as not to disturb Henry with her cough), so I slept on the sofa in the drawing-room where we had made love. I didn't want to stay the night, but he begged me to.

We must have drunk a bottle and a half of whisky between us. I remember Henry saying, 'It's strange, Bendrix, how one can't be jealous about the dead. She's only been dead a few hours, and yet I wanted you with me.'

'You hadn't so much to be jealous about. It was all over a long time ago.'

'I don't need that kind of comfort now, Bendrix. It was never over with either of you. I was the lucky man. I had her all those years. Do you hate me?'

'I don't know, Henry. I thought I did, but I don't know.'

We sat in his study with no light on. The gas-fire was not turned high enough to see each other's faces, so that I could only tell when Henry wept by the tone of his voice. The Discus Thrower aimed at both of us from the darkness. 'Tell me how it happened, Henry.'

'You remember that night I met you on the Common? Three weeks ago, or four, was it? She got a bad cold that night. She wouldn't do anything about it. I never even knew it had reached her chest. She never told anybody those sort of things' – and not even her diary, I thought. There had been no word of sickness there. She hadn't had the time to be ill in.

'She took to her bed in the end,' Henry said, 'but nobody could have kept her there, and she wouldn't have a doctor – she never believed in them. She got up and went out a week ago. God knows where or why. She said she needed exercise. I came home first and found her gone. She didn't get in till nine, soaked through worse than the first time. She must have been walking about for hours in the rain. She was feverish all night, talking to somebody, I don't know who: it wasn't you or me, Bendrix. I made her see a doctor after that. He said if she'd had penicillin a week earlier, he'd have saved her.'

There wasn't anything to do for either of us but pour out more whisky. I thought of the stranger I had paid Parkis to track down: the stranger had certainly won in the end. No, I thought, I don't hate Henry. I hate You if you exist. I remembered what she'd said to Richard Smythe, that I had taught her to believe. I couldn't for the life of me tell how, but to think of what I had thrown away made me hate myself too. Henry said, 'She died at four this morning. I wasn't there. The nurse didn't call me in time.'

'Where's the nurse?'

'She finished her job off very tidily. She had another urgent case and left before lunch.'

'I wish I could be of use to you.'

'You are, just sitting here. It's been an awful day, Bendrix. You know, I've never had a death to deal with. I always assumed I'd die first – and Sarah would have known what to do. If she'd stayed with me that long. In a way it's a woman's job – like having a baby.'

'I suppose the doctor helped.'

'He's awfully rushed this winter. He rang up an undertaker. I wouldn't have known where to go. We've never had a trade-directory. But a doctor can't tell me what to do with her clothes – the cupboards are full of them. Compacts, scents – one can't just throw things away. . . . If only she had a sister. . . .' He suddenly stopped because the front door opened and closed, just as it had on that other night when he had said, 'The maid,' and I had said, 'It's Sarah.' We listened to the footsteps of the maid going upstairs. It's extraordinary how empty a house can be with three people in it. We drank our whisky and I poured another. 'I've got plenty in the house,' Henry said. 'Sarah found a new source . . .' and stopped again. She stood at the end of every path. There wasn't any point in trying to avoid her even for a moment. I thought, why did You have to do this to us? If she hadn't believed in You she would be alive now, we should have been lovers still. It was sad and strange to remember that I had been dissatisfied with the situation. I would have shared her now happily with Henry.

I said, 'And the funeral?'

'Bendrix, I don't know what to do. Something very puzzling happened. When she was delirious (of course, she wasn't responsible), the nurse told me that she kept on asking for a priest. At least she kept on saying, Father, Father, and it couldn't have been her own. She never knew him. Of course the nurse knew we weren't Catholics. She was quite sensible. She soothed her down. But I'm worried, Bendrix.'

I thought with anger and bitterness, You might have left poor Henry alone. We have got on for years without You. Why should You suddenly start intruding into all situations like a strange relation returned from the Antipodes?

Henry said, 'If one lives in London cremation's the easiest thing. Until the nurse said that to me, I'd been planning to have it done at Golders Green. The undertaker rang up the crematorium. They can fit Sarah in the day after tomorrow.'

'She was delirious,' I said, 'you don't have to take what she said into account.'

'I wondered whether I ought to ask a priest about it. She kept so many things quiet. For all I know she may have become a Catholic. She's been so strange lately.'

'Oh no, Henry. She didn't believe in anything, any more than you or me.' I wanted her burnt up, I wanted to be able to say, Resurrect that body if you can. My jealousy had not finished, like Henry's, with her death. It was as if she were alive still, in the company of a lover she had preferred to me. How I wished I could send Parkis after her to interrupt their eternity.

'You are quite certain?'

'Quite certain, Henry.' I thought, I've got to be careful. I mustn't be like

Richard Smythe, I musn't hate, for if I were really to hate I would believe, and if I were to believe, what a triumph for You and her. This is to play act, talking about revenge and jealousy: it's just something to fill the brain with, so that I can forget the absoluteness of her death. A week ago I had only to say to her 'Do you remember that first time together and how I hadn't got a shilling for the meter?' and the scene would be there for both of us. Now it was there for me only. She had lost all our memories for ever, and it was as though by dying she had robbed me of part of myself. I was losing my individuality. It was the first stage of my own death, the memories dropping off like gangrened limbs.

'I hate all this fuss of prayers and grave-diggers, but if Sarah wanted it, I'd try to get it arranged.'

'She chose her wedding in a registry office,' I said, 'she wouldn't want her funeral to be in a church.'

'No, I suppose that's true, isn't it?'

'Registration and cremation,' I said, 'they go together,' and in the shadow Henry lifted his head and peered towards me as though he suspected my irony.

'Let me take it all out of your hands,' I suggested, just as in the same room, by the same fire, I had suggested visiting Mr Savage for him.

'It's good of you, Bendrix.' He drained the last of the whisky into our glasses, very carefully and evenly.

'Midnight,' I said, 'you must get some sleep. If you can.'

'The doctor left me some pills.' But he didn't want to be alone yet. I knew exactly how he felt, for I too after a day with Sarah would postpone for as long as I could the loneliness of my room.

'I keep on forgetting she's dead,' Henry said. And I had experienced that too, all through 1945 – the bad year – forgetting when I woke that our love-affair was over, that the telephone might carry any voice except hers. She had been as dead then as she was dead now. For a month or two this year a ghost had pained me with hope, but the ghost was laid and the pain would be over soon. I would die a little more every day, but how I longed to retain it. As long as one suffers one lives.

'Go to bed, Henry.'

'I'm afraid of dreaming about her.'

'You won't if you take the doctor's pills.'

'Would you like one, Bendrix?'

'No.'

'You wouldn't, would you, stay the night? It's filthy outside.'

'I don't mind the weather.'

'You'd be doing me a great favour.'

'Of course I'll stay.'

'I'll bring down some sheets and blankets.'

'Don't bother, Henry,' but he was gone. I looked at the parquet floor, and I remembered the exact timbre of her cry. On the desk where she wrote her letters was a clutter of objects, and every object I could interpret like a code. I thought, She hasn't even thrown away that pebble. We laughed at its shape and there it still is, like a paper-weight. What would Henry make of it, and the miniature bottle of a liqueur none of us cared for, and the piece of glass polished by the sea, and the small wooden rabbit I had found in Nottingham?

Should I take all these objects away with me? They would go into the waste-paper basket otherwise, when Henry at last got around to clearing up, but could I bear their company?

I was looking at them when Henry came in burdened with blankets. 'I had forgotten to say, Bendrix, if there's anything you want to take ... I don't think she's left a will.'

'It's kind of you.'

'I'm grateful now to anybody who loved her.'

'I'll take this stone if I may.'

'She kept the oddest things. I've brought you a pair of my pyjamas, Bendrix.'

Henry had forgotten to bring a pillow and lying with my head on a cushion I imagined I could smell her scent. I wanted things I should never have again – there was no substitute. I couldn't sleep. I pressed my nails into my palms as she had done with hers, so that the pain might prevent my brain working, and the pendulum of my desire swung tiringly to and fro, the desire to forget and to remember, to be dead and to keep alive a while longer. And then at last I slept. I was walking up Oxford Street and I was worried because I had to buy a present and all the shops were full of cheap jewellery, glittering under the concealed lighting. Now and then I thought I saw something beautiful and I would approach the glass, but when I saw the jewel close it would be as factitious as all the others – perhaps a hideous green bird with scarlet eyes meant to give the effect of rubies. Time was short and I hurried from shop to shop. Then out of one of the shops came Sarah and I knew that she would help me. 'Have you bought something, Sarah?' 'Not here,' she said, 'but they have some lovely little bottles further on.'

'I haven't time,' I begged her, 'help me. I've got to find something, for tomorrow's the birthday.'

'Don't worry,' she said. 'Something always turns up. Don't worry,' and suddenly I didn't worry. Oxford Street extended its boundaries into a great grey misty field, my feet were bare, and I was walking in the dew, alone, and stumbling in a shallow rut I woke, still hearing, 'Don't worry,' like a whisper lodged in the ear, a summer sound belonging to childhood.

At breakfast time Henry was still asleep, and the maid whom Parkis had suborned brought coffee and toast in to me on a tray. She drew the curtains and the sleet had changed blindingly to snow. I was still bleary with sleep and the contentment of my dream, and I was surprised to see her eyes red with old tears. 'Is anything the matter, Maud?' I asked, and it was only when she put the tray down and walked furiously out that I came properly awake to the empty house and the empty world. I went up and looked in at Henry. He was still in the depths of drugged sleep, smiling like a dog, and I envied him. Then I went down and tried to eat my toast.

A bell rang and I heard the maid leading somebody upstairs – the undertaker, I supposed, because I could hear the door of the guest-room open. He was seeing her dead: I had not, but I had no wish to, any more than I would have wished to see her in another man's arms. Some men may be stimulated that way: I am not. Nobody was going to make me pimp for death. I drew my mind together, and I thought, Now that everything is really over, I have got to begin again. I have fallen in love once: it can be done again. But I was unconvinced: it seemed to me that I had given all the sex I had away.

Another bell. What a lot of business was going on in the house while Henry slept. This time Maud came to me. She said, 'There's a gentleman below asking for Mr Miles, but I don't like to wake him.'

'Who is he?'

'He's that friend of Mrs Miles,' she said and for the only time admitted her share in our shabby collaboration.

'You'd better show him up,' I said. I felt very superior to Smythe now, sitting in Sarah's drawing-room, wearing Henry's pyjamas, knowing so much about him while he knew nothing about me. He looked at me with confusion and dripped snow on to the parquet. I said, 'We met once. I'm a friend of Mrs Miles.'

'You had a small boy with you.'

'That's right.'

'I came to see Mr Miles,' he said.

'You've heard the news?'

'That's why I came.'

'He's asleep. The doctor gave him pills. It's been a bad shock to all of us,' I added foolishly. He was staring round the room: in Cedar Road, coming out of nowhere, she had been as dimensionless, I suppose, as a dream. But this room gave her thickness: it was Sarah too. The snow mounted slowly on the sill like mould from a spade. The room was being buried like Sarah.

He said, 'I'll come back,' and turned drearily away, so that his bad cheek was turned on me. I thought: that was where her lips rested. She could always be snared by pity.

He repeated stupidly, 'I came to see Mr Miles and say how sorry . . .'

'It's more usual on these occasions to write.'

'I thought I might be of some use,' he said weakly.

'You don't have to convert Mr Miles.'

'Convert?' he asked, ill at ease and bewildered.

'To the fact that there's nothing left of her. The end. Annihilation.'

He broke suddenly out, 'I wanted to see her that's all.'

'Mr Miles doesn't even know you exist. It's not very considerate of you, Smythe, to come here.'

'When is the funeral?'

'Tomorrow at Golders Green.'

'She wouldn't have wanted that,' he said and took me by surprise.

'She didn't believe in anything, any more than you claim you do.'

He said, 'Don't any of you know? She was becoming a Catholic.'

'Nonsense.'

'She wrote to me. She'd made up her mind. Nothing I could have said would have done any good. She was beginning – instruction. Isn't that the word they use?' So she still had secrets, I thought. She had never put that in her journal, any more than she had put her sickness. How much more was there to discover? The thought was like despair.

'That was a shock for you, wasn't it?' I jeered at him, trying to transfer my pain.

'Oh, I was angry of course. But we can't all believe the same things.'

'That's not what you used to claim.'

He looked at me, as though he were puzzled by my enmity. He said, 'Is your name Maurice by any chance?'

'It is.'

'She told me about you.'

'And I read about you. She made fools of us both.'

'I was unreasonable.' He said, 'Don't you think I could see her?' and I heard the heavy boots of the undertaker coming down, and I heard the same stair creak.

'She's lying upstairs. The first door on the left.'

'If Mr Miles . . .'

'You won't wake him.'

I had put on my clothes by the time he came down again. He said, 'Thank you.'

'Don't thank me. I don't own her any more than you do.'

'I've got no right to ask,' he said, 'but I wish you'd – you loved her, I know.' He added as though he were swallowing a bitter medicine, 'She loved you.'

'What are you trying to say?'

'I wish you'd do something for her.'

'For her?'

'Let her have her Catholic funeral. She would have liked it.'

'What earthly difference does it make?'

'I don't suppose any for her. But it always pays us to be generous.'

'And what have I to do with it?'

'She always said that her husband had a great respect for you.'

He was turning the screw of absurdity too far. I wished to shatter the deadness of this buried room with laughter. I sat down on the sofa and began to shake with it. I thought of Sarah dead upstairs and Henry asleep with a silly smile on his face, and the lover who had employed Mr Parkis to sprinkle his door-bell with powder. The tears ran down my cheeks as I laughed. Once in the blitz I saw a man laughing outside his house where his wife and child were buried.

'I don't understand,' Smythe said. He held his right fist closed as though he were prepared to defend himself. There was so much that neither of us understood. Pain was like an inexplicable explosion throwing us together. 'I'll be going,' he said and reached for the door-knob with his left hand. A strange idea occurred to me because I had no reason to believe he was left-handed.

'You must forgive me,' I said. 'I'm rattled. We're all rattled.' I held out my hand to him: he hesitated and touched it with his left. 'Smythe,' I said, 'what have you got there? Did you take anything from her room?' He opened his hand and showed a scrap of hair. 'That's all,' he said.

'You hadn't any right.'

'Oh, she doesn't belong to anybody now,' he said, and suddenly I saw her for what she was – a piece of refuse waiting to be cleared away: if you needed a bit of hair you could take it, or trim her nails if nail trimmings had value to you. Like a saint's her bones could be divided up – if anybody required them. She was going to be burnt soon, so why shouldn't everybody have what he wanted first? What a fool I had been during three years to imagine that in any way I had possessed her. We are possessed by nobody, not even by ourselves.

'I'm sorry,' I said.

'Do you know what she wrote to me?' Symthe asked. 'It was only four days ago,' and I thought with sadness that she had had time to write to him but not to telephone to me. 'She wrote – pray for me. Doesn't it seem odd, asking *me* to pray for her?'

'What did you do?'

'Oh,' he said, 'when I heard she was dead, I prayed.'

'Did you know any prayers?'

'No.'

'It doesn't seem right praying to a God you don't believe in.'

I followed him out of the house; there was no point in remaining till Henry woke. Sooner or later he had to face being on his own, just as I had. I watched Smythe jerking his way across the Common ahead of me, and I thought, An hysterical type. Disbelief could be a product of hysteria just as much as belief. The wet of the snow, where the passage of many people had melted it, worked through my soles and reminded me of the dew of my dream, but when I tried to remember her voice saying, 'Don't worry,' I found I had no memory for sounds. I couldn't imitate her voice. I couldn't even caricature it: when I tried to remember it, it was anonymous – just any woman's voice. The process of forgetting her had set in. We should keep gramophone records as we keep photographs.

I came up the broken steps into the hall. Nothing but the stained glass was the same as that night in 1944. Nobody knows the beginning of anything. Sarah had really believed that the end began when she saw my body. She would never have admitted that the end had started long before: the fewer telephone calls for this or that inadequate reason, the quarrels I began with her because I had realized the danger of love ending. We had begun to look beyond love, but it was only I who was aware of the way we were being driven. If the bomb had fallen a year earlier, she wouldn't have made that promise. She would have torn her nails trying to release me. When we get to the end of human beings we have to delude ourselves into a belief in God, like a gourmet who demands more complex sauces with his food. I looked at the hall, clear as a cell, hideous with green paint, and I thought, she wanted me to have a second chance and here it is: the empty life, odourless, antiseptic, the life of a prison, and I accused her as though her prayers had really worked the change: what did I do to you that you had to condemn me to life? The stairs and banisters creaked with newness all the way upstairs. She had never walked up them. Even the repairs to the house were part of the process of forgetting. It needs a God outside time to remember when everything changes. Did I still love or did I only regret love?

I came into my room and on the desk lay a letter from Sarah.

She had been dead for twenty-four hours and unconscious for longer than that. How could a letter take so long across a strip of common? Then I saw that she had put my number wrong, and a little of the old bitterness seeped out. She wouldn't have forgotten my number two years ago.

There was so much pain at the idea of seeing her writing that I nearly held the letter to the gas-fire, but curiosity can be stronger than pain. It was written in pencil, I suppose because she was writing in bed.

'Dearest Maurice,' she wrote, 'I meant to write to you the other night after you had gone away, but I felt rather sick when I got home and Henry fussed about me. I'm writing instead of telephoning. I can't telephone and hear your voice go queer when I say I'm not going to come away with you. Because I'm not going to come away with you Maurice, dearest Maurice. I love you but I can't see you again. I don't know how I'm going to live in this pain and longing and I'm praying to God all the time that he won't be hard on me, that he won't keep me alive. Dear Maurice, I want to have my cake and eat it like everybody else. I went to a priest two days ago before you rang me up and I told him I wanted to be a Catholic. I told him about my promise and about you. I said, I'm not really married to Henry any more. We don't sleep together – not since the first year with you. And it wasn't really a marriage, I said, you couldn't call a registry office a wedding. I asked him couldn't I be a Catholic and marry you? I knew you wouldn't mind going through a service. Every time I asked him a question I had such hope; it was like opening the shutters of a new house and looking for the view, and every window just faced a blank wall. No, no, no, he said, I couldn't marry you, I couldn't go on seeing you, not if I was going to be a Catholic. I thought, to hell with the whole lot of them and I walked out of the room where I was seeing him, and I slammed the door to show what I thought of priests. They are between us and God, I thought; God has more mercy, and then I came out of the church and saw the crucifix they have there, and I thought, of course, he's got mercy, only it's such an odd sort of mercy, it sometimes looks like punishment. Maurice, my dearest, I've got a foul headache, and I feel like death. I wish I weren't as strong as a horse. I don't want to live without you, and I know one day I shall meet you on the Common and then I won't care a damn about Henry or God or anything. But what's the good, Maurice? I believe there's a God – I believe the whole bag of tricks, there's nothing I don't believe, they could subdivide the Trinity into a dozen parts and I'd believe. They could dig up records that proved Christ had been invented by Pilate to get himself promoted and I'd believe just the same. I've caught belief like a disease. I've fallen into belief like I fell in love. I've never loved before as I love you, and I've never believed in anything before as I believe now. I'm sure. I've never been sure before about anything. When you came in at the door with the blood on your face, I became sure. Once and for all. Even though I didn't know it at the time. I fought belief for longer than I fought love, but I haven't any fight left.

'Maurice, dear, don't be angry. Be sorry for me, but don't be angry. I'm a phoney and a fake, but this isn't phoney or fake. I used to think I was sure about myself and what was right and wrong, and you taught me not to be sure. You took away all my lies and self-deceptions like they clear a road of rubble for somebody to come along it, somebody of importance, and now he's come, but you cleared the way yourself. When you write you try to be exact and you taught me to want the truth, and you told me when I wasn't telling the truth. Do you really think that, you'd say, or do you only think you think it? So you see it's all your fault, Maurice, it's all your fault. I pray to God He won't keep me alive like this.'

There wasn't any more. She seemed to have had a knack of getting her prayers answered even before they were spoken, because hadn't she started dying that night when she came in out of the rain and found me with Henry?

If I were writing a novel I would end it here: a novel, I used to think, has to end somewhere, but I'm beginning to believe my realism has been at fault all these years, for nothing in life now ever seems to end. Chemists tell you matter is never completely destroyed, and mathematicians tell you that if you halve each pace in crossing a room, you will never reach the opposite wall, so what an optimist I would be if I thought that this story ended here. Only, like Sarah, I wish I weren't as strong as a horse.

Chapter Two

I was late for the funeral. I had gone into town to meet a man called Waterbury who was going to write an article on my work in one of the little reviews. I tossed up whether I'd see him or not: I knew too well the pompous phrases of his article, the buried significance he would discover of which I was unaware and the faults I was tired of facing. Patronizingly in the end he would place me – probably a little above Maugham because Maugham is popular and I have not yet committed that crime – not yet, but although I retain a little of the exclusiveness of unsuccess, the little reviews, like wise detectives, can scent it on its way.

Why did I ever trouble to toss up? I didn't want to meet Waterbury, and certainly I didn't want to be written about. For I have come to an end of my interest in work now: no one can please me much with praise or hurt me with blame. When I began that novel about the civil servant I was still interested, but when Sarah left me, I recognized my work for what it was – as unimportant a drug as cigarettes to get one through the weeks and years. If we are extinguished by death, as I still try to believe, what point is there in leaving some books behind any more than bottles, clothes or cheap jewellery? and if Sarah is right, how unimportant all the importance of art is. I tossed up, I think, simply from loneliness. I hadn't anything to do before the funeral: I wanted to fortify myself with a drink or two (one may cease to care about one's work, but one never ceases to care about conventions, and a man must not break down in public).

Waterbury was waiting in a sherry-bar off Tottenham Court Road. He wore black corduroy trousers and smoked cheap cigarettes, and he had with him a girl much taller and better-looking than he was who wore the same kind of trousers and smoked the same cigarettes. She was very young and she was called Sylvia and one knew that she was on a long course of study that had only begun with Waterbury – she was at the stage of imitating her teacher. I wondered where, with those looks, those alert good-natured eyes and hair the gold of illuminations, she would end. Would she even remember Waterbury in ten years and the bar off Tottenham Court Road? I felt sorry for him. He was so proud now, so patronizing to both of us, but he was on the losing side. Why, I thought, catching her eye over my glass at a particularly fatuous comment of his about the stream of consciousness, even now I could get her from him. His articles were bound in paper, but my books were bound in cloth. She knew she could learn more from me. And yet, poor devil, he had the nerve to snub her when occasionally she made a simple human unintellectual comment. I wanted to warn him of the empty future, but instead I took another glass and said, 'I can't stay long. I have to go to a funeral in Golders Green.'

'A funeral in Golders Green,' Waterbury exclaimed. 'How like one of your own characters. It would have to be Golders Green, wouldn't it?'

'I didn't choose the spot.'

'Life imitating art.'

'Is it a friend?' Sylvia asked with sympathy and Waterbury glared at her for her irrelevance.

'Yes.'

I could see that she was speculating – man? woman? what kind of a friend? and it pleased me. For I was a human being to her and not a writer: a man whose friends died and who attended their funerals, who felt pleasure and pain, who might even need comfort, not just a skilled craftsman whose work has greater sympathy perhaps than Mr Maugham's, though of course we cannot rank it as high as . . .

'What do you think of Forster?' Waterbury asked.

'Forster? Oh, I'm sorry. I was just wondering how long it took to Golders Green.'

'You ought to allow forty minutes,' Sylvia said. 'You have to wait for an Edgware train.'

'Forster,' Waterbury repeated irritably.

'You'll have to take a bus from the station,' Sylvia said.

'Really, Sylvia, Bendrix hasn't come here to talk about how to get to Golders Green.'

'I'm sorry, Peter, I just thought . . .'

'Count six before thinking, Sylvia,' Waterbury said. 'And now can we get back to E. M. Forster?'

'Need we?' I asked.

'It would be interesting as you belong to such different schools. . . .'

'Does he belong to a school? I didn't even know that I did. Are you writing a text-book?'

Sylvia smiled and he saw the smile. I knew from that moment he would grind sharp the weapon of his trade, but it didn't matter to me. Indifference and pride look very much alike, and he probably thought I was proud. I said, 'I really ought to be going.'

'But you've only been here five minutes. It's really important to get this article right.'

'It's really important for me not to be late at Golders Green.'

'I don't see why.'

•Sylvia said, 'I'm going as far as Hampstead myself. I'll put you on your way.'

'You never told me,' Waterbury said with suspicion.

'You know I always see my mother on Wednesdays.'

'Today's Tuesday.'

'Then I needn't go tomorrow.'

'It's very good of you,' I said, 'I'd like your company.'

'You used the stream of consciousness in one of your books,' Waterbury said with desperate haste. 'Why did you abandon the method?'

'Oh, I don't know. Why does one change a flat?'

'Did you feel it was a failure?'

'I feel that about all my books. Well, good-bye, Waterbury.'

'I'll send you a copy of the article,' he said as though he were uttering a threat.

'Thanks.'

'Don't be late, Sylvia. There's the Bartok programme on the Third at six-thirty.'

We went together into the débris of Tottenham Court Road. I said, 'Thank you for breaking up the party.'

'Oh, I knew you wanted to get away,' she said.

'What's your other name?'

'Black.'

'Sylvia Black,' I said, 'it's a good combination. Almost too good.'

'Was it a great friend?'

'Yes.'

'A woman?'

'Yes.'

'I'm sorry,' she said, and I had the impression that she meant it. She had a lot to learn, in the way of books and music and how to dress and talk, but she would never have to learn humanity. She came down with me into the crowded tube and we strap-hung side by side. Feeling her against me I was reminded of desire. Would that always be the case now? Not desire, but only the reminder of it. She turned to make way at Goodge Street for a newcomer, and I was aware of her thigh against my leg as one is aware of something that happened a long time ago.

'This is the first funeral I've ever been to,' I said to make conversation.

'Are your father and mother alive, then?'

'My father is. My mother died when I was away at school. I thought I'd get a few days' holiday, but my father thought it would upset me, so I made nothing out of it at all. Except I was let off prep. the night the news arrived.'

'I wouldn't like to be cremated,' she said.

'You'd prefer worms?'

'Yes, I would.'

Our heads were so close together that we could talk without raising our voices, but we couldn't look at each other because of the press of people. I said, 'It wouldn't matter to me one way or the other,' and wondered immediately why I had bothered to lie, because it *had* mattered, it must have mattered, for it was I in the end who had persuaded Henry against burial.

Chapter Three

On the afternoon before, Henry had wavered. He had telephoned asking me to come over. It was odd how close we had become with Sarah gone. He depended on me now much as before he had depended on Sarah – I was somebody familiar about in the house. I even pretended to wonder whether he would ask me to share the house when once the funeral was over, and what answer I would give him. From the point of view of forgetting Sarah there was nothing to choose between the two houses: she had belonged to both.

He was still hazy with his drugs when I arrived, or I might have had more trouble with him. A priest sat rigidly on the edge of an arm-chair in the study: a man with a sour gaunt face, one of the Redemptorists probably who served up Hell on Sundays in the dark church where I had last seen Sarah. He had obviously antagonized Henry from the start and that had helped.

'This is Mr Bendrix, the author,' Henry said. 'Father Crompton. Mr Bendrix was a great friend of my wife's.' I had the impression that Father Crompton knew that already. His nose ran down his face like a buttress, and I thought, perhaps this is the very man who slammed the door of hope on Sarah.

'Good afternoon,' Father Crompton said with such ill-will that I felt the bell and the candle were not far away.

'Mr Bendrix has helped me a great deal with all the arrangements,' Henry explained.

'I would have been quite ready to take them off your hands if I had known.'

There had been a time when I hated Henry. My hatred now seemed petty. Henry was a victim as much as I was a victim, and the victor was this grim man in the silly collar. I said, 'You could hardly have done that surely. You disapprove of cremation.'

'I could have arranged a Catholic burial.'

'She wasn't a Catholic.'

'She had expressed the intention of becoming one.'

'Is that enough to make her one?'

Father Crompton produced a formula. He laid it down like a bank note. 'We recognize the baptism of desire.' It lay there between us waiting to be picked up. Nobody made a move. Father Crompton said, 'There's still time to cancel your arrangements.' He repeated, 'I will take everything off your hands,' repeated it in a tone of admonition as though he were addressing Lady Macbeth and promising her some better process of sweetening her hands than the perfumes of Arabia.

Henry said suddenly, 'Does it really make much difference? Of course, I'm not a Catholic, father, but I can't see . . .'

'She would have been happier. . . .'

'But why?'

'The Church offers privileges, Mr Miles, as well as responsibilities. There are special Masses for our dead. Prayers are regularly said. We remember our dead,' he added, and I thought angrily, how do you remember them? Your theories are all right. You preach the importance of the individual. Our hairs are all numbered, you say, but I can feel her hair on the back of my hand: I can remember the fine dust of hair at the base of her spine as she lay face down on my bed. We remember our dead too, in our way.

Watching Henry weaken I lied firmly, 'We've absolutely no reason to believe she would have become a Catholic.'

Henry began, 'Of course the nurse did say,' but I interrupted him, 'She was delirious at the end.'

Father Crompton said, 'I would never have dreamed of intruding on you, Mr Miles, without serious reason.'

'I had a letter from Mrs Miles written less than a week before she died,' I told him. 'How long is it since you saw her?'

'About the same time. Five or six days ago.'

'It seems very odd to me that she didn't even mention the subject in her letter.'

'Perhaps Mr . . . Mr Bendrix, you hadn't her confidence.'

'Perhaps, father, you jump a little too quickly to conclusions. People can be interested in your faith, ask questions about it, without necessarily wishing to become Catholics.' I went quickly on to Henry, 'It would be absurd to alter everything now. Directions have been given. Friends have been invited. Sarah was never a fanatic. She would be the last to want any inconvenience caused for the sake of a whim. After all,' I drove on, fixing my eyes on Henry, 'it will be a perfectly Christian ceremony. Not that Sarah was even a Christian. We saw no signs of it anyway. But you could always give Father Crompton money for a Mass.'

'It isn't necessary. I said one this morning.' He made a movement with his hands in his lap, the first break in his rigidity: it was like watching a strong wall shift and lean after a bomb had fallen. 'I shall remember her every day in my Mass,' he said.

Henry said with relief as though that settled matters, 'Very good of you, father,' and moved a cigarette-box.

'It seems an odd and impertinent thing to say to you, Mr Miles, but I don't think you realize what a good woman your wife was.'

'She was everything to me,' Henry said.

'A great many people loved her,' I said.

Father Crompton turned his eyes on me like a headmaster who hears an interruption at the back of the class from some snotty youngster.

'Perhaps not enough,' he said.

'Well,' I said, 'to go back to what we were discussing. I don't think we can alter things now, father. It would cause a great deal of talk too. You wouldn't like talk, would you, Henry?'

'No. Oh no.'

'There's the insertion in *The Times*. We should have to put in a correction.

People notice that kind of thing. It would cause comment. After all you aren't unknown, Henry. Then telegrams would have to be sent. A lot of people will have had wreaths delivered already to the crematorium. You see what I mean, father.'

'I can't say that I do.'

'What you ask is not reasonable.'

'You seem to have a very strange set of values, Mr Bendrix.'

'But surely you don't believe cremation affects the resurrection of the body, father?'

'Of course I don't. I've told you my reasons already. If they don't seem strong enough to Mr Miles, there's no more to be said.' He got up from his chair, and what an ugly man he was. Sitting down he had at least the appearance of power, but his legs were too short for his body, and he rose, unexpectedly small. It was as if he had suddenly moved a long way off.

Henry said, 'If you'd come a little sooner, father. Please don't think . . .'

'I don't think anything wrong of you, Mr Miles.'

'Of me perhaps, father?' I asked with deliberate impertinence.

'Oh, don't worry, Mr Bendrix. Nothing you can do will affect her now.' I suppose the Confessional teaches a man to recognize hate. He held his hand out to Henry and turned his back on me. I wanted to say to him, You're wrong about me. It's not Sarah I hate. And you are wrong about Henry too. He is the corrupter, not me. I wanted to defend myself, 'I loved her', for surely in the Confessional they learn to recognize that emotion too.

Chapter Four

'Hampstead's the next stop,' Sylvia said.

'You've got to get out to see your mother?'

'I could come on to Golders Green and show you the way. I don't usually see her today.'

'It would be an act of charity,' I said.

'I think you'll have to take a taxi if you are to be on time.'

'I suppose it doesn't really matter missing the opening lines.'

She saw me to the courtyard of the station, and then she wanted to go back. It seemed strange to me that she had taken so much trouble. I have never seen any qualities in me for a woman to like, and now less than ever. Grief and disappointment are like hate: they make men ugly with self-pity and bitterness. And how selfish they make us too. I had nothing to give Sylvia: I would never be one of her teachers, but because I was afraid of the next half hour, the faces that would be spying on my loneliness, trying to detect from my manner what my relations with Sarah had been, who had left whom, I needed her beauty to support me.

'But I can't come in these clothes,' she protested when I begged for her company. I could tell how pleased she was that I wanted her with me. I knew I could have taken her from Waterbury there and then. His sands had already run out. If I chose he would listen to Bartok alone.

'We'll stand at the back,' I said. 'You might be just a stranger walking round.'

'At least they are black,' she said, referring to her trousers. In the taxi I let my hand lie on her leg like a promise, but I had no intention of keeping my promise. The crematorium tower was smoking, and the water lay in half-frozen puddles on the gravel walks. A lot of strangers came by – from a previous cremation, I supposed: they had the brisk cheerful air of people who have left a dull party and can now 'go on'.

'It's this way,' Sylvia said.

'You know the place very well.'

'Daddy was done here two years ago.'

As we reached the chapel everyone was leaving. Waterbury's questions about the stream of consciousness had delayed me just too long. I had an odd conventional stab of grief – I hadn't after all seen the last of Sarah, and I thought dully, so it was her smoke that was blowing over the suburban gardens. Henry came blindly out alone: he had been crying and he didn't see me. I knew nobody else, except Sir William Mallock, who wore a top hat. He gave me a look of disapproval and hurried on. There were half a dozen men with the air of civil servants. Was Dunstan there? It wasn't very important. Some wives had accompanied their husbands. They at least were satisfied with the ceremony – you could almost tell it from their hats. The extinction of Sarah had left every wife safer.

'I'm sorry,' Sylvia said.

'It wasn't your fault.'

I thought, if we could have embalmed her, they would never have been safe. Even her dead body would have provided a standard to judge them by.

Smythe came out and splashed quickly away among the puddles, speaking to nobody. I heard a woman say, 'The Carters have asked us for the week-end of the tenth.'

'Would you like me to go?' Sylvia asked.

'No, no,' I said, 'I like having you around.'

I went to the door of the chapel and looked in. The runway to the furnace was empty for the moment, but as the old wreaths were being carried out, new ones were being carried in. An elderly woman was kneeling incongruously in prayer like an actor from another scene caught by the unexpected raising of a curtain. A familiar voice behind me said, 'It's a sad pleasure to see you here, sir, where bygones are always bygones.'

'You've come, Parkis,' I exclaimed.

'I saw the announcement in *The Times*, sir, so I asked Mr Savage's permission to take the afternoon off.'

'Do you always follow your people as far as this?'

'She was a very fine lady, sir,' he said, reproachfully. 'She asked me the way once in the street, not knowing, of course, my reason for being around. And at the cocktail party she handed me a glass of sherry.'

'South African sherry?' I asked him miserably.

'I wouldn't know, sir, but the way she did it – oh, there weren't many like her. My boy too. . . . He's always speaking about her.'

'How is your boy, Parkis?'

'Not well, sir. Not at all well. Very violent stomach-aches.'

'You've seen a doctor?'

'Not yet, sir. I believe in leaving things to nature. Up to a point.'

I looked round at the groups of strangers who had all known Sarah. I said, 'Who are these people, Parkis?'

'The young lady I don't know, sir.'

'She's with me.'

'I beg your pardon. Sir William Mallock is the one on the horizon, sir.'

'I know him.'

'The gentleman who's just avoided a puddle, sir, is the head of Mr Miles's department.'

'Dunstan?'

'That's the name, sir.'

'What a lot you know, Parkis.' I had thought jealousy was quite dead: I had thought myself willing to share her with a world of men if only she could be alive again, but the sight of Dunstan woke for a few seconds the old hatred. 'Sylvia,' I called, as though Sarah could hear me, 'are you dining anywhere tonight?'

'I promised Peter. . . .'

'Peter?'

'Waterbury.'

'Forget him.'

Are you there? I said to Sarah. Are you watching me? See how I can get on without you. Is isn't so difficult, I said to her. My hatred could believe in her survival: it was only my love that knew she existed no more than a dead bird.

A new funeral was gathering, and the woman by the rail rose in confusion at the sight of the strangers coming in. She had nearly been caught up in the wrong cremation.

'I suppose I could phone.'

Hate lay like boredom over the evening ahead. I had committed myself: without love I would have to go through the gestures of love. I felt the guilt before I had committed the crime, the crime of drawing the innocent into my own maze. The act of sex may be nothing, but when you reach my age you learn that at any time it may prove to be everything. I was safe, but who could tell to what neurosis in this child I might appeal? At the end of the evening I would make love clumsily, and my very clumsiness, even my impotence if I proved impotent, might do the trick, or I would make love expertly, and my experience too might involve her. I implored Sarah, Get me out of this, get me out of it, for her sake, not mine.

Sylvia said, 'I could say my mother was ill.' She was ready to lie: it was the end of Waterbury. Poor Waterbury. With that first lie we should become accomplices. She stood there in her black trousers, among the frozen puddles, and I thought, this is where a whole long future may begin. I implored Sarah, Get me out of it. I don't want to begin it all again and injure her. I'm incapable of love. Except of you, except of you, and the grey old woman swerved towards me, crackling the thin ice. 'Are you Mr Bendrix?' she asked.

'Yes.'

'Sarah told me,' she began, and while she hesitated a wild hope came to me that she had a message to deliver; that the dead could speak.

'You were her best friend – she often told me.'

'I was one of them.'

'I'm her mother.' I hadn't even remembered her mother was alive: in those years there had always been so much to talk about between us that whole areas of both our lives were blank like an early map, to be filled in later.

She said, 'You didn't know about me, did you?'

'As a matter of fact . . .'

'Henry didn't like me. It made it rather awkward, so I kept away.' She spoke in a calm reasonable way, and yet the tears came out of her eyes with an effect of independence. The men and their wives had all cleared off: the strangers picked their way among the three of us, going into the chapel. Only Parkis lingered, thinking, I suppose, that he might yet be of use to me in supplying further information, but he kept his distance, knowing, as he would have said, his place.

'I've a great favour to ask of you,' Sarah's mother said. I tried to remember her name – Cameron, Chandler, it began with a C. 'I came up today from Great Missenden in such a hurry. . . .' She wiped the tears out of her eyes indifferently as if she were using a washcloth. Bertram, I thought, that was the name, Bertram.

'Yes, Mrs Bertram,' I said.

'And I forgot to change the money into my black bag.'

'Anything I can do.'

'If you would lend me a pound, Mr Bendrix. You see, I have to get some dinner in town before I leave. It's early closing at Great Missenden,' and she wiped her eyes again as she spoke. Something about her reminded me of Sarah: a matter-of-factness in her grief, perhaps an ambiguity. Had she 'touched' Henry once too often? I said, 'Have an early dinner with me.'

'You wouldn't want to be bothered.'

'I loved Sarah,' I said.

'So did I.'

I went back to Sylvia and explained, 'That's her mother. I'll have to give her dinner. I'm sorry. Can I ring you up and make another date?'

'Of course.'

'Are you in the book?'

'Waterbury is,' she said gloomily.

'Next week.'

'I'd love it.' She put her hand out and said, 'Goodbye.' I could tell that she knew it was one of those things that had missed the moment. Thank God, it didn't matter – a mild regret and curiosity as far as the tube station: a cross word to Waterbury over the Bartok. Turning back to Mrs Bertram, I found myself speaking again to Sarah: You see, I love you. But love had not the same conviction of being heard as hate had.

As we approached the crematorium gates, I noticed that Parkis had slipped away. I hadn't seen him go. He must have realized that now I had no more need of him.

Mrs Bertram and I had dinner at the Isola Bella. I didn't want to go anywhere I had ever been with Sarah, and of course at once I began to compare this restaurant with all the others we had visited together. Sarah and I never drank Chianti and now the act of drinking it reminded me of *that* fact. I might as well have had our favourite claret, I couldn't have thought of her more. Even vacancy was crowded with her.

'I didn't like the service,' Mrs Bertram said.

'I'm sorry.'

'It was so inhuman. Like a conveyor belt.'

'It seemed suitable. There were prayers after all.'

'That clergyman – was he a clergyman?'

'I didn't see him.'

'He talked about the Great All. I didn't understand for a long time. I thought he was saying the Great Auk.' She began to drip again into her soup. She said, 'I nearly laughed and Henry saw me. I could see that he put that against my account.'

'You don't hit it off?'

'He's a very mean man,' she said. She wiped her eyes with her napkin and then she rattled her spoon fiercely in the soup, stirring up the noodles. 'I once had to borrow ten pounds from him because I'd come to London to stay and forgot my bag. It could happen to anybody.'

'Of course it could.'

'I always pride myself on not having a debt in the world.'

Her conversation was like the tube system. It moved in circles and loops. I began by the coffee to notice the recurring stations: Henry's meanness, her own financial integrity, her love for Sarah, her dissatisfaction with the funeral service, the Great All – that was where certain trains went on to Henry.

'It was so funny,' she said. 'I didn't want to laugh. Nobody loved Sarah more than I did.' How we all, always, make that claim and are angered when we hear it on another's tongue. 'But Henry wouldn't understand that. He's a cold man.'

I made a great effort to switch the points. 'I don't see what other kind of service we could have had.'

'Sarah was a Catholic,' she said. She took her glass of port and swallowed half of it in a gulp.

'Nonsense,' I said.

'Oh,' Mrs Bertram said, 'she didn't know it herself.'

Suddenly, inexplicably, I felt fear, like a man who has committed the all-but-perfect crime and watches the first unexpected crack in the wall of his deception. How deep does the crack go? Can it be plugged in time?

'I don't understand a thing you're saying.'

'Sarah never told you I was a Catholic – once?'

'No.'

'I wasn't very much of one. You see, my husband hated the whole business. I was his third wife, and when I got cross with him the first year, I used to say we weren't properly married. He was a mean man,' she added mechanically.

'Your being a Catholic doesn't make Sarah one.'

She took another gulp at her port. She said, 'I've never told another soul. I think I'm a bit tight. Do you think I'm tight, Mr Bendrix?'

'Of course not. Have another port.'

While we were waiting for it, she tried to switch the conversation, but I brought her relentlessly back. 'What did you mean – Sarah was a Catholic?'

'Promise you won't tell Henry.'

'I promise.'

'We were abroad one time in Normandy. Sarah was just over two. My husband used to go to Deauville. So he said, but I knew he was seeing his first wife. I got so cross. Sarah and I went for a walk along the sands. Sarah kept on wanting to sit down, but I'd give her a rest and then we'd walk a little. I said, "This is a secret between you and me, Sarah." Even then she was good at secrets – if she wanted to be. I was scared I can tell you, but it was a good revenge, wasn't it?'

'Revenge? I don't understand you very well, Mrs Bertram.'

'On my husband, of course. It wasn't only because of his first wife. I told you, didn't I, that he wouldn't let me be a Catholic? Oh, there were such scenes if I tried to go to Mass, so I thought, Sarah's going to be a Catholic, and he won't know and I shan't tell him unless I get really angry.'

'And didn't you?'

'He went and left me a year after that.'

'So you were able to be a Catholic again?'

'Oh well, I didn't *believe* much, you see. And then I married a Jew, and he was difficult too. They tell you Jews are awfully generous. Don't you believe it. Oh, he was a mean man.'

'But what happened on the beach?'

'Of course, it didn't happen on the beach. I only meant we walked that way. I left Sarah by the door and went to find the priest. I had to tell him a few lies – white ones of course – to explain things. I could put it all on my husband, of course. I said he'd promised before we married, and then he'd broken his promise. It helped a lot not being able to speak much French. You sound awfully truthful if you don't know the right words. Anyway he did it there and then, and we caught the bus back to lunch.'

'Did what?'

'Baptized her a Catholic.'

'Is that all?' I asked with relief.

'Well, it's a sacrament – or so they say.'

'I thought at first you meant that Sarah was a real Catholic.'

'Well, you see, she was one, only she didn't know it. I wish Henry had buried her properly,' Mrs Bertram said and began again the grotesque drip of tears.

'You can't blame him if even Sarah didn't know.'

'I always had a wish that it would "take". Like vaccination.'

'It doesn't seem to have "taken" much with you,' I couldn't resist saying, but she wasn't offended. 'Oh,' she said, 'I've had a lot of temptations in my life. I expect things will come right in the end. Sarah was very patient with me. She was a good girl. Nobody appreciated her like I did.' She took some more port and said, 'If only you'd known her properly. Why, if she'd been brought up in the right way, if I hadn't always married such mean men, she could have been a saint I truly believe.'

'But it just didn't take,' I said fiercely, and I called the waiter to bring the bill. A wing of those grey geese that fly above our future graves had sent a draught down my back, or else perhaps I had caught a chill in the frozen grounds: if only it could have been a deathly chill like Sarah's.

It didn't take, I repeated to myself all the way home in the tube, after depositing Mrs Bertram at Marylebone, and lending her another three pounds 'because tomorrow's Wednesday and I have to stay in for the char'. Poor Sarah, what had 'taken' had been that string of husbands and step-fathers. Her mother had taught her effectively enough that one man was not enough for a lifetime, but she herself had seen through the pretence of her mother's marriages. When she married Henry she married for life, as I knew with despair.

But that wisdom had nothing to do with the shifty ceremony near the beach. It wasn't You that 'took', I told the God I didn't believe in, that imaginary God whom Sarah thought had saved my life (for what conceivable purpose?) and who had ruined even his non-existence the only deep happiness I had ever experienced: oh no, it wasn't You that took, for that would have been magic and I believe in magic even less than I believe in You: magic is your cross, your resurrection of the body, your holy Catholic church, your communion of saints.

I lay on my back and watched the shadows of the Common trees shift on my ceiling. It's just a coincidence, I thought, a horrible coincidence that nearly brought her back at the end to You. You can't mark a two-year-old child for life with a bit of water and a prayer. If I began to believe that, I could believe in the body and the blood. You didn't own her all those years: I owned her. You won in the end, You don't need to remind me of that, but she wasn't deceiving me with You when she lay here with me, on this bed, with this pillow under her back. When she slept, I was with her, not You. It was I who penetrated her, not You.

All the light went out, darkness was over the bed, and I dreamed I was at a fair with a gun in my hand. I was shooting at bottles that looked as though they were made of glass but my bullets bounded off them as though they were coated with steel. I fired and fired, and not a bottle could I crack, and at five in the morning I woke with exactly the same thought in my head: for those years you were mine, not His.

Chapter Five

It had been a macabre joke of mine when I thought that Henry might ask me to share his house. I had not really expected the offer and when it came I was taken by surprise. Even his visit a week after the funeral was a surprise: he had never been to my house before. I doubt whether he had ever come much nearer to the south side than the night I met him on the Common in the rain. I heard my bell ring and looked out of the window because I didn't want to see visitors – I had an idea it might be Waterbury with Sylvia.

The lamp by the plane-tree on the pavement picked out Henry's black hat. I went downstairs and opened the door. 'I was just passing by,' Henry lied.

'Come in.'

He stood and dithered awkwardly while I got my drinks out of a cupboard. He said, 'You seem interested in General Gordon.'

'They want me to do a Life.'

'Are you going to do it?'

'I suppose so. I don't feel much like work these days.'

'It's the same with me,' Henry said.

'Is the Royal Commission still sitting?'

'Yes.'

'It gives you something to think about.'

'Does it? Yes, I suppose it does. Until we stop for lunch.'

'It's important work anyway. Here's your sherry.'

'It won't make any difference to a single soul.'

What a long way Henry had travelled since the complacent photograph in the *Tatler* that had so angered me. I had a picture of Sarah, enlarged from a snapshot, face-down on my desk. He turned it over. 'I remember taking that,' he said. Sarah had told me the photograph had been taken by a woman-friend. I suppose she had lied to save my feelings. In the picture she looked younger and happier, but not more lovely than in the years I had known her. I wished I had been able to make her look that way, but it is the destiny of a lover to watch unhappiness hardening like a cast around his mistress. Henry said, 'I was making a fool of myself to make her smile. Is General Gordon an interesting character?'

'In some ways.'

Henry said, 'The house feels very queer these days. I try to keep out of it as much as possible. I suppose you aren't free for dinner at the club?'

'I've got a lot of work I have to finish.'

He looked round my room. He said, 'You haven't much space for your books here.'

'No. I have to keep some of them under the bed.'

He picked up a magazine that Waterbury had sent me before the interview to show an example of his work and said, 'There's room in my house. You could have practically a flat to yourself.' I was too astonished to answer. He went rapidly on, turning over the leaves of the magazine as though he were really uninterested in his own suggestion, 'Think it over. You mustn't decide now.'

'It's very good of you, Henry.'

'You'd be doing me a favour, Bendrix.'

I thought, Why not? Writers are regarded as unconventional. Am I more conventional than a senior civil servant?

'I dreamed last night,' Henry said, 'about all of us.'

'Yes?'

'I don't remember much. We were drinking together. We were happy. When I woke up I thought she wasn't dead.'

'I don't dream of her now.'

'I wish we'd let that priest have his way.'

'It would have been absurd, Henry. She was no more a Catholic than you or me.'

'Do you believe in survival, Bendrix?'

'If you mean personal survival, no.'

'One can't disprove it, Bendrix.'

'It's almost impossible to disprove anything. I write a story. How can you prove that the events in it never happened, that the characters aren't real? Listen. I met a man on the Common today with three legs.'

'How terrible,' Henry said seriously. 'An abortion?'

'And they were covered with fish scales.'

'You're joking.'

'But prove I am, Henry. You can't disprove my story any more than I can disprove God. But I just know he's a lie, just as you know my story's a lie.'

'Of course there are arguments.'

'Oh, I could invent a philosophic argument for my story, I daresay, based on Aristotle.'

Henry abruptly changed the subject back. 'It would save you a bit if you came and stayed with me. Sarah always said your books weren't as successful as they should be.'

'Oh, the shadow of success is falling upon them.' I thought of Waterbury's article. I said, 'A moment comes when you can hear the popular reviewers dipping their pens for the plaudits – even before the next book's written. It's all a question of time.' I talked because I hadn't made up my mind.

Henry said, 'There's no ill-feeling left, is there, Bendrix? I got angry with you at your club – about that man. But what does it matter now?'

'I was wrong. He was only some crazy tub-thumping rationalist who interested her with his theories. Forget it, Henry.'

'She was good, Bendrix. People talk but she was good. It wasn't her fault I couldn't, well, love her properly. You know I'm awfully prudent, cautious. I'm not the sort that makes a lover. She wanted somebody like you.'

'She left me. She moved on, Henry.'

'Do you know I read one of your books once – Sarah made me. You described a house after a woman in it had died.'

'*The Ambitious Host.*'

'That was the name. It seemed all right at the time. I thought it very plausible, but you got it all wrong, Bendrix. You described how the husband found the house terribly empty: he moved about the rooms, shifted chairs, trying to give an effect of movement, of another being there. Sometimes he'd pour himself drinks in two glasses.'

'I forget it. It sounds a bit literary.'

'It's off the mark, Bendrix. The trouble is, the house doesn't seem empty. You see, often in the old days I'd come home from the office, and she would be out somewhere – perhaps with you. I'd call and she wouldn't answer. Then the house was empty. I almost expected to find the furniture gone. You know I did love her in my way, Bendrix. Every time she wasn't there when I came home those last months I dreaded to see a letter waiting for me. "Dear Henry" . . . you know the kind of thing they write in novels?'

'Yes.'

'But now the house never seems empty like that. I don't know how to express it. Because she's always away, she's never away. You see, she's never anywhere else. She's not having lunch with anybody, she's not at a cinema with you. There's nowhere for her to be but at home.'

'But where's her home?' I said.

'Oh, you've got to forgive me, Bendrix. I'm nervy and tired – I don't sleep well. You know the next best thing to talking *to* her is talking about her, and there's only you.'

'She had a lot of friends. Sir William Mallock, Dunstan . . .'

'I can't talk about her to them. Any more than to that man, Parkis.'

'Parkis!' I exclaimed. Had he lodged himself in our lives for ever?

'He told me he'd been at a cocktail party we gave. The strange people Sarah picked up. He said you knew him too.'

'What on earth did he want with you?'

'He said she'd been kind to his little boy – God knows when. The boy's sick. He seemed to want something of hers for a momento. I gave him one or two of her old children's books. There were a lot of them in her room, all scrawled over in pencil. It was a good way of getting rid of them. One can't just send them to Foyle's, can one? I don't see any harm in it, do you?'

'No. That was the man I put to watch her, from Savage's detective agency.'

'Good God, if I'd known. . . . But he seemed really fond of her.'

'Parkis is human,' I said. 'He's easily touched.' I looked around at my room – there wouldn't be any more of Sarah where Henry came from: less perhaps, for she would be diluted there.

'I'll come and stay with you, Henry, but you must let me pay some rent.'

'I'm so glad, Bendrix. But the house is freehold. You can pay your share of the rates.'

'Three months' notice to find new digs when you marry again.'

He took me quite seriously. 'I shall never want to do that. I'm not the marrying kind. It was a great injury I did to Sarah when I married her. I know that now.'

Chapter Six

So I moved to the north side of the Common. I wasted a week's rent because Henry wanted me to come at once, and I paid five pounds for a van to take my books and clothes across. I had the guest-room and Henry fitted up a lumber-room as a study, and there was a bath on the floor above. Henry had moved into his dressing-room, and the room they had shared with the cold twin beds was left for guests who never came. After a few days I began to see what Henry meant by the house never being empty. I worked at the British Museum until it closed, and then I would go back and wait for Henry, and usually we went out and drank a little at the 'Pontefract Arms'. Once when Henry was away for a few days at a conference at Bournemouth, I picked up a girl and brought her back. It wasn't any good. I knew it at once, I was impotent, and to save her feelings I told her that I had promised a woman I loved never to do this with anyone else. She was very sweet and understanding about it: prostitutes have a great respect for sentiment. This time there had been no revenge in my mind, and I felt only sadness at abandoning for ever something I had enjoyed so much. I dreamed of Sarah afterwards and we were lovers again in my old room on the south side, but again nothing happened, only this time there was no sadness in the fact. We were happy and without regret.

It was a few days afterwards that I pulled open a cupboard in my bedroom and found a pile of old children's books. Henry must have looted this cupboard for Parkis's boy. There were several of Andrew Lang's fairy books in their coloured covers, many Beatrix Potters, *The Children of the New Forest, The Golliwog at the North Pole*, and also one or two older books – Captain Scott's *Last Expedition* and the Poems of Thomas Hood, the last bound in school leather with a label saying that it had been awarded to Sarah Bertram for proficiency in Algebra. Algebra! How one changes.

I couldn't work that evening. I lay on the floor with the books and tried to trace at least a few features in the blank spaces of Sarah's life. There are times when a lover longs to be also a father and a brother: he is jealous of the years he hasn't shared. *The Golliwong at the North Pole* was probably the earliest of Sarah's books because it had been scrawled all over, this way and that way, meaninglessly, destructively, with coloured chalks. In one of the Beatrix Potters her name had been spelt in pencil, one big capital letter arranged wrongly so that what appeared was SAЯAH. In *The Children of the New Forest* she had written very tidily and minutely 'Sarah Bertram Her Book. Please ask permission to borrow. And if you steal it will be to your sorrow'. They were the marks of every child who has ever lived: traces as anonymous as the claw marks of birds that one sees in winter. When I closed the book they were covered at once by the drift of time.

I doubt whether she had ever read Hood's poems: the pages were as clean as when the book was handed to her by the headmistress or the distinguished visitor. Indeed as I was about to put it back in the cupboard a leaf or print dropped on the floor – the programme probably of that very prize-giving. In a handwriting I could recognize (but even our handwriting begins young and takes on the tired arabesques of time) was a phrase: 'What utter piffle'. I could imagine Sarah writing it down and showing it to her neighbour as the headmistress resumed her seat, applauded respectfully by parents. I don't know why another line of hers came into my head when I saw that schoolgirl phrase with all its impatience, its incomprehension and its assurance: 'I'm a phoney and a fake.' Here under my hand was innocence. It seemed such a pity that she had lived another twenty years only to feel that about herself. A phoney and a fake. Was it a description I had used of her in a moment of anger? She always harboured my criticism: it was only praise that slid from her like the snow.

I turned the leaf over and read the programme of july 23rd 1926: the Water Music of Handel played by Miss Duncan, R.C.M.: a recitation of 'I wandered lonely as a cloud' by Beatrice Collins: Tudor Ayres by the School Glee Society: Violin Recital of Chopin's Waltz in A flat by Mary Pippitt. The long summer afternoon of twenty years ago stretched out its shadows towards me, and I hated life that so alters us for the worse. I thought, that summer I had just begun my first novel: there was so much excitement, ambition, hope, when I sat down to work: I wasn't bitter, I was happy. I put the leaf back in the unread book and thrust the volume to the back of the cupboard under the *Golliwog* and the Beatrix Potters. We were both happy with only ten years and a few counties between us, who were later to come together for no apparent purpose but to give each other so much pain. I took up Scott's *Last Expedition*.

That had been one of my own favourite books. It seemed curiously dated now, this heroism with only the ice for enemy, self-sacrifice that involved no deaths beyond one's own. Two wars stood between us and them. I looked at the photographs: the bears and goggles, the little cairns of snow, the Union Jack, the ponies with their long manes like out-dated hair-dressings among the striped rocks. Even the deaths were 'period', and 'period' too was the schoolgirl who marked the pages with lines, exclamation marks, who wrote neatly in the margin of Scott's last letter home: 'And what comes next? Is it God? Robert Browning.' Even then, I thought, *He* came into her mind. He was as underhand as a lover, taking advantage of a passing mood, like a hero seducing us with his improbabilities and his legends. I put the last book back and turned the key in the lock.

Chapter Seven

'Where have you been, Henry?' I asked. He was usually the first at breakfast and sometimes he had left the house before I came down, but this morning his plate had not been touched and I heard the front door close softly before he appeared.

'Oh, just down the road,' he said vaguely.

'Been out all night?' I asked.

'No. Of course not.' To clear himself of that charge he told me the truth. 'Father Crompton said Mass today for Sarah.'

'Is he still at it?'

'Once a month. I thought it would be polite to look in.'

'I don't suppose he'd know you were there.'

'I saw him afterwards to thank him. As a matter of fact I asked him to dinner.'

'Then I shall go out.'

'I wish you wouldn't, Bendrix. After all, in his way, he was a friend of Sarah's.'

'You aren't turning a believer too, are you, Henry?'

'Of course I'm not. But they've as much right to their views as we have.'

So he came to dinner. Ugly, haggard, graceless with the Torquemada nose, he was the man who had kept Sarah from me. He had supported her in the absurd vow which ought to have been forgotten in a week. It was to his church that she had walked in the rain seeking a refuge and 'catching her death' instead. It was hard for me to show even bare politeness and

Henry had to shoulder the burden of the dinner. Father Crompton was not used to dining out. One had the impression that this was a duty on which he found it hard to keep his mind. He had very limited small talk, and his answers fell like trees across the road.

'You have a good deal of poverty around here, I suppose?' Henry said, rather tired, over the cheese. He had tried so many things – the influence of books, the cinema, a recent visit to France, the possibility of a third war.

'That's not a problem,' Father Crompton replied.

Henry worked hard. 'Immorality?' he asked with the slightly false note we can't avoid with such a word.

'That's never a problem,' Father Crompton said.

'I thought perhaps – the Common – one notices at night . . .'

'You get it happening with any open space. And it's winter now anyway.' And that closed that.

'Some more cheese, father?'

'No, thank you.'

'I suppose, in a district like this, you have a good deal of trouble raising money – for charity, I mean?'

'People give what they can.'

'Some brandy with your coffee?'

'No thank you.'

'You don't mind if we . . .'

'Of course I don't. I can't get to sleep on it, that's all, and I have to get up at six.'

'Whatever for?'

'Prayer. You get used to it.'

'I'm afraid I've never been able to pray much,' Henry said, 'since I was a boy. I used to pray to get into the second XV.'

'And did you?'

'I got into the third. I'm afraid that kind of prayer isn't much good, is it, father?'

'Any sort's better than none. It's a recognition of God's power anyway, and that's a kind of praise, I suppose.' I hadn't heard him talk so much since dinner had started.

'I should have thought,' I said, 'it was more like touching wood or avoiding the lines on the pavement. At that age anyway.'

'Oh well,' he said, 'I'm not against a bit of superstition. It gives people the idea that this world's not everything.' He scowled at me down his nose. 'It could be the beginning of wisdom.'

'Your church certainly goes in for superstition in a big way – St Januarius, bleeding statues, visions of the virgin – that sort of thing.'

'We try to sort them out. And isn't it more sensible to believe that *anything* may happen than . . .?'

The bell rang. Henry said, 'I told the maid she could go to bed. Would you excuse me, father?'

'I'll go,' I said. I was glad to get away from that oppressive presence. He had the answers too pat: the amateur could never hope to catch him out, he was like a conjuror who bores one by his very skill. I opened the front door and saw a stout woman in black holding a parcel. For a moment I thought it was our charwoman until she said, 'Are you Mr Bendrix, sir?'

'Yes.'

'I was to give you this,' and she thrust the parcel quickly into my hand as though it contained something explosive.

'Who's it from?'

'Mr Parkis, sir.' I turned it over in perplexity. It even occurred to me that he might have mislaid some evidence which now too late he was handing over to me. I wanted to forget Mr Parkis.

'If you'd give me a receipt, sir? I was to put the parcel into your own hands.'

'I haven't a pencil – or paper. I really can't be bothered.'

'You know how Mr Parkis is about records, sir. I've got a pencil in my bag.'

I wrote the receipt out for her on the back of a used envelope. She stowed it carefully away and then scuttled to the gate as though she wanted to get as far as possible as quickly as she could. I stood in the hall weighing the object in my hand. Henry called out to me from the dining-room, 'What is it, Bendrix?'

'A parcel from Parkis,' I said. The phrase sounded like a tongue twister.

'I suppose he's returning the book.'

'At this hour? And it's addressed to me.'

'Well, what is it then?' I didn't want to open the parcel: weren't we both of us engaged in the painful process of forgetting? I felt as though I had been punished enough for my visit to Mr Savage's agency. I heard Father Crompton's voice saying, 'I ought to be off now, Mr Miles.'

'It's early yet.'

I thought, if I stay out of the room, I shan't have to add my politeness to Henry's, he may go sooner. I opened the parcel.

Henry was right. It was one of the Andrew Lang fairy books, but a piece of folded notepaper stuck out between the leaves. It was a letter from Parkis.

'Dear Mr Bendrix,' I read, and thinking it was a note of thanks my eyes impatiently took in the last sentences. 'So under the circumstances I would rather not have the book in the house and hoping that you will explain to Mr Miles that there is no ingratitude on the part of yours truly, Alfred Parkis.'

I sat down in the hall. I heard Henry say, 'Don't think I've got a closed mind, Father Crompton . . .' and I began to read Parkis's letter from the beginning:

'Dear Mr Bendrix, I am writing to you and not Mr Miles being assured of your sympathy due to our close even though sad association and you being a literary gentleman of imagination and accustomed to strange events. You know my boy has been bad lately with awful pains in his stomach and not being due to ice-cream I have been afraid of appendicitis. The doctor said operate, it can't do any harm, but I have great fear of the knife for my poor boy, his mother having died under it due to negligence I am sure, and what would I do if I lost my boy the same way? I would be quite alone. Forgive all the details, Mr Bendrix, but in my profession we are trained to put things in order and explain first things first, so the judge can't complain he hasn't been given the facts plainly. So I said to the doctor on Monday, let's wait until we are quite certain. Only I think sometimes it was the cold that did it and he waiting and watching outside Mrs Miles's house, and you will forgive me if I say she was a lady of great kindness who deserved to be left alone. You can't pick and choose in my job, but ever since that first day in Maiden Lane I wished it was any other lady I had the watching of. Anyway my boy was upset terribly when he heard how the poor lady had died. She only spoke to him once, but somehow he got the idea, I think, that his mother had been like her, only she wasn't, though a good true woman in her way too whom I miss every day of my life. Well, when his temperature was 103 which is high for a boy like him, he began to talk to Mrs Miles just the same as he had done in the street, but he told her he was watching her which of course he wouldn't do, having professional pride even at his age. Then he began to cry when she went away, and then he slept, but when he woke up, his temperature being still 102, he asked for the present she had promised him in the dream. So that was why I bothered Mr Miles and deceived him of which I am ashamed there not being a professional reason, only my poor boy.

'When I got the book and gave it him he became calmer. But I was worried because the doctor said he would not take any more risks and he must go to hospital on Wednesday and if there had been an empty bed he would have sent him that night. So you see I couldn't sleep for worrying because of my poor wife and my poor boy and being afraid of the knife. I don't mind telling *you*, Mr Bendrix, that I prayed very hard. I prayed to God and then I prayed to my wife to do what she could because if there's anyone in heaven, she's in heaven now, and I asked Mrs Miles if she was there, to do what she could too. Now if a grown man can do that, Mr Bendrix, you can understand my poor boy imagining things. When I woke up this morning, his temperature was ninety-nine and he hadn't any pain, and when the doctor came there wasn't any tenderness left, so he says we can wait a while and he's been all right all day. Only he told the doctor it was Mrs Miles who came and took away the pain – touching him on the right side of the stomach if you'll forgive the indelicacy – and she wrote in the book for him. But the doctor says he must be kept very quiet and the book excites him, so under the circumstances I would rather not have the book in the house. . . .'

When I turned the letter over there was a postscript. 'There is something written in the book, but anyone can see that was many years ago when Mrs Miles was a little girl, only I can't explain that to my poor boy for fear the pain might return. Respectfully, A.P.' I turned to the fly-leaf and there was the unformed scribble with indelible pencil just as I had seen it before in the other books in which the child Sarah Bertram had composed her mottoes.

'When I was ill my mother gave me this book by Lang.
If any well person steals it he will get a great bang,
But if you are sick in bed
You can have it to read instead.'

I carried it back with me into the dining-room. 'What was it?' Henry asked.

'The book,' I said. 'Did you read what Sarah had written in it before you gave it to Parkis?'

'No. Why?'

'A coincidence, that's all. But it seems you don't need to belong to Father

Crompton's persuasion to be superstitious.' I gave Henry the letter: he read it and handed it to Father Crompton.

'I don't like it,' Henry said. 'Sarah's dead. I hate to see her being bandied about. . . .'

'I know what you mean. I feel it too.'

'It's like hearing her discussed by strangers.'

'They aren't saying anything ill of her,' Father Crompton said. He laid the letter down. 'I must go now.' But he made no move, looking at the letter on the table. He asked, 'And the inscription?'

I pushed the book across to him. 'Oh, it was written years ago. She wrote that kind of thing in a lot of her books like all children.'

'Time's a strange thing,' Father Crompton said.

'Of course the child wouldn't understand it was all done in the past.'

'St Augustine asked where time came from. He said it came out of the future which didn't exist yet, into the present that had no duration, and went into the past which had ceased to exist. I don't know that we can understand time any better than a child.'

'I didn't mean . . .'

'Oh well,' he said, standing up, 'you mustn't take this to heart, Mr Miles. It only goes to show what a good woman your wife was.'

'That's no help to me, is it? She's part of the past that has ceased to exist.'

'The man who wrote that letter had a lot of sense in him. There's no harm in praying to the dead as well as for them.' He repeated his phrase, 'She was a good woman.'

Quite suddenly I lost my temper. I believe I was annoyed chiefly by his complacency, the sense that nothing intellectual could ever trouble him, the assumption of an intimate knowledge of somebody he had only known for a few hours or days, whom we had known for years. I said, 'She was nothing of the sort.'

'Bendrix,' Henry said sharply.

'She could put blinkers on any man,' I said, 'even on a priest. She's only deceived you, father, as she deceived her husband and me. She was a consummate liar.'

'She never pretended to be what she wasn't.'

'I wasn't her only lover—'

'Stop it,' Henry said. 'You've no right . . .'

'Let him alone,' Father Crompton said. 'Let the poor man rave.'

'Don't give me your professional pity, father. Keep it for your penitents.'

'You can't dictate to me whom I'm to pity, Mr Bendrix.'

'Any man could have her.' I longed to believe what I said, for then there would be nothing to miss or regret. I would no longer be tied to her wherever she was. I would be free.

'And you can't teach me anything about penitence, Mr Bendrix. I've had twenty-five years of the Confessional. There's nothing we can do some of the saints haven't done before us.'

'I've got nothing to repent except failure. Go back to your own people, father, back to your bloody little box and your beads.'

'You'll find me there any time you want me.'

'Me want you, father? Father, I don't want to be rude, but I'm no Sarah. No Sarah.'

Henry said with embarrassment, 'I'm sorry, father.'

'You don't need to be. I know when a man's in pain.'

I couldn't get through the tough skin of his complacency. I pushed my chair back and said, 'You're wrong, father. This isn't anything subtle like pain. I'm not in pain, I'm in hate. I hate Sarah because she was a little tart, I hate Henry because she stuck to him, and I hate you and your imaginary God because you took her away from all of us.'

'You're a good hater,' Father Crompton said.

Tears stood in my eyes because I was powerless to hurt any of them. 'To hell with the lot of you,' I said.

I slammed the door behind me and shut them in together. Let him spill his holy wisdom to Henry, I thought, I'm alone. I want to be alone. If I can't have you, I'll be alone always. Oh, I'm as capable of belief as the next man. I would only have to shut the eyes of my mind for a long enough time, and I could believe that you came to Parkis's boy in the night with your touch that brings peace. Last month in the crematorium I asked you to save that girl from me and you pushed your mother between us – or so they might say. But if I start believing that, then I have to believe in your God. I'd have to love your God. I'd rather love the men you slept with.

I've got to be reasonable, I told myself going upstairs. Sarah has been dead a long time now: one doesn't go on loving the dead with this intensity, only the living, and she's not alive, she can't be alive. I mustn't believe that she's alive. I lay down on my bed and closed my eyes and I tried to be reasonable. If I hate her so much as I sometimes do, how can I love her? Can one really hate and love? Or is it only myself that I really hate? I hate the books I write with their trivial unimportant skill, I hate the craftsman's mind in me so greedy for copy that I set out to seduce a woman I didn't love for the information she could give me, I hate this body that enjoyed so much but was inadequate to express what the heart felt, and I hate my untrusting mind, that set Parkis on the watch who laid powder on door bells, rifled waste-paper baskets, stole your secrets.

From the drawer of my bedside table I took her journal and opening it at random, under a date last January, I read: 'O God, if I could really hate you, what would that mean?' And I thought hating Sarah is only loving Sarah and hating myself is only loving myself. I'm not worth hating – Maurice Bendrix, author of *The Ambitious Host, The Crowned Image, The Grave on the Water-Front*, Bendrix the scribbler. Nothing – not even Sarah – is worth our hatred if You exist, except You. And, I thought, sometimes I've hated Maurice, but would I have hated him if I hadn't loved him too? O God, if I could really hate you. . . .

I remembered how Sarah had prayed to the God she didn't believe in, and now I spoke to the Sarah I didn't believe in. I said: You sacrificed both of us once to bring me back to life, but what sort of a life is this without you? It's all very well for you to love God. You are dead. You have him. But I'm sick with life, I'm rotten with health. If I begin to love God, I can't just die. I've got to do something about it. I had to touch you with my hands, I had to taste you with my tongue: one can't love and do nothing. It's no use your telling me not to worry as you did once in a dream. If I ever loved like that, it would be the end of everything. Loving you I had no appetite for food, I felt no lust for any other woman, but loving him there'd be no pleasure in anything at all with him away. I'd even lose my work, I'd cease to be Bendrix. Sarah, I'm afraid.

That night I came wide-awake at two in the morning. I went down to the larder and got myself some biscuits and a drink of water. I was sorry I had spoken like that about Sarah in front of Henry. The priest had said there was nothing we could do that some saint had not done. That might be true of murder and adultery, the spectacular sins, but could a saint ever have been guilty of envy and meanness? My hate was as petty as my love. I opened the door softly and looked in at Henry. He lay asleep with the light on and his arm shielding his eyes. With the eyes hidden there was an anonymity about the whole body. He was just a man – one of us. He was like the first enemy soldier a man encounters on a battlefield, dead and indistinguishable, not a White or a Red, but just a human being like himself. I put two biscuits by his bed in case he woke and turned the light out.

Chapter Eight

My book wasn't going well (what a waste of time the act of writing seemed, but how else could time be spent?) and I took a walk across the Common to listen to the speakers. There was a man I remembered who used to amuse me in the pre-war days and I was glad to see him safely back on his pitch. He had no message to convey like the political and the religious speakers. He was an ex-actor and he just told stories and recited snatches of verse. He would challenge his audience to catch him out by asking for any piece of verse. 'The Ancient Mariner,' somebody would call, and at once, with great emphasis, he would give us a quatrain. One wag said, 'Shakespeare's Thirty-Second Sonnet' and he recited four lines at random and when the wag objected, he said, 'You've got the wrong edition.' I looked around at my fellow listeners and saw Smythe. Perhaps he had seen me first, for he had the handsome side of his face turned towards me, the side Sarah had not kissed, but if so he avoided my eye.

Why did I always wish to speak to anybody whom Sarah had known? I pushed my way to his side and said, 'Hullo, Smythe.' He clamped a handkerchief to the bad side of his face and turned towards me. 'Oh, it's Mr Bendrix,' he said.

'I haven't seen you since the funeral.'

'I've been away.'

'Don't you still speak here?'

'No.' He hesitated and then added unwillingly, 'I've given up public speaking.'

'But you still give home-tuition?' I teased him.

'No. I've given that up too.'

'Not changed your views, I hope?'

He said gloomily, 'I don't know what to believe.'

'Nothing. Surely that was the point.'

'It was.' He began to move a little way out of the crowd and I found myself on his bad side. I couldn't resist teasing him a little more. 'Have you got toothache?' I asked.

'No. Why?'

'It looked like it. With that handkerchief.'

He didn't reply but took the handkerchief away. There was no ugliness to hide. His skin was quite fresh and young except for one insignificant spot.

He said, 'I get tired of explaining when I meet people I know.'

'You found a cure?'

'Yes. I told you I've been away.'

'To a nursing home?'

'Yes.'

'Operation?'

'Not exactly.' He added unwillingly, 'It was done by touch.'

'Faith-healing?'

'I have no faith. I'd never go to a quack.'

'What was it? Urticaria?'

He said vaguely, to close the subject. 'Modern methods. Electricity.'

I went back home and again I tried to settle to my book. Always I find when I begin to write there is one character who obstinately will not come alive. There is nothing psychologically false about him, but he sticks, he has to be pushed around, words have to be found for him, all the technical skill I have acquired through the laborious years has to be employed in making him appear alive to my readers. Sometimes I get a sour satisfaction when a reviewer praises him as the best-drawn character in the story: if he has not been drawn he has certainly been dragged. He lies heavily on my mind whenever I start to work like an ill-digested meal on the stomach, robbing me of the pleasure of creation in any scene where he is present. He never does the unexpected thing, he never surprizes me, he never takes charge. Every other character helps, he only hinders.

And yet one cannot do without him. I can imagine a God feeling in just that way about some of us. The saints, one would suppose, in a sense create themselves. They come alive. They are capable of the surprizing act or word. They stand outside the plot, unconditioned by it. But we have to be pushed around. We have the obstinacy of non-existence. We are inextricably bound to the plot, and wearily God forces us, here and there, according to his intention, characters without poetry, without free will, whose only importance is that somewhere, at some time, we help to furnish the scene in which a living character moves and speaks, providing perhaps the saints with the opportunities for *their* free will.

I was glad when I heard the door close and Henry's footsteps in the hall. It was an excuse to stop. That character could remain inert now till morning: it was the hour at last for the 'Pontefract Arms'. I waited for him to call up to me (already in a month we were as set in our ways as two bachelors who have lived together for years), but he didn't call and I heard him go into his study. After a while I followed him: I missed my drink.

I was reminded of the occasion when I came back with him first; he sat there, beside the green Discus Thrower, worried and dejected, but now watching him I felt neither envy nor pleasure.

'A drink, Henry?'

'Yes, yes. Of course. I was only going to change my shoes.' He had his town and his country shoes and the Common in his eyes was country. He bent over his laces: there was a knot that he couldn't untie – he was always bad with his fingers. He got tired of struggling and wrenched the shoe off. I picked it up and uncoiled the knot for him.

'Thank you, Bendrix.' Perhaps even so small an act of companionship gave him confidence. 'A very unpleasant thing happened today at the office,' he said.

'Tell me.'

'Mrs Bertram called. I don't think you know Mrs Bertram.'

'Oh yes. I met her the other day.' A curious phrase – the other day, as though all days were the same except that one.

'We've never got on very well together.'

'So she told me.'

'Sarah was always very good about it. She kept her away.'

'Did she come to borrow money?'

'Yes. She wanted ten pounds – her usual story, in town for the day, shopping, run out, banks closed. . . . Bendrix, I'm not a mean man, but I get so irritated by the way she goes on. She has two thousand a year of her own. It's almost as much as I earn.'

'Did you give it her?'

'Oh yes. One always does, but the trouble was I couldn't resist a sermon. That made her furious. I told her how many times she'd done it and how many times she had paid me back – that was easy, the first time. She took out her cheque book and said she was going to write me a cheque for the whole lot there and then. She was so angry that I'm certain she meant it. She'd really forgotten that she had used her last cheque. She had meant to humiliate me and she only succeeded in humiliating herself, poor woman. Of course, that made it worse.'

'What did she do?'

'She accused me of not giving Sarah a proper funeral. She told me a strange story. . . .'

'I know it. She told it to me after a couple of ports.'

'Do you think she's lying?'

'No.'

'It's an extraordinary coincidence, isn't it? Baptized at two years old, and then beginning to go back to what you can't even remember. . . . It's like an infection.'

'It's what you say, an odd coincidence.' Once before I had supplied Henry with the necessary strength; I wasn't going to let him weaken now. 'I've known stranger coincidences,' I went on. 'During the last year, Henry, I've been so bored I've even collected car numbers. That teaches you about coincidences. Ten thousand possible numbers and God knows how many combinations, and yet over and over again I've seen two cars with the same figures side by side in a traffic block.'

'Yes. I suppose it works that way.'

'I'll never lose my faith in coincidence, Henry.'

The telephone was ringing faintly upstairs: we hadn't heard it till now, because the switch was turned off in the study.

'Oh dear, oh dear,' Henry said, 'I wouldn't be a bit surprized if it were that woman again.'

'Let her ring,' and as I spoke the bell stopped.

'It isn't that I'm mean,' Henry said. 'I don't suppose she's borrowed more than a hundred pounds in ten years.'

'Come out and have a drink.'

'Of course. Oh, I haven't put on my shoes.' He bent over them and I could see the bald patch on the crown of his head: it was as though his worries had worn through – I had been one of his worries. He said, 'I don't know what I'd do without you, Bendrix.' I brushed a few grains of scurf off his shoulder. 'Oh well, Henry . . .' and then before we could move the bell began to ring again.

'Leave it,' I said.

'I'd better answer. You don't know . . .' He got up with his shoe-laces dangling and came over to his desk. 'Hello,' he said, 'Miles speaking.' He passed the receiver to me and said with relief, 'It's for you.'

'Yes,' I said, 'Bendrix here.'

'Mr Bendrix,' a man's voice said, 'I felt I'd got to ring you. I didn't tell you the truth this afternoon.'

'Who *are* you?'

'Smythe,' the voice said.

'I don't understand.'

'I told you I'd been to a nursing home. I never went to one.'

'Really it couldn't matter less to me.'

His voice reached for me along the line. 'Of course it matters. You aren't listening to me. Nobody treated my face. It cleared up, suddenly, in a night.'

'How? I still don't . . .'

He said with an awful air of conspiracy, 'You and I know how. There's no getting round it. It wasn't right of me keeping it dark. It was a . . .' but I put down the receiver before he could use that foolish newspaper word that was the alternative to 'coincidence'. I remembered his clenched right hand, I remembered my anger that the dead can be so parcelled up, divided like their clothes. I thought, He's so proud that he must always have some kind of revelation. In a week or two he'll be speaking about it on the Common and showing his healed face. It will be in the newspapers: 'Rationalist Speaker Converted by Miraculous Cure'. I tried to summon up all my faith in coincidence, but all I could think of, and that with envy, for I had no relic, was the ruined cheek lying at night on her hair.

'Who is it?' Henry asked. I hesitated a moment whether to tell him, but then I thought, No. I don't trust him. He and Father Crompton will get together.

'Smythe,' I said.

'Smythe?'

'That fellow Sarah used to visit.'

'What did he want?'

'His face has been cured, that's all. I asked him to let me know the name of the specialist. I have a friend . . .'

'Electric treatment?'

'I'm not sure. I've read somewhere that urticaria is hysterical in origin. A mixture of psychiatry and radium.' It sounded plausible. Perhaps after all it was the truth. Another coincidence, two cars with the same number plate, and I thought with a sense of weariness, how many coincidences are there going to be? Her mother at the funeral, the child's dream. Is this going to continue day by day? I felt like a swimmer who has overpassed his strength and knows the tide is stronger than himself, but if I drowned, I was going to hold Henry up till the last moment. Wasn't it, after all, the duty of a friend, for if this thing were not disproved, if it got into the papers, nobody could tell where it would end? I remembered the roses at Manchester – that fraud had taken a long time to be recognized for what it was. People are so hysterical in these days. There might be relic-hunters, prayers, processions. Henry was not unknown; the scandal would be enormous. And all the journalists asking questions about their life together and digging out that queer story of the baptism near Deauville. The vulgarity of the pious Press. I could imagine the headlines, and the headlines would produce more 'miracles'. We had to kill this thing at the start.

I remembered the journal in my drawer upstairs and I thought, That has to go too, for that could be interpreted in their way. It was as though to save her for ourselves we had to destroy her features one by one. Even her children's books had proved a danger. There were photographs – the one Henry had taken: the Press mustn't have that. Was Maud to be trusted? The two of us had tried to build a makeshift house together, and even that was being broken up.

'What about our drink?' Henry said.

'I'll join you in a minute.'

I went up to my room and took the journal out. I tore the covers off. They were tough: the cotton backing came out like fibres; it was like tearing the limbs off a bird, and there the journal lay on the bed, a pad of paper, wingless and wounded. The last page lay upwards and I read again, 'You were there teaching me to squander, so that one day we might have nothing left except this love of You. But You are too good to me. When I ask You for pain, You give me peace. Give it him too. Give him my peace – he needs it more.'

I thought, you've failed there, Sarah. One of your prayers at least has not been answered. I have no peace and I have no love, except for you, you. I said to her, I'm a man of hate. But I didn't feel much hatred; I had called other people hysterical, but my own words were over-charged. I could detect their insincerity. What I chiefly felt was less hate than fear. For if this God exists, I thought, and if even you – with your lusts and your adulteries and the timid lies you used to tell – can change like this, we could all be saints by leaping as you leapt, by shutting the eyes and leaping once and for all: if *you* are a saint, it's not difficult to be a saint. It's something He can demand of any of us, leap. But I won't leap. I sat on my bed and said to God: You've taken her, but You haven't got me yet. I know Your cunning. It's You who take us up to a high place and offer us the whole universe. You're a devil, God, tempting us to leap. But I don't want Your peace and I don't want Your love. I wanted something very simple and very easy: I wanted Sarah for a lifetime and You took her away. With Your great schemes You ruin our happiness like a harvester ruins a mouse's nest: I hate You, God, I hate You as though You existed.

I looked at the pad of paper. It was more impersonal than a scrap of hair. You can touch hair with your lips and fingers and I was tired to death of the mind. I had lived for her body and I wanted her body. But the journal was all I had, so I shut it back in the cupboard, for wouldn't that have been one more victory for Him, to destroy it and leave myself more completely without her? I said to Sarah, all right, have it *your* way. I believe you live and that He exists, but it will take more than your prayers to turn this hatred of Him into love. He robbed me and like that king you wrote about I'll rob Him of what he wants in me. Hatred is in my brain, not in my stomach or my skin. It can't be removed like a rash or an ache. Didn't I hate you as well as love you? And don't I hate myself?

I called down to Henry, 'I'm ready,' and we walked side by side over the Common towards the 'Pontefract Arms'; the lights were out, and lovers met where the roads intersected, and on the other side of the grass was the house with the ruined steps where He gave me back this hopeless crippled life.

'I look forward to these evening walks of ours,' Henry said.

'Yes.'

I thought, in the morning I'll ring up a doctor and ask him whether a faith cure is possible. And then I thought, better not; so long as one doesn't *know*, one can imagine innumerable cures. . . . I put my hand on Henry's arm and held it there; I had to be strong for both of us now, and he wasn't seriously worried yet.

'They are the only things I do look forward to,' Henry said.

I wrote at the start that this was a record of hate, and walking there beside Henry towards the evening glass of beer, I found the one prayer that seemed to serve the winter mood: O God, You've done enough, You've robbed me of enough, I'm too tired and old to learn to love, leave me alone for ever.